Jack,

December 2018

INNOCENTS TO THE SLAUGHTER

INNOCENTS TO THE SLAUGHTER

HELEN MASKEW

This edition first published in 2018

Unbound

6th Floor Mutual House, 70 Conduit Street, London W1S 2GF

www.unbound.com

All rights reserved

© Helen Maskew, 2018

The right of Helen Maskew to be identified as the author of this work has been asserted in accordance with Section 77 of the Copyright, Designs and Patents Act 1988. No part of this publication may be copied, reproduced, stored in a retrieval system, or transmitted, in any form or by any means without the prior permission of the publisher, nor be otherwise circulated in any form of binding or cover other than that in which it is published and without a similar condition being imposed on the subsequent purchaser.

ISBN (eBook): 978-1-912618-79-8
ISBN (Paperback):978-1-912618-78-1

Design by Mecob

Printed in Great Britain by Clays Ltd, Elcograf S.p.A.

To the Lit Chicks' Book Club – always the best of friends.

Dear Reader,

The book you are holding came about in a rather different way to most others. It was funded directly by readers through a new website: Unbound.

Unbound is the creation of three writers. We started the company because we believed there had to be a better deal for both writers and readers. On the Unbound website, authors share the ideas for the books they want to write directly with readers. If enough of you support the book by pledging for it in advance, we produce a beautifully bound special subscribers' edition and distribute a regular edition and e-book wherever books are sold, in shops and online.

This new way of publishing is actually a very old idea (Samuel Johnson funded his dictionary this way). We're just using the internet to build each writer a network of patrons. Here, at the back of this book, you'll find the names of all the people who made it happen.

Publishing in this way means readers are no longer just passive consumers of the books they buy, and authors are free to write the books they really want. They get a much fairer return too – half the profits their books generate, rather than a tiny percentage of the cover price.

If you're not yet a subscriber, we hope that you'll want to join our publishing revolution and have your name listed in one of our books in the future. To get you started, here is a £5 discount on your first pledge. Just visit unbound.com, make your pledge and type LAWES18 in the promo code box when you check out.

Thank you for your support,

Dan, Justin and John
Founders, Unbound

Super Patrons

Carolyn Box
Jack Brawn
Julie Hallam
Dan Kieran
Nicky Martin
Helen Maskew
Kathleen McLuskie
John Mitchinson
Sue Napier
Carlo Navato
Justin Pollard
Lesley Taylor
Anna Whiteoak
Edward Young

FOREWORD

There was a hanging today, a chilly May Friday overcast with threats of rain. They had provided all the trappings that made it an official execution. Surrounded by soldiers and officials, the prisoner came out through the prison gates into its yard where the temporary wooden scaffold had been erected the night before. The condemned's arms were pinned to the side with a leather belt; the head and neck bare. It was an unimpressive sight. To the disappointment of the expectant crowd, the prisoner showed no reaction, no twitching or resistance as the soldiers each side of their captive moved swiftly until the foot of the scaffold was reached. There the condemned stood, silent and expressionless, head erect and staring out into the sea of people.

The waiting crowd of about 500, all of whom had previously been gossiping in the yard while anticipating the event, now fell silent, their attention drawn to the centrepiece of the spectacle. Tension became palpable; the atmosphere was imbued with hostility and loathing. As the prisoner mounted the steps of the scaffold and appeared into view, the militia-men, drafted in to provide a barrier against which the crowd could move no further forward, brought their muskets to the ready in anticipation of a surge. But it was not forthcoming; the crowd remained hushed and still, but watchful. As the executioner moved to place the prisoner over the trapdoor the spectators watched with intense curiosity. Standing behind, he attempted to slip a cloth bag over the head, but it was vehemently shaken away and those closest heard the murmur, 'I won't have it!' With a shrug of indifference, the hangman took the noose hanging from the main beam and placed it around the neck. The chaplain stepped forward with his book and opened his mouth to pray, but again there was another shake of the head from the prisoner. 'There'll be no cant here! I'll take my chances.' Then there was a cry for all to hear: 'Take your God to the devil and go with him!' There was a gasp from the crowd, many of whom shook their heads in disgust; some crossed themselves.

Checking one further time that he had correctly positioned the noose, then tightening the rope and adjusting the knot until it rested on the back of the neck, the hangman moved to the side of the scaffold where he paused briefly until the clock in the prison tower struck the first of ten strokes; then at a nod from the prison constable he pulled the lever. The trapdoor opened with a clatter and the body fell through the hole to oblivion.

Chapter 1

LONDON

Pyecombe House,
Devon

Friday, 8 March 1839
  To Mr Ambrose Hudson,
  I write from my family seat, Pyecombe House, as George Montague Harnet, aged 10 years and son and heir of Lord George Harnet. I seek your assistance in a matter of some urgency, having heard that you investigate reports of cruelty to children. I want to report to you that I have been oppressively treated by my father. My tutor, Mr Barraclough, advised me to write and invite you to take up my case.
  Lord George Snr has stopped my monthly allowance in a most peremptory manner, just because he heard me swearing at a footman. I admit my language was sharp, but the man is in a servile position and should expect to be admonished from time to time by members of the family who employ him.
  My father has threatened to continue to withdraw monies from me until I apologise – an action I am totally unwilling to carry out.
  If you could see fit to contact me so that I can make arrangements for you to visit I would be grateful. As you will understand, until the matter is put right and I am again in funds I will not be able to reimburse you for your expenditure; but a note of hand will, I am sure, suffice until you are successful in bringing my father to his right mind.
  Your servant,
  Geo. Montague Harnet

Spiking the unsolicited note on top of a pile of others, James

McNiece, Ambrose's editor, sighed. 'Pompous young pup!' he thought. 'The tutor's put him up to this for a joke. I've a good mind to send it back to his father and ask him whether he knows his son's using the family seal. It's all very well my journalist gaining a reputation as a crusader, but unwanted petitioners are time-wasting.' The *Escritoire* was receiving at least five a week among the more genuine reports that needed following up. The reason the editor was at his desk on a Sunday afternoon in March was mainly to deal with such unsought correspondence. In all courtesy they were due a reply and he was now a past master at the short response, which was something in the order of: 'We thank you for your enquiry, but Mr Hudson is unable to follow up personal requests now.'

There was a further motive for attendance at the office. Mrs McNiece had invited their daughter and five grandchildren to the house. Now James could deal with Emma and one or two of her children at one sitting, but five little ones were excessive. As soon as was courteous after their arrival he had excused himself on the grounds of an urgent need to visit his workplace, to which he then walked to find some peace and quiet – even if it meant dealing with absurd requests such as the one he had just placed on the discard pile.

However, his visit to the office had not been a complete waste of time; among the dross there were some communications of real relevance. A member of parliament from a distant county was looking for help in a case of suspected illegal child labour in the coal mines. His report was long and distressing, but James knew that Ambrose would baulk at working underground – if that was the necessary means to bring in evidence. However, as always, he would talk to Hudson and see how that issue could be resolved. A second large packet contained correspondence that was much more likely to be of interest and which would probably bear fruit. So, taking up both packets, he walked around the corner from the paper's office in Fleet Street down Ludgate Hill to St Paul's and then to his sister Agnes Bridie's house in Gresham Street where Ambrose Hudson had lodgings.

He knew he would receive a warm welcome from Agnes. She was a constant refuge from the sometimes overwhelming demands of his large family. Her house provided an oasis of calm; besides, Ambrose

Chapter 1

always kept a bottle of good French brandy. As usual Agnes embraced him affectionately and they had a brief conference on family matters before he went up the stairs to the first floor and Ambrose's rooms and knocked. The occupant responded with a cheerful command for his visitor to enter, immediately offering a seat and the anticipated spirits. It was obvious from the state of Ambrose's large, shabby, leather-topped desk that he was hard at work on a piece. Scraps of paper covered a table, some falling to the floor; others were pinned up round the room.

McNiece got straight to the point. 'We've had the usual cascade of requests and reports – most of which require absolutely no following up. But opening our correspondence this afternoon I find we've been sent a couple of interesting possible assignments.' He waved the packages and Ambrose cleared a corner of the desk. 'The first concerns child labour in a Northumbrian coal mine. I know it's an area where you've never been involved before, either geographically or professionally, and I'm not sure if you've changed your mind about working underground – no pun intended! It certainly wouldn't appeal to me. But having read the man's observations, you may well be persuaded. I think I might almost be – in your shoes.'

Ambrose thought for a moment and then said, 'Leaving the issue of working underground aside for a moment, what's the other assignment?'

McNiece picked up a letter and handed it to him. 'What do you make of that?'

Sitting back in his chair Ambrose read the following:

Richmond Woollen Mill,
Bingley,
Yorkshire

Friday, 8 March 1839
  Dear Mr Hudson,
  Recently I read with great interest your account of Seddon Union and the negligent treatment of its inmates. Your report on the events and mismanagement by its board of guardians was

as exemplary as your followers would expect and I congratulate you, both on your assiduous seeking after justice and fair treatment for young children who have no voice, and in the quality of your account which I consider cannot fail to move even the hardest of hearts, but which unfortunately still does not include those of our legislature.

I have followed most of your previous reporting and know you have been particularly interested in the plight of some of the children in the textile mills of Lancashire. I have read thoroughly accounts of your time there in the first few years of the decade. My present concerns are entirely related to your enterprises in the region. I will try to be brief, but the reasons for this letter are serious and I have no wish to trivialise them.

I am an overseer at the above address. My first task in this correspondence is to assure you that not all overseers are evil men who are paid to put the workers under the lash – in fact very few I know of fit that description. As always, it is the few who besmirch the rest of us. I see one of my duties, and not the least, as that of care of my workers – completely rational since they provide the profits by which the mills are kept running. But in this instance, I am particularly concerned about the well-being of the youngsters who work at the mill in which I am employed.

Unfortunately, my masters – the owners and shareholders – are not so troubled. You will be aware that the legislation of 1833 was drawn up to include all textile mills. Now no child under nine should be employed in the industry and children between nine and eleven cannot work longer than a nine-hour day. There are also supposed to be neutral inspectors to enforce the laws. I believe it was only because of men like Michael Sadler and the Earl of Shaftesbury that such regulations were passed – as well as the groundwork of men like you who put themselves in harm's way to report on what is happening.

In that regard, I regret to say that at this mill – and others I can name – the laws are not adhered to. It is easy to understand

Chapter 1

why – no one can really ascertain the age of a child simply by looking at them. My masters are not conscientious in their enquiries about children brought in by their parents and others to work. It is known that many are not beyond seven or eight. In one instance, a child was rumoured to be but five years old. I understand the parents' often desperate attempts to get money to feed their families, but there are men – and women – working in this area who profiteer from that need. They agree to take children from their parents, paying them very small sums of money and promising to find their offspring adequate food and lodging. The children are put to work for long hours and the men keep their wages in lieu of their 'expenses'. The children live in dreadful conditions when they are not working. These men are therefore nothing other than the equivalent of slave traders. When such a scoundrel makes an approach to the foreman it is claimed that the parish records have been checked and show the children are all the required legal age to work. The 'no questions asked' policy dominates the employment system in the mills. The neutrality of the inspectors is suspect – some of them are local men with ties either of kinship or finance to the mill owners.

There is a second issue, and one that is much darker. Indirectly related to the scandal of child labour we have an 'outbreak' of baby farming in the Bingley district. Those who procure young children for the factories, as I have described above, are also running profitable enterprises in the exploitation of young women and their offspring. The enormous increase in populations of the mill towns in the north, both east and west, has led to much social distress, not least the numbers of illegitimate babies born to unfortunate women. As you know, the repercussions of bearing a bastard child are merciless. No woman with a small baby and without a husband can work to feed herself or it; the woman must seek to beg – or apply to the workhouse. Hence, they make use of the baby farms.

Although I feel sure you are probably well acquainted with how these inhuman enterprises are arranged, in case you have forgotten I will refresh your memory. Usually advertisements are placed in local papers by women claiming to want to 'care for' children – for a price. This is not illegal. They require an annual single charge of, say, twelve pounds to take the baby at birth and foster or adopt it for at least a year. But the ill-treatment it receives usually results in its death and the baby farmer pockets the fee unearned. The mother, either relieved at the opportunity to delegate responsibility for the unwanted child to another or too distracted by other young mouths to feed, relies on the woman to do her best for her baby. Infant mortality is such a common occurrence in the slums of our towns that such deaths are only briefly mourned. The mother, accepting this fact of life, does not seek to make too close enquiry as to the manner of her baby's death. This is a national scandal. As I have said, fostering is not illegal, but the murdering of babies is. There have been reports, especially in London and other large cities, of unidentified naked little corpses floating in rivers, or wrapped in paper and thrust into privies and onto midden heaps.

Having, I hope, achieved your attention I will now go on to explain the situation here in Bingley. I believe the same people are involved in both scandals. They take a percentage of the fees and in return provide accommodation and basic set-up costs for the women who run them. I have other details in my possession which I will be pleased to share with you.

I hope I have adequately described as well as I can on paper the two iniquities that are being perpetrated here. We might say these little ones are 'innocents to the slaughter'; but perhaps we have all lost our innocence in these mechanical times. In your practical way, I hope you will agree to help uncover the actual horrors being enacted daily and which for sheer wickedness far exceed my powers of description with this pen.

If you are able and willing to help investigate these scandals please write care of the Fountain Inn, Bingley, and address your

Chapter 1

correspondence to a name I will use for anonymity – Randal Saunders. There are serious risks in trying to expose the perpetrators of such dreadful practices and those among them who will stop at nothing to preserve both their businesses and their status.

I remain in anticipation of your reply,
Your humble servant,
Donald Thwaites

Ambrose was silent as he considered for a while and then re-read the letter more slowly. 'It seems to me these are very serious issues. What he's alleging is truly shocking, but I can't think why a man would write such a letter unless he has substantial reasons for doing so. He's also clearly worried about identifying himself as an informer.' He looked questioningly at McNiece. 'What do we know about baby farmers? It's not something I've come across personally – although I've heard the term.'

McNiece sat back in his chair. 'Thwaites – or Saunders – has described what happens very accurately, as far as I understand it. It's a vile trade and one we should all be ashamed of.'

Ambrose considered the letter again. 'Thwaites is also concerned about the use of under-age labour which, despite the recent legislation, is obviously still happening. Now that's something I know about. I must admit, James, I'm really tempted to consider this one. But obviously Donald Thwaites's two concerns are connected and investigating both might have to be a two-hander – something I've never undertaken before. I'm much better working alone – it's less complicated. Besides, I can't think of anyone who would want to take the sort of risks this man's hinting at. You wouldn't…?'

McNiece jumped in swiftly. 'Oh, no! You're the "doer" in this partnership, I'm the "talker". I think I've passed the age for adventures and it's not something we've ever contemplated before – working together in that way. I'm more use here!' He thought for a moment. 'What about your friend in Suffolk – Edgar Lawes? You say he's told you how much he envied your undercover role in the Seddon Union affair. With his money, he obviously has the luxury and freedom of time.'

'I think – between you and me – that was just armchair wishes! Besides, his life's tied up with official and estate business. I doubt he'd really have the time for something like this, although I don't doubt his courage – he's young and can look after himself. Anyway, I'll sleep on this and give it more thought tomorrow. Whatever happens I'll respond to Thwaites's letter and tell him I'm interested. It looks as though I'm already talking myself into a trip to Yorkshire!'

Over several more brandies James promised he would draft a reply to the Northumbrian MP suggesting that they had not turned his request down completely but were otherwise immediately engaged on another equally pressing matter. That was not to say they wouldn't be interested in following it up later in the year. Ambrose could never say 'no', even to a request that might result in some personal hardship; but he had a chronic antipathy towards dark, enclosed spaces.

By the time he left his sister's house to walk home, McNiece was in that pleasant state of the semi-oblivion several glasses of good spirits provide – not too drunk to make a fool of himself, but happy enough to ride out the storm from his wife at the lateness of the hour of his return and the unfortunate fact that he had missed saying goodnight to his daughter and grandchildren.

Ambrose arrived at the office of the *Escritoire* early next morning and immediately set about composing a letter to Thwaites.

The Escritoire,
Fleet Street

Monday, 11 March 1839
Dear Mr Saunders,
I address you by your pseudonym as it will be less confusing in the future for us both to use one familiar name each, and probably less dangerous if what you say is true. As you see I have sent this under seal and write under the name Frank Barrett, a new identity for me. I'm afraid my professional name suffers from a certain notoriety, my accounts having been published and read nationally. As I note, you are concerned about the vested

Chapter 1

interests underlying these cases and therefore discretion is clearly advisable by us both.

I read your letter with great interest and concern. As you acknowledge, I have much experience in the business of child labour in the textile mills of Lancashire, but my understanding of the vile practice of baby farming is less complete, although I will immediately begin researching all that I can find on the subject.

To be brief – I am very interested in meeting you and hearing what you must say before fully committing myself. In the meantime, I would like to discuss the matter with a close and trustworthy friend – one who is a Justice of the Peace and shares with me the same wish: that is to achieve justice for the poor and particularly their unfortunate children. Putting it plainly, to investigate both aspects that you describe would need the involvement of two people. I'm not certain whether he will be willing to assist – and must first show him your letter. This may take a little time.

I am aware of the risks you are running and to reduce them I think it best that correspondence between us is kept to a minimum. Therefore, it is unnecessary for you to respond to this letter, unless there are aspects with which you disagree, in which case I would be obliged if you would reply by return before I make approaches to the third party. If I receive no response from you within seven days, that is by the 18th, then I will assume I may go ahead and seek help from my friend and between us, if he is willing, plan for our journey north. I will write from my colleague's home in Suffolk letting you know when we will arrive in Bingley and arranging a date for you and me to meet at the Fountain, if that is appropriate – and still safe. You may find it easy to identify me by my height, which is considerably taller than average!

In the meantime, please take all considerations necessary for your safety.

I remain your servant,
Frank Barrett

Ambrose was not entirely certain that Edgar would want to be part of this investigation; estate or court matters might be so pressing he couldn't give up the time. But from what his friend had told him last Christmas when he was his guest in Suffolk, time was not a problem. He was then three months away from the end of his year as Guardian of Seddon Workhouse and had almost decided to give up his place on the board; particularly now that the new chairman, and his friend, the farmer Edward Lake, a staunch supporter of humanitarian change, were both very actively involved in its daily running. He told Ambrose that he felt he could now step back – being on hand if necessary as a JP with special status which allowed him to visit the workhouse whenever he felt it was necessary.

Ambrose considered Edgar a man of infinite good sense. Although sometimes too cautious – he was a lawyer after all – he certainly had an acute sense of the injustices meted out by greedy and wicked people, particularly on children with no power to protest. The more he thought it through, the more likely he considered Edgar would be incensed at the idea of babies being sold for profit, maltreated and, even worse, murdered.

Ambrose waited anxiously for the post each day, but there was no response from Donald Thwaites. After the seven days had passed he penned a letter to Edgar Lawes, laying out briefly the background, and his concerns and thoughts as to possible action. Without divulging too many details of his planning – which was now well underway in his head – he put it simply to Edgar that he might like to join him in this enterprise which, he warned, would not be without some danger. If Edgar was interested Ambrose went on to suggest that he would visit Seddon Hall as soon as convenient. Within four days Edgar replied that he was delighted to hear from his friend, pleased to offer him all the hospitality he was able and intrigued by the prospective undertaking. If his friend would write back immediately

Chapter 1

and let him know when he would arrive in Ipswich he would ensure his coach and four were at his disposal.

Responding straight away, Ambrose told Edgar that he would take a couple of weeks to prepare himself physically for the investigation and therefore to expect him on the mail-coach arriving on Saturday, 6 April, a week after Easter.

During this time, he read all he could about the recent changes in legislation, although as a professional journalist he always followed parliamentary proceedings closely. More to the point, he collected and examined as many advertisements for child-fostering as he could find. James was right in that respect: it was an open and booming business. The numerous women who advertised made no bones about the fact that they sought money in return for the care or adoption of babies. A typical example was as follows:

> *A widow with a little family of her own would be glad to accept the charge of a young child, age no object. If sickly, would receive a mother's care. Terms fifteen shillings a month. Would adopt entirely if under a month old for the small sum of twelve pounds.*

A desperate young girl with no means of supporting herself or her baby would understand the significance of the advertisement. No questions would be asked as to the child's origins. All that was required was ready money.

As always, Ambrose endeavoured to look the part he should be playing.

He gathered together a good supply of workman's clothing and two pairs of stout boots. As a working man seeking new employment he could present himself as well set up according to his station. Indeed, it was necessary that he build up some muscle if he was to be a credible labourer. He realised how out of condition he was as a result of his sedentary trade as a writer, although his height and build were such that he could never be considered fat. He took steps to tone up, but limited time meant he would have to keep up his exercises until he arrived in Bingley. Perhaps while he was in Suffolk he could get in some riding if Edgar would lend him the ambling mare. But he had to start the physical process immediately and so he asked his landlady whether she had any physical jobs she needed doing.

'What about these logs, Mrs Bridie? They must need splitting.' And he pointed out the large pile that was delivered fortnightly and lay mounting up in the back yard.

'Young Thomas comes to do that, Mr Hudson. I couldn't possibly put him out of a job. He needs the money.'

'What if I was to pay him what he would have earned, plus a small bonus for inconvenience, and tell him to take the time off?'

'I'm sure he wouldn't argue with that, Mr Hudson,' said his landlady with a laugh.

The lad didn't argue and went off to find paid occupation elsewhere for the two weeks. Now they were both happy: the boy was well in pocket and swinging the large axe twice daily did wonders for Ambrose's physique – even in a couple of weeks.

Acknowledging Ambrose's letter, Edgar confirmed he would himself come to meet him in Ipswich and they could talk in private on the journey back to Seddon Hall. So, very early on Friday, 5 April, Ambrose, with all that he hoped would be necessary for his assignment, left London on the mail-coach for Suffolk.

Chapter 2

SUFFOLK

A warm April day with all the expected signs of spring. The Ipswich post-house was busy and Edgar's driver was pressed to find a parking space close to the entrance where the mail-coach would pull in. There was some time to wait – coaches were invariably late because of hold-ups on the road, and the London coach pulled in with horns blowing an hour after time.

Edgar immediately recognised his friend – well over 6 feet and still without much flesh, he stood out from the crowd most easily. Likewise, Ambrose had no difficulty in perceiving his host and raised his hand in acknowledgement as he waited for his boxes to be thrown down. Edgar's coachman loaded them on the back of the carriage and as soon as they could make their way through the mass of horses, carriages and carts they drove out of the post-house entrance onto the road.

Having completed the normal courtesies, Edgar was anxious to learn more about the undertaking. But before Ambrose expanded on what he had already divulged, he was just as anxious to hear about Peter Samuels and William Tuttle, the two young boys they'd rescued from the Seddon workhouse the previous year.

Edgar told him that it was all good news. 'William remains with the Lodges, Fred and Amy and their two lads. And he's really come on in all departments. Good food, fresh air and above all a loving family have done wonders. I swear he's grown at least 2 inches. He's certainly tall for an 11-year-old.'

'That's good news, Edgar. He writes regularly to tell me how lucky he thinks he is and how much he owes to Fred and Amy. Does he mention the workhouse at all? Or has he buried it away out of memory?'

'I'm not sure. He's still occasionally withdrawn and when he first arrived was very shy and suspicious of strangers; he was reluctant to step outside the Lodge House and clung to Amy.'

'That's not unusual – it was all so sudden.'

'Although it took two or three weeks of adjustment, once William was out of the atmosphere of the workhouse he seemed to blossom very quickly. But he has also had to cope with some other changes. My steward Sam Saunby retired in October and moved into a cottage in Boxford. Fred has now officially taken on the role of my estate manager and the family moved into the estate house when Sam vacated it. It's a very good size; it's large enough for Amy to run a school there for 10 children.'

'A school? Well, you always said the village children should have one. Amy's the perfect teacher, I suppose?'

'Yes, none better. Will attends and is a great favourite with all the other children; Amy's older boy Frederick hero-worships him. William's reading and writing are coming on very well, no small thanks to your consistent correspondence with both him and Peter.'

'Yes, Peter; how is he faring?'

'As you know, when we took him out of the workhouse he went to live with Harry Valentine and his wife Mary, where he's thriving. Having placed him as an apprentice stable boy, Harry and I have been surprised how he shows an incredible affinity with the horses.'

'Really? Where do you think that comes from?'

'Animals don't judge, Ambrose. Peter trusts them like he never trusted a human being. I would say they "don't let you down"! But of course they can do – literally. After a few spills, he's become confident enough to handle some of Harry's more challenging animals and we never had to put him on the "ambling mare" as you call her! Now Harry's showing Peter how to break in a horse for riding.'

'I suppose you could say the hardship of the union would make or break a child. I always knew Peter was a fighter. This just shows how determined he is to make the best of things.'

'The lad will be 16 this year and I have to tell you – is in love!'

That did surprise Ambrose. It was difficult to imagine the young, scowling scruffy lad he remembered from their days as inmates together as being 'in love'.

'Is it anyone you know?' he asked.

'Certainly is! You must remember Caroline Alfrey? She of the

Chapter 2

symmetrical features and luminescence; at least that was how you described her – and her mother – in your journal! Peter has met her several times at the Lakes' farm suppers, and he was invited with me, as my protégé, to Hugh and Deborah Bradshaw's garden party in the summer, where the young couple were seen to be particularly friendly.'

'They're very young for any serious consideration of marriage, surely? Do you think a match between them would be suitable?'

'Why not? Consider their backgrounds: they share a similar history and have both suffered because of their parents' misfortunes. They've now put that life behind them and embarked on another more fortunate one. If they should find mutual attraction in each other, I can see no harm. But I agree with you, I think for two 15-year-olds marriage is a way away yet. Let's see if the affection withstands the test of time.'

'He's not likely to have his heart broken, is he?' asked Ambrose anxiously.

'Deborah Bradshaw says Caroline has told her that she has great affection for him. It was interesting how they came together, again another outcome of their time in the House. You may remember that Peter's mother is buried in St Mary's churchyard and that he regularly visits her grave.'

Ambrose nodded. 'Yes, when he was a workhouse boy Amy Lodge gave him time to do it when we walked over to the church for a Sunday service. It was one of the questions he asked when you offered him the apprenticeship – would he still be able to visit the grave?'

'Yes, well, Caroline Alfrey's father Richard is also buried nearby; unfortunately as a suicide his body's outside consecrated ground in the field adjoining the churchyard, but the site had a wooden marker. That's how they met – both visiting their parents' graves.'

Ambrose was silent for a moment as he thought of his friend Richard Alfrey and the terrible circumstances that led him to take his own life.

Edgar went on. 'They immediately knew they had much in common and were able to appreciate each other's loss and its circumstances. Obviously, Peter was attracted to Caroline's beauty, and he's not such a bad-looking young chap himself. In fact, they make a handsome couple.'

Ambrose laughed. 'It seems like a match made in heaven! Although its wellspring – the workhouse – was its very antithesis. But personally, I hope they don't tie the knot too soon – they're both very young and should enjoy their situations for a while longer before they settle to domesticity and family life.'

'You speak as though that were a life sentence. Have you never thought of marriage yourself?'

'Once or twice there has been someone – but my work doesn't incline to the settled life; it's erratic and I'm often away for weeks on end. I think I'll become a crusty old bachelor – I'm nearly 40 after all! But what about you? You're in a far better situation to settle down, and I'm sure there are plenty of young women who would be very willing to take on the name of Lawes!'

'One of the disadvantages of belonging to an aristocratic family – even a cadet branch – is that there are too many predatory mothers out there waiting to pounce. You've met one of them – Lady Somerset and her two ugly daughters. Unfortunately, she doesn't have a Cinderella. As far as I can see my county is devoid of beautiful luminescent women, at least those available for matrimony. Believe me – I keep my eyes open; but I've found none to tempt me yet.'

'Perhaps Yorkshire will be more fruitful!'

'Ah yes – Yorkshire. Tell me more about this enterprise, which does sound like something to tempt me.'

Ambrose enlarged on what he had already described in his letter. His proposal was first to meet with Donald Thwaites to ascertain names, places and details that the man had promised to pass on. 'Without that information we can't proceed, so we must meet him face to face. Depending on your willingness to become involved, I'll write to him and arrange a meeting in this tavern – the Fountain – which is in the town of Bingley. Not a place I know at all, so we'll have to do a little research first.'

'We should ask Hugh Bradshaw. He'll have information about the place in his extensive library – even if it's only Farley's *Domesday!*'

'Good idea. As I mentioned, the reason I'm anxious for your help is

CHAPTER 2

that the investigation is twofold: the illegal child labour and the business of baby farming. I'm best placed to investigate factory workings – having done it often before, I know what to look for. What I need is someone who'll discreetly follow up these allegations of baby farming outside the confines of the mill; I can do anything required from the inside. How we proceed separately needs much more discussion and planning. But are you willing to help?'

He stopped and looked challengingly at Edgar. He was certain of his friend's moral commitment to righting issues of injustice, but he had never really been tried in a practical way. It was true that he had dramatically set the ball rolling at Seddon with his investigation of the adulteration of the food in the establishment – but that hardly put his personal safety at risk. When it came to it, was Mr Lawes JP an armchair philosopher, enlightened in mind but perhaps unable to transfer his philanthropy into actions, especially ones that invited danger?

As though reading his thoughts, Edgar sat back in the carriage and looked directly at Ambrose. 'I know you have doubts as to whether I can exchange the comfortable life for a disagreeable one – even if only for a little while. I think you perceive me to be rather – shall we say soft, the result of a privileged upbringing. Admittedly, I've never been tested – never fought a battle, or even been involved in a brawl, not since childhood anyway. But I have a very good aim with a pistol and can fence with the best. About my personal courage – you'll have to take my word that I'll do my best not to let you down in a fight. That's really all the assurances I can give you. As for "roughing it", I can get my hands dirty when necessary. I'm no fop, believe me; Harry Valentine and I have often ended up in the mud together working with fractious horses.' He raised his eyebrows quizzically. 'Have I said enough to convince you?'

'You don't have to say anything to me about your personal integrity – I know you're a man of your word and would try never to let anyone down once you've given it. As for physical courage, none of us knows our breaking points. In truth, I've only been in a few fights myself – mostly unconnected with investigations and usually because of intervening foolishly in tavern brawls where I would've done better to mind my own business. I don't seek out trouble while

I'm on assignments; the whole idea of working incognito is to be unobserved and discreet. If you really want to be involved I can't think of anyone else I'd rather have with me.' He held out his hand and Edgar shook it firmly.

The drive to Seddon took some hours as en route they stopped to bait the horses and themselves. By the time they reached the Hall it was late and dark. The servants carried Ambrose's boxes to his room and he washed, changed and went downstairs to find Edgar in his library where cold food and a good claret were waiting for him. His host suggested that they leave all discussion of the forthcoming enterprise until the morning; it had been two long days of travelling for his guest. Having refreshed themselves they parted company.

At breakfast, they planned the day. 'I'm anxious to let Donald Thwaites know of your willingness to be involved and to arrange a meeting between us as soon as possible. If you'll allow me use of your library, I'll write to him now.' Having discussed itinerary and schedule with Edgar previously, he told Donald that the pair proposed to arrive in Yorkshire no later than 15 April and he would send word to meet him somewhere close to 16 or 17 of the month – he could be no more specific than that.

It was a bright April Sunday and reminded Ambrose of his first few weeks in Seddon House a year previously. Although he had no wish to dwell on the events of the last twelve months, it was difficult not to with all the reminders around him. The letter to Thwaites having been sent, Edgar asked his friend how he wanted to spend the day.

'I'd like to visit Peter and William beyond anything else.'

'You do realise that your arrival here will be common gossip by now and there'll be several people anxious to see you since your visit at Christmas.'

'Hmm! I was hoping to avoid too many social calls.'

'I'm afraid in a close-knit community like Seddon that isn't possible. Curiosity – I call it just plain nosiness – will fuel everyone's determination to meet you again.'

'So long as we can limit it to short visits for tea or some such; I rule out dining and cards!'

Chapter 2

Visiting Peter took no time as he was busy in the stables at the back of the Hall. Apart from the animals used for drawing and hacking, Edgar Lawes kept a small but thriving string of racehorses, some of which he used for breeding, others he trained and raced. He was beginning to be recognised in the county as something of an expert and had good connections with many of the stables in Newmarket. One of his young mares was a third-generation offspring of Wizard, the winner of the first 2,000 Guineas race in 1809 on Newmarket Heath. Valentine's view was: 'With that pedigree she'll make you a packet, sir!'

They found Peter mucking out a stable and so intent on his work that he was unaware of Ambrose walking up behind him.

'Just can't keep away from that straw, can you?'

Peter looked up with a start and then his intense, serious face broke into a beaming smile. 'Mr Hudson – it's you! Mr Lawes said you were expected.'

Ambrose held out his hand and Peter took it firmly and pumped it up and down in delight at seeing his old friend once again. Standing back and looking at the boy, Ambrose could see that Edgar was right. Peter was growing into a physically powerful young man; he seemed to have shot up by another inch since he last saw him at Christmas and was also filling out proportionately. There was every reason why Caroline Alfrey might return his affection; he was a fine young man altogether, with his clear grey eyes and a reddish tinge to his hair. His expression, which had been furtive and mistrusting when he was an inmate in the House, had cleared and was now open and frank. The Valentines had done a good job in building not only his physique but his confidence. Peter now looked Ambrose fully in the face.

At that moment, Harry had come around the corner to investigate the sound of voices and Ambrose held out his hand in greeting. 'Good morning, Harry; good to see you again.'

'Likewise, Mr Hudson,' and Harry Valentine shook the hand offered with a hard grip.

'If it's all right with you both I'd like to take this young man off for a few hours – perhaps ride over to the Lodges to see William.'

'How are you on a horse these days?' asked Edgar. 'Riding was never a favourite pastime of yours as I remember!'

'I'm no better than I was last time I rode. I've no need to keep a horse in London – there's no point when there are plenty of street vehicles for hire. I still have a healthy respect for anything on four legs that is taller and stronger than I am!'

Harry laughed. 'You should take the ambling mare, Mr Hudson. Peter will ride something more in line with his abilities.'

Edgar said, 'I'll leave you both to it. I've some papers to see to. Be careful with my beast, Ambrose! She'll tell me if you mishandle her!'

The docile, plodding, dun-coloured horse was saddled and Ambrose, who was no rider, felt distinctly uncomfortable as he was sure she was looking disdainfully at him down her emblazoned nose. He was certain she recognised and remembered him from his lack of skills on outings last winter. Peter rode a young bay he was responsible for training.

'I'll lead the way, Mr Hudson.' And, with a sensitivity unusual in a young man, carefully kept his more impatient mount in check, while allowing Ambrose's mare to set her own gentle pace.

'Which route would you prefer, sir? There are several possible tracks to the Lodges' house.'

Ambrose said he would first like to visit the churchyard at St Mary's. So, the two trotted quietly across to the Norman church where they dismounted at the lychgate and tied the horses to a low-hanging branch of a willow newly flushed with catkins. The local parishioners were all at prayer, at least the godliest, and no one observed them as they walked along the pathway leading to the church door. They could see that many of the old graves were now mostly grassed over; the more recent had customary signs of remembrance – little bunches of spring flowers placed against the headstones.

'Let's go and see your mother's grave.'

Silently the boy led him to a secluded – and calculatedly excluded – corner of the graveyard. This was where inmates of the House were buried, well away from the rest of the parish community. There were different arrangements here; none of the graves were marked; they were simply mounds covered in grass. Peter's mother's grave was the

Chapter 2

exception. As they walked towards it Ambrose could see a smart granite headstone with a large bunch of fresh daffodils arranged in a little pot at its foot. He bent over to read what was inscribed and a lump came into his throat:

> *In memory of Janet May Samuels*
> *Died 5 July 1837*
> *Aged 32 years*
> *Loving mother of Peter Samuels*
> *She will always be with the angels*

'That's a beautiful headstone,' he murmured.

'Mr Lawes paid for it. He went to a lot of trouble to find out when Ma was exactly born and died.'

'Who chose the words?' asked Ambrose.

'I did. Mrs Lodge said I was good enough to write down what I would like written on it and give it to the stonemason. That was about the time I was learning my letters – she did give me some help. But they're my own words. She will be – won't she?'

'What's that?'

'Always with the angels.'

Ambrose could not bring himself to speak safely so he nodded and squeezed Peter's arm. They stood in respectful silence for a while and then Ambrose suggested that Peter showed him Richard Alfrey's grave which was on the other side of the churchyard wall. They retraced their steps down the path and back out of the gate.

They found the grave which looked rather incongruous isolated up against the wall – excluded from any contact with those in hallowed ground; but it also bore a headstone. The memories came flooding back to Ambrose. How he had found Richard hanging from a beam in the workhouse yard, his final act of desperation as he faced the fact that he was unable to protect his wife and daughter. How Calman, the master of the House, had cut him down and between them they had laid him on a stable door. The cursory nature of the inquest which found Alfrey to be temporarily deranged, and the swiftness of his consignment to a hole in the ground dug by inmates directed to do so. There had been no service, no blessing; no acknowledgement that all men, regardless of their final condition, deserve a dignified interment. The only mourners had been his wife and daughter and Ambrose who, as well as being part of the work detail left behind to fill in the hole, had been the man's only friend in that bleak institution. But where he remembered a bare newly dug patch of earth surrounded by pasture, there was now a neatly edged plot and a recently erected headstone. It was inscribed with the words:

> *Here lies Richard Alfrey aged 37 years*
> *Died 28 May 1838*
> *Loving and gentle*
> *Husband of Emily*
> *and*
> *Father of Caroline*
> *May he finally rest in peace*

This was a fitting epitaph for a man who certainly merited the description. Ambrose promised himself he would return with flowers, although they were plentiful already; it was clear that mother and daughter were regular visitors. He asked Peter if Mr Lawes had organised this headstone as well.

'Mr Lawes and Mr Bradshaw arranged things together,' Peter told him.

The pair walked together in silence back to the tethering place, immersed in their own thoughts. Indeed, after having mounted up and ridden off, it was some quarter of an hour before either spoke.

Their thoughts were running along the same tracks and, with some prompting, Peter was eager to tell Ambrose how he was thoroughly immersed in his stable work. 'It's as though I was born to it, at least that's what Mr Valentine says. He thinks I could end up with stables of my own one day.'

'Is that what you would like?' asked Ambrose.

'I'd like it very much especially if it meant…' And his voice trailed off.

Ambrose immediately guessed what the lad was thinking but

Chapter 2

decided not to enquire into the current situation as far as Peter's feelings for Caroline Alfrey were concerned. He would find the right moment for a proper conversation on that score. He was happy the boy had found a soulmate but concerned that he might rush into marriage and all it entailed when he was still too young. Besides, Peter was not able to earn anything like enough money to support a wife – and children. No, he would wait a day or two before broaching the subject.

Arriving at the Lodges' house which, as Edgar had described, was a substantial one, they were immediately met by William Tuttle and Fred and Amy Lodge's two young boys playing together in the garden surrounding the building. Throwing down a stick that he was using as a sword, he ran over to greet the two riders – recognising Peter immediately, but uncertain about Ambrose.

As Peter dismounted he called to his friend, 'Will! Here's a surprise. Mr Hudson's come to see us again. You remember, Mr Lawes said he was coming soon.'

William rushed to the gate and then, suddenly becoming shy, hung back as Ambrose strode through. The meetings between them had generally started off awkwardly as Will was still getting used to his good fortune and occasionally thought it was either a dream or he would be taken back to the House by someone in a tall hat and black boots.

Ambrose put him at his ease by holding out a hand and greeting him fondly. 'Hello, Will! I told you at Christmas I'd be back as soon as I could. I hope you've been getting my letters. I've kept all of yours – I don't think you've missed a week, so I have quite a pile now. I must say, your writing's almost as good as Mrs Lodge's and Mr Lawes always said she has the best hand in the district. You couldn't have had a better teacher. And you are looking very well.'

Indeed, he was. The small, thin and pinched boy he had known in the House had grown rapidly in a short space of time. His tow-coloured hair was thick and neatly clipped to a collar length. His face had filled out, along with the rest of him, thanks to good feeding. But it was the difference in his expression and demeanour that struck Ambrose most acutely. Like Peter, he had lost the untrusting, sceptical look of a boy who lacked any care or affection. He also returned Ambrose's smile with a charming one of his own, which lit up his face. Within a few minutes they were chatting together as they had done at Christmas. By this time Fred, Amy Lodge and Fred's uncle Ted Lake had come out of the house to see what the noise was about and after greetings had been exchanged everyone moved through the front door into the large hall.

It was, as one might expect from its inhabitants, a place of warmth and comfort, bearing all the usual signs of untidiness in a house with three young boys romping around it.

'Come in and welcome!' Amy Lodge led them all into a large sitting room with comfortable chairs and a wood fire; for despite it being early spring there was still a winter chill in the air. 'Sit down, everyone, I'll arrange for refreshments to be brought in.'

William had disappeared for a few minutes but returned carrying a large flat folio tied with tape. He placed it on the table. 'Here's my scrap book, Mr Hudson; I've pasted every letter you've ever sent me, even the first one you wrote while Peter and me were still in the House. Look – they're all in order according to their dates. Mrs Lodge told me that was the best way to keep them.'

As Ambrose opened the book his eyes fell on the first inclusion and he was momentarily overcome when he saw a small paper label with two pin holes; on the label was written in very faded ink: 'William Tuttle'. This scrap of paper was the only evidence that William had of his family name. It had been found pinned to his blanket after someone, presumably his mother, had left him at the gates of the workhouse, having decided for one reason or another that she could no longer take care of him. A few weeks after the boys had left the workhouse Edgar had made enquiries about their pasts.

'I was successful as far as Peter was concerned, but not for William. I drew a blank everywhere I looked,' he told Ambrose in a letter. 'There was no mention of any Tuttles in the records of the local parishes that made up the Seddon Union. That tiny scrap of paper pinned on the blanket was the only clue as to who he was. How he's kept it safe for 11 years is miraculous, but he lived in hopes of tracing her whereabouts one day.'

Chapter 2

Ambrose was particularly interested in how William was doing at school.

'I go with Mr and Mrs Lodge's two boys, Fred and Tom.'

'How many children are in the school, William?'

'Eight boys and two girls. Did you know, all of us can read – and write quite well, including the youngest who's only six.'

'Why don't you show me how well you can read; perhaps from the book you're reading now. What is it?'

'It's called *Midshipman Easy* by a man called Captain Marryat.'

'Oh yes, and what's it about?'

'A boy who joins the navy during some wars—'

'I think they were called the Napoleonic Wars, William. But tell me a little of the story.' Ambrose was impressed with William's fluency and the fact that he had grasped some of the more difficult ideas in the book. He turned to Amy and said, 'You've taught him well. It's only been just over nine months since he came to you and already he's a confident reader – and understands what he's reading.'

'William's one of the fastest learners I've come across,' she said. 'It's as though he's always been thirsting to learn. I had no difficulty in getting him to remember his alphabet and your letters to him helped considerably. He was quite desperate to read them for himself. The fact that you kept your promise and wrote every week gave him a real incentive to practise – and that's all learning to read really is, practising every day. Now William takes books that interest him off the shelf. He likes this book because of the adventures Jack Easy has, especially rescuing the lady from a Spanish ship and fighting pirates. He reads some of it each night to Fred and Tom and now they're all mad to go to sea!'

'From what I've heard about the treatment of sailors in the British navy, I think it would be a good idea to discourage such notions!' Ambrose laughed. 'In fact, I once thought I'd do a piece on an ordinary sailor's life on a British frigate, but when I listened to some of their stories in the taverns round the London docks I soon changed my mind. Apart from the conditions I'd have to live in, I'm a poor sailor; once there was the slightest swell I'd be on my back suffering in my hammock.'

The conversation turned to reminiscences about the events and people connected with the Seddon Union. Fred could tell them little. 'Since I left being its porter I've had little contact with any of our mutual acquaintances. I did hear through local gossip that one or two of the inmates, females mostly, had managed to get out. One's been lucky in that her sister came into some money from a grateful employer and she's been able to offer her a home while she seeks work to keep herself.'

'It's always good to hear that someone managed to get out,' said Ambrose. 'What else is new there?'

'The surgeon's infirmary was built just in time, as three of the inmates contracted consumption. They were the first to be nursed in it by a woman with real nursing skills. Sadly, three other inmates died – the reforms to their diet had been too little and too late for some of them.'

'And what about the officials – Jennie and John Calman, for example? Anyone heard of them since we threw them out?'

'Nothing. They seem to have disappeared without trace. There've been various rumours as to their whereabouts, but no sightings have ever been confirmed. For most of us it was good riddance! The surgeon Matthew Burgwin continues to treat the inmates, as well as extending his practice in the Seddon parishes. He's now engaged to Robert Bignell's eldest daughter, but they won't marry for at least two years until Robert's satisfied his future son-in-law can keep his daughter in a condition to which her father had accustomed her.'

'So, apart from the infirmary and the doctor doing a proper job at last, what about the new officials? How are they settling in?'

'As you know, the union has a new master and matron who immediately replaced the Calmans. They are a married couple with previous experience in charge of running a large country house in Norfolk. They are both well thought of. Nothing like the Calmans!'

'Thank God for that!' said Ambrose. 'And how's the new chairman doing?'

'Very energetically, Mr Hudson! He and my uncle here' – and he waved his hand at Ted Lake – 'have introduced all the reforms

Chapter 2

that were suggested, mostly accepted with a good grace by the other guardians and officials.'

'Good. Glad to hear it.'

'After all the serious events of the previous year, a representative of the Poor Law Commissioners made a visit – announced well in advance – and found everything to be "in order".'

'Just as one might expect,' muttered Ambrose.

'You might have guessed that nothing was said in criticism of the previous chairman, Colonel Jack Shepherd.'

'I am surprised!' said Ambrose sarcastically. 'Is he still devoting his energies to his position as Master of Foxhounds of the Seddon Hunt?'

'That and hounding poachers,' said Fred. 'The commissioners entirely overlooked his mismanagement of the House. But overall, the union workhouse is slowly pulling itself into a semblance of normality, leastways as normal as such an institution could ever be.'

Peter and Ambrose spent a pleasant afternoon with the Lodges, but finally it was time to leave.

'Will you be back soon, sir?' asked William, with a touch of anxiety in his voice.

'I can't be certain when exactly, but sometime in the summer perhaps,' was the best Ambrose could promise.

The boy looked disappointed.

Peter led the way back at a pace that he felt Ambrose could manage, although both horses automatically quickened their trot, energised with a kind of equine sixth sense as they anticipated a good feed and clean stables. As he gazed through the ears of the ambling mare Ambrose found the rhythm of the horse helped with the flow of ideas that he intended to discuss with Edgar that evening.

Peter had his own thoughts also as they rode back through the bridleways to Seddon Hall. Mostly they were centred on Caroline Alfrey, which was not unusual because he rarely thought of much else – apart from the racing mare that was in foal; he had high hopes her offspring would turn out to be a winner. But Caroline was certainly already a winner in his mind. He thought, as always, of his first meeting with her; both were carrying bunches of summer flowers. The gardener at Seddon Hall had given him some dwarf dahlias from the borders of the walled garden. Caroline had brought some bright orange marigolds. He had seen her over the wall as she kneeled to arrange the flowers in a pot at the foot of the headstone. Her nimble fingers were skilful and soon she had a pretty arrangement, its colour making a startling contrast to the dark granite of the stone. As she stood their eyes met, and she blushed slightly at his wide-eyed gaze. Immediately aware that he might have offended her by staring, he dropped his eyes and went pink himself.

At a loss as to what to do next both spoke at once: 'I'm just putting—' They laughed out loud together and, needing no further prompting, Peter leaped over the wall and stood at the foot of Richard Alfrey's grave. 'I come here often, but I've never seen you. Mr Edgar Lawes arranged for my mother's headstone – but I made up the words.'

Caroline looked over the wall. 'Yes, I've seen them – they are beautiful words. I'm sure she's always with the angels. I hope my father is too. Sometimes I come with my mother, but mostly on my own. It still upsets her to see his grave outside the churchyard – like he was an outcast who no one cares about but us. We were so grateful when Mr Lawes and Mr Bradshaw provided him with a headstone like your mother's. It makes a great difference having a marked grave. It gave my father some dignity at last.'

Peter nodded sympathetically, at least he hoped it would come across that way. 'We must come on different days. I always notice the flowers on the grave and how well they've been arranged. Not like my efforts which seem all the clumsier compared with yours. I'm all fingers and thumbs!'

Caroline thought for a moment and then said, 'Shall I come over and we could work on them together? They're such pretty flowers – I'm very fond of dahlias and they're not too difficult to arrange. How do you like it at Seddon Hall?'

He was suddenly aware she was looking at him for a response but, as he hadn't heard the question, he just continued staring.

Chapter 2

'I heard you'd left the workhouse and went to Seddon Hall to become a stable boy,' she said.

Pulling himself up from the ground where he had been kneeling beside her, he said quickly, 'I'm an apprentice groom and stable hand. I'm looking after Mr Lawes's racehorses. It's a good job and he says I'm learning fast. I've fallen off a few times, but I'm quite a good rider now – leastways that's what Mr Valentine the stable manager says! I really love horses, although until last year I didn't know anything about them, let alone having ridden one.'

Caroline smiled. 'I've heard that you're doing well. Mr Bradshaw often has Mr Lawes to visit and he talks about you all the time. It seems we've both been lucky since we left the union. My mother and I were found places by Mr Lawes at the Bradshaws'. They are very kind people. My mother is now companion to Miss Deborah Bradshaw and I help her brother Mr Hugh with his books. When I first went there I was a parlour maid, but he caught me looking through his library – I love books – and kindly allowed me to borrow them when I wanted to. He taught me to write properly, and now I help him catalogue his books.'

Peter felt a surge of jealousy at the thought of Caroline closeted in a library with another man, but then he remembered that Hugh Bradshaw was at least 60 – indeed he'd seen him at the workhouse when the gentleman attended the board of guardians' meetings. That thought brought his mind to his time in Seddon and how strange it was that they had never met there since she was an inmate at the same time. But then he remembered it was not so odd because there was strict segregation of men and women in all the workhouses. From the time they were admitted Mrs Alfrey and her daughter didn't see their husband and father until they identified his body three months later. He had taken his own life by hanging, and everyone knew it was because he felt helpless in the face of the overseer Robert Enderby's assault on his wife and the threats he made about his daughter.

Now here the pair were face to face and he was tongue-tied. As if appreciating his confusion, Caroline said, 'I must be off home now, but I expect we'll meet here again, if only by accident.'

Striving not to appear overeager, Peter agreed that it was most likely he would return soon – perhaps they could arrange it together and she could help him with the flowers next time. Nodding prettily, Caroline held out her small hand and Peter took it carefully in his large rough one; he handled it as though it were a piece of porcelain that he might easily drop. They smiled at each other and Peter hopped back over the wall to the other side of the churchyard and watched her walk back down the field path towards the town.

So that's how they met, she arranging a riot of blooms – orange, red and yellow in a pot; he struck dumb in admiration of her beauty. How could he possibly become a friend – and perhaps more – to such a creature? He was a ragamuffin boy from the workhouse. It was only by good fortune that he was settled and had a job that he loved, surrounded by people who accepted him for what he had been, but believing in him to the extent of giving him a home. They had so much faith in him he sometimes wondered if he had as much in himself. For most of his life he'd had no one to whom he could show any consideration, apart from William, and no one who'd ever lavished affection on him. He often thought he must be unlovable. Now new feelings were stirring in him, ones he'd never experienced before. Was this love? He had no way of knowing. But when he looked at Caroline Alfrey his chest seemed to want to burst and the blood pumped in his head. He knew it was not the same feeling as anger – he had felt that emotion more times in his life than a boy of his age should. He remembered Enderby's bullying and how useless he had been against it. That had made his heart race also – but not like this. He was covered in a kind of warmth of happiness when he looked at her.

He remembered how he had almost skipped all the way back to Seddon Hall, and how Harry Valentine – a very astute man – had looked him up and down and said, 'Something's up, young man. You've got a spring in your step that wasn't there when you went out. I won't ask, but I might guess. One day you'll tell me what it is and I'll know I'm right!' Well, it was eight months later and everyone knew that Peter Samuels loved Caroline Alfrey and it was pretty much around the town that she returned his affection. Harry Valentine claimed to have been the first to know!

Chapter 2

Peter realised he had drifted off in his own thoughts and completely forgotten about the ambling mare and her mount. Turning around anxiously, he was relieved to see Ambrose safely on board and in an equal brown study, clearly with many things on his mind. They continued in a companionable silence until they reached a place where they could ride side by side and pass the time of day. But each kept their private thoughts to themselves.

Chapter 3

On their return to the Hall their ways parted. Peter and Ambrose dismounted and the boy led both horses back to their stables. Ambrose walked through the front door to be met by Foster, Edgar's manservant.

'Mr Lawes has visitors, Mr Hudson. Lady Somerset has called, with her two daughters.'

Ambrose groaned inwardly. He would have to spend at least an hour being polite to plump Miranda and Esther with the receding chin. Lady Somerset had clearly got wind of the fact that Ambrose was back. As he entered the drawing room, the two young ladies immediately looked coy.

The amply proportioned Lady Somerset bore down on him with gloved hand outstretched. 'Mr Hudson, you are among us again! Are you on an assignment, or is this a purely social visit? I do hope, whichever it is, that you'll be able to dine with us and tell us more of your splendid adventures in the wilds of the north!'

Edgar directed a meaningful glance at his friend which, as Ambrose interpreted it, said, 'Don't blame me, I couldn't keep them away. These are two marriageable women who can't find mates. We're all fair game!' Aloud, Edgar said, 'We'll be delighted to dine tomorrow evening if that's convenient. Otherwise I'm afraid we will have to decline as both of us have several commitments before Ambrose leaves us; unfortunately, none of them can be rearranged.'

'Oh! Such a shame, we are already dining with family over in Ipswich tomorrow and will not be back for two days. Perhaps when you are next here, Mr Hudson, you will put us in your diary – as a priority!'

Ambrose smiled and made polite noises about not wanting to miss an evening with the Somerset ladies etc. etc. The girls looked extremely disappointed at another missed opportunity. He felt somewhat sorry for them. What were two plain girls to do who could not find suitable men to marry? Custom dictated they would have to remain at home and care for their mother.

After a good dinner Edgar and Ambrose took two bottles of old tawny port into the library. Edgar was anxious to hear what Ambrose had in mind for him as part of the assignment. There was a fire and Foster had ensured all the lamps were lit. The room smelled of old leather – the books and chairs – and Ambrose had always considered it one of the most comfortable rooms he had ever encountered. 'I wish I had a library, Edgar; a place to escape to! I have to make do with an untidy study, although I have invested in a very comfortable chair.'

Edgar leaned forward in his chair. 'Now, tell me about this journey to Bingley. Is it all organised?' he asked eagerly.

'Yes. You realise the journey to Yorkshire will be a long one. I intend to take the York stage as far as Leeds and then hire a carriage to Bingley where we'll stay the night at a coaching inn. I expect Thwaites to provide instructions as to where the Fountain is and we can put up as close as possible to that venue. Once I've heard from Thwaites I'll write back giving brief descriptions of us and arranging to meet in the public bar of the inn on or around the afternoon of 16 or 17 April if we're delayed on the road.'

'Look, I have an idea that might speed up our journey and solve the problem of where we should stay. I have connections stretched all over the country in indirect ways, as a member of one of the many branches of the extended Lawes family; we're spread up and down the country. Among my innumerable cousins and second cousins is one living up on moorland outside Bingley. His name is George Lawes, a widower; he holds large stretches of land, farming sheep extensively; but his greatest interest is in breeding racehorses.'

'I see, so he could be useful to us how?'

'I'm in regular correspondence with him and visited once in the last three years. When you described this venture of yours I wrote to my cousin, in anticipation that you would agree, that I could visit while I was in the area and bring a good friend with me.'

'You obviously gave no hint of what we were about?'

'Of course not. But George is a "good sort" who'll be prepared to accommodate us as necessary and ask no questions as to either our business or movements, which I've explained might be erratic – that is we might disappear for days and then turn up unexpectedly.'

Chapter 3

'Will he agree to that? It does sound as though we'll be using his house like a hotel.'

'As I say, he is very accommodating, although, if our mission is successful, George should be the first to hear all the details before you and McNiece get it into print.'

'That's absolutely reasonable. This will certainly make our business easier – having a decent place to stay and on the doorstep too, and I don't see any reason why we shouldn't tell him why we've come to Bingley. It's all going on in his neighbourhood after all.'

'You're right – and I'd be happy with that. I have another idea to put to you, one you may not agree with – until you've thought about it. As you know, Harry Valentine is training Peter up to be a racing stable master. I've recently had it in my mind to take the lad up north sometime to see some larger racing establishments; Wetherby is closest to Leeds and has an excellent history of racing and some famous studs. My cousin is also a recognised horse breeder in the area and, as we'll be in the district, from my point of view it would be useful to take the boy with us.'

Ambrose felt a flash of concern. 'You don't have any idea of involving him in our assignment, do you? I have an instinct that this one will probably produce more danger than some others I've been involved with. I wouldn't like Peter mixed up in it in any way.'

'Certainly not! It never crossed my mind that would be the case – it's simply an expediency. As we're travelling there, he might as well come with us and take the opportunity to expand his knowledge. My cousin George will be happy to put him up and supervise any visits to Wetherby.'

Ambrose frowned. 'Just as long as Peter's well out of it. Until I know all about the characters we'll be getting involved with and can estimate how dangerous it will be going underground, I can't make exact plans. It'll be a matter of "wait and see" until I speak to Donald Thwaites. Reading his first letter it's quite clear the people he knows who are involved in these activities are ruthless and nasty. I'm sure they'd stop at nothing to protect themselves or their enterprises. I was going to warn you to come armed – knife and pistols. Having lived and worked in the filthy overcrowded streets of Burnley and Manchester I know how risky it can be. Life is cheap for some people – especially those with nothing to lose.'

'Well, I hope it never comes to me using either, but I am prepared, although I still need to hear what you've planned – as far as you can, that is,' said Edgar quizzically.

'I suggest we leave on Friday, the 12th. My estimation is we should arrive in Leeds three days later; it depends how the mail's running. The journey's well over 200 miles by coach and requires at least two overnight stops, maybe three. We have a difficulty getting from Seddon to a stop on the Great North Road to catch it, but I've planned a route that gets us to Yorkshire no later than the 15th. I've already told Thwaites we hope to be in Bingley by that day or the next.'

'Here's another suggestion: it'll make our journey much quicker and easier if I provide the coach and we travel privately. We can still take the mail route which is the most direct but there'll be less waiting around. We can hire changes on the way up and my drivers can collect the horses on their way back as we'll only stop at the most reputable staging inns. My drivers are very knowledgeable about ostlers and stabling. In that way we can drive straight to my cousin's place at Bingley without having to take horses from Leeds. I know you aren't a keen rider, but while we have a couple of days I do advise you to let Peter give you some instruction. We're bound to have to use horseback at some point, and I can't guarantee you an ambling mare! We'll probably have to take what we can get.'

'I take your point and I'll ask Peter to give me some tips about how to stay on any mount I might be forced to take. Thanks for your offer. A journey that doesn't rely on public stagecoaches will be a real advantage; it'll give us flexibility – particularly when and how long we stop at each stage.'

'Tomorrow first thing in the morning we'll walk round to the stables and I'll talk to Harry about Peter's absence, which I'll say could be – what do you think – three or four weeks?'

'Better make it a month. I can never be sure how long these investigations will last. If it looks as though this will be a long one, then I suppose Peter can always be driven home earlier?'

Chapter 3

'Peter has a mare that'll be foaling in a couple of months – he'll definitely want to be back for that.'

'I hope we don't take two months over this. I have no intention of working flat out in a woollen mill any longer than I have to.'

'You've never really talked much about your times in the Lancashire cotton mills, although, of course, I've read your articles. What is it really like?' And as the journalist described the conditions under which the factory workers operated he became increasingly ashamed of the grasping owners and shareholders who allowed such desperate conditions to continue.

'Many of these owners are men of my own class. I shouldn't be, but I'm still amazed at the human capacity for callousness. And now we have this business of women involved in the bartering of tiny babies, and possibly killing them for money. It makes me feel physically sick.'

Whether it was the tenor of the conversation or that he had had too much of the second bottle of port, Edgar went to bed feeling distinctly depressed.

Peter was delighted with the idea of teaching Ambrose some equestrian skills. In addition, the news that he would be travelling with them to Yorkshire was an exciting prospect. The furthest he had travelled had been to Ipswich with Harry when they went to bargain with a feed merchant. Since he left the Seddon workhouse he had enjoyed more comfort and happiness in nine months than he had experienced in all his years before. The opportunity to make a new life was not wasted on him. He was determined to carve out a future for himself and certainly – in his own mind – for Caroline. He had a pang of sadness that he would be leaving her behind 'for a few weeks' as Mr Lawes had explained to him. But now that he could write a good hand he would be able to send her letters every day. Mr Lawes had already given him a smart leather writing case which he would certainly take with him. He had never heard of Yorkshire and had no idea where it was. The concept of north and south was new to him. His whole universe was centred on Seddon and its surrounding parishes; anywhere outside that sphere was a mystery.

Being away so long he would have to ask Caroline to take responsibility for his mother's grave; it certainly could not go untended. The gardener at the Hall always supplied him with whatever fresh flowers were in season and the boy visited the churchyard at least once a week and had never failed. He was sure she would be glad to do it; it would present no difficulty for her as she just as regularly tended her father's plot.

Having come to terms with a separation from his beloved, his thoughts turned to his other major concern which was the mare who was in foal. He had been there early last August when she had been covered by the stallion and then had seen that his work was good as the mare's belly swelled; Harry estimated the birth would be in the first week of July. Peter had expressed concern to Harry that they might be away at the vital time.

'Mr Lawes has already assured me that you'll be back in time for the birth and if there's any necessity for Mr Hudson and himself to stay longer in Yorkshire then you'll be sent home ahead. Can't have you being away when this foal is born. I've a feeling it's going to be a great flat racer. With my help you're going to bring it on just fine!'

The fact that Harry Valentine, a well-established trainer with an enviable reputation across the county, wanted to take trouble to train a workhouse boy was a constant source of wonder to Peter. Both Mr Valentine and Mr Lawes chided him when he referred to himself that way – they said his qualities were such that wherever he had come from he was a strong enough young man to overcome his background and succeed. His memories of Seddon Union workhouse were always conflicting. He still viewed with horror the treatment meted out by the likes of the overseer, Robert Enderby, and the master, John Calman, but his thoughts always returned to the fact that if he had not been an inmate then Mr Lawes and Mr Hudson would never have been able to rescue him and provide him with all these opportunities. Above everything else, he would never have met Caroline.

Four days before they were due to leave, Edgar sought Peter in the stables where he was cleaning tack while, as usual, enjoying thoughts of Caroline. 'You have three days to try to turn Mr Hudson into a reasonable rider – that is, able to handle a strange horse with confidence. Do you think you can do it?'

Peter was silent for a moment. 'Well, as long as Mr Hudson's really keen to learn, I'm sure he'll make headway. I suppose you would always choose the mount for him – not put him on anything too lively, sir?'

'Certainly; as I said, an "average horse". Give him the skills to control it that's all.'

'You know he's not confident around them, sir?'

'Oh yes, he's told me many times. Still – it's important he can ride with some confidence. We'll be relying on horseback where we're going. Wild moorland country; you'll enjoy it, Peter – plenty of good gallops in open spaces!'

'We should leave old Ambler in the stables then. Mr Hudson has no fear of her – but then Tom Lodge could ride her without any risk!'

'Good. I suggest he starts with Megan – she's big enough for him.'

'Very good, sir.'

So, the ambling mare remained in her stable while Peter put Ambrose through several tough paces in the paddock. Only comparatively recently had Peter learned to ride himself, but he was a natural, lithe and supple and above all young. Ambrose was a man nearing 40, who, while keeping himself fit, was no gymnast. For a man of supreme self-confidence and brio, he had at last met his match. His approach to riding was fearful as he realised he could very likely lose control of a large animal that had a mind of its own.

Peter tried to relieve his fear. 'Most domestic animals pick up on people's feelings, Mr Hudson. Horses can always tell when they have a novice on their back. If the animal has a mind not to be ridden it will try to throw its burden off. That's what Mr Valentine told me anyway,' he said cheerfully.

'Well, that's very encouraging, Peter,' said Ambrose.

'The trick is, sir, to give the impression you're not scared; be firm from the off. That way the horse will get the idea that you know what you're doing and will go along with the commands you give it.'

'It sounds like a good theory – let's hope it works!'

Theory was one thing, practice another. The first two days were ones that Ambrose sincerely wished to forget. Fortunately, Peter had never allowed him to pick up any speed before he was thrown off, landing bruised and undignified in the paddock grass, but fortunately with nothing broken. However, such was Peter's patience, pace and clearness of instruction, by the third day his pupil remained upright in the saddle for the whole of the morning and afternoon sessions, had moved from trot to canter out on the adjoining pasture, and was ready to try a gallop the next day. Edgar decided to make an occasion of it and invited Ted Lake and Will to come along, together with the stable hands.

Ambrose wasn't so keen. 'I feel like a performer in a circus!'

'Nonsense, I'm sure you'll come up to the mark. You already look far more confident on horseback than I've ever seen you. We'll have you out hunting before you know where you are!'

'That I will never do – on principle and to protect my neck!'

Fortunately, Ambrose acquitted himself well. He sat upright and looked confident – although inwardly quaking – and with Peter alongside guided the horse through her paces until she reached a full gallop. As Peter reined in his own mount, Ambrose's horse slowed too and allowed her rider a graceful finish.

Puffing from exhilaration and effort Ambrose said, 'Well, I never thought I'd enjoy myself on the back of a horse, but that was one of the best experiences of my life! I think I could repeat the exercise on my own now.'

'Perhaps you should change horses, sir – get the feel of different animals?' suggested Peter.

'Good idea!' said Edgar, although Ambrose looked apprehensive. However, by evening he had mastered three mounts, each presenting with different temperaments but all of which he succeeded in handling successfully.

'What do you think, Peter? Can we call him a "competent rider"?'

'If he keeps at it, I'm sure he can handle any mount you choose for him, Mr Lawes.'

'Then you can consider you've done your job, Peter. Well done!'

If Ambrose was considerably stiff after these sessions he did his best not to show it.

Chapter 3

When not on horseback Ambrose was waiting anxiously for a confirmation from Donald Thwaites. By late afternoon on 10 April a short note arrived post-haste from Bingley which was brought to Edgar in the library.

Fountain Inn,
Bingley

8 April, 10pm
  Dear Mr Hudson,
  I found your letter here this evening and as you requested I reply immediately. First, may I thank you for agreeing to investigate the facts as I originally described.
  I acknowledge that you hope to arrive in Yorkshire on Sunday 14. I have much information for you but will not trust it to a letter as I am increasingly aware of hostility towards me from some quarters and fear that my correspondence with you may have been compromised in some way, although I have no evidence that seals have been tampered with here. I have delivered this into the hands of a trusted friend who will see to it that it is safely on its way.
  You will find me here at six in the evening of the 15th. If you have been delayed I will return the next evening. I will approach you. On no account ask for me by name, I am not sure who is listening here. We can go separately to another establishment where I hope we will be able to converse in safety.
  If all this sounds clandestine and somewhat dangerous, I can only hope it will not discourage you. We need your help – and that of your friend. God willing you have a safe journey,
  I remain your humble servant,
  Donald Thwaites

Passing the letter to Edgar, Ambrose said, 'I think the man's been spotted by those he wishes to expose. If that's the case the game's up and he's in some danger and so will we be. Are you sure you still want to proceed, Edgar? I wouldn't blame you if you felt it was too risky.'

The two men were sitting in front of the usual good fire, the lamps had been lit and the brandy glasses reflected the half-light of the room. There was an immediate change in the atmosphere between the two men.

Edgar bristled. 'I hope you're not having second thoughts about my involvement. I'm fully prepared for anything that might happen.'

Ambrose looked at him squarely. 'No one can be "fully prepared" for anything. That's the first thing you learn in this kind of enterprise. We're at the mercy of those we're investigating. We go where they go, usually with no idea what will happen next, although I always try to be mentally one step ahead. I point this out because I want you to be under no illusions that this is a sort of lark. As I have said before, I've no concerns over your personal courage – it is simply your lack of experience that worries me.'

Edgar responded quickly. 'I resent that you think I even consider this as a diversion. Of course, you're right – I've never had to match my wits against those who are so bent on evil, although I have met plenty face to face when they've appeared in the dock before me. I think I have a reasonable supply of common sense and, while I'm under no misapprehension of the dangers that might ensue, I'm fully prepared to bow to your experience and take orders from you as necessary.'

'Edgar, I'll be delighted to have your company. I couldn't contemplate this enterprise without a second party to help me. But, as I've planned it we won't be working side by side, but each on the two enterprises, although I imagine they'll overlap. The focus for you will be the baby farmers who clearly have a complete absence of morality and respect for life. But all I want you to do is just to collect the evidence in whatever way you can. As a lawyer, your skills will be invaluable.'

'I take it from what you've just said that you do consider me sufficiently capable to be included in your plans? I was a little upset – perhaps unjustifiably so – that you had doubts as to my abilities in a tight spot. As I've already admitted, I've no experience in unarmed combat

Chapter 3

of any kind but I would never walk away from a fight when it was necessary.'

Ambrose took a long pull from his glass. 'I'm sorry if you thought I was questioning your courage, Edgar; it was certainly not my intention. Look – there's no one I'd rather have alongside me than yourself. Let's say no more about it.' He put out his hand which Edgar shook.

They settled down to making plans for the journey.

Edgar sought out Ambrose in the stables, where his friend was keeping company with the ambling mare. 'I've had a positive response from my cousin in Bingley. He'll be delighted to put us up. I've decided to take the everyday coach and four. It has no livery, so is plain enough to escape attention on the road. We'll take my own driver, but also hire another reputable one as a relief. They'll both be armed – as is normal in any case.'

'Well, we should take all the precautions necessary – coach travel's still not a safe affair even in 1839.'

'I've also consulted my driver on the best route using the Great North Road. He suggests two overnight stops, one at Grantham and the next at Pontefract, which is only 30 miles, or a three-hour drive, to Bingley. This means we'll arrive at George Lawes's farmstead about midday on Sunday, the 14th, allowing us time to make acquaintances and settle Peter in before you and I ride off to Bingley on the following day. It's unfortunate that the 14th is a Sunday and we might arrive just as everyone's in church, but there's no avoiding it.'

'Have you decided how you're going to kit yourself out? You obviously can't dress like a young aristocrat.'

'I thought something inconspicuous that gives nothing away about my status. So, out go the smart jackets and well-tailored breeches; the decorative neckties stay in the drawer. I'll use plain linen ones. It just shows how much we judge each other by appearance! Simply by a change in cut of jacket and trousers, and downgrading to more humble cloth and less flamboyant colours, visually I could become a member of another class altogether.'

'Well, up to a point,' said Ambrose. 'The one element over which you have no control is that you are still a well-fed, healthy-looking man with an indefinable aristocratic bearing.'

'You mean arrogant?'

'Certainly not – it's just a confidence that comes from years of giving orders and assuming control of events and other people's lives. You can't lose that, any more than a working man can lose a certain servile look in the presence of his employer – forelock-tugging I mean! You'll have to try to adjust your appearance somewhat, like I'm struggling to master equestrian skills.'

So, Edgar practised for an acting role. He spent some time before the mirror rehearsing a slightly less erect carriage; he also adopted a quizzical look by screwing up his eyes, a gaze somewhat shielded by a cap and one that gave nothing away. Ambrose said there was not enough time for him to work on his voice, and better for him to keep his mouth shut in unfamiliar company when he would probably get away with non-committal grunts.

The final sacrifice to his role and one that touched his vanity was having his collar-length curls clipped into a short shaggy style, much to the bemusement of his valet who had not been let into details of the forthcoming enterprise. Indeed, very few of the staff at the Hall had any idea that their master was undertaking a hazardous adventure, apart from Foster and Harry Valentine who would nominally oversee the house and stables in Edgar's absence. Fred Lodge had been given some sketchy details of what was afoot and was prepared to manage the estate for 'a few weeks' on his own. At first both Ambrose and Edgar had decided not to inform Peter about their reasons for travelling north, and asked Harry not to talk about it at any cost. Later Ambrose reflected on this.

'Look, Edgar, I think we should tell Peter something of what we are about. After all, the boy will inevitably overhear our conversation when we're travelling together in the coach; we can't stay silent on the subject for two days while we're on the road. He's sure to be curious as to what we're discussing.'

'You're right of course. I suggest we give him an outline of the reasons for the journey and explain some of the circumstances that led to it.'

Chapter 3

On the night before they were due to set off they took the boy into their confidence. Peter listened but said nothing.

'Now you've heard what we are about, do you have any questions? Anything you're not clear about?' Ambrose asked him.

To Ambrose's surprise he asked, 'How can you be sure these men don't already know they're being watched?'

The journalist hadn't expected that one; rather he thought Peter would concentrate on the risk they were running, and what steps they would be taking to minimise it. He looked at Edgar who raised his eyebrows and shook his head in place of an answer.

'Edgar and I believe that's a possibility. The man who first asked me to consider things has written only lately and said he was worried that he might be being watched. In one sense, it's a good thing.'

'How can that be?' asked Peter. 'Surely you want to take them by surprise. If they know you're coming they'll be on their guard – it'll put you in even more danger!'

'Yes and no. It puts us on extra-special alert. Anyway, as far as we can be sure, they have no knowledge of who we are. I work under a pseudonym—'

'What's that?'

'A false name. I'm taking the name Frank Barrett.'

Edgar asked, 'Anyone you know?'

'A neighbour of mine – but it's not an uncommon name.'

'Will you need a pseudonym?' asked Peter of Edgar.

'I can't think why I would – my role is simply keeping an eye out for evidence. Besides, very few people know me in Yorkshire; like Barrett, Lawes is not an unusual name and I am genuinely related to a local squire of that name. There are lots of us all over the country. I'm not as well-practised as Mr Hudson at living with a different name. I'd be bound to forget it at the wrong moment.'

Ambrose thought for a while. 'I think you're right. As you say, the name Lawes is well known round the Bingley district where we're likely to be operating and people will make the connection with your cousin George; but you can still remain unobtrusive.'

Peter immediately asked what that meant. He was developing a distinct liking for unfamiliar words and had begun to slip those he remembered into conversations when he felt it was appropriate. This sometimes amused, sometimes irritated Harry Valentine, who was usually on the receiving end of these small literary pearls which often seemed to crop up inappropriately when they were both deeply involved in the task of mucking out.

The consequence of their discussion was that Edgar could be himself: a horse-dealer and a relation of George Lawes. Some in George's neighbourhood would remember him from previous visits. As he was involved in the business already he had all the experience necessary; no one could question his bona fides.

Anxious not to be excluded, Peter asked, 'Can I use a pseudo – a different name?'

'That won't be at all necessary, Peter,' Ambrose told him. 'You'll most definitely not be involved in any of our business. You're going with us because Mr Lawes thinks it's an opportunity for you to visit some of the best stud farms and training stables in the north. You'll be as far away from trouble, if there was any, as we can possibly manage.'

Quietly disappointed that he obviously had no role to play in this adventure, Peter nonetheless resolved to learn every scrap of information he could from the two men about their forthcoming mission as they travelled together side by side for three days in the coach. He was beginning to work out a set of subtle questions, hoping his probing would be 'unobtrusive' enough to fool both, but particularly Ambrose who Peter estimated as one not easily deceived by anyone, let alone a 15-year-old boy. However, Peter had learned some lessons during his time in the workhouse, principally how to survive and for that he had often needed to be devious. He was confident he could match his wit to Ambrose on that score. His only regret was that he had been sworn to secrecy and that he could have no discussion either with William or, most especially, Caroline, about the true objectives of Mr Hudson and Mr Lawes's journey north. He felt his relationship with her was built on a mutual trust and shared experiences, so the thought of dissembling was uncomfortable. But he was very aware of the seriousness with which the men impressed the need for concealment and such was his respect for them both it never crossed his mind to divulge even a hint of what they were about. He spent much of the after-

Chapter 3

noon before they were due to set out tending the pregnant mare; as he worked on her chestnut coat she was the only friend to whom he laid bare all he knew.

Chapter 4

YORKSHIRE

The journey had been long, tedious and uneventful. Starting out at four o'clock on a frosty Friday morning they travelled with stops and changes throughout the day and evening until they finally arrived in Grantham at about ten o'clock, where they spent the night at the main post-house – tolerably clean but not luxurious. Anxious to keep to their schedule and with the weather in their favour, dry and windless although still cold for springtime, the drivers kept up a brisk pace the following day, crossing the border into Yorkshire late in the afternoon and arriving in Pontefract close to six o'clock. The travellers took rooms for the night and, at first light the following morning, with a fresh team of horses, the trio set out on the 30-mile journey to Bingley.

For much of the previous two days Peter had been a passenger inside the coach, but on several occasions Edgar suggested he might like to sit up aloft with the coachman and even try his hand at driving. The boy was torn between the opportunity to take control of a team of horses for the first time or remaining in the coach where he might pick up some snippets of conversation. He felt sure Edgar's offer of a chance to extend his knowledge of horsemanship was a genuine one, but the boy was canny enough to guess that the two men wanted some time to themselves to discuss tactics out of his earshot.

On those occasions when talk had been free-flowing in the coach Peter had gathered most of the story and the general purpose for which they were heading north. When baby farming was explained to him he became particularly exercised.

'That's one of the cruellest things I've ever heard of!' he protested. 'When I think of how Will was left at the gates of the House, at least his mother didn't farm him out to evil, grasping women who most probably would have let him die. I hope you catch whoever's doing this, put a stop to it and have those involved transported thousands of miles away or at least sent to prison.'

Child labour was something he had heard of. From his own experience in the workhouse he knew that young children were often apprenticed from there to cruel masters who cared nothing for their welfare. They often worked them until they were too weak to carry on and then sent them back like unwanted goods. There were regulations which the union masters were supposed to follow but because the supervision of workhouses was often lax they were insufficient to protect children from what was often gross mistreatment. According to what he overheard from the conversation between Mr Lawes and Mr Hudson, in the factories the law had recently been changed to prevent the employment of children under nine years old. But, again from his own experience, Peter could see how little children might still be employed, especially if the people who were inspecting the factories were not doing their job properly, something else Mr Hudson had told him. Thinking about it he became angry; but he had every confidence that Mr Hudson could bring justice for those children and have the wrongdoers punished, like the baby farmers.

From his corner of the coach, while pretending to sleep, he gathered from what Mr Hudson was saying that he was already prepared to go undercover in the woollen mill where Mr Randal Saunders worked.

As Ambrose explained to Edgar, 'I've researched the mechanisms of the textile trade during my time in Lancashire, but I haven't been able to try my hand at one of the new power looms. I think my best approach will be to put myself in the way of general labouring – carrying bales of cloth and sacks of wool rather than setting myself up to fail as an experienced machinist.'

'I can see the sense in that.' Edgar nodded.

'There are other advantages in that tactic: I'll be more flexible and able to move freely round the factory rather than standing static at one position for hours on end. I'll also be able to make acquaintances and pick up information much more casually and with less suspicion.'

Peter became fascinated with the way Ambrose recognised a difficulty and immediately seemed to be able to work through to a solution. He also had a practical knack of being able to foresee problems before they might arise; a useful skill, Peter thought, and one well

Chapter 4

worth learning. During the long journey, the boy discovered much about the two men, and was struck by how well they seemed to get along, despite their difference in status. There was no doubt that Mr Lawes was an aristocrat, very well provided for and with a well-established standing in his local society and further abroad. On the other hand, Mr Hudson, as Peter knew, was the son of an artisan miller, self-taught in journalism. But his style of life had made him a man of the world with a great all-round experience of people and places. He seemed at ease with everyone, not only Lady Somerset and her two snooty daughters, and Mr Hugh Bradshaw, who was a real gentleman in every sense of the word, but also Mr Lodge and Harry Valentine who both worked with their hands for their livings. Peter had also been impressed with his friend's approach to learning to ride. He could tell immediately that he was afraid of horses, but that had not stopped him trying to improve by throwing himself into it totally – another lesson that Peter absorbed and resolved to apply to himself.

For their part, as they had already agreed, the two men included Peter in much of their discussions although they did not spend the whole journey dissecting their enterprise. Much of it was passed in exchanging views of current news, both national and international, and the state of the world generally.

'You must admit, Edgar,' Ambrose said, 'there's a general momentum for reform across the whole country, led by articulate men with means which allows them the luxury of time to pursue their ideals.'

'I don't deny it, Ambrose, but I sometimes have concerns as to their methods. Stirring up trouble only leads to violence in the end. Then the authorities have all the excuse they need to crack down on genuine dissent.'

'But it's only through their passion that they're able to inspire and radicalise less literate yet intelligent men and women. Tell me, how else is the power of the poor to be harnessed in the future? If they could unite and stand up against the masters, there might be hope for significant change, not only in their working conditions and wages, but also indirectly to real parliamentary reform. You know my views on reform well by enough by now, Edgar. It's the only way essential social changes will come about.'

'Although I broadly agree with your aims, and certainly hope for very similar outcomes, like my father, I'm a pragmatist rather than an idealist. It's my belief the status quo will be very difficult to change at the rate you hope for. Custom, tradition – call it what you will – have guided and shaped social conditions through a millennium and won't be swept away suddenly unless we see a repeat of the events in France 50 years ago.'

'Of course, no one wants that kind of barbarity in England, Edgar, but unless change comes who knows what men will do if they are pushed to desperation.'

'I've always thought a revolution here in England would be most unlikely. Our government has always been clever enough to bend slightly whenever agitation for change rises to dangerous levels.'

'Well, legislation against sedition and combination has been draconian,' Ambrose reminded him.

'Yes, but, as I said, on other occasions the authorities have been forced to bow to reason, release the valves in the engine of state a fraction and reduce the pressure, just enough to prevent an explosion.'

Ambrose frowned with frustration. 'Unless we step up the pace we'll both be below ground before we see any fair treatment of the poor. I don't understand why you don't see that!'

'I'm sorry, but I can't agree with you. I truly believe that reform should evolve slowly, carefully and thoroughly. In that way, it can be established on solid foundations that won't be shifted lightly in the future.'

There was the usual silence when they came to a point when they knew they would never agree on the means, although there was no problem with the ends.

In the meantime, Peter became selective in what he absorbed. Discussions of deep political theory were all very well, and he did find some of it interesting, particularly when Ambrose described in graphic detail the living and working conditions of the labourers in the Manchester cotton mills. They sounded appalling, even worse than Seddon Union workhouse. As far as he could understand it, he agreed with Mr Ambrose. There was no point hanging about waiting for things to happen. Look at him and Caroline. If he hadn't taken

Chapter 4

action she would never know how he felt about her. Mr Ambrose was right – what did he say? That was it: 'deeds not words'! As the conversation began to get bogged down in politics, he fell into a deep sleep. But he was wide awake when sitting above with the driver, a kindly man who took it upon himself to educate Peter on the finer points of coach management as well as the geography of some of the towns they passed through. By the time they reached Pontefract there was little Peter had not heard about the characters running the post-houses and inns where they stopped. These were often racy stories of adultery and petty crime, with a few gruesome accounts of travellers waylaid by footpads and murderers which Peter found much more interesting than talk of Chartism and the Reform Acts.

But back inside the coach he listened very carefully whenever the subject of the mission was raised. In his own mind, he was determined to be involved in some way, although Mr Lawes had been unequivocal in his demand that Peter put all such thought out of his head. He was sending the boy to Yorkshire to improve his knowledge of the racing world and as such Peter would be kept very occupied and well away from any action of the kind he and Ambrose were anticipating. But Peter continued quietly to garner all the information he could, storing it in his mind with the thought that he might find it useful sometime soon.

George Lawes's farmstead and stables, known locally as Hoyles, were on the edge of the hills and valleys of Ilkley Moor and just skirting a small hamlet called High Eldwick, some 3 miles from Bingley. As their coach passed through that small town, built on the hills of the Pennines, they saw evidence of how, despite its location, it was growing substantially. Over-topping all the buildings were several tall chimneys which Ambrose identified as belonging to the new mills built to process wool into cloth, in the same manner as cotton goods were produced in the mills of Lancashire. The town was still not large, at least in comparison with industrial towns like Manchester and Glasgow, but it was clear that there was an increasing population as more people drifted in from the outlying countryside to seek work in these new factories. Set within the backdrop of wild moorland that seemed to stretch away beyond sight, Bingley was ramshackle in outward appearance; shacks and simple dwellings had found their places on what had previously been open country. There were also signs of more permanent buildings, small terraces back to back; basic structures but where families lived with less temporary amenities. Apart from the mills, the most important development had been the building of a canal connecting the mill town of Leeds in the north-east to the port of Liverpool in the north-west. Edgar explained how it had been cut out by thousands of Irish men called navigators who dug their way with much sweat and toil through the land.

'So, what happened to all the navigators when the canal was finished?' asked Peter.

'Some of them decided to stay and take advantage of the opportunities for work on new housing as the town has developed; a few have taken up factory work themselves. The town is increasing in size very rapidly.'

Although the route their driver was following took them quite close to the canal Peter had no view of it. Neither could he see much of the streets from the small windows of the coach, although he was aware by their erratic speed, that they were travelling up and down what was clearly steep hilly terrain; but he could hear feet clattering on little stone cobbles and imagined a throng of people passing to and fro. The hardened surfaces of the streets of his small market town of Seddon were the result of earth trampled down by feet, both human and animal over hundreds of years, plus an accumulation of straw and dung from a constant procession of stock of all kinds driven through the main street to market or the shambles for slaughtering. The sounds of Seddon's streets were consequently muffled, unlike here where there was the constant noisy tapping and scraping of the iron rings that raised the walkers' wooden-soled pattens above the cobbles. Sometimes, through the open window of the coach and above the sound of feet, he caught a different type of language, one that he could barely understand. It would take him several days before he could work out what was being said to him by these strange northern men and women.

They drove through Bingley and on for a couple of miles until they

Chapter 4

came to the small hamlet of High Eldwick, by which time it was midday. The coach veered off the main road onto a long rutted track with grass at its centre. Still hampered by his restricted view through the coach windows, Peter had no visual idea of the kind of terrain they were travelling over, although his body told him it was considerably bumpy, until finally the driver reined in the team and the coach came to rest. Stiff and weary from their long journey, the three travellers climbed out. Peter's first impression was that Hoyles was a set of long, low and functional buildings, all dark grey stone with slate roofs. There were so many buildings it was difficult to tell which one was the main house, until a large wooden door was opened in a more substantial dwelling and a generously built man appeared in its doorway.

As they came down from the coach he walked towards them with a smile on his weather-beaten face and his hands extended, crying, 'Welcome, welcome!' and Peter and Ambrose caught not the sound of the Yorkshire timbre that they expected, but a well-modulated and educated voice such as that of Mr Edgar Lawes. It seemed somehow out of place in this wilderness, which was Peter's first impression of the countryside around him. Beyond the buildings all he could see were acres and acres of wild, barren undulating country with tops of grey stone pushing up through the grass and intermittent stands of spiky bright green rushes. There were no enclosures, no hedges and just a few small bushy trees, stunted by what seemed to be a constant wind that whined through the chimney tops of the farmstead. The land stretched away seemingly for ever and the boy thought how careful one would have to be not to wander too far and become lost among those desolate grey crags. The brightness of the rushes told him that there would most likely be dangerous bogs. It was not for nothing that back in Suffolk his friend Ted Lake's farm was called Rushie Farm. But there the land had long since been drained for cultivation and very few marshy areas now remained. In this wilderness, the land had been left untouched, wild and untended other than by the persistent nibbling of sheep and cattle, some of which he could see grazing in the distance. But what firmly caught his eye was a group of five or six horses loose in a paddock adjoining what he presumed were the stables, a large set of stone buildings that stood apart from the rest.

While Peter was assessing his surroundings Edgar and Ambrose had gone ahead into the farmhouse with their host, George Lawes. Ambrose's first impression of the interior was one of starkness, which surprised him as he understood Edgar's cousin to be a man of means. Like Edgar he was the local Justice of the Peace with a considerable status in the community, but it soon became clear to Ambrose that the man's establishment was not designed for the purposes of show. As they moved through the main door they were confronted with a large lobby full of boots hung up in pairs on pegs, walking sticks, shepherd's crooks, riding whips, all upright and ready at hand in stands against the walls; on numerous pegs hung sturdy jackets useful against the rain and persistent wind. They were both forced to stoop through a low door into a large living room which appeared to be the centre of the farm's operations. Like the lobby, the floor here was flagged and carpetless. The main feature of the room was a large inglenook fireplace showing a good blaze of wood and coal. An enormous and sturdy deal table dominated the centre with numerous plain wooden chairs tucked under it. There were no pictures or portraits on the unplastered walls; instead many shelves hung upon them, some with books and piles of journals laid flat, others with crockery, pewter and a few well-polished trophies. Apart from these last, with their obvious signs of care born of pride, there was certainly no evidence of any feminine touches to this room – no ornaments or flowers, although there were pairs of neat well-washed curtains hanging at all three windows. It was a working environment where men, who spent most of their time outdoors, came in for respite, food and an escape from the weather.

Before they left for Yorkshire Edgar had given Ambrose some details about George Lawes. 'My cousin's in his late forties and is a widower. He moved to Yorkshire 10 years ago from Norfolk after his wife died. It had always been a love match and he couldn't bring himself to marry a second time, even though he has no children. He bought Hoyles and now devotes all his energies to enlarging it and

Chapter 4

making it profitable; he invested much of his money in breeding racehorses in which he's always been involved.'

'So, did he start from scratch up here, or was there an existing stud?'

'Hoyles was just sheep and cattle when he bought it and he started the business from nothing. This area's a centre for horse breeding but, since he's been here, George has made a considerable name for himself locally and, it's rumoured among the Lawes family, a great deal of money.'

Remembering what Edgar had told him, looking around the room, Ambrose could see no evidence of luxury – indeed almost the opposite. The room gave all the indications of frugal living. To tell the truth he was a little disappointed and hoped that the level of hospitality on offer wouldn't reflect the plain physical features evident from where he was standing. However, the room was warm and cheerful enough in its limited way and he was heartened when shown to his own bedroom which was well-furnished with a large comfortable bed, useful cupboards and above all a neat little writing desk under the small casement window which, like all the rest of the windows in the house, overlooked the vast expanse of the moors. A fire blazed in the hearth which immediately raised his spirits. However, there was a significant drawback. The room was in the roof space, as all the bedrooms were. This presented a problem to a man such as Ambrose who was well over 6 feet. Wherever he went he was forced to stoop through low-set doorways and had had more bumps to his head than he cared to remember; sleeping in a room with such a low ceiling meant keeping his wits about him.

Returning to the main living room slightly less apprehensive as to the quality of his host's hospitality, Ambrose wondered what the standard of cuisine would be in an establishment where food might be considered simply as fuel for work. He needn't have worried. George Lawes knew his duty as to his guests' and his men's comfort. Within half an hour the table was set with enough food to feed a small battalion. Just as well, because at the sound of a bell outside, six men entered in stocking-feet and took their places round the table. Before they sat down George said, 'My cousin Mr Lawes and Mr Hudson and Peter Samuels here will be staying with me for a few weeks. My cousin's particularly interested in the horses and will probably want to spend some time in the stables. They have free rein to go where they like, and to use the horses – although not the bloodstock of course!' He laughed and turned to Edgar. 'I won't waste time introducing all my men; I'm sure you'll get to know everyone over the course of time. I imagine you're all hungry after such a journey, so let's get on.'

With the master at the head of the table, the housekeeper and cook ladled out thick potage into large bowls, too hot for the men to even sip without blowing on it first. Trays of fresh-baked crusty bread were placed at either end of the table within easy reach of everyone, as were pats of yellow butter. Whenever either Ambrose, Peter or Edgar were given soup their thoughts always returned to the Seddon workhouse and the thin apology that was the dreadful substitute dished up to the inmates, along with the adulterated bread. But the soup from the Hoyle's kitchen was a total contrast, yellow with the thickening of chickpea and brimming with onions, carrot and mutton. Along with the soup there was cold game pie and home-made chutneys; an apple cake with cream rounded off a substantial meal. Although it was Sunday, there was still basic work to do and the men were served with mugs of weak beer brewed in one of the outbuildings.

Conversation was sparse, the men concentrating solely on their food, although there was the usual assessment of the weather, now and to come, and a report to the master on what had been achieved from the morning's work. Talk of horses and sheep was too technical as far as Ambrose was concerned, although he made the appearance of listening and nodding intently; they were all three supposed to be interested in livestock, after all. But Edgar and Peter became very absorbed in how the farm was managed and genuinely impressed with the depth of knowledge George's stockmen exhibited. Apart from the usual politeness required when family and friends have been apart for some time, George Lawes held off any detailed discussion with his cousin and companions. He was anxious not to invite too many casual enquiries from his men during conversation.

When the meal was over the stockmen took themselves off to complete their chores.

'After work they'll go off and are free to make their own arrange-

Chapter 4

ments for Sunday worship – or not. Most of them go with their families to the Methodist chapel in Bingley; others use their time to make up lost sleep. A few remain to feed the stock and eventually shut up the horses for the night. Sunday is a quiet day in this part of the world.'

As the men filtered out of the farmhouse George signalled to the housekeeper who brought in a fine silver and glass claret jug with matching glasses. It seemed oddly out of place on the plain deal table, but the wine inside certainly reflected the quality of its container.

Edgar sat back in his chair and held his glass to the light. 'I must congratulate you on your cellar, George. This is as fine a wine as I've tasted for a long time.'

'Even though I might live plain, Edgar, I've never forgotten what good wine should be!' And he pushed the jug towards Ambrose. 'Now, assuming you're well satisfied with food and wine, let's talk about your purpose for being here. You've briefly outlined some facts, although have not gone into specifics.' He took Edgar's letter from his notecase. 'You say that you and Ambrose are to investigate issues in the local mills – particularly illegal child labour. Personally, I haven't come across any cases in my court, but that's not to say it doesn't go on. The mills have not been open for as long as those in places like Manchester, and perhaps bad habits haven't had the chance to become widespread. Your source, who you don't name, obviously has inside knowledge and it seems to me he's put himself in some degree of danger. My knowledge of people around here is that there are very few who are vicious characters – you might say that's true of anywhere – but overall there are some exceptionally strong and determined people in the area; it may be living in a harsh landscape that shapes them into such, I don't know. But my advice is to tread very carefully.'

Edgar looked at Ambrose who nodded. 'Edgar may have told you that I've experience of similar situations in the cotton mills of Manchester. You're quite right. Many of the men involved in these activities feel they've nothing to lose. Indeed, they know if they're caught they'll be transported – or worse if they've committed murder, as many of them have, both directly and indirectly by their actions.'

'I suppose you know your business best, Mr Hudson – or Frank

Barrett as I presume you would prefer to be called here. All I can offer is the hospitality of this house, and any local information I can give you. Gossip is plentiful, more so than you might expect in an isolated community like this. People's movements don't pass unobserved or unheeded, as they certainly do in large cities. Here we're aware of most of what's going on. Anyone wishing to keep their doings secret must work hard at it. For example, I've put it about to my neighbours that I'll have visitors for the next few weeks who have business hereabouts and will be flitting from place to place looking at stock and land. You've no need to worry about questions; I've given them sufficient information for them to assume that you're bona fide guests of mine. You may see this as a gross intrusion on our privacy, but that's the best way to tackle nosiness here – feed them enough information to satisfy them. I've managed to avoid arranging any social gatherings where you may be quizzed on business of which you've no experience or knowledge. I've said you are both using Hoyles as a convenience and will most likely be absent for much of the time.'

Edgar said, 'I'm exceedingly grateful, George. That's exactly what we need – to avoid unwanted questions as to why we're here. I knew I could rely on you to pave our way.'

Ambrose nodded in agreement. 'As to my alias – I would be glad if, as you acknowledge, it can be used at all times. Using a pseudonym is difficult at first, but with use it becomes commonplace. I now respond quite happily to Frank Barrett!'

George looked at Edgar. 'Despite your appearance – what happened to the Byronic curls, by the way? – you'll be recognised, so how you manage your part of the investigations is something to think about. Given your standing within your own community – and as a cousin of mine – I don't think people will question anything you do, provided it's not too outrageous! Perhaps your best approach would be one of subtlety and anonymity.'

'I've considered how best to cover my traces in view of the fact that I'm already known here. I have a genuine wish to look at your stables and perhaps visit others in the district. This will provide me with a cast-iron reason for my presence. Added to which I've brought young Peter who, as you have kindly suggested, will work alongside your

Chapter 4

stable master for the duration of our stay.' He looked at Peter who had been sitting quietly attentive to all that was passing between the three men. 'You understand that this is a good opportunity to increase your skills with really good racehorses?'

Peter nodded.

George looked across at Peter and smiled. 'I hope to take you with us to Wetherby to see some racing and experience the bloodstock sales. There's not much my stablemen can't tell you about the racing game. Mr Lawes tells me you're a natural with horses, despite only just coming into the business – and it is a business: lots of money in it if you have the know-how and skills.'

'Lots of money lost if you don't!' murmured Ambrose.

'Quite right, but we use Yorkshire common sense up here. I personally don't put money on horses – well, only very small amounts. I make my money from breeding the beasts. In that way, I'm sure not to lose. But now we've finished the claret I'll take you on a tour of the farm and stables and you can see for yourselves the arrangements here. As I told you, my men are mostly resting, working or taking Sunday worship.'

'Don't you attend church yourself, George?' asked Edgar. 'Suffolk society demands its local landowners show their faces regularly at services.'

'I get away with a fortnightly appearance. Most of the village populations – and many of the workers in Bingley – are Nonconformists. The congregations in the Anglican establishments are quite small here. I do my best to support the local parson, but I must confess religion doesn't play a great part in my life. If I want a spiritual experience I come out and look at a field of fine racehorses and thank the Almighty for his inspirational gift!'

Buttoning coats against the stiff breeze, which was blowing unremittingly round the buildings, the four made their way outside. They were taken first to the stables where Peter was dumbstruck when he saw how many horses there were, several in the stalls being groomed, but at least 12 out grazing in fenced-off pasture with new spring grass. The stables themselves were tidy and well-organised. Two men were mucking out, cleaning tack and generally keeping the yard to a high standard. He noticed what he at first took to be two young boys, but on closer inspection they turned out to be young men very short in stature – obviously the riders of these magnificent animals. George Lawes ordered one of them to bring out a mount to show his guests. It was a beautiful grey gelding and Peter, even with his inexperienced eye, could tell from its proportions it was a fine animal for racing. Ambrose, although now used to the proximity of horses, stepped back a pace as the horse approached. It seemed to him to be full of pent-up energy and, as far as he was concerned, might possibly take it into its head to bolt at any time.

George noticed his nervousness and said quietly, 'Come now, Mr Barrett, don't tell me you're shy of horses? Everyone rides here – there's no other way to get about these moors. Some of the tracks will take a horse and cart – just – but mostly it's bridleways that have long existed and provide safe routes around marshes and bogs.'

Ambrose shook his head. 'I'm a city man, Mr Lawes.'

'George, please,' said his host.

'George. As I explained to Edgar, normally I've had no need to acquire any skills of horsemanship where there's always transport to hand. But, at my friend's far-sighted insistence, I've recently improved my riding skills thanks to this young fellow,' he said, nodding towards Peter. 'He's certainly given me confidence. I think he considers me an adequate rider – but on the right mount!'

'We can certainly provide you with that. But in view of the fact you're supposed to be here looking at stock, perhaps we'd better stick to the story that it's sheep and cattle that interest you, not horses. Later this afternoon perhaps with Peter and a stable lad you could try out a few horses to see which suits. Edgar, I have a superb one for you – one you may be interested in buying from me!'

'George, you've become a typical Yorkshire horse-dealer, despite your aristocratic connections. Do you ever let slip an opportunity to make a deal? I knew there would come a time when we'd talk horses, but I'd not anticipated it so soon!'

'I make money by making opportunities, Edgar. Anyway, let's move on to the rest of the farm. We have cattle here also, but mostly we graze sheep. I now provide quality Yorkshire wool not only to the

Chapter 4

new mills in Bingley but also Leeds and Bradford, all conveniently nearer than transporting it abroad or south to Oxfordshire where I originally had contracts. The new machinery is eating the stuff up and sometimes the raw supplies run out, so I've put money into more sheep and less cattle. In fact, the small herd we keep is mixed dairy and beef and mostly serves the farm and some of the outer hamlets.'

At a swift pace for a generously proportioned man, George led the way round the stockyards and barns until his guests had been acquainted with the lie of the land immediately surrounding the farmstead, as well as being given the chance to admire the range of stock. As they looked across the moor they could see numerous white dots among the grey-green of the ground almost as far as the eye could see. Peter could not even begin to estimate how many sheep there might have been. As if reading his mind, George told them that his land stretched for nearly 2,000 acres north and west, mostly unfenced and it was only through the skills of his men that the sheep were kept safe and within bounds. He employed three shepherds and working with each was an apprentice, known as a shepherd's page. Having taken them round in a circle, they found themselves back at the stables where George went off to discuss likely mounts, particularly one suitable for a novice rider in the saddle. While maintaining an outward composure, inwardly Ambrose was anticipating the coming few hours with more than a little trepidation.

The following morning, while Peter was introduced to the stable hands and stable master Charlie Anderson, George organised mounts for Edgar and Ambrose. Edgar's cousin chose two nondescript hacks on which they might ride over to the town later in the afternoon. They tried out their horses, although Edgar was certainly in no need of practice, but rode alongside Ambrose as encouragement.

'George has chosen a quiet, well-behaved beast for you, Ambrose. She won't baulk if you occasionally pull at her mouth.'

'I'm pleased to hear it!' said Ambrose, gripping the animal with his knees and trying to test Peter's theory about 'seeming confident and in charge'.

The pair returned to the house for the midday meal which this time they took in a small dining room off the main eating area, away from the farmhands so that they could discuss their tactics in private. Ambrose reminded Edgar of his advice on the intricacies of clandestine living and how to fend off awkward questions.

'The trick is,' he said, 'always stick as close to the truth as you can. Building a web of deceit only results in having to remember the lies you've told already. It makes it more likely you'll slip up and be caught out. For example, if anyone asks me where I'm from I'll tell them London. If they persist and enquire further I'll tell them I've been a carpenter and odd job man in the city, have never married and consequently have no wife or children. In the past I've always tramped around the country to get work and I've come north to look for it in the new industries. If they insist on probing further the one piece of deception I'll use is to say that some years ago I once worked in a woollen mill in Oxfordshire and hope they're satisfied. I think that county is sufficiently far away for there to be no connections with this area – I would be unlucky if there were.'

As the meeting with Thwaites was at six o'clock and Bingley only a couple of miles or so, they set off just after the stable clock struck five. Edgar had estimated that it would mean a comfortable unhurried ride for both them and their horses on regular tracks. That way they could accustom themselves to manoeuvring horses on moorland terrain. George had drawn a route for them, one that he told them was clearly waymarked. The late afternoon was dry, although persistently cold and both Edgar and Ambrose had dressed as inconspicuously as they could while making sure they were warm. If the meeting with Thwaites took time, it might be too dark to set off back to Eldwick and it was more than likely they would have to stay the night somewhere, and not in a local inn where their appearance might prompt curiosity. Experience had taught Ambrose that preparation was everything, so into saddlebags they slung a couple of blankets, candles and some food that needed no preparation and were soon ready to leave. Peter came to see them off – asking no questions, but still quietly absorbing everything he saw.

Their ride to the outskirts of Bingley was uneventful. They saw a

Chapter 4

few people en route, mostly farm workers and particularly shepherds who were at their busiest with lambing. They heard the town church clock chime the three-quarter hour just as they came into sight of the town, which sloped on the south side of the Pennine Hills while still surrounded by moorland. Donald Thwaites had told them that the Fountain Inn was halfway down the main street through the middle of the town and could not be mistaken with its simple painted sign outside. It was still light as they entered the street and slowly began to make their way down to its centre, Edgar looking left and Ambrose to the right. The cobbled street, for all it was a major thoroughfare, was comparatively narrow and their progress was so impeded by those on foot that Edgar soon indicated they should dismount and lead the horses.

As they passed by an alleyway a tall woman, with her head covered in a grey shawl, moved out of a doorway and seemed almost to collide with Ambrose. He stopped to make way, but instead of moving on, she asked quietly, 'Frank Barrett?'

With consummate professional control, he did not move a muscle, just said, 'You have the advantage of me, miss.'

'My name is Rosalie Thwaites. I think you've been corresponding with my brother.'

Reluctant to exchange any confidences with this stranger Ambrose thought quickly. How was he to know this was not a trick? Perhaps someone had intercepted his correspondence with Thwaites and knew of their assignation.

The woman, whose face was still hidden, whispered, 'I believe you're really known as Ambrose Hudson, you're a journalist from London and my brother contacted you because he had information about criminals operating in the mill where he was an overseer. I've nothing to identify myself with, other than a packet of letters he has given to me to pass on to you.' She briefly took out a brown package from under her shawl and just as swiftly put it away again.

Ambrose was aware that they were not in an ideal position to maintain the conversation, which had opened within the confines of the narrow street; the woman, the two men and their horses were all beginning to impede the normal flow of people and animals and likely soon to attract attention from irritated passers-by.

Conscious of this herself, the woman said, 'Follow me out of the street and we'll find a place where it's easier to talk.'

Still apprehensive and on his guard, Ambrose indicated to Edgar that they should follow her, but he was sufficiently prepared to check he had his knife handy in case they were walking into an ambush. The woman led them at a steady pace through the main street, straight past the venue for their meeting and continued for almost a quarter of a mile until they were out of the main area of the town and verging on countryside again. All the time she kept her shawl about her head and neither man caught any sight of her face. Even when they stopped beside some trees where they tethered their horses, she kept her face hidden. It became clear to Ambrose that they were not being led into a trap; there was plenty of open space and no sign that anyone had followed them.

'This is not what my friend and I were expecting. Where's your brother, Miss Thwaites – as I presume you are?'

'My brother is dead, Mr Barrett. I'll call you by the name agreed with him. Donald was killed three days ago.'

'Dead? Killed?'

'I say "killed", and there is no doubt in my mind that he was murdered.'

'Murdered by whom?' asked Edgar.

'Look – this public thoroughfare is not the place to talk. If you'll continue to trust me you should ride on from here for at least 2 miles until you come to the first main track on your right. Take it and you'll arrive at a barn. I've arranged with the farmer for you to stable your horses there for as long as you need; he's family and trustworthy. I'll catch up with you on foot, but I must tell you I'm not sure whether I was followed into town, so I'll be taking certain measures to throw anyone with that idea off my scent. That'll take me a little extra time, so expect me in just over an hour, when it will be darker.' She pulled her shawl more closely around her head and set off back down the road and into the town.

'This is desperate news, but at the back of my mind I thought this might happen. It means, of course, if they know about Donald, they possibly know about us.'

Edgar nodded. 'It's an appalling thing – the man murdered like that. But what now? Do we trust her? Are your instincts telling you anything?'

'They tell me to be very disconcerted that she knows all about us. It certainly could be a trap, but now she's left us to our own devices I'm of a mind to think she's genuine. After all, if she had other ideas she would probably lead us to this barn to make sure we arrived and were then ambushed. I can only suggest we do as she says; but keep your eyes open and your knife and pistol handy.'

Just as she had described, half-an-hour's ride down the road they came to a well-used track leading right. Three-quarters of a mile on they came across the barn which was substantial and with a pair of stout doors that were wide open. Before he dismounted Ambrose stopped and listened very carefully for any signs of life, but there were no sounds other than the familiar chirping of numerous sparrows disturbed in their roost. Nodding to Edgar that it was safe to dismount, they tethered the horses outside to an overhanging branch and side by side walked slowly through the doorway looking right and left. The rafters of the barn were high; half their area was covered with a platform now clear of last year's hay; animal stalls made up the main ground area. Investigating thoroughly every corner and stall, they found the place to be deserted.

'It looks clear, Edgar!' he said, with a sigh of relief. 'We should bring the horses in. It appears the farmer has left water, feed and hay ready – which is gratifying. He's also left us two lanterns.'

Edgar untacked their mounts and made sure both were installed and with access to everything they needed. In the meantime, settling on a spot at the back of a stall hidden from the entrance, Ambrose opened the saddlebags, took out the blankets and set out some food.

'Damn it! Do you realise we've not eaten properly since we left Eldwick? In all the excitement of the last hour I'd forgotten how famished I am! You know, we're probably going to end up spending the night here. Just as well we came prepared. By the time the woman returns – if she does – it'll be well past seven, and obviously she'll have much to tell. It'll be fully dark before we would be ready to leave. Much better to stay, sleep and return at first light.'

'That's a good idea. At least we have enough provisions to last us for the next few hours and we can buy more in the town tomorrow.'

'How are you in terms of sleeping rough, Edgar? To me, this barn is the height of luxury compared to some of the places I've slept.'

'Do you know, Ambrose, since I was a boy I've always dreamed about spending the night in the open with my horse.'

'Are you being ironic or is that a real ambition?'

'Truthful. I always thought it would be a great adventure.'

'Then, why didn't you?'

'An over-protective mother. I'm sure my father would have been perfectly happy, but my mother considered I'd be prey to any passing fox or – worse – vagabond!'

The hour passed and they began to listen for signs of Miss Thwaites. They had spent the time speculating on the dramatic announcement of her brother's death.

Ambrose said, 'If, as she claims, it was murder, then that would confirm everything Donald described in his first letter. The men he had been observing are obviously ruthless in the extreme.'

'The lady was clearly on her guard and if, as she thought, she might have been followed, I hope that her meeting with us hasn't aroused too much suspicion,' observed Edgar.

'Well, thinking about the encounter with her, she came out of the shadows and was hidden from the crowded main street by our horses. She kept her face concealed and our conversation was of the briefest. However, it'll be a serious matter if all our attempts at concealment go for nothing and it's already known a journalist from London is here on an investigation.'

'Is that likely, do you think?'

'I have a maxim to never worry about anything I've no control over; rather to make the best of what I can manipulate. Let's wait and see if the woman reappears and then hear her account.'

After well over an hour they heard someone enter the barn. Crawling as silently as they could from their hiding place, to the relief of both men they saw it was the woman. She came towards them and for

Chapter 4

the first time they could see her face as she took the shawl from her head and slipped it round her shoulders. She was, as their first impression had noted, a tall woman, slender with dark hair of some length tied in a knot on the base of her neck. They could not at a distance immediately make out her features in the gloom of the barn, but as she drew nearer they saw she was not beautiful in the conventional sense, but had a face lively with character, orchestrated most noticeably by finely arched eyebrows over a pair of deep brown eyes that looked with candour at the two men. Ambrose introduced his friend Edgar, who held out his hand and which she took in a firm grip.

'My apologies for all the previous precautions which may have seemed unnecessary to you both, but believe me, when you hear what I have to tell you, you'll understand why we have to be on our guard at all times.'

'I take it you're certain you weren't followed?' asked Edgar.

'I can confirm that no one shadowed me here. I know that my brother was watched by someone from the mill, but until just before his death he could never identify them. In the letters I've found since he died he has named a person whom he was sure was involved in some dreadful crimes. Working at the mill myself, I know the man and have kept him under surveillance since then. Now that you are here I wished to be certain that he's no longer suspicious, having successfully plotted and brought about my brother's death.'

Ambrose interrupted her: 'On behalf of us both, may we offer our condolences, Miss Thwaites.'

'Thank you. His loss has been a profound shock to me; we were very close. But, to continue, knowing you had planned to meet Donald in the Fountain I was unsure whether the man already knew you were coming and was waiting for you. I kept him under view in the tavern until six o'clock when I came out onto the street to find you. Fortunately, it was crowded with workers and I was unobserved in the throng. My brother's description of you as an exceptionally tall man, Mr Barrett, enabled me to identify you quite easily, although I took a risk approaching you, I admit. Having put you on the road to this place I returned to the town to make sure he had not moved. Sure enough I found him in the same tavern getting steadily drunk.

I moved within sight of him and he was oblivious to my presence. I consider we are now safe.'

Both men thought simultaneously that the man must have been blind. Miss Thwaites's physical charms were not those that deserved such indifference.

'But it was a risky strategy. Was it necessary to put yourself in the way of such danger? What would you have done if you were challenged?' asked Ambrose.

'There were enough people about for me to either slip away quickly or stand and make a commotion, which would have discomforted him I'm sure!'

Edgar was astonished, thinking he had never come up against a woman with such pluck.

Ambrose became practical. 'Come and sit with us. We have food for you and we can eat while we talk.'

'I'll be brief because I must return home tonight. There must be no suspicion attached to me and I don't want anyone enquiring about my movements. The details of my brother's murder are simple, as told to the coroner at least. He was asked to look at one of the driving belts for the engines that are situated high up on the top storey of the mill. It's claimed he was thrown backwards by the force of the belt which had slipped off its wheel. He fell down three storeys over the protective balustrade.'

'What evidence do you have that this wasn't the case?' asked Edgar – the magistrate in him coming to the fore.

'Two reasons why I'm certain it wasn't an accident. First, my brother was an experienced engineer and understood machinery very well. He always treated it with great respect and would never have attempted any adjustment to a driving wheel without stopping the machine first at the main control. He would also get someone to assist him. In this case, they said the engine hadn't been stopped or was "accidentally" turned on again while he was investigating the problem, and that is why he was supposedly thrown off. Second, common sense tells me that the sequence of events doesn't ring true. The balustrade is too high for anyone to fall over on their own, even with such a mechanical momentum behind them. The only possible way

Chapter 4

he could have gone over is by being deliberately forced – and it would have taken more than one person. At the short inquest that took place yesterday the witnesses called all reported an identical story, as though they had been primed. Either they are implicated in his death, or have been scared into lying.'

Ambrose nodded. 'Given that when he first wrote to me a month ago he mentioned how ruthless the men concerned are, from your reasoning it seems most unlikely that his death was an accident.'

Rosalie gave a sigh of relief. 'You're the first to acknowledge to me that must be the case. Everyone in the mill has been trying to assure me that was what it was – an accident.'

'How much did your brother confide in you, Miss Thwaites?' asked Edgar.

'I knew something of my brother's concerns, although he was careful not to acquaint me with all he knew; he hinted it was because he was concerned for my safety. Since his death I've become increasingly aware of the need to be discreet. I've no idea whom I can trust among his colleagues; I avoid gossip and speculation which are rife among those I work with – I'm employed at the factory as a power-loom weaver.'

'I thought it was the men who were the weavers,' said Edgar, surprised.

'Hand-loom weaving has always been done by men, but new inventions have speeded up the process and made it easier for women to manage the large machines, which is cheaper for the owners. The hand-weavers could claim high wages for their skills, and they were – are – still powerful among the workers here in the north. But I can see that their skills will eventually become unwanted as the machines take over completely. You would have seen how that has happened over in Lancashire I think, Mr Barrett – or should I call you Mr Hudson?'

Ambrose was taken aback. It was clear that his journalistic experiences early in the decade must have been a subject of discussion between Miss Thwaites and her brother. Either that or she had been able to find out for herself. If that was the case he wondered what her sources were, but he restrained himself from asking as he was most anxious for her to continue with her story.

'Once again, I'm very sorry for your loss. I wish I could have met your brother who, it seems to me, has risked his life and ultimately lost it – and, between us, it's Ambrose Hudson, please.'

Edgar nodded in agreement.

Ambrose went on, 'Mr Lawes and I are here to help his cause, and if, along the way, we can bring the perpetrators of his murder to justice in the courts we'll gladly do so. In the meantime, you have correspondence from your brother for me, I understand?'

Slipping her hand into the deep pocket of her skirt, she brought out a thick, sealed packet which was rather crumpled and covered in streaks of what looked like soot. 'I've been carrying this around for the last three days. My brother had left instructions with me to seize it from his house if anything untoward happened to him. He had concealed it well, because when I went to look for it someone had been there before me. The rooms had been ransacked, but the packet was well hidden behind a brick in the chimney, along with a small cash box that contained his savings. Fortunately, only he and I knew of this hiding place. He never married and so his belongings are now legally mine as his nearest family.' She handed the packet to Ambrose. 'As I said, my brother has told me a little of the contents and not enough for me to be in any danger – he never divulged any names to me when he was alive, but reading letters he left me it seems he was sure that one man and one woman are deeply involved.'

Spreading their blankets over some straw bales to make a comfortable place to sit, Edgar propped himself up next to Ambrose and watched as he broke open the seal and took out a sheaf of papers. Edgar could see among them that one was an ink sketch of something or some place. He and Rosalie remained silent while Ambrose read Donald Thwaites's covering letter.

Richmond Mill,
Bingley

11 April
  Dear Mr Hudson,
    I hope I will be able to hand these papers to you personally on the 15th as we have already agreed. In case for whatever reason I

Chapter 4

cannot keep our arrangement at the Fountain, this letter contains all the information I would have shared with you when we met.

I have put down as many details of what I know of both illegal child labour and the baby fostering 'service' as I have discovered and, on a separate sheet, some indication of that business's actual location. It has taken me many weeks to gather this information which I hope will speed up your own investigation should you pursue it once you know the risks. I do not think we are dealing with a vast conspiracy in Bingley; rather it begins and ends with one man and one woman. There may be those who collude with them – certainly there are women in the town who are used by them to provide local information and some of the workers in the mill are aware of those children they work alongside who they must know should not be employed because they are clearly too young.

The parents of those children certainly do, but you must remember that their decisions are always based on economic necessity. As I mentioned in my first correspondence with you, children as young as five are currently employed here, mostly doing fetching and carrying work but some are put to the more dangerous tasks of cleaning waste from round the machines. It is the poor wages that drive the workers to seek additional income, seemingly at any cost to their offspring. You may think we are dealing with small amounts, but cumulatively those who organise it are certainly making more each week than their wages as labourers. For them it is additional income. The mill manager, who must certainly be involved, asks no questions about the children's ages, requires no baptismal certificates as proof and certainly never asks to see an official birth certificate which have been available for over a year now. The reason that this practice can continue unchallenged is because the inspection process here is inadequate and corrupt. When inspectors are due – there are as yet no unannounced inspections – the mills are literally whitewashed – tidied up and made, as they say, shipshape. The children do not appear on those days; rather they are told to stay at home, unpaid. This is reminiscent of the way the union workhouses are inspected – as I read in your riveting account of your time in one.

The outcome of this is that the man involved is making large amounts of money over time and the children are at significant risk both from the treatment they receive from their 'overseers' and the poorly guarded machinery they work around. To my knowledge four such young children have been killed since September last year. When a child dies in the factory, the body is 'found' elsewhere outside the precincts of the premises. There is therefore no connection with the mill. Each time the coroner's verdict has been 'death by natural causes', an assumption that the child has died directly from hunger and its associated diseases. The parents, complicit in breaking the law, can say nothing let alone make accusations. Such is the explosion of population numbers in these factory towns that there are always plenty of replacements. Many parents of young children do not seem deterred by these dreadful outcomes and will put their youngest to work out of desperation to feed themselves and the rest of their families. As far as this illegal employment is concerned, up to now no one has ever been challenged let alone prosecuted. I believe they have corrupt protection, either from the mill owner or, sadly, one or some of the local justices. It is true that here both owners and local officials are often one and the same.

While not wishing in any way to diminish the viciousness of this practice, I believe an even more serious and criminal enterprise is the appalling activity of baby farming which has recently found its way into this district. In my earlier correspondence with you I explained how the system works, and I am sure you will have researched for yourself information about such practices. It is my opinion that here in Bingley the root causes of why women resort to the 'services' of 'child-minders' is that the wages of our mill workers are totally inadequate to sustain a

Chapter 4

decent living and the conditions in which their families live are dire – although you must have observed this in Lancashire where conditions are almost identical. It is often the overcrowding that adds to the distress of the poor, particularly the women. Such continual close and intimate proximity within families leads to an obvious outcome which is that of many pregnancies – the majority unwanted. Because the women must work they seek care for their newborns from women who will accept payment for their time and effort. I must stress that I have discovered some good women who strive to look after other women's children as they would their own. But their honesty and skills are much in demand and they cannot accommodate as many as there are requests. The baby farmers are then open to make advances to the most desperate mothers promising them, in return for a fee, that they will take care of their babies for as long as necessary. I have been able to put a name to the woman who runs the organisation – and it is organised – and she is particularly cunning. Her name is Fairfax. The man in the case I am not so certain of but am pursuing strong leads which may show he is the same villain implicated in illegal child labour. I believe the farming is operated from an abandoned homestead out on the moors far beyond Bingley. Two days ago, I managed to follow the woman to the place unobserved and later made some discreet enquiries about it. It is a place called Rickard's and provides a perfectly secluded spot that is totally unobserved. What she does there I cannot begin to imagine. I enclose a rough sketch of where it is, but my geography is poor and you may find the scale unhelpful!

She has evidently infiltrated the neighbourhood network of women in the shanties, tenements and courts which is an ideal arrangement by which she can gather information, aided by the local male accomplice from the mill. By such means the woman is informed of any mother – or sometimes expectant mother – who might need her services; she then visits them in their homes where she entices the desperate women into agreeing to give up their babies – for a price. Her prior knowledge means she knows exactly when to strike – when her quarry is most tired and vulnerable and can see no other option than fostering out her child to another. In Bingley, this has the makings of a profitable business, although fortunately it is only in its infancy. I am hoping your investigation will bring it to an immediate halt; but I warn you the pair in control are ruthless and well provisioned. One of them, or both, must have had money to set up the business in the first place.

For the last few weeks, as my enquiries have progressed I have felt continually threatened. Perhaps it is my own fault as I have been perhaps too persistent. I am sometimes aware of being followed, never by the same man and no one I can identify by name. Some weeks ago, I received a cryptic note warning me off and graphically describing what might happen if I continue asking questions. There are now very few people around me I can trust, apart from my sister Rosalie, who will in the event of anything happening to me relay this correspondence to you and answer any questions she can, although I have taken pains not to reveal anything that might cause her harm if she was ever in the unfortunate position of having to explain her actions.

I must assume that if you are reading this in Rosalie's presence I must be unable for whatever reason to speak to you face to face; but you must have already decided, with your companion Mr Lawes, that you are willing and able to become involved. These two matters I leave to you in the knowledge that your previous experience in Lancashire leaves you far more accomplished in this area than I can ever be – the reason I wrote you in the first place. My starting point was to keep my ears and eyes open as to new child employees, their origins and particularly the availability of documents that might prove their ages. I have provided you with a list of the names of three children whom I know to be under the age of nine and who are at present working on the power-loom floor of the factory. I also made

Chapter 4

myself aware of how they were brought into employment in the first place, taking note of who introduced them and who they are placed with.

As for the second area of my concern, it was not difficult as overseer to engage some of the women machinists in conversation about their families and to extract gossip about others in their lodging houses. It may have been this engagement that alerted the perpetrators to my interest. Perhaps I was too inquisitive and it was reported back to those concerned. You, I know, are unlikely to make that kind of mistake. Thus, the professional will always trump the keen amateur!

One person you may rely on is my sister Rosalie, but I beg you not to bring her into any danger. We are – were – extremely close and have worked in the woollen industry together since childhood. There is very little she does not know about factory life and the area around Bingley. Although we do not live together, she will have full access to my house, money and effects in the event of my death. She will also be able to recommend safe accommodation for yourself and Mr Lawes, as well as advising you on the best way to gain access as a worker in the mill.

I wish you God speed in your enterprise. Assuming I have met my end, I trust you to take up where I have been forced to leave off. All I seek is justice for those poor children without a voice and punishment for those whose cruelty towards them is so unremitting.

I remain your humble servant,
Donald Thwaites

While Edgar and Rosalie waited in silence during the minutes Ambrose read the letter, they noticed that it was growing dark and lit the two small lamps attached to the nearest stall so that Ambrose could continue reading. When he had finished he passed it to Edgar without comment and then took the other sheets and looked at them also. In the deepening gloom the scratchy sketch was difficult to follow, and even Edgar with his sharp eyesight was only just able to scan the long letter in the less than adequate light of the lamps. The men were both shocked and moved by the letter. It spoke strongly of a courageous man who, although threatened, had been prepared to brush aside the risk and pursue his mission unfalteringly.

Ambrose became aware that Rosalie would have to walk almost 3 miles back in the dark to where they had started out in the town. He had no idea how far away from Bingley she lived – in fact he suddenly realised how remiss he had been in not finding out more about her circumstances. They had all three exhibited some tension caused not only by the danger of their meeting, but the fact that Edgar and he were complete strangers to her, as she was to them; nor had either of them expected a different third party to be involved and he wondered what role she could possibly play. It was clear her local knowledge would be invaluable, but she obviously was known to the man or men involved, both as Donald's sister, and as a worker in the mill. The woman was at risk – but would she be *a* risk?

'It's getting dark. How far from home are you? Under the circumstances you shouldn't be walking back alone. I suggest that Edgar takes you back to town on his horse and then returns here. Before you go we must arrange to meet again as soon as possible.'

'I'm still working at the mill – I have to eat after all. I've been given some time off to arrange Donald's funeral on Thursday and settle his affairs.'

At the mention of the funeral the two men were brought up sharply. They had overlooked that Rosalie was in mourning, despite her black gown and grey shawl. They had been so intent on finding out what progress Donald Thwaites had made that both had completely forgotten to follow appropriate etiquette and enquire about her state of mind after the death of her brother.

Edgar immediately voiced his sympathy: 'Ambrose and I have been terribly remiss in not acknowledging your loss adequately. Please excuse our lapse. I know I speak for my friend when I commend you on your dignified behaviour. Are you sure you wish to continue to be involved in this – particularly now?'

'I want nothing more than to be a part of bringing the murderers of my brother to justice, and to help pursue his cause which he has more

Chapter 4

than adequately described in his letter. He shared it with me before he sealed it. He was right in what he said, I do know this area and the woollen industry as well as anyone, and I'll be able to guide you at the beginning. We'll meet here tomorrow. I presume you'll be spending the night here – it's too dark and probably too dangerous for you to ride back across moorland with which you're not acquainted. There's no reason for Mr Lawes to carry me back to the town. I can ride sufficiently well to get myself there and back. Besides, I'll need to bring you some provisions for tomorrow. Have you any objections to my borrowing one of your horses?'

Edgar was nonplussed for a moment, and lied when he said, 'Not at all. Take Ambrose's – she's not as lively as the other, but as you say you can ride, this one will be comfortable for you.' He went to the stall and saddled up the mare and brought her out to the front of the barn. It was now very gloomy – with no sign of the moon.

Rosalie took the reins and placed her foot in the stirrup; with a leg-up from Ambrose, she scrambled into the saddle. 'I'll be here at dawn tomorrow when there'll be very few people around, although I'm certain I wasn't followed in town yesterday. The farmer won't disturb you; I paid him for the use of the barn for a couple of days, not knowing exactly when you might arrive or for how long you might need it.'

Edgar adjusted the stirrups to her height and she flicked the reins, waved her hand and trotted off down the track. They watched her until she was out of sight in the darkness and then turned back into the dimly lit barn, Ambrose musing on a pair of fine brown eyes and an expressive face; Edgar wondering how he had come to allow a stranger use of a mount that was not even his. Indeed, he had not had the wit to ask her where she would be stabling her for the night.

Chapter 5

Watching the two men move off from the stable yard on the evening of 15 April, Peter hoped they weren't riding into danger. He knew from what he had overheard that they were to meet with Ambrose's original contact at an inn in Bingley. He also recognised that Ambrose was apprehensive about the practical matter of riding over unknown ground, but had put a brave face on things when he saddled up and mounted his hack; Mr Hudson was so good at everything and knew so much but it was comforting to know that riding was an activity where he held the advantage.

He turned and walked back into a stable to continue grooming one of Mr George Lawes's thoroughbreds under the supervision of Charlie Anderson. When Peter had been introduced to the horses in the yard, he had rapidly become enamoured of the feel and smell of the animals, prompted by an immediate sense of their innate nobility. When he had first sat on one he had been very afraid, sensing its strength and power beneath him. It had taken some time and several tumbles before he had gained the confidence to put himself in charge and direct the animal where he wanted it to go, rather than the reverse. Now he was at home on most mounts, although not yet trusted with any of George Lawes's racehorses; but he had been promised this was something for the near future when he had shown the stablemen what he could do. For the next week he was to follow the same duties as the other stable boys, mucking out, grooming and cleaning tack.

The two brothers he was working with, Jem and Matthew, were friendly enough. At first they were most curious about Peter's Suffolk accent, teasing him that he might as well have been speaking French for all they could understand him. On strangers' territory, the boy wisely refrained from making similar observations about their Yorkshire drawl.

It wasn't long before they started to probe him about his background. Although he was quite honest in his answers, he was never prepared to talk about his time before he had gone to live on the Lawes's estate and, lacking detailed information, the stable lads assumed that he was, like them, the son of an estate worker who had been taken on to work in the owner's stables – the usual scheme of things. Indeed, Matthew and Jem were the sons of a shepherd, but while their elder brother had taken on an apprenticeship to work with the estate flock, they had opted to work with the horses and had been doing so since they were 11. Both boys were ambitious to ride in races and were at the point of being trained in those skills.

'We're set on racing – both of us. We've been out on the gallops many times,' Matthew told him. 'There's nothing like it!'

They clearly lived and breathed horses, and most of their conversation concerned racing, racecourses and all the gossip of the horse-breeding world. Rarely did they talk of girls, although both were well into their teens. Peter wondered if either of the boys could read or write, but it was not the kind of question to ask in these early days when their acquaintance was in its infancy.

On the morning that Edgar and Ambrose left, firmly and rhythmically brushing the flanks of a superb grey, Peter became absorbed in his own thoughts which always turned to one topic. With his usual thoughtfulness, Mr Hudson had provided him with pen, ink and sealing wax to complement his new writing case. Ambrose knew how important it would be for Peter to keep in touch with Caroline. He also knew that the boy's writing skills had sufficiently progressed for him to produce a fair hand and one he was proud of.

As soon as Peter had finished his work and in the short period before supper he determined he would write a letter and arrange for its posting as soon as possible. What to say? He had never written to a sweetheart before. His correspondence with Ambrose had been man to man, generally on topics he thought might interest his mentor. He wondered what she would be interested to hear. Not too much about the horses, but enough for her to understand what he was doing and to achieve a picture in her mind of his surroundings. That was it – he could describe the bleakness of the moors, and how much more beautiful they would be if she were with him! Thus, he had the theme of his correspondence and the grey benefited from an extra polishing as Peter mentally polished his letter.

The next morning neither Mr Lawes nor Mr Hudson appeared for

Chapter 5

breakfast, nor did they show themselves all morning. As he knew their meeting had not been until six the previous evening Peter assumed they'd stayed the night in Bingley – he noticed they'd taken a quantity of provisions and clothing in anticipation that this might be necessary. But as they'd not shown by early afternoon he began to worry. He was in the unfortunate position of a little knowledge being a disturbing thing. Although aware what their enterprise was, he had not been included in their planning and therefore had no idea how they were to carry it out. To his relief at about four in the afternoon he heard horses arriving in the stable yard and recognised the voices of his two friends. Jem and Matthew were already on hand to take the horses from their riders, and Peter heard Ambrose give a sigh of relief as he slipped out of the stirrups and saddle and felt the ground beneath him.

'Thank God for that!' he said. 'I don't know about you, Edgar, but I need a drink and then a hot bath!'

The boy went out to greet the men and saw they were both grubby and dishevelled: Edgar with his cropped hair and cap pulled over his eyes, and Ambrose in working clothes with straw attached. They told him nothing of where they'd been, only that they'd spent the night in a barn.

Peter finished his work at six and walked across to the house. There was no sign of his friends, so he went up to his garret room and fulfilled the promise he'd made to himself. In his long, descriptive letter to Caroline he tried to convey how much he was missing her, without overstepping proprieties. Having washed and changed he went downstairs to the main dining room where other workers were gathering for the evening meal. Evidently Edgar and Ambrose were taking dinner with George Lawes in the small dining room. Peter felt excluded, but Ambrose had made it very clear that he did not want Peter involved in what was plainly going to be a dangerous adventure. The less he knew, the safer he would be. The men obviously wished to talk over the day's affairs without him. To his mind, that meant there had been progress or even action in the last 24 hours, but what it was would not be shared with him.

Indeed, that is precisely why Edgar and Ambrose moved swiftly into the house, took a bath and tidied themselves up before presenting themselves to their host in the small dining room. George Lawes, ready with a bottle of sherry from which he poured them generous measures, was anxious to hear what the meeting had produced. Over dinner the pair related to their host their first encounter with Rosalie Thwaites and how she had produced her brother's letter with its enclosures, which explained everything he had discovered. Ambrose went on to describe the events of Donald Thwaites's death.

George shook his head. 'This man's death was shocking. I heard rumours of what was described to me as "a fatal incident" at Richmond Mill, but nothing much was made of it; accidents in the mills aren't uncommon and coroners are always swift to bring in verdicts of accidental death, mainly to placate the mill owners who certainly don't want investigations into the management of their mills. Even though I'm a JP I don't have any dealings with the industry in Bingley; most of my cases concern the farming community. I don't like to think of any locals being involved in such ruthlessness, but the man's sister obviously knows what happened and why.'

'I think Thwaites knew he was a marked man and wanted to protect his sister. His letter to us was very explicit.'

'Will you share the letter with me?'

'Here, you may read it at your leisure. It'll be helpful; with your local knowledge, there's a possibility you may recognise the name Rickard's which Thwaites identifies as the place where the Fairfax woman maybe living. He's tried to draw a sketch map – but it is just that – sketchy!'

George took the letter. 'I'll read it later. But I do recognise that name; it's a small piece of moorland often rented by my neighbour's chief shepherd. The owner has recently re-let it for a year because the shepherd has been moved to a larger holding closer to where the sheep are lambing this season. Thwaites's intelligence is accurate. I'm sure I have it placed on a map somewhere, let's see.'

Anxious not to be sidetracked for the moment, Ambrose intervened. 'That will be very useful, George, but now we've had our meeting with Rosalie Thwaites, Edgar and I have begun to formulate

Chapter 5

a plan that we need to share with you. First, we had a comfortable night bedding down with the remaining horse among the straw with enough food to satisfy us. It was a novelty for Edgar, but not so for me. Sleeping on any kind of straw takes me back immediately to my experience in the Seddon Union workhouse last year. Anyway, the night passed peacefully enough and Rosalie was as good as her word, returning at dawn this morning.'

At that point Edgar broke in as the issue of lending his cousin's horse to a stranger was playing on his conscience, although George had not seen fit to mention it. 'She was clearly a proficient rider; the mare was in very good condition when she returned her. Apparently, Rosalie lives just outside the town on a smallholding with her father. Her brother was always interested in engineering and preferred to work in the factories, so he left their holding, found a position in Richmond Mill and went to live in a house in Bradford which he rented from a relative. Rosalie works in the same factory, but still lives at home and cares for her father who is just about able to manage their small piece of land. She assured me the horse was well taken care of.'

George grunted and refilled their glasses. 'While you are my guests you have free run of the place – especially in view of what you have come here to do. You can raid the kitchens for food – use any horses you want – even take some of my men if it comes to a fight. But one thing I can't allow is you using any of my thoroughbreds!'

'Wouldn't dream of it, George,' said Edgar, and Ambrose nodded.

'So, tell me, what's all this about? What have you let yourselves in for?'

Edgar looked at Ambrose who took up the story. 'There's no doubt that illegal child labour is going on in this particular mill – and probably many others. Mr Thwaites has provided us with some names of children he suspects are under-age for work. The men he had been investigating were aware that he had at best guessed, or at worst from their point of view had evidence of what they were doing. To be completely sure of keeping his mouth shut they killed him or had him killed. Donald was sure there is one man at the head of this gang of ruffians and was pursuing the idea that the same man is involved with the woman organising the baby farming. The whole business is based on exploitation – of the parents of the children involved, and the children themselves.'

'Yes, but we have new legislation now that prohibits young children working in factories. I know all about it, I've read the Act – had to as a magistrate.'

'These regulations are flouted time and time again.'

'But there's an inspection process that is designed to police the Act surely?'

'I think we all know the inspection process is rigged, George—'

Edgar broke in: 'Three children illegally employed can add at least seven extra shillings a week to a family income. The men ensure the children are kept out of the way when the inspectors come which, as the rogues see it, maintains the jobs of the children by protecting from prosecution the mill owners, who are generally careless in their use of information about their employees. In other words, no one knows or checks how old these children are. There's no excuse for that now that we have the official birth certificates – but many parents don't register their children's births, so there's no written proof of age.'

'The whole system is corrupt, George,' said Ambrose. 'Very often the inspectors are bribed to look the other way on their visits. It's the man who organises this business who must be stopped, and employers must be made more aware of the ages of the children they are employing. That's what Donald was trying to instigate with my help.'

'I must say I'd be surprised if Samuel Richmond knows any of this,' said George with a shake of his head. 'He always seems a decent sort to me. Perhaps he doesn't take as much interest in the mill as he used to. I believe he's recently remarried; she's a wealthy woman and a pillar of the Church and Samuel has become caught up in that somewhat. I think he would be horrified if he felt his mill was being used for anything other than its proper purpose. He's not an avaricious man and would play no part in profiteering from other folk's misery. But if what you say is true, he should return his gaze more sharply to the business. He must have wondered at the manner of Thwaites's death, although as the coroner's verdict was unequivocal, he probably took it for what it was worth. Anyway – what do you intend to do about

Chapter 5

all this and how will you go about it? What's your plan?' asked the ever-practical Yorkshire man.

'Infiltrate myself into the factory – as I did before in Lancashire. Donald had primed his sister as to how I might get work there and she already had some suggestions for me. First, I need to be taken on at the hiring fair in Bingley where, as you know, the unemployed – mostly unskilled labourers – apply for work by the day. After Miss Thwaites reappeared just as the sun was rising we had a very useful talk. The woman is extremely inventive and has great common sense—'

'As well as a fine pair of brown eyes and a handsome figure,' muttered Edgar.

Ignoring him, Ambrose continued. 'She agrees I should present myself as a strong man willing to work at anything in the mill that doesn't require too many mechanical skills. This will enable me to move about the place quite naturally. I'll be known as Frank Barrett and keep to my story. She's also found me somewhere to live – a room in a lodging house in a quiet part of the town, not too close to the mill but within walking distance. We were late back this afternoon because we've spent much of the day on foot walking around Bingley getting our bearings. We located the factory easily enough and the lodging house which is about twenty minutes' walk from it. I'll make discreet enquiries about the hiring fair when I've established myself in my lodgings early tomorrow morning.'

'I've heard there are more workers putting themselves up than the mills can take. Can you be sure you'll get a place easily?' asked George.

'According to Miss Thwaites, Richmond Mill is an unpopular place to work in now. There's a superstition about it; as well as the children who've been killed, two adults have died working the machines in the last six months and her brother's death is still considered a mystery by some. The workers are beginning to think the place is cursed and would rather avoid it. If anyone questions why I'm putting myself up to work there it'll be because I'm a stranger in the district and don't know any better. It's likely I'll miss the fair tomorrow morning and will have to try the next day, although it's a pity I have to waste time. If I'm taken on maybe the workers will have Donald Thwaites's funeral on their minds, and pay little attention to a new man. He was popular apparently. Early tomorrow I'll walk to Bingley from here which will take me about an hour. So I'll be disappearing for maybe a few weeks. But we do need to have a means of keeping in touch. Anyone have any ideas how best we can do that?'

The other two considered for a moment then George leaned forward on his chair. 'I send regular deliveries of wool to the mills in Bingley. The men I use have been with me for years and I trust them entirely. I'm supposing that you'll not want a regular correspondence – as I see it, the more clandestine contacts there are the more risk is run. But if it's a matter of urgency then you can get a note out through one of my delivery men when they are in the district. I'll give you a schedule of their movements and introduce you to my senior man, John Walters, who's watertight when it comes to keeping his mouth shut. He can be your go-between.' Notwithstanding his bluff, open appearance, George Lawes had acquired a forensic grasp of Ambrose's need for complete anonymity.

The conversation turned to the subject of baby farming and Ambrose described its workings to George.

'The woman we're after is called Fairfax and she's manipulating a small number of women living within the tenements and shacks of Bingley who identify potential mothers desperately in need of her "services". As word's passed from one woman to another everyone in the community now knows where to go if they feel despairing enough to want to relieve themselves of their unwanted offspring. For the most part, it's young women who've been abandoned by the children's fathers. There were a few cases that Thwaites had heard of when mothers didn't want to pass off their children to another woman, but financial circumstances forced them into it. These were generally older women with more children than they could possibly maintain; very often they were widows. But whatever their condition, their plight was the same – what they did was out of pure economic necessity. The last baby is often the last straw and the baby farmers know that's the time to strike.'

'So how do you hope to infiltrate this gang then, Ambrose?'

Chapter 5

'The three of us talked it through and we thought it wasn't a good idea for Edgar to become actively involved. In fact, it would probably be impossible. First, he was too much of a stranger with a strikingly Suffolk accent that wouldn't go unnoticed however much he tried to disguise it; second, this was really a business conducted by and with women and it was unlikely there would be any role for him to play in the operation.'

Edgar said, 'As we see it the solution is for me to secretly observe what's going on. Fortunately, included in Thwaites's papers was this outline of the homestead from which he had discovered the business may be operating. I could place myself in a position on the moor and record the daily comings and goings at the cottage and take any opportunity to collect evidence which will be useful if the miscreants are brought to court.'

Ambrose nodded. 'We agreed this would be a better option and less dangerous – as long as Edgar confines himself to simply observing. Now, I know you're anxious to get started on this enterprise, Edgar, but I'm going to suggest that you do nothing this end until you hear from me. It's important we don't waste time chasing hares and so we must first confirm the connection between Rickard's and the Fairfax woman and try to ascertain who her contact is in the mill. It may mean waiting a few days while I am investigating, but as soon as I have enough information then you can start surveillance of the cottage. In the meantime, perhaps you can tell us something about the place, George?'

Edgar passed George the sketch map and he examined it closely. 'Well, I can just about make out where it might be. As the crow flies it's not far from the Cat Stones and close to the old coal pits, although it's too far to walk; you'll need a horse to get there; most is high moorland belonging to one of my neighbours. He uses it for grazing his sheep and then only in the summer. For now he has his shepherd living in a lambing hut for the season. I know the man – he's taciturn and isolates himself, so his occupation suits him well. My neighbour has several such buildings dotted about the moor – as I have myself. The shepherds spend most of the spring and summer out there with the flocks. Look, what if I identify a decent, weatherproof hut for

Edgar to operate from – as close to the centre of the operation as possible?' He raised his head from the map and turned to Edgar. 'The moor's an enormous place but that would enable you to have a base from which you could make sorties to spy on our villains; it must be somewhere accessible to Rickard's, but well hidden from it.'

Ambrose was somewhat gratified to hear George including himself in the operation, and privately acknowledged that without their host's help and local knowledge they would have much more to do themselves; in fact, he was an invaluable asset.

Although disappointed that he was not to set out immediately, Edgar appreciated Ambrose's reasoning; wild-goose chases were not part of the plan. But all the same, even if he did have to wait, inwardly he was becoming quite excited. The night in the barn among the straw and farm equipment, with the occasional restless movement of his horse next to him, had given him great pleasure; especially when he had risen in the night and opened one of the barn doors and looked out. It was a crisp, April night – almost frosty; the clouds had rolled away and there were magnificent stars and a full moon. He had a great sense of well-being and was at peace with himself. As he lay back on the straw and pulled the blanket over his shoulders he began to anticipate what he called privately his 'great adventure'. Now George's suggestion, that he camp out for days or even weeks on an empty, desolate moor, had become strangely appealing. This was something he hadn't recognised in himself before: the relish of a secret life where he was out of the gaze of his relations, friends and employees, even if only for a short time.

'I think that's a good idea,' he said, 'but how do I pass myself off to your friends and neighbours? As you've said – this is a very close community. I imagine your acquaintances will soon become curious about the strange man living out on the moor. Is there any way I can keep myself secret? It's going to be hard to establish a credible story to explain my presence. We need to come to some definite conclusion about this if you're away tomorrow, Ambrose.'

His friend thought for a moment. 'Although I'm making a start in the morning you need to take a few days to establish a story that will satisfy the nosiest of locals. George, your stable hands and shepherds

Chapter 5

know he is a relation of yours. How about the idea that he also takes an interest in sheep husbandry? They already know he keeps horses, but he also runs a large flock back in Suffolk. We could say he's interested in breeding from the hardier varieties raised around here. In that way, he can go out with one of your shepherds and then it can be suggested he tries some shepherding himself. That will mean he'll be regularly toing and froing and soon be ignored. Even though your employees might think it's strange for someone of Edgar's station to want to rough it like that, you have very good credibility among your workers and neighbours and it seems likely they'll accept any story you put forward. Besides, as I understand it from talking to your workers, you're a landowner who uses his practical skills, not simply a landlord idly raking in the rents. Edgar, it would mean you would have to really roll up your sleeves and learn the elements of the business before isolating yourself out on the moor.'

'Doubts about my ability to immerse myself – again!' Edgar laughed. 'Have no fear, I'll plunge into this wholeheartedly and might even learn something to take back to my shepherds.'

George nodded. 'This would work, as long as it's planned properly. There's no doubt I'll be able to convince my neighbours there's nothing untoward about your presence here, Edgar. If we don't rush into things, just establish yourself quietly and when you finally move off to the hut there will be little comment or interest. It should only take a few days. You've come looking the part – with your shorn locks. My men know you're an able horseman with a good eye. You'll not have to pretend on any score, I'm sure. I'll put you with James Macintyre, my chief shepherd. He's been with me for years, is loyal and as a bonus keeps his mouth shut, which is a rarity among stock workers in these parts; rural working life is hard and men have little free time for fancy activities. Small talk in the ale-house is mostly what passes for recreation and this certainly includes speculation about strangers. I'll alert Macintyre to the need for discretion and as Ambrose has pointed out – and he's quite right – the nearer the truth we can give the less likely we are to make mistakes which would soon be detected. Now, before you both retire I'll call in my delivery man. You need to be introduced, Ambrose. Walters is also a man who can keep his mouth shut, although there's no need to give him too much information. He's about the yard somewhere – I'll call him in.'

John Walters was a sturdy, thick-set man; open-faced and with a firm handshake, Ambrose immediately felt this was a man who could be trusted.

'John, Mr Barrett's hoping to start work at Richmond's, if they'll take him on. He needs to keep in touch with my cousin here and will be passing you a packet or two; you don't need to know too much – other than it's nothing illegal. You being such a good Methodist, I just assure you of that!'

Walters raised his eyebrows slightly, then touched his cap and nodded. 'Very good, sir. I'll look out for him.'

Feeling they had made considerable progress, the three men sat for a further hour or two over a bottle of George's best port, but both Ambrose and Edgar had finally to confess real weariness after the long day's activities and went off to bed. George joined his stable manager in smoking a cheroot together as they made their customary late evening walk round the stables.

Chapter 6

Early the following morning, well before dawn, Ambrose took up his old and shabby pack in which he had stowed a set of work clothes and everything else he would need for time away. On the scrubbed wooden kitchen table was a bowl and spoon for a serving of the porridge simmering slowly on the hob. His one luxury was a good pair of work boots – not new but well worn-in and very comfortable. From now on his activities would all be conducted on foot, somewhat of a relief for him from horseback.

In almost complete darkness he slipped out of the front door away from the dogs kennelled near the stables who kept their ears permanently cocked for noises recognised as out of the ordinary. Although they had been mutually introduced and the dogs had familiarised themselves with his scent, he was keen to avoid waking them up and rousing the household; he wanted to be out and on the road, unobserved by any of George's workers. Fortunately, the weather was dry, but in the coldness of a pre-dawn April day he pulled a threadbare coat around him and, with his cap pulled well round his ears, set off towards Bingley to seek out his new lodgings and present himself at the hiring fair.

He arrived in the outskirts of the town just before six. Rosalie had recommended a lodging house in James's Row, a street about a mile from the town centre; indeed she had gone so far as to reserve a room for him. Thomas Jolly, the lodge-house keeper, was a good friend of Miss Thwaites's father – they had both been in the army together and seen action in Spain – and she had known the man since she was a child. His name belied his nature, which veered towards the lugubrious, but he was someone who could be trusted and – a rarity in the district – never indulged in gossip, although there were plenty of strangers coming in and out of his door. These were of intense interest to his neighbours who thirsted for information, but who were always disappointed when Mr Jolly remained closed-lipped about them. Edgar and Ambrose had already externally surveyed the place during the previous afternoon and found it to be ideally situated.

Therefore, Ambrose had no difficulty locating number five, a tall tenement fronting directly onto the street with a small flight of steps up to a front door that had clearly seen much wear and tear as over time the inhabitants passed in and out in a continuous stream. Banging the iron knocker on the paint-peeled wood, he waited a few seconds until the handle turned and the door opened. A short, fat, grey-haired woman peered out.

Ambrose took off his cap and made his introduction: 'Good morning, ma'am! I'm Frank Barrett and I've a room reserved here.'

She looked him up and down with an inscrutable expression, nodded and opened the door sufficiently to let him into a narrow and dingy entrance hall. There was a door immediately left of a right-hand staircase and the hall then became a passageway extending into darkness beyond his sight somewhere to the back of the house. He could hear sounds of occupation through thin walls as the lodgers in their various rooms upstairs and down prepared themselves for the day's work. Silently she indicated he should follow her up the stairs and two flights later he came to the top of the house. She unlocked a door into an attic room and Ambrose inwardly groaned at the thought of the vulnerability of his forehead. He had hoped, after his experiences in George Lawes's garret, that he would find himself in a room with a roof space in which he didn't have to double over to move around and a door through which he could pass without bending from the waist.

The interior of the room was large enough for his needs and the furniture adequate: a small pallet-type bed with a flock mattress, a pillow and a couple of blankets, a table and chair, a washstand, a bucket and chamber pot. There was no fire, but as summer was approaching the garret would soon be one of the warmest rooms, if not the stuffiest room in the building. Light entered by means of a small skylight on the south side of the roof. Experience of living in such spartan quarters as these had taught him to remember to bring an adequate supply of candles. These were expensive and generally not included with the rent; neither was there any means of heating food, so clearly he would be eating elsewhere. As he intended to spend the least time possible here he was quite prepared to put up with the inconveniences, as he

Chapter 6

always did when he was on such an investigation. Passing the woman a handful of coins which covered his rent for four weeks, he muttered that the room was as he had expected. She handed him a key. The woman had not introduced herself and he presumed she was Mrs Jolly, who appeared to be as unsociable as her husband.

He had to ask where the privy was and for the first time her face showed some reaction as she said with surprise, 'At the bottom of the garden, where it always is! The pump's a few yards down the street. You fetch your own water and make your own arrangements for washing. There's a tin bath in the kitchen you can use, but it must be shared on a first come first served basis. You can heat your water in the copper in the kitchen, but it's ninepence for half a bag of coal.'

She left him to unpack his small amount of luggage. He realised he'd had nothing to eat since he'd left Hoyles and thought he would try to find food in the tavern in the centre of town where he should have had his assignation with Donald Thwaites. It would be a good opportunity to enquire about the hiring fair and to gauge the customers; perhaps pick up local gossip, not only general but anything particularly concerning that gentleman's death. After spending a good hour settling in and leaving his bag with spare clothing, but with his money in a belt strapped round his waist, he locked the door, passed down the stairs, through the hall and out of the front door without seeing a sign of a soul. He was aware that the noises he had noted when he entered the house had all but diminished and he presumed everyone was by now at work. It was interesting that there were evidently no families living here as there were no sounds of small children. The place must solely cater for single working men and women. Pulling his cap down over his brow, he set off for the town centre where soon he was on familiar ground, aware that this was where he and Edgar had travelled two days before. He came to the main street and found the place outside the tavern where Rosalie had first waylaid them; the sign hanging from the front wall of the inn above the main door showed an ornate fountain in full spate.

Ambrose entered to be met with a buzz of talk and laughter. Despite it being a working day, he had to elbow his way through the crowd to the only bar, where he waited to be served; looking around him he could see this was a tavern for shift-working men. They were a rough-looking bunch, many emaciated through lack of food and over-indulgence of alcohol; all had either bad teeth or toothless gums and, as he came within smelling distance of them, foul breath and malodorous bodies. In fact, the place was full of unsavoury smells and Ambrose wondered what the beer and food would be like. When he was eventually served with a pint of home-brewed ale he was pleasantly surprised by its quality. He sat himself down at the corner of a table occupied by two men and a young boy who were having a fierce argument over something or someone. He nodded but they ignored him as he waited for his food which was poor and expensive – tasteless bread and hard cheese costing him thruppence.

As their energies over their disagreement dissipated, the two men began to take an interest in the stranger at their table. The more open-faced of the two, said "Ow do?' and Ambrose nodded back. The man opened the conversation: 'Stranger in town? I suppose you're looking for work?'

'Yes. I've come up from London. Not much doing down there so I thought I'd try my luck here. What's about – anything?'

'Depends what you want. There's a queue waiting to get on the new machines in most of the factories. The work pays well – that's when they're working that is. We've all been laid off for a time recently since the market slumped, or so the bosses tell us. It's just beginning to pick up. They always want general labourers to do the fetching and carrying. You look strong; you could be lucky.'

Ambrose took a chance: 'Someone recommended the Richmond Mill as a place that sometimes needs labourers – what do you know about it? Are they right?'

The man looked surprised for a moment and narrowed his eyes. 'Don't know who told you that, but seemingly they're right. They've been taking on.'

'What about any of the other mills locally? I've rented some lodgings here in the town so don't want to be too far out.'

'You should know in this business you take what you can get. Some of us with families walk miles for work. You got a family?'

'No, single man, never married; always been able to find work

Chapter 6

because I can move around. But I hoped to get myself settled in Bingley – who knows, I might find a wife here!'

'The mill girls are always on the lookout for a feller, but you need to find work first; they won't take one on without a wage coming with them. Our Yorkshire lassies are a careful lot!'

The second man was looking Ambrose up and down with some curiosity. 'Have you done factory work before?'

Sticking to his principle of always telling as much of the truth as possible, Ambrose explained he had worked for a while in mills in Lancashire, but was not a skilled man with machines; rather he stuck to labouring work.

'Try the hiring fair tomorrow – you've missed this morning's. If you get into town early you can get a good spot to be seen, although with your height that won't matter too much. Make sure the overseer can see your hands and feet. It's size that matters in labouring!' He laughed. 'But then, you should know that.'

'Thanks for the advice,' murmured Ambrose and offered them all another drink, which they had no hesitation in accepting. They had reached the point of introductions and, now well used to his alias, Ambrose automatically gave his name as Frank Barrett. They introduced themselves as Jimmy Cardine and Dick Butcher. The lad was Dick's son Ted and Ambrose estimated him to be about the same age as his young friend William Tuttle – about 11. It seemed they all worked at different jobs in Richmond Mill. Ambrose saw this as a tremendous piece of luck and he would try to take full advantage of the opportunity presented to him. They told him they had been on a night shift – hence their recourse to the tavern after work.

Coming back from the bar with the drinks, he started to probe gently for information about the mill and its workers. Richmond Mill was considered of small size; that is, it employed under 200 workers. The complete processes in the production of cloth were undertaken on the premises, apart from the initial cleaning of the fleeces; partly-cleaned wool arrived in the mill in hessian sack bundles and it was then carded, spun and woven into cloth. Richmond Mill produced fine strong worsted cloth from the wool of long-haired rough fell sheep abundant in the district. Assuming that he had previous experience of mill work, the men were not inclined to take Ambrose through the whole process. Instead, in the way that all men like to gossip over a pint of ale, they began to speak of some of the personalities he might come across if he were taken on.

The name Tom Sizewell was mentioned as someone responsible for hiring and firing. He was the manager and their estimation of him was that he was tricky and moody; one who would as soon lash out for seemingly no reason. This unpredictability made him untrustworthy in their eyes and they warned Ambrose to keep his distance whenever possible. Feeling it incumbent upon him to maintain a friendship with the pair, Ambrose was quite free with his money and it was not long before both men were somewhat the worse for drink. Consequently, their conversation began to veer towards the maudlin and Ambrose could see that he would gain nothing further by staying. Thanking them for the advice and hoping his luck would be in and he would soon see them on the premises as an employee, he rose to leave.

'Watch out for Sizewell – he may be only the size of a rat, but he's got sharp teeth. Keep out of his way!' Dick looked Ambrose up and down. 'No doubt you can handle yourself, but if you get the job and want to keep it, steer clear is my advice.'

Ambrose waved a hand and walked out into the street. By this time it was late morning, and he had the rest of the day to explore the town and its surrounding countryside.

He was aware that tomorrow, Thursday, was the day of Donald Thwaites's funeral and he made a point of visiting All Saints' Church where the burial was to take place. He sat on a headstone which, of great age, had fallen over and was balanced against the churchyard wall. He could hear the voices of the sexton and his lad, evidently digging Thwaites's grave. There was the usual peace and quiet of such places – a contrast to the racket and din of the mill where Donald had once spent his days. 'Perhaps this is what we all crave – ultimate peace. But not gained in such a fashion!' Ambrose thought. He sighed and thought of Rosalie and how she might be thinking at this moment. Would she be thinking of him, perhaps? But no – why should she? All thoughts would be for her lost brother.

Chapter 6

He sat for half an hour before moving off back to his lodgings, many unfamiliar thoughts circling in his head.

Next morning, as the church clock struck the half before nine, he arrived in the central area that accommodated the Thursday market. It was a large, wide-open space at the bottom of a steep hill, crowded and busy with people of all descriptions. The fair started at nine and to pass the time he found a corner in the tap room of a back-street tavern and bought himself a pint of ale of mediocre quality and something to eat. The place was already beginning to fill up with sundry workmen, some coming off shift and needing the restorative properties of alcohol before they trudged back to their dwellings. From previous experience in the similar environment in Lancashire, Ambrose recognised how many of these men preferred the dubious cleanliness and comfort of a crowded tavern to the filthy conditions in which most of them lived in the shanties, tenements and cellars of any small industrial town. Their wives were probably working their own shifts by now and had left the youngest children with slightly older ones – too young to work but old enough to be reckoned capable of looking after their younger siblings; the age when children assumed serious responsibilities had always been very young. Labouring families in agricultural communities heaped duties on their children from a young age. Bird scaring and stone picking provided mundane employment which required little skill for a child of four or five and at least it was in the fresh air. In this urban setting tasks were carried out in appalling and desperate conditions. Children had to grow up quickly, learning all the skills necessary to survive.

Ambrose had often reflected on the conundrum of whether this early pressure to contribute to family survival helped the children become more self-reliant and thereby better able to cope with what life threw at them, or simply drained away all energy, aspiration and hope of bettering their condition. Like his friend Edgar he considered the most important thing a child could receive, apart from the unwavering love and care of its parents, was an education. Without the opportunities for learning, no child could possibly hope for any self-improvement. He hoped that one day education would become free and compulsory for all children. Until that day came, they would continue to be ruthlessly exploited in the ways that he had experienced in the mills of Lancashire, and those that Donald Thwaites had discovered in Bingley.

Sipping slowly to make his pint last as long as he could while observing the other customers, he finally judged it timely to move himself into position at the hiring fair. He was not the first; there were at least 20 men already standing in a ragged line in the square and continually jostling for prime positions, like a flock of birds seeking the best places to roost on a branch. Ambrose had previous experience of these selective procedures and knew that, for a man of his height and size, the best place to stand was somewhere near the centre of the line. He always dominated a group; his height never went unnoticed. As he reckoned it, those scanning the workers often passed by the first in line in the hopes there would be someone fitter, stronger, larger further down. Standing at the end of the line was equally disadvantageous, giving an impression of second-best, and perhaps too late for selection. The centre ground was the best place, and effective use of his elbows and shoulders saw him as near as he could manage in that position. Remembering Dick Butcher's advice, he made sure the overseer would have a clear view of his hands and feet, so stood with his legs slightly apart and his hands to the front. There was a swarthy man to his left who, although lacking height, was well-built. To his right he was relieved to see a thin, pale man with a crippled hand. He was sorry for him, but in the cut and thrust of the search for work he couldn't afford to be sentimental. He must get employment at the Richmond Mill. The town clock struck nine and five minutes later a man strode purposefully from a side street and approached the line.

Earlier in the tavern he had listened in on conversations, which all centred on mill gossip. He noted that the manager Tom Sizewell was coming to the hiring and, from the brief description given by Dick Butcher, recognised him now; Butcher was right, the man was 'rat-like'. He was of medium height but skinny with the blue nose of a drinker and pock-marked skin. He was moving down the line towards Ambrose and had already picked out a man for some purpose.

To Ambrose's relief the manager stopped in front of him, looked

Chapter 6

him up and down and said brusquely, 'What do you do? You look strong enough. Any experience of mill work? Let's look at your hands.'

Ambrose obediently stretched out his arms, the cuffs of his shabby jacket riding up to reveal a pair of massive hands on strong wrists.

Without touching them the man eyed the calluses carefully, as though measuring each one as a signal of previous experience. Then he stepped back and took in Ambrose's physique, as if he were judging a bull at market, although he stopped short of running his hands down his flanks. 'We need a general labourer today to fetch stuff in and out of the factory. You look as though you could handle heavy weights.' He shouted to a man in the crowd who was carrying a large, bulky and awkwardly shaped bundle of cloth.

The man responded by stepping forward and throwing the bundle hard at Ambrose, who whirled round and quick as a flash caught it in the crook of his left arm, steadied it with his right hand, clasped it to his chest with both arms and then presented it to the under-manager.

The man nodded. 'You'll do. Report to my overseer and sign on for the day. If you're any good we'll keep you at least till we don't need you.'

He passed on, rejecting the workman next to Ambrose; the man sighed with frustration and melted back into the crowd. Doubtless he would be back next day and Ambrose hoped he would have better luck. In fact, most of the labourers who had put themselves forward were passed over. Admittedly they were generally a poor set physically and he predicted to himself that their next move would be to seek outdoor relief from the Relieving Officers attached to the local workhouse. 'Poor bastards!' he thought.

Following on behind Sizewell was a tallish man with shaggy hair and narrow eyes who carried himself with some authority and it was soon evident that he was one of the overseers. Ambrose stepped into line with two other men who had been picked out for temporary work and, as they gathered themselves together, the overseer gave them instructions as to where they were to go and who they were to ask for. Fortunately for Ambrose both men had worked at the mill previously and were well acquainted with its location and many of its workers. To his great relief they had no desire for small talk; there was not even an exchange of identities; it was a cheerless group that trudged along, each man deep in his own thoughts. Twenty or so minutes later they arrived at the top of a side street, where facing them were the iron gates of Richmond Mill.

From the front, the building presented an even smaller perspective than Ambrose remembered from first viewing it two days previously. His experience in Manchester had been in a very large and substantial factory with hundreds of workers. He had realised earlier that this could be an advantage. Fewer people would make his investigation more manageable; he could quickly get to know and observe people. But, conversely, in this small community might not everyone get to know and observe him? He would possibly be of special interest as a newcomer, as there was a permanent turnover of casual workers who were frequently employed, worked briefly and then discharged. They seemed to be regarded as of not much account, hired purely for their ability to fetch and carry; but the very temporary nature of his employment threw up the same dilemma. The longer he stayed the more were his chances of gathering the evidence he needed. But equally the more permanent his position became the more others would be curious about him. If that were to be the case he had to make sure both his alias and story were unimpeachable.

He followed his two companions and the overseer through the gates and into a yard bustling with activity where horse-drawn carts were being loaded in one area with bales of woollen cloth and, in another, bundles of wool were lifted with chains and wooden hoists up into the first floor of the building. From the hinterland behind the warehouse the noise of machines dominated the air. It was a sound that brought back memories. The rattle and whirring of wheels, cogs, frames and shuttles were so like the sounds he had experienced previously in Manchester. There were some differences between the operations of power looms for cotton manufacture and those in the woollen mills, but the basic principle of weaving was the same; it was only the raw material, its preparation and its products that varied.

As a journalist, he tried to make sense of the place, and his five senses came into play immediately. Apart from his immediate vision

Chapter 6

of the yard, the dominant impression arose from the smell. Hanging in the air was an unfamiliar stench that was almost tangible. He realised it came from a greasy aura that pervaded the yard and, puzzling it out, decided it must come from the wool, which, despite having been scoured of superficial dirt before it was delivered, was still in a semi-raw state. There was a taste to it that hit the back of his throat and he was instantly reminded of the similar effect of stale urine that had hung in the air from straw mattresses soaked with the stuff on the beds in Seddon workhouse. He observed clumps of fleece lying loose across the floor of the yard, and small particles drifted in the light breeze where they had escaped from the bales as they were heaved out of carts and onto the hoists. He felt a stickiness already clinging to his eyebrows and hair when he put his hand to his face to wipe away wisps of wool. Comingling with these filaments was the additional smell and accumulation of smoke and soot coming from the large chimneys that took up the exhaust from the coal-fired machinery. This turned the escaping cream-coloured wool smoky grey as it wafted in the air. Finally, he picked up a set of two orchestrated noises. The chains on the hoists cranked and creaked as they took up the bundles and, almost in harmony, the men's pattens clattered on the cobblestones as they moved about the yard, although their speech was muffled by the quantities of bales and bundles that absorbed it. But the dominant noise was from the first floor where the power looms were situated. There was a permanent din and racket which escaped through open doors and pervaded all parts of the yard and building. All these sensations were experienced within seconds of him entering the premises.

There were four horse-drawn carts in the yard and consequently there were piles of droppings among the lumps of wool. No attempt was made to clear them away; the dung was simply packed down, layer upon layer where the horses stood until someone decided it was becoming an impediment and occasionally shovelled it up into sacks. Someone told him later that it was sold off to the local gentry estates for their gardens. Slinging his pack down in a corner, Ambrose presented himself to the overseer who tersely explained how his first job was to begin moving bales of cloth from the hook of the hoist and load them into the back of the wagon. The weights the horses were required to pull seemed excessive to Ambrose and he reflected that industry made no exceptions to exploitation; man and animal were ill-used in equal proportions. His job was a simple exercise and only required brute strength, just like the horses. The carts came and went twice a day and in between Ambrose was set to work moving bundles and bales to different areas in the mill.

He entered the building by means of an external staircase that took him all the way up to the second floor where the wool was carded and combed ready for spinning. This process had recently been mechanised and he discovered that the processes on this floor were mostly done by women and children. He immediately realised that this would be where the main source of cheap child labour might be found and where any illegal employment would take place. The first floor was occupied by the power looms, again mostly operated by women, but with some men assisting. Overall, as he moved around the establishment he estimated that women and children outnumbered the men by about a dozen to one. Men seemed to be mostly employed as overseers of each section.

As this was his first day he was anxious to make a positive impression and increase the chances of being taken on permanently. Aside from his initial sensory reactions to the surroundings he spent little time assessing particulars; rather as he worked his way around the building he took in as much of the general as he could without drawing attention to himself. He estimated there were possibly 120 workers. There was a tension in the air, not least because of stringent time-keeping for working hours and the ever-present risk of machine failure. Coupled with the noise, the single-minded attention to the tasks in hand obviated conversation between any of the mill workers. There were few exchanges other than the cussing at children when they were either in the way or had disappeared when they were needed to unclog a particularly difficult section of machine.

Ambrose's comprehension of the whole working arrangement was that it was under constant stress to meet production requirements as laid down by the owner, regardless of risk. The processes were dangerous for everyone and made worse by the heavy machinery which was all unguarded. It was clear that output outweighed any safety considerations. Neither was there much regard for the workers' welfare. For example, he couldn't ascertain how and when workers stopped for food or breaks; there seemed to be no uniformity. They were allowed a few minutes for the privy and to take some basic refreshment, but had to arrange for someone else to have oversight of the running of their machines which were never switched off. The drudgery was unremitting and Ambrose recalled to mind as he always did when confronted with such images William Wordsworth's poetic plea for a reconsideration of the effects of mechanisation: 'Enough of science and of art; close up those barren leaves.'

During the day, as he walked from floor to floor lifting and carrying, he became aware of how vulnerable the whole building was to fire. He had heard that some mills in West Yorkshire had been burned to the ground by incendiary sparks that set alight inflammable material within their wooden structures. Because of these local experiences there were strict rules about the use of naked flames and harsh penalties for anyone caught smoking or lighting a fire of any kind. It was instant dismissal and blacklisting, so that not only would the culprit lose his immediate job but would be refused employment elsewhere. The workers generally agreed with these draconian punishments as they recognised it was their lives that were being put at risk. Besides, if the mill went up in a conflagration, there would be no employment for anyone. Consequently, they didn't scruple to report anyone causing a fire hazard. The place was as dry as a tinder box and the fire risk exacerbated by the oily atmosphere from the wool. Had there been a fire, those on the upper floors would have stood very little chance of escape. The only exit was the external stairs and workers trying to get out would have to avoid the wool and metal obstructions littering the spaces between the machines.

However, the inherent risk of fire was outweighed by the imminent dangers of the working conditions of the women and children. He was used to the arrangements of machinery inside the mills of Lancashire and they didn't differ to any large degree in Richmond Mill, the only exception being that cotton fibres were replaced by wool, and instead of large bags of raw cotton, creamy fleeces burst out of rough hessian sacking and spewed across the second floor where the combing and spinning processes were in operation. This was the greasiest area of the whole establishment and the air was full of the oily residues of fleece. Space was tight between machines and there was little room for the workers to move freely. The noise of the machines was considerable and there was no chance for conversation. Instead the women worked doggedly, eyes on the task and at one with the mechanical pace of their machines. The heat in the room with its high, small barred windows was intense, even though it was a cool April day outside. It was also airless, as could be seen by the scant movement of fibres that hung in the air, like snowflakes indecisive of where to land. He was not shocked by the insanitary and crowded conditions he observed, having previously experienced the like elsewhere. He made a mental note that there were two privies outside in the yard and a pump for water that served all the workers. Breaks to visit the privy or get a drink strictly chimed with the rhythm of production and many of the young children denied the call of nature were permanently wetting and even soiling themselves, their clothing soaked and stained.

As he moved discreetly round the building, his previous experience in the cotton mills had shown him what to look for; the technical principles were the same and a requirement for small digits common to both. He was most attentive in his observation of the children and made a mental note of how many there were and their ages. As a precaution, he had left at his lodgings the list Donald Thwaites had provided of those most likely to be under-age, but had memorised a few in the event he could identify them. Ambrose took into consideration how ill-nourishment stunted growth and that it was likely that small children could be older than their height or bulk implied. But previous experience told him he could be certain that at least six or seven of those he could see scrabbling around on the floor could not possibly be more than four or five years old and had been put to work illegally by their parents with the full complicity of the overseers and possibly the owner. Known as 'scavengers', the smallest of all these little ones were specifically employed in cleaning beneath the machines where remnants of fibres could clog the workings and halt produc-

Chapter 6

tion. This was a dangerous occupation that entailed reaching into the smallest apertures among the cogs and wheels that whirred and clattered unremittingly. Their hands were tiny enough, but the risks to their fingers were acute. He was always amazed that more of them were not amputated, although he had seen tiny tots with fingertips missing.

On one occasion as he was delivering bundles of carded wool he almost knocked over a young girl scurrying back to her machine after a privy break. 'Hey!' he cried. 'Steady!'

'Steady yourself!' she replied with a scowl. 'You should be more careful.'

Ambrose noticed she had a deep and livid scar on her left arm. 'That looks nasty,' he said with a smile, 'how did that happen?'

'Same way it always does – you should know. The machine got in my way. Now you're in my way, I'm late back and will lose money.'

She was evidently not going to stay and chat. He watched her as she took her place at the machine managed by a large plump woman. 'The girl's a piecer,' he realised. She was one of the taller children who worked with the women at the machines; their job was to lean over the great spinning machines and mend any broken strands – 'pieces' of thread. Their small nimble fingers were also ideal for the intricate winding of the thread into a whole again. Such was their proximity to moving parts that they were also at constant risk of severe injury, as he had just seen. He knew those who were seriously harmed were quickly sent home, discarded as so many pieces of jetsam – out of sight and out of mind. Profit was the master here; those who provided it were indispensable until they became unfit for the great drive to swollen bank accounts.

By and large all the workers were dressed uniformly in grey cast-off clothing; the girls in tattered remnants of garments, cut-down versions of their mothers' dresses to a descending scale of age and size; some had acquired ragged shawls, pieces of cast-off cloth with which they covered their heads to keep their hair out of the machinery, a lesson learned the hard way as Ambrose had heard reports of women and children being scalped as they leaned too close to rollers and shuttles. The boys wore jackets and trousers of varying sizes – all handed down through the males in the family from the father to the eldest son and on to the next, until the cut-down garment, reaching the end of its useful life and full of snags and holes, just about decently covered the youngest. On their feet, most wore the uniform pattens, but some went barefoot.

On this first day, being content to observe, Ambrose hardly engaged in any conversation with anyone, male or female, aside from general questions like: 'Where do you want this?' as he brought in another supply of wool; or friendly comments about the heat in the place and how he wished he could have a pull of ale. He spent his time shifting bags and bales, employing a steady rhythm that was not criticised, so he presumed his work-rate was acceptable. Twelve hours of labour found him outside the factory gate at 10 that night with wages of a shilling and, to his great relief, promise of more work for the next five days, but on the cheapest daily rate. During the day, he had discovered that the male overseers earned between fifteen and twenty-two shillings a week; men working in the weaving sheds received ten shillings, while the women were paid about eight. Girls and boys received five shillings or less. His rate was therefore something in between that of a child's wage and a skilled female machinist. Since money was the least of his concerns he felt fortunate when he compared his situation with those who depended utterly on these pittances that had to stretch to pay rent, fuel and food, most usually for large families. He had noticed the poor quality of the food that the workers brought with them in their dinner pails – generally bread and some hard cheese and little sign of any meat. Most brought in flagons of cold tea; alcohol was not allowed – primarily because of the need for sober hands to manage large, complicated machinery, but also because public drunkenness at any level was socially frowned on, especially on the premises of respectable mill owners. What their employees did with their money, and how they behaved in their own quarters in the town was their business, but it had to be out of sight.

Ambrose had never taken a good meal for granted. His investigative work had mostly sent him to places where the quality of food matched the misery of the workers. He could subsist on very little, but he recognised that under these circumstances he would have to

Chapter 6

maintain a level of nutrition to match the work he was required to do. He had taken the precaution of packing up a supply of staples such as porridge, bread and cheese, but he would try to arrange with Rosalie Thwaites to leave fresh supplies at his lodgings whenever possible. As he walked back to the Jollys' tenement through the town's unlit streets it occurred to him how much he would be glad to see her again. He thought about her steady gaze, honest expression and quiet but confident voice and he experienced an unfamiliar thrill of anticipation. 'Will she be pleased to see me?' he wondered 'and if she is, what do I do? Where will this go?' His experience with women was limited. His lifestyle had not been conducive to the usual run of domestic relationships – wooing, engagement, marriage and children. Much of his time was spent outside the capital, and when at home in London he was too busy writing to take on much of a social round. Besides, he was choosy about his friends and took the view that casual and superficial acquaintances were time-wasting. Neither was he one to make friends for personal advantage or ostentation; better to have a few firm and long-standing companions than a host of hangers-on. Edgar had what Ambrose considered was essential for a friendship to flourish: loyalty and discretion. He would not have involved him in their current enterprise if he could not have relied on such qualities.

Ambrose remembered that this afternoon Miss Thwaites would have attended her brother's funeral and wondered how many others would have been there. He had heard very few speak in the mill either about the man or his end, although that may have been out of respect; it was the day of the funeral after all. He had not broached the subject with any of his fellow labourers as he purposed to maintain a discreet presence. Ambrose could not be sure that either the manager or even the owner might attend, although he thought it was unlikely. He would ask her when they next met. But he was sure she would not have been alone at the ceremony; her father would have been there and she and her brother must have friends and neighbours. He realised how little he knew about her, but now he sincerely hoped that over the time available he might alter that situation.

Back in his room, having first trekked down to the pump in the street and hauled a bucket of water for washing and drinking up the two flights of stairs, he made himself some cold porridge in a small saucepan he had brought for the purpose and ate some cold meat and bread he had purchased earlier. While he was eating he mulled over the events of the day, taking stock of the operation in the mill, its squalor, racket and depressing atmosphere. He knew he had the beginnings of a useful report for McNiece and entered all he could remember in his notebook which he had tucked behind a loose piece of wainscot hidden by the table. He was adept at finding such hidey-holes, since he never underestimated the opposition, and if any suspicions were aroused as to his identity and purpose then it was wise to take as many precautions as possible to protect his evidence. Once he had built up a good body of information he would take steps to pass it on to George Lawes's man, John Walters, who would be delivering fleeces to the mill every day except Tuesdays.

In his methodical way, he had devised a strategy for the next few days; his priority was to start engaging other workers in general conversation, gaining their trust and by those means gradually chipping away at what they knew about the running of the mill in respect of the employment of children. With any luck, he might even hear gossip about the manner of Donald Thwaites's death. His approach to digging out information had always been to initiate contact and then let his unwary source simply prattle on. Among the dross of personal views and reminiscences there would always be a nugget of useful information, especially as he was a master at gently steering a conversation in the direction he wished it to flow. Thus, after an initial mutual set of grumbles together about the weather, bosses, pay and working hours, he would enquire about his companion's family in the natural and casual way of continuing a conversation. His experience previously had been that it would not be long before full details of wife and children were laid bare and, with gentle prompting, Ambrose would soon gather information as to their ages and whether they were working. He would be selective about who he lighted upon for his first 'interrogation'; if he was doing his job effectively his quarry should walk away having no knowledge that he had been quizzed.

Sanguine about his progress after this first day, he took off his

Chapter 6

shabby jacket and trousers which had both absorbed the oil and odour of the fleeces, washed his face and hands in cold water, turned back the grubby blanket and threw himself onto the hard truckle bed. Snuffing out his stub of candle he wondered how much longer he would want to submit himself to long bouts of privation. As he lay in the dark his thoughts formed themselves into a chain of connections which started with the disagreeable situation of his current state and ended with a picture of domestic happiness – a bright fire and a pair of fine brown eyes looking at him from across the hearth.

Chapter 7

Saturday at daybreak brought wet weather, made the more uncomfortable by a fresh easterly wind. Ambrose woke to the sound of a loose shutter banging somewhere in the building. Looking at his watch he noted it was six o'clock, so he swung his long legs off the bed, pulled on his trousers and shirt and found his boots. Quietly he went down the stairs and out through the scullery door to the privy at the end of the garden; as he came out there was already a wet and bedraggled queue forming. Instead of going back to his room, he went through the front door and made his way to the communal pump in the street, where he put his head under the cold water, wiped his face with the tail of his shirt, ran his fingers through his wet hair and, refreshed, made his way back to his room. Throughout the lodging house he heard others rising and preparing for work. He had a scanty breakfast of bread and yet more cold porridge which he ate standing up. Whenever he ate porridge his mind went back to Seddon, and the awful gruel and foul bread they served to the inmates. After packing up food for his midday meal in a cloth bag that he hung round his shoulder, he headed for the stairs, locking his room carefully behind him. Proceeding down the two flights towards the front door he saw he was not alone; it seemed every occupant of the lodging house was on the move.

Within 15 minutes he arrived at the mill and presented himself to the foreman who oversaw the loading bays. Having done almost two full days' work he had so impressed the man with his strength and willingness to work that he was offered further employment over the coming week. He had spent the previous day trying to establish himself with his immediate workmates, but his efforts had not been particularly rewarding. Friday was busy and there had been few opportunities to sit and talk; food was taken 'on the wing'. Besides, it had been payday and all thoughts were on how much would be coming in and whether it would be enough to cover what had to go out. Today he planned to make a deeper acquaintance of one or two. As it was Saturday and all thoughts were on the day of rest to come, with the assistance of a mug or two of ale after work, and when the men were in a more relaxed frame of mind, he was certain he would hear much more local gossip about the management of the mill.

His political antennae were also alert to the possibility of picking up signals of radicalism. Were the workers at Richmond submissive to its regime or, as in Manchester, were there some among them who advocated union membership and were advancing demands for better pay and conditions? Perhaps this relatively new mill was ideal for the purposes of infiltration by those sympathetic to the Chartist cause. Weighing it up he thought this second possibility would not be the case; the mill was too small, the workers mostly known to each other and the mill owner did his best to keep a tight grip on his profits. Besides, factory work was late in coming to Yorkshire and local people were still moving in from the villages and thankful for the work.

After a morning lifting, carrying and loading bales and bundles, the twelve o'clock whistle blew for dinner-time and with a sigh of relief he sat down on a bundle and unwrapped a piece of bread and the inevitable yellow cheese. He didn't know it yet, but it was at this point he had the most incredible stroke of luck. One of those rare occurrences that would push his investigation on faster than he could have ever expected.

A couple of other labourers sat nearby and one called across, 'Hey, Frank! What have you got? Does your wife feed you well?'

Ambrose grunted and said, 'No wife – I do for myself.' He made no move towards them, but with the innate desire to know all about strangers in the district, one of them crossed to share Ambrose's bale.

'Jed Stow – I heard a big man had been taken on. Saw you yesterday. You've come back then.'

'Frank Barrett. You're right, and I'm glad for the work.'

'You don't sound as though you're from round these parts. I'd put you down as a southerner.'

'Right again! London and the south coast. Not much doing there so I thought I'd try my luck here.'

With the customary local suspicion of strangers, Stow probed him hard, but Ambrose had his story down pat and soon the man took him for what he was – just another casual employee. Letting the man

CHAPTER 7

guide the conversation, Ambrose listened carefully for anything that might be useful. The half-hour break was soon up and as they walked back to their respective workstations Jed, who appeared to have taken a liking to this tall open-faced man who listened rather than rattled on, suggested they met up for a drink after work. Pleased that it had been so easy to make his first real acquaintance, Ambrose spent the rest of the day mechanically lifting, stowing and reminiscing about his last meeting with Rosalie.

The man was waiting for Ambrose by the mill gates and the pair walked off into the town to a tavern which, to Ambrose's relief, was relatively clean and quiet. Stow was gratified to note that Ambrose was the first with his hand in his pocket. They took their drinks to an empty table, which was lucky as the place was beginning to fill up. When Ambrose could clearly offer no more about himself his companion started to talk about the mill, other workers and finally his family. He admitted he had no desire to rush home; as he explained, what was there to go back for – a whining wife, six brats and one of them a screaming baby!

'I wonder if anyone has ever told him how these things happen, and that he's had a major hand in it!' Ambrose thought, but did not say it.

Stow rattled on, expressing the wish that his wife would follow the advice she had given to their niece who had got herself into trouble with a local lad and was now living with the consequences.

Ambrose immediately paid more attention and probed discreetly. 'What does a girl do in that situation? I'm not married so fortunately I've not come up against that kind of thing.'

'So, you've never got a girl into trouble! Well – you're either slow or lucky! It's no joke when the silly bitches fall for a baby. Her mother, my wife's sister, is dead so we're the only family she's got and we can't afford to feed another brat – and a bastard at that. But, anyway, I had a stroke of luck. When I first heard about it I was angry and had a row at work with the father of the lad concerned. He wouldn't do anything and we almost came to blows. Sizewell, the manager – the one who took you on – came between us and, blaming me, told me to back out of it or I'd be sent home. He asked me if the problem was to do with work, and before I knew what I was doing I'd told him the situation. I don't normally talk about family business, but I was desperate to do something; we've got too many mouths to feed as it is. To my surprise he seemed concerned and said he might know someone who could help – perhaps mind the child until it was old enough to work. That seemed a really good idea to me, so I went home that night and spoke to Janet, that's my wife. She said I should find out more. In the meantime, she'd been asking around and found the names of a couple of women who might help. But when she visited them they told her they were "no longer in the business". Someone else had moved in and taken the fostering over – a woman called Fairfax.'

Ambrose stiffened imperceptibly, recognising the name immediately. This was too good to be true – to meet a family involved with the woman whose trail they were following. He hid his excitement and let Stow continue the tale, with a little prompting on his part. 'What happened next? Have you met the woman?'

'Well, I went back to Sizewell and asked him if he could get the woman to call. He said we'd have to get the money together first and as soon as we had it I should bring it to him. Mind you, it was a high price, ten pounds.'

'That's a sum of money to find! How did you manage it?'

'We scraped it together somehow – my wife did most of it. When we had it all I took it to Sizewell and he said the woman, Mrs Fairfax, would be calling to pick the brat up. I think she came around Thursday. I was out and the wife dealt with her. Good riddance! But we're still left with one of our own that screams!'

'Did you trust Sizewell? After all, he could have taken the money and then denied everything.'

'I thought of that, but it's a new business they've set up. If there was any fraud going on it would soon get around the town and then they would be finished. We're unforgiving around here if people try to do us down. It's every man for himself – as you must know. Besides, I wasn't that stupid that I didn't make enquiries about the woman first. It was easy. I found out she's helped at least three others and they all seemed satisfied. Unwanted brats are a problem for us all.'

Chapter 7

Ambrose digested this information carefully while he was sipping his ale and letting Jed Stow run on. The Fairfax woman had collected his niece's child two days previously. Anything might have happened to it since then.

Eventually, after an hour and more drinks than Ambrose felt were good for him, he suggested to his new friend that it might be time to go home. By now, cloaked in the comforting warmth of semi-drunkenness, with its temporary illusion of security and well-being, Jed Stow made no opposition; he was still in that half-inebriated state that imbued good intentions towards his fellow man.

'Come back with me, Frank – the missus will find you something to eat.' Jed was suddenly anxious to invite this new-found friend back to his house. In truth, he had taken a liking to Ambrose with his willingness to put his hands in his pocket and stand his round with affability, and he was easy to talk to. Not many men wanted to hear about the trials of family life, they had enough of their own. Stumbling out of the tavern and walking unsteadily in front of Ambrose, he led the way to the outskirts of the town via a deeply rutted road down a steep hill to low ground where the water from summer and winter torrents accumulated to form muddy pools which persisted, even in the hottest weather.

The whole area was damp and insanitary, made worse by the excessive overcrowding of the population that had taken the area for its own. The houses, or shacks as they should have been more accurately described, had a squalid, untrimmed look about them, which spoke as much of want of care by the occupants as of cash. There was clearly an abrogation of responsibility in terms of communal behaviour. No tenement inhabitant felt any obligation to clear the filth that accumulated outside their door and through which dogs and pigs rummaged at will. Ragged clothes hung out of doors indicating futile attempts at washing garments. As late as it was, infants crawled among the debris, along with hopeful mangy cats and curs. The whole place reeked of a multitude of evil smells which trumped even the stiffest breeze that might have brought fresh air. The source of the malodour was a large dunghill at the bottom of the street that oozed a chocolate-coloured liquid at its base. There were a few thinly-clad children playing among the detritus, their mothers oblivious to the risk of injury or disease.

The tenements were wooden, with shuttered windows, no glass, and from which little or no light escaped or entered. Approaching a shabby doorway, Jed called out drunkenly to his wife, 'I've brought a mate; we want some food! Open the door!'

In response a small, wizened woman appeared out of the gloom, stared at Ambrose and glared at her husband but said nothing. Bending double through the doorway, Ambrose stepped into what he recognised as a typical slum hovel of the factory workers. It was no different from what he had seen in Manchester: the same dirt floor, broken furniture and jumble of filthy rags covering raised wooden boards that served as beds. From previous experience he quickly worked out the sleeping arrangements. He took it that five of the children must sleep in one bed, top to toe, and the parents and the baby used a small area at the back of the room which was curtained off with a cotton sheet. A weak fire burned in the grate and a pan of soup was on the boil. He imagined any handy vegetable would be thrown in to be cooked to death in the sludgy mixture. There was a cheap, functional table and two rickety chairs.

The Stow family was typical of the neighbourhood. It was clear from what Jed had already given away in conversation that all his children were under 10 years old and three already worked in the mill. Around the same time as having given birth to their sixth child, two months previously, Janet Stow had sustained an injury to her leg in the factory. 'It's left us short of a wage,' he told Ambrose, 'but she was counted a good worker and has managed to find some piece-work from one of the local independent weavers. She works at home until her leg mends.'

On the crowded table was evidence of her activity, a bolt of woollen cloth and cropping scissors to trim it to a fine finish.

Ambrose had a few polite words with her while Jed Stow took off his jacket and fell into the only reasonable chair that was close to the meagre fire. He took a bowl of the slops bubbling over the fire and slurped it noisily from a spoon. Ambrose, considerably less drunk than his companion, and with his mind sharpened to observe and absorb

Chapter 7

all that was relevant to his purpose, was all the time planning how he would broach the subject of the predicament of Mrs Stow's niece and her unwanted baby without antagonising his companion.

The problem was more easily solved than he could have wished for. They hadn't long been cramped into the tiny living quarters when Jed Stow, having swallowed down the last of the slops, promptly fell asleep in front of the miserable fire. Very soon Ambrose was certain he was in a deep slumber – head back, mouth wide open and snoring rhythmically. Janet Stow seemed disposed not to let her visitor return to his lodgings and began to question him about his family. He could give a brief and evidently satisfying account which she didn't follow up too deeply. This allowed him to open his own subtle interrogation of the Stow family history. It was a common story – the family had moved from Hull to Bingley to find work some years before.

'How many of you came here?' asked Ambrose.

'There were five of us then – we've added three more since. My sister Jean and her daughter came with us and our mother too. Jean was a widow with no money and thought there would be better prospects in the mill. She died not long after they got here. I'm not sorry she never knew what happened to her daughter. She would've wished she'd stayed in Hull.' Having introduced the subject of her niece's troubles, like her husband, Mrs Stow seemed pleased to talk about it, even with a stranger; it was evidently still very much on her mind.

'The three eldest are all working so I use my niece Meg Foley, who lives next door with my mother who's crippled, to help me mind the younger ones, when she's not working. It's Meg who's just given up her baby to this woman who fosters. She's not cheap – we had to find ten pounds a year for it to be looked after. As the girl's family, we couldn't bear the disgrace and inconvenience of a bastard child so we all begged, borrowed and scraped up the fee between us. We managed it in the end, although it was tight. The child was collected two days ago.'

Ambrose grunted and nodded his head encouragingly.

'It's the oldest story. Meg was my sister's only child and she met a smooth-talking bastard – about a year ago it was. He was a local man, twice her age – she's 14. I don't need to spell out the rest. It wasn't long before I noticed her swelling belly and confronted the girl. Meg had no idea what had happened – I'm not sure she even knew how it came about, but there it was. She was obviously in trouble and it was too late to do anything about it. My husband went to the father of the brat and asked for help, but he denied all knowledge and gave him a mouthful; there was no help coming from that quarter and Jed nearly got the sack for causing trouble at work.'

Ambrose remained silent, but with a serious of sympathetic nods and an attentive and interested expression encouraged her to continue uninterrupted.

'The whole family got together to decide what to do. My Jed was all for throwing her out, but Mam and I persuaded him that we would take care of it and he needn't be involved. We'd heard of fostering – several of my friends pay women to look after their children when they're at work – but we decided to try to find a full-time foster mother as Meg will have to go back to work. It's certain she couldn't manage a small baby as well – one without a father.'

For the first time Ambrose broke in. 'How did you find the woman – I think Jed told me her name was Fairfax? Was it word of mouth?'

'Yes, it was Mrs Fairfax. We asked about and Tom Sizewell, one of the bosses, told Jed he'd heard of a woman who took in very young babies and raised them for a year – at a price. She was new to the district, but we found out her name and she came to see us. I told Jed to check she was honest; he asked around and everyone said she gives babies a good home while the mothers need it – for a price of course.'

'What did Meg think about handing over her baby to a stranger?'

'We didn't give her a chance to think about it. No sooner was it born than we paid the money over to Sizewell. The woman came and collected her – Meg called the baby Margaret after her grandmother.'

'What sort of woman was Mrs Fairfax? Motherly, I expect, if she's taking on tiny newborn babies.'

'Well, no! She seemed more business-like; a small woman and very tidy in her dress. She said she had plenty of help with the children and they were just like one big happy family all living together in a big house. She was very quick, I must say, and seemed anxious to be off. She didn't even stay for a tea.'

Chapter 7

'I suppose Meg can go and see the baby when she likes?'

'No, the mothers don't get involved. The woman said they get upset and so do the babies. It's better to make a clean break. Besides, Meg couldn't travel to where the woman lives without money for fares.'

Ambrose ventured a more searching question. 'How far away does Mrs Fairfax live then?'

'We don't really know. She said it was on the Bradford side of Bingley.'

'Don't you have an address?'

'No, although Jed picked up some word that she might be out near Ilkley. To tell the truth we were so relieved to be without the problem of another mouth to feed we just gave her the child and let her go. Anyway, just for now Meg stays at home minding my youngest three, but Jed has set about trying to get her work again so she can be earning her keep. I can mind the three others while I'm working at home. But I keep in touch with the overseers at the mill; I collect the three children at the end of their shift and bring them home safely.'

'What would happen if Meg was able to look after the child? I mean, say her luck changed and she got hold of some money somehow. How could she go and get her back if she doesn't know where she is?'

'Well, she said we could have the baby back at any time if we could pay money for "the inconvenience", but that's not likely to happen, I can tell you. Meg must work at something, and I'm not prepared to look after another child. Margaret can stay where she is, comfortable and fed better than she would be here.' But, for an instant, Janet Stow's ageing wizened face softened; perhaps it was identifying the child by name that produced a wave of sentiment. 'I suppose the baby'll be well looked after, we've paid the woman enough. It took less than ten pounds to raise all my babies put together, I'm sure.'

Just as Ambrose was about to enquire further, Stow woke from his drunken sleep and, with no memory of having invited Ambrose into his house, began to ask questions aggressively as to what he was doing there. Ambrose felt it was time to withdraw. Wishing them goodnight he retreated through the door and out into the equally foetid air of the street. He had mixed feelings as he hurried back to the centre of the town. Glad to have made a useful contact who he felt would produce much more information – and so easily; but also a revisiting of the anger he had felt in Manchester when confronted with the identical living conditions of the mill workers there. What depressed him most was that he knew if he were to visit every other tenement in the row he would be confronted with the same sights.

Not for the first time he wondered what it was in the Englishman's mentality that would prompt him to take up musket, pike and billhook and join a civil war to depose and execute a king over religion, but prevented him combining with others to bring on a revolution for social justice. Given the circumstances in which most industrial workers – and many agricultural labourers – existed, this was a most startling anomaly. It was also a paradox that people were prepared to act when they were affected personally; the example of Jed Stow physically challenging a neighbour over a domestic matter came into his head, as well as the issue of overcrowding which regularly led to confrontations, verbal and then physical. But it seemed this frustration stretched only as far as the communal living areas as they struggled to maintain their local territorial integrity. It was true, he observed to himself, that tolerance proportionately diminishes as density increases. Beyond the impoverished streets, for some reason he had not yet fathomed, the impetus for wider reform dissipated as fog before a breeze.

On his way back to the lodging house he thought again of Rosalie and whether it would be possible to find out exactly where she lived. It would be difficult for him to ask about her in the mill without drawing attention to himself. Remembering that the funeral had been held on the previous Thursday, he wondered if she had revisited her brother's grave. With an hour to spare before he must return to his room for the night – there were strict rules that prevented the lodgers from coming and going at will – he made a small diversion to the outskirts of the town and visited All Saints' Church and its churchyard for a second time. The burial ground had been used for generations and many of the graves were unmarked. In any case it was by now too dark to read their inscriptions, but even in the gloom he could see that the most recent were on the south side and, keeping to the main

Chapter 7

path that ran through the churchyard, it was not long before he found the only newly dug grave. On close inspection of a wooden marker he was just able to determine that Donald Thwaites was buried there. A few small bunches of garden flowers had been left on the mound; they were already past their best. Perhaps she would attend a service tomorrow; if so she would surely visit the grave again to refresh them. He resolved to go himself, three times if necessary if she had a preferred service.

Back in his lodgings he took out ink and paper and wrote a letter to Edgar giving details of his new source of information and all that he had gathered from it. George's man, John Walters, would be delivering to the mill on Monday and he would slip the letter to him for delivery to Hoyles.

On Sunday morning before five Ambrose brushed his clothes into respectability and, knotting a clean handkerchief around his neck, strolled off to All Saints' Church and joined a very small congregation as it filed into the grey stone building to take early communion. He stood by the lychgate as though waiting for someone. She was not among them and he could do nothing else but return to his lodgings and wait for morning service.

At eleven o'clock he entered the church and took up a place in one of the rear pews close to the doors. As he looked around he despaired of seeing her, even if she came. The place was now very well-attended – mostly people of the middling sort in their finery. Right up to the last moment, just before the service began, people continued to fill the pews and, as he wondered whether he could creep out undetected, to his great relief and joy he saw her enter supporting an elderly man. Strikingly tall and dressed in the black of mourning, from veiled bonnet to shoes, she retained the air of quiet dignity that had impressed him so much on their first acquaintance. Her father looked frail, tired and drawn and Ambrose understood just from his physical demeanour that he was mourning the loss of his son deeply. The couple occupied a pew some rows up to the left of him, and it was impossible from his vantage point to catch her eye. Instead he was forced to follow polite ecclesiastical conventions, mouthing the well-remembered hymns and Anglican responses, and sitting back with eyes closed as though ruminating on the tenets of the sermon when he was in fact almost asleep.

As the service ended, the rector led the way out followed by the congregation in the customary order of social hierarchy. Anxious to be at the door to intercept her, Ambrose had swiftly left his pew minutes before the service ended, brushing past the other worshippers and reaching the porch before she and her father had risen from their own position. He waited close to the entrance and, as they appeared, made his way forward and gently touched her elbow.

Preoccupied with keeping her father safely upright, Rosalie was disconcerted when his hand found her arm, but looking up to see who was being so intrusive, she instantly recognised him and with a smile of recognition said, 'Oh! It's you.'

Ambrose took off his cap and nodded. 'I've been anxious to see you to ask about the funeral and whether you and your father are keeping well – as well as can be expected under the circumstances.'

Rosalie turned to her father and said, 'Pa, this is Mr Barrett. He started work at the mill a short time ago; he was one of Donald's friends.' She turned to Ambrose. 'Father's not so well, but insisted we come today so that he can visit the grave once again.'

Ambrose held out his hand to the old man who shook it limply and replied so softly that Ambrose had to incline his head downwards to hear him.

'I'm pleased to make the acquaintance of anyone who was a friend to Donald. His death has been a blow to my daughter and me.' He faltered, 'I'm not sure how we'll get on without him.' He seemed to retreat into himself and, taking his arm once again, Rosalie led him to a bench by the wall of the churchyard.

'Pa, sit here for a little, I'm going to walk down to the grave. Have a rest and I'll come and fetch you in a minute.' She indicated to Ambrose that he should follow her down the grass track to the newly dug mound of black peaty earth. She seemed very eager as she pulled back her veil and said, 'I'm glad we've met here. I had considered coming to your lodgings, but that might have caused unwanted

Chapter 7

curiosity. The last thing we want is people asking questions as to how we come to know each other. Have you any news, or is it too early?'

'I've had two strokes of great luck! I've been taken on for a week's work and I've also struck up an acquaintance with a mill-hand who has direct knowledge of the baby farming. It couldn't have been more fortunate to meet him and he's free with his tongue, especially after he's had a drink or two. Last evening we drank together for a couple of hours and as I was about to leave he invited me back to his family lodgings. By this time he was drunk and almost reeling; I had paced myself – one pint to every two of his – but remained more or less sober.'

Ambrose went on to describe briefly Jed and Janet Stow's story. 'It's easy to understand how they got themselves involved with this business, and it seems there are others who have given their babies away. It's understandable – the conditions they live in.'

This was not news to her; after all, she had lived all her life near the town and had seen the shanty huts spring up unregulated. The consequences of neglect and despair were obvious for all to see. She was disappointed when he told her he had not yet broached the subject of her brother's death with his new colleague.

'I don't know him well enough to start asking questions about something that has caused gossip and rumour . Outside the mill men are still reluctant to speculate. But I intend to keep up this contact and as soon as I feel it's the right moment, I'll open the subject and see what he knows – I promise.'

She sighed. 'I despair of getting to the truth when everyone has been threatened with dismissal if they gossip about Donald's death. It seems to me that if they're so anxious to keep things quiet, there must have been something suspicious about it. Someone knows what really happened.'

'I agree with you and I'll do everything I can to find out who did this, and bring them to justice. Don't forget, I have two JPs on my side. And don't forget either the good news about the other affair. Coming across someone who has been involved with Mrs Fairfax like that has moved things on considerably. Just as important is the clear link between the Fairfax woman and Tom Sizewell. However, when

I think about it perhaps it is not so surprising considering this is a small town and everyone knows everyone else's business. Sooner or later someone would have let something slip. I think the woman has been fortunate in settling in Bingley. From what I gather, fostering of babies and young children has become much more common as more and more young women come into the town seeking work. It also seems as though she's elbowed some of the regular fosterers out.'

Rosalie raised an eyebrow. 'I'm not surprised that Sizewell's involved in it. He's not a man to be trusted and, although I've no proof, I feel sure he's mixed up in my brother's death in some way or another. I wish there was more I could do!'

'I feel we've made a good start and now have something positive to work on. Having established myself in the mill, tomorrow I'll set about gathering as much information as I can. I'm hoping early this week Mr Lawes will be settling himself somewhere out on the moors in sight of the Rickard's place your brother identified in his letter. I'll pass on to him all that I know in a letter, which he should receive tomorrow.'

She nodded and then asked, 'Have you eaten today? Why don't you come to the house and let us give you dinner? We're returning home now and you're very welcome to join us. But it would be as well if we are not seen walking together, so perhaps you could follow a little later. We're not far away and there'll be plenty of time for you to take a meal with us before you have to return to your lodgings.'

Ambrose considered this to be an excellent idea: not just because of its practicality, but it would mean time spent with Rosalie – time to get to know her and for her to know him. He left them at the church gate after she had given him directions to their property which was about 2 miles out of the town. He walked back to James's Row and in the confines of his room made another effort to tidy himself up, although he despaired that his meagre clothing was not especially fit to impress. The best he could do was to discipline his unruly hair with water, tie his kerchief in a jaunty knot and polish his boots with spit and elbow grease.

Uncertain as to what he might expect, he set out with a spring in his step to walk to the Thwaites's smallholding. The weather was calm

Chapter 7

and cool, with a touch of fresh April air which raised his spirits even further. On his way, he found a bank of primroses, yellow as butter with their innocent faces turned to the light. He picked a handful and arranged them as best he could manage into a bouquet. Feeling self-conscious as a middle-aged man might when he goes a'courting, he hoped no one would pass him on the road; but Sunday afternoon was a quiet time and he met no other travellers. He recognised the place as soon as he saw it. Rosalie had described it as small, single-storey with a slate roof and one large chimney. There was a sign on the gate that gave it away – 'Parsloes' – the name of their landlord. After walking up the path to the front door, Ambrose took the metal knocker and announced his arrival. Opening the door, Rosalie gave him a smile of welcome.

Awkwardly he thrust the flowers into her hands. 'I had nothing else to bring – but they are bright-eyed and reminded me…' He trailed off and stood squirming with the embarrassment of a schoolboy meeting his first sweetheart.

But smiling at him she put him at his ease as he stuffed his cap in his pocket while she led him into the parlour. The furniture was old and well-used; the place somewhat disorderly, although warm and not uninviting. She found him a cushioned seat and offered him some ale. 'We are not as you might usually find us. Things are rather disorganised; Donald's death has left a large hole that is difficult to fill.'

'What will you do now? If you're working and, as I couldn't help observing, your father doesn't look at all well, who'll manage the smallholding? You surely can't take on both mill work and the livestock.'

'Fortunately, we have good neighbours and an understanding landlord. Parsloe has arranged for one of his farmhands to come over and deal with the pigs and our few sheep. We keep a house cow and I can milk her in the morning and evening before and after work. Of course, this is only a temporary arrangement. I may give up the work in the mill and take up the smallholding full-time. There's enough land for a decent living for two; all our surplus can be sold off to pay the rent.'

'It'll be a hard life,' commented Ambrose.

'No harder than working on the looms. At least I'll be in the fresh air away from the dirt and grease.'

Looking at the determination in her face, Ambrose had no doubt she could run the place on her own. It was clear that her father would be of little help; in fact, he was going to need some looking after. He wondered if the man had had a seizure after his son's death. He was certainly very withdrawn and hardly said a word all through their supper which they ate round the kitchen table – a simple meal of chicken soup and pork pie, finished off with a slice of cake made with the honey from their own bees. It was evident Rosalie was not at all house-proud, but she could certainly cook, a valuable facility which he guiltily stored away in the back of his mind.

After they had eaten and she had seen her father upstairs to his room, they talked until about six in the evening. From the outset they were comfortable in each other's company, although as a matter of habit, in any discussions with someone of whom he knew little, he reverted to his journalistic method, listening rather than asking and having a keen ear for the spaces between the words, because often what was left unsaid was most revealing. He always found it interesting how it was that, once people started to talk about themselves, their lives and ideas, they became quite content to reveal much of themselves to relative strangers. Once he had picked up a body of knowledge he could then gently home in on those areas that were most relevant to his enquiries. In this instance, he was interested in why and how Rosalie and her brother came to work at the mill, her thoughts on its functioning, and, most importantly, what her ideas were as to why her brother had been killed and by whom.

'Neither of us was particularly keen to work the land. When we first moved into Parsloes, Father was fit and well able to manage the place, with some help from us when we were available. We both had had an education; Donald went to school and later, having shown real talent in his understanding of engineering, was apprenticed at 12 to a machine builder in Bradford. Seven years later he was a master engineer and had overseer work in a factory in Leeds.'

'So why did you move to Bingley?'

'Father had a mind to run a smallholding. He thought it made sense

Chapter 7

for us to have a source of income outside the factory. When he heard about this place he went for it immediately. Donald had no difficulty getting work at Richmond Mill.'

'Did you go to school?'

'No, my mother taught me to read and write. But when she died unexpectedly I took on the role of housekeeper. For my mother's sake, I've kept up my reading and Donald was more than generous in supplying money for me to buy a few books.'

'When did you start work at the mill?'

'I was 14 and Donald suggested I might like to earn money for myself as a machinist. At first it didn't seem possible that I could abandon the smallholding, but Father encouraged me to take it on. I must admit, the housekeeping suffered somewhat, but the men didn't seem to notice and we all muddled along together. Father was even capable of doing some washing on occasions! Anyway, the extra money went into purchasing livestock and improving the smallholding generally until it now produces a good surplus. So, with that source of income we could save. But now Donald's dead things must change.'

'Will you be able to manage?'

'For the moment, yes; we're sufficiently cushioned from debt by a healthy sum of spare cash. This will tide us over until I can establish myself back on the farm and run it properly. But as for the future, well, I'm not sure after what has happened.' She fell silent, and Ambrose could tell she was thinking of her brother and the family's loss.

'Are you sure you've no idea who actually pushed Donald over the railings?' asked Ambrose.

'As I've told you, I have suspicions, but no proof. There are a few men in the mill whom I've taken a profound dislike to and certainly don't trust. But just because I find them unpleasant doesn't make them murderers. What I'm sure of is that his death is connected to the illegal employment of under-aged children. Whether they're working for the owner or whether this is private enterprise I'm not sure. Supervision by the mill manager is slack and I've only seen the owner in the mill about once every year since I've been there. Mr Richmond has many other financial interests and is inclined to leave the whole management of the place to Tom Sizewell, a man I really detest. Now you've told me about his connection to the Fairfax woman, my opinion has been vindicated.'

'Any particular reason why you disliked him – before you knew of his acquaintance with Mrs Fairfax, that is?' asked Ambrose.

'You're experienced in the treatment of workers in the mills in Lancashire. Things are no different here. Workers are exploited, particularly the women. As you must be aware, many of the young girls are considered easy prey by the men and resistance is useless, especially if they want to keep their jobs. I've been lucky, perhaps because they know I wouldn't be scared to speak out, as well as being able to read and write, which they are suspicious of. I hold my own with them, so they find me difficult and generally steer clear. It's the very young vulnerable girls who are caught. They're powerless – often don't even realise what's happening to them as they're handed around among the men like so many rag dolls.'

'It's appalling that this is going on, and no action being taken against these men. They seem to be able to get away with murder – literally.'

Rosalie nodded. 'You're right, and I'm sure my brother was right too; Sizewell is involved in allowing under-aged children to work. He certainly turns two blind eyes to everything vicious that goes on in the mill, although he doesn't participate himself; probably thinks as a manager he's too grand.'

'He sounds like the type who would let others do his dirty work for him. I've met a few of them in my time.'

'Well, I think he runs a few men who are capable of anything – from simple fiddling of weights and measures to ravishing of small girls, and ultimately to murder if it's a question of protecting themselves. Now we know he's involved in baby farming and deeply involved with Mrs Fairfax.'

Ambrose said, 'We must find out how far that is as soon as possible. What else do you know about him?'

'As I said, the man has this little group of hangers-on who follow him around like puppets on strings. They're mixed up in all sorts – dog fighting, gaming, anything that makes easy money. I'm sure

Chapter 7

they're at least guilty of colluding with him in anything else. Sizewell's responsible for hiring and firing and never asks questions when the men and women bring the children in, although he made sure they were off the premises when we had an inspection last year.'

'That's common practice in the mills everywhere. So, where does he live? Does he have a family?'

'I don't know. If he does he can't spend much time with them. He has a house in the town but he's generally at work, in the tavern or at dog fights and card schools. He's never short of money and that's how he keeps his followers – very generous in the local inns I understand.'

They stayed in the parlour until the small clock on the mantelpiece struck half past six and Ambrose realised he should be getting back to town before dark. Reluctantly he rose to go. She touched his arm and said, 'Mr Hudson – or Barrett – you've been very clever in getting me to reveal all kinds of things that I wouldn't generally share with a stranger. You've given me no chance to ask you about yourself. I don't even know your real Christian name.'

'It's Ambrose. What else would you like to know?'

'Well – do you have a family?'

'You mean, am I married?'

'Not necessarily. I imagine your line of work makes it difficult to keep a wife; your being away from home wouldn't be easy for her.'

'Well, rest your mind, I don't have a wife and that's one of the reasons – I don't think many women would put up with me being away half the year. Besides, I've never met one who would have me!'

'Why do all bachelors say that?'

'We're bachelors because it's true!' He laughed. Taking her hand and looking her full in the face he said, 'Thank you for the meal and your company. My kind of work is lonely and I don't have many friends, although I've been fortunate in meeting Edgar Lawes and we seem to get along very well. I've enjoyed the last few hours immensely and hope I can consider you as another – er – friend from now on.'

She smiled and nodded, her eyes wrinkling in a most attractive way.

By God! She's really beautiful, he thought, holding her gaze until she began to flush pink. He cleared his throat and said, 'My reasons for coming to Yorkshire in the first place were clear – to investigate two illegal practices. But I can promise you that there is a third: that of finding your brother's killer or killers. I'll do everything in my power to get justice for you.' He found her hand was still inside his own and she had made no move to withdraw it. Unusually flustered, with his other hand he fumbled for the cap in his pocket.

She took her hand away, stepped back a pace and moved to the door. 'Goodnight, Ambrose,' she said and – perhaps he was mistaken, he was not sure –he thought he saw tears in her eyes.

He stooped under the low lintel of the front door and at the gate turned back to see her framed against the light of the oil lamp inside. She raised her hand and he waved in response as he clicked the gate behind him and turned onto the track.

It was a gloomy evening, cloudy and the light was fading. He heard the fluting of a diligent song thrush, which was full-throatily pronouncing its territory when every other bird had gone to roost, and the bleating of sheep as they made connection with each other in their flock. He trudged on, deep in his thoughts, for at least a mile and met no other travellers until, out of the silence, he heard the faint jingle of a harness and the thump and rattle of a cart coming towards him. It was apparently travelling at some speed because within a minute he perceived it in the gloom. It had no lamp but, even in the darkness, he could see it was an open dog cart with a single horse and one occupant. It occurred to him that he must be invisible to the driver as the cart was coming straight at him.

Realising it was not going to stop to allow him to pass and that there was no room for them both on the track, he quickly stepped aside into a shallow ditch, cursing as his boots squelched in deep muddy water. At the last second the driver became aware of him, and pulled on the brake but without much force. The horse, completely confused by the lack of clear command, took off, reins flapping and unmanaged. As he looked up from the ditch Ambrose could see it was a woman driving. With no control over the beast or the cart the inevitable happened and the vehicle tipped itself over on its side and the horse, dragging on the reins and halter, was brought to a stop in a sweat, but fortunately still upright.

Chapter 7

They were now some way from Ambrose down the track. Without a moment's thought he raced towards the cart to offer the driver help. However, before he reached her and to his great surprise she had extricated herself from the seat, snatched up a large box that had fallen to the ground, got herself off the cart and, clearly unharmed, was off up the track at lightning speed, skirts flapping and bonnet flying. All he could ascertain in the gloom was that she was of small stature, and in the few seconds he looked at her he was unable to make out her features clearly. But he had the briefest of images in his mind and felt he might have seen her somewhere before. By the time he reached the cart she had disappeared round a bend in the track.

He turned his attention to the poor animal, which stood trembling, sweating and rolling its eyes. He wished Edgar or Peter had been with him. He was unsure what to do but common sense told him he should try to calm the beast and tether it to the hedge before attempting to pull the cart upright. It was a light vehicle and the wheels seemed undamaged. With a struggle, he should be able to set it right on the track since the ditch was fortunately shallow. He took his courage in his hands and approached the horse. 'There, there!' he said ineffectually. He stretched out his hand to stroke its nose, but the animal rolled its eyes, shook its head and pricked back its ears. Eventually, with soothing noises and by gently stroking its neck he calmed it to the point where it stopped trembling and he could safely tie the reins to a stout branch in the hedge.

Now much calmer, the animal began to nibble at the fresh green hawthorn shoots. Satisfied that it was fully occupied, Ambrose felt ready to tackle the cart. As he anticipated, this was not difficult and soon he had it upright and could carefully manoeuvre the horse back between the shafts. Having righted the thing Ambrose wondered what to do with the vehicle. He could see lettering on the side: *Right's Carts of Halifax* and presumed it had been hired from that source. In view of his desire to maintain his anonymity he had no wish to get involved in its return, when there would be the inevitable questions as to where it was found and how he came to be there. But he was interested in who the woman was and particularly why she was in such a hurry to be off – abandoning a cart that was not hers. Rosalie might be able to help. Untethering the animal, he took the bridle and, coaxing the reluctant creature away from its browsing, led it and the equipage back down the track to Parsloes. The door was open as Rosalie had just let the two dogs out. Parking the vehicle in front of the gate he went up to the door and tapped it. She was startled to see him again, but after he had related the events she came out to look at the horse.

'There's no harm been done to the animal fortunately,' she said as she ran her hands down its flanks, 'apart from being terrified, that is. Why would anyone run off and leave a valuable horse and cart like that?'

'I've no idea, but she definitely didn't want to stay and speak to me.'

'Well, I know the hire people and I'll get one of my neighbours to take it back tomorrow. In the meantime, we'll stable the horse here for the night.'

'Thank you, that's a relief. I was beginning to think I'd have to take it back myself and under the circumstances that would have been very inconvenient. Perhaps you could ask your neighbour if he could ascertain from Mr Right who the hirer was – just to satisfy our curiosity. You know, I have a strange feeling I've seen the woman before – but I just can't place her.'

Rosalie laughed. 'Perhaps it'll come back to you tomorrow – these things often do after a night's sleep.'

'Talking of sleep, it's time I made my way back before the lodging door is locked. I want to add a postscript to my letter to Edgar.'

'Well, goodnight then.' And she nodded and turned back to the cottage.

'Goodnight, Rosalie. If you find out who this careless woman is who can abandon carts like that please let me know!'

'I certainly will,' she said.

Back on the track again he stepped up his pace. Besides writing to Edgar, Ambrose also wanted to write up his daily journal, a purely practical exercise by which he kept track of events as and when they happened. But he didn't use it to record his thoughts about the fine eyes and svelte figure of a beautiful woman. Those he kept locked in his head.

Chapter 8

Monday morning. Ambrose heard a church clock chime five and rolled over, pulling up the meagre blanket which had slipped off onto the floor. 'Just five minutes more,' he thought to himself, although he knew he would have to make the effort to get up sooner or later. He'd had a restless night. The bed was far too small, and every toss and turn was recorded in his long limbs. At one point, he'd had such bad pins and needles in his left foot he was forced to get up and walk across the room a few times to relieve it. His physical discomfort was not helped by the agitation of his mind which insisted on revisiting the events of the day, not least his visit to Rosalie and the pleasant evening they had spent together. He was also puzzled why he was so sure he had seen the woman in the cart before. He had met many women during his work, some he had known well but he was certain she was not one of them. Admittedly it had been a very fleeting glimpse in the dark, and he had not seen her face clearly; but there was something about her outline that struck a definite chord with him. Perhaps it was someone he had seen in a factory in Lancashire on a previous assignment.

As he approached the gates of Richmond Mill he had already decided he would spend the day assessing the employment conditions of the children, as much as he was able from his position in the loading bay.

In order to achieve this he must increase his legitimate access to the interior of the building. On occasions he was asked to carry goods or messages inside the machine shops where he might rub shoulders with the workers, mostly women and children. He had the names of three youngsters identified as under-age by Donald Thwaites. The difficulty was how to find them. He could hardly stand at the power-loom door and shout for them to come forward. Again, it would require some luck if he came across them by accident. He determined to spend more time inside the mill and use his listening skills. He might just pick up a name, or identify a young-looking child whom he might casually quiz. Walking across the yard to receive his instructions from the foreman, he reminded himself he must be sure to keep an eye open for John Walter's wagon; the letter to Edgar was ready in his back pocket.

Not for the first time he wondered what his friend was doing. He was certain Edgar would be engrossing himself in the affairs of the district and planning how to observe while not getting too deeply involved; he had seemed very taken with the idea of bringing miscreants to book. Ambrose considered this unsurprising since, as a magistrate, Edgar was usually at the end of the justice process – dispensing punishment for crimes that others had investigated beforehand. He had rarely been involved in the process of gathering the evidence to bring criminals to court, although in his position as the local JP he was often party to the decision to prosecute after an enquiry came to fruition. Following the process through from beginning to end would be a new experience and one he would relish. Ambrose was sure that Edgar appreciated the danger involved but hoped his friend had taken notice of his warnings and would avoid any risks. There was an extreme ruthlessness about this whole business here in Bingley and it might be that Edgar was in a more exposed position than he was; the moors were lonely places where bodies could be disposed of without risk of discovery. He shivered as he thought of how the 'farmers' might get rid of unwanted babies.

Looking around the loading yard, he found his luck was in. First, there was George's delivery man Walters standing by his cart full of fleeces. The foreman called Ambrose over and told him to get shifting. Having previously been identified to John Walters at Hoyles and, without any hint of recognition, the delivery driver simply nodded to Ambrose and they began to pull bundles off the back of the wagon. In the bustle of activity, it was not difficult for Ambrose to slide the letter into the man's hand as they grabbed and lifted the heavy sacks together and put them on barrows where he wheeled them off to the hoists. Ambrose was kept busy in the yard for most of the morning and had no official access to any of the factory floors. It was not until two o'clock, an hour after dinner, when at last he was sent onto the spinning-machine floor to assist in some heavy work. While waiting for additional help he was unsupervised and left to his own devices

Chapter 8

for 10 minutes or so. Pretending to 'look busy' he walked among the clattering billies, the machines used for spinning woollen yarn.

He observed a dozen or so small children working as scavengers and piecers. Walking in the narrow aisle between billies he nearly tripped over one little mite who, tiny as she was, had to crawl out from beneath a machine clasping a handful of dirty, greasy fleece that she would deposit into an adjacent wicker basket. As she staggered to her feet and tottered to the container he put out an arm to steady her and said, 'Careful, little lady! What's the rush?' She did not reply but looked up at him with a frown of annoyance, pushing past his long legs with some desperation. Ambrose thought either she was in fear of the overseer, or she didn't have a full command of speech. He estimated she couldn't have been more than four, although she might have been a very stunted six-year-old. In any case, she was certainly too young to be working legally. Now back from the basket, she disappeared under the spinning machine and, bending double and down on his haunches to see exactly where she had gone, he saw she had crawled into a space between the large iron feet of the billy which raised it just a few inches from the ground. Seeing that he was not overlooked, he went down on his hands and knees and peered into the small cavern where the child had vanished.

'Hello!' he shouted above the racket, but there was no answer. He could see a pair of tiny unshod feet protruding from beneath the skirt of a grubby ragged black dress; he noticed how blue they looked. Inside this minute space she lay on her front and, with her tiny fingers, he imagined she was nimbly picking out wool waste from between the rollers, belts and chains that carried the force of the steam power into productive motion. What Ambrose could see was the danger of this operation; the child was constantly at risk of being knocked by all the moving parts and he was amazed that, young as she was, she had learned so quickly how to avoid contact while concentrating on her work. This was her life for six days a week and at least 12 hours a day, unremitting in its danger and tediousness. He felt, as he had done many times before, a rush of anger at those who tolerated and even revelled in this enterprise. As far as he was concerned there was certainly no justification for employing children to carry out work such as this. He thought of Will and Peter and their life in the workhouse which, although harsh and bleak, allowed them often to work outside together in the vegetable garden, breathing in fresh air and feeling the warmth of the sun on their backs. Here in a room with tiny barred windows there was little light, and even less inside the bowels of the machinery; there could be no pleasure from the power of the sun. Its sole purpose here was as the source of the energy chain that fuelled the looms.

When after a few minutes she slithered out to throw more waste into her basket he stood up straight and then bent down towards her again. She flinched and cowered back against the frame of the machine. Cupping his hands to his mouth he shouted as loudly as he dared, 'Don't be frightened, I'm not going to hurt you! What's your name?'

She looked up at him in bewilderment and fear. Her little face was pinched and grey and her mousy hair filthy and straggled. Barely audible against the background of the deafening noise she said defiantly in the high pitch of a young child, 'Tilly, and I'm nine!'

Ambrose immediately recognised a stock answer when he heard one. The child had been schooled to reply to any enquiry about her age. He also recognised the name. She was one of three children identified by Donald Thwaites – Matilda Matthews, probably aged five.

It was not the place to have any kind of conversation with the child and, in any case, it was certain she was not in a mind to respond to him.

So, here was Tilly, 'aged nine', who obviously belonged to someone, but had been put to work almost as soon as she could stand to make an early contribution to her family's purse. It would be a useful starting point to discover who was responsible for her and where she came from. He didn't imagine she would find her own way home; surely there were other members of her family working here who would collect her at the end of the day. He decided to try to keep an eye out for her when the whistle went and see who turned up to escort her home.

Half an hour later, having completed his task of moving machinery, Ambrose returned to the yard and was immediately accosted by Jed

Chapter 8

Stow who told him the foreman had been looking for him and said, 'You'd better get along sharpish if you want to keep your job!' Making an excuse to the boss that he had been helping elsewhere, he was set to work moving yet more equipment and that kept him occupied all the afternoon until the factory whistle went at six o'clock and his shift ended.

Stationing himself in the shadow of the factory gates, he watched as the stream of workers, old and young, passed him by, funnelling through and beyond the entrance and into the streets around the mill. He had to keep his eyes permanently on the rhythmically moving crowd and it was difficult to isolate individuals among the mass of people and impossible to pick out the small figure of Matilda Matthews. There was a depressing homogeneity of dress and demeanour in this bunch of humanity and no relief from its oppressive drabness. Faces were thin, drawn and devoid of any indication that they had feelings of joy or anger. Emotionless, the throng made its way as one body, streaming to the gates and release from the tyranny of the machines and their masters. The only noise Ambrose heard was the orchestrated clatter of pattens on the cobbles and he was most struck by the absence of any rumble of speech; there was no conversation between these comrades in adversity – even as they linked up with family members. The imperative was to get out: for the women to their homes and those members of the family who remained behind there; the men, in the main, took direct and well-worn routes to the numerous inns and taverns that had grown up in the surrounding streets as adjuncts to the new mills. Ambrose was aware how these bars offered warmth and escape from both work and domestic difficulties.

From his vantage point in the shadows he saw Jed Stow purposefully making his way through the gates. Ambrose stepped out and touched his arm. 'Are you going to the Cow and Calf?'

'Might be.'

'Mind if I join you later? I've something to do first, but I'll stand you a drink in about half an hour.' Knowing that once Jed Stow was ensconced in the bar he would be unlikely to shift for several hours, and neither would he pass up the offer of a drink, Ambrose considered he would have plenty of time to discover more about Tilly's family, particularly where she lived. The easiest method would have been to make enquiries of his fellow workers, but he remained committed to his anonymity. As always when on investigations he knew his best mode of action was to discreetly follow, observe and listen.

Almost on the verge of giving up any sighting of Tilly, he was relieved to see some stragglers bringing up the rear. Among them was a small group of women who were evidently waiting for someone. Finally, Tilly and a couple of other children appeared and joined with their mothers, aunts and older sisters in the walk to the gates. She was dragging her feet wearily as she held the hand of a thin, hawk-featured woman who pulled at her with a curse whenever she faltered. 'For God's sake – keep up, Tilly! We won't get home till morning at this rate and then it'll be time to come back.'

'I'm tired, Ma!'

'We're all tired. When we get home, after you've helped your sisters get the wood and water and dinner on for your dad and brothers, maybe you can go to bed a bit earlier.' The child said nothing and the woman gripped her hand determinedly, keeping up her brisk pace.

Ambrose fell in behind the group which continued walking through the main street to the slum area where the Stows lived. Indeed, their destination was only a few doors away. There the party split into two groups; Tilly's mother and her two sisters shoved their way through a broken door that was half off its hinges and into an interior that shed no light. The door was pushed shut and Ambrose could discern nothing more of the family. But he felt it would not be difficult to encourage a drunken Jed to gossip about his neighbours.

He retraced his steps through the town and found the tavern and his colleague next to the bar. By this time Jed had swallowed two pints of porter in quick succession and, with his immediate working-day thirst quenched, was settling to the pleasant side of drinking, but at a steadier pace that would see him though the rest of the evening.

Spotting Ambrose at the door, Jed waved a greeting and indicated his almost empty glass. 'Just in time – I'll have an ale!'

Obliging his friend, Ambrose called on the barman to pour two more glasses and now, well equipped with liquor, they made their

Chapter 8

way to a rough round table and two small stools. Ambrose hated sitting on stools – it made his back ache, and they were always too short for his long legs; adjusting himself as best he could he endeavoured to open a sensible conversation with Stow. Passing over the preliminary conventions as quickly as possible he enquired casually how Mrs Stow and the children were. 'I haven't yet been able to see her or where they all work.'

'They're in the spinning shop mostly. My three eldest – one boy and two girls – work all over. The youngest is a scavenger, the older boy wants to train up as a loom operator, but I think the boss would rather have women doing it because he can pay them less. Between them they make us a few shillings a week; you know we've got three more at home to feed? I'm trying to arrange for the next eldest to be taken on with her sister on the billy.'

Ambrose was immediately attentive. He knew the young child Jed was referring to could have been no more than five. 'Isn't she a bit young?' he ventured tentatively.

Jed Stow was unconcerned. 'Not here she's not. Once they can get on their feet and while they're small enough to get inside the billy they can be taken on.'

Ambrose raised an eyebrow and took the plunge. 'I thought the law had been changed and they had to be a certain age before they could be employed? Bosses down south were grumbling about it.'

'No one takes notice of that here. There are too many mouths to feed. Everyone must play their part – young and old. You must know that – as you say you've worked in mills before.'

'I didn't see much of the inside of the mill in Oxford,' Ambrose explained. Anxious to move away from his own history he asked, 'What about the government inspectors?'

Jed frowned at his new friend. 'Well, as I said, you know yourself, working in mills, the regulations mean nothing. How many inspections have you seen? Not many I'm sure. When we get them, we know well in advance. All the very young ones are sent home – which causes us aggravation because they lose a day's pay. The bosses take a risk with any who are a bit on the young side but can fool the inspectors by telling them to say they're nine or ten. These government men don't know what a nine-year-old should look like. Besides, most of them know the owners and don't ask a lot of questions. Look, it's time for another one – your round, I think!'

Cheated by an astute drinker into paying more than his dues and spending more money than he meant to, Ambrose was relieved an hour later when Jed, decidedly the worse for drink, agreed to call it a night and return home. Ambrose offered to walk with the man and see him to his door in the hope of more information. But Stow was by now incapable of speech and Ambrose realised there would probably be little else that Jed's wife could reveal. She clearly had no knowledge as to the whereabouts of Mrs Fairfax; neither was the family inclined to seek further contact. The link was Sizewell who had initially put Jed Stow onto the fostering arrangements; he would have the precise details. But how to set about any enquiry into him needed careful thought. It appeared it would be down to Edgar to pursue the investigation of Mrs Fairfax from his vantage point out on the moor. The place Rickard's was their best bet to locate her and any of her accomplices.

It was well past nine o'clock by the time they reached Stow's lodgings. Ambrose pushed the door open and called to Mrs Stow that her husband was home and then set out to walk back to his own lodgings. As he passed the broken door of number 12 he wondered about Tilly and the Matthews family. Was she getting a good night's sleep? In all likelihood she was not.

Chapter 9

Edgar felt he had been kicking his heels at Hoyles for the past week, even though, with Peter, he had been enjoying the experience of a bustling and thriving racing stables. In his own less extensive way, he too aspired to produce first-class racers, but seeing George's operation at Hoyles made him realise how far he had to go to emulate his cousin's achievements. But, as George remarked, there was time enough on his side in which to increase his stock of breeding mares and his reputation. Both men were most pleased with Peter's reaction to George's enterprise; the boy was completely enamoured of everything he saw and impressed his host with his enthusiasm and energy. They both agreed that the lad had the real potential to become an excellent trainer. The only disappointment for Edgar and Peter was that they had not managed any visits to other stables.

Opportunity was found during the week for Edgar to visit some of the distant flocks, accompanying one of George's more taciturn shepherds. The man was bemused that a gentleman should take such a practical interest in sheep farming, but asked no questions, just followed his master's instructions and explained how they did these things in Yorkshire.

Edgar was uncertain when Ambrose would write and he was determined to be on hand to receive a letter. It was not until the evening of Monday, 22 April, just before dinner, that he finally received a package; after breaking the seal he read its contents eagerly, hoping this would be the signal for action he had been waiting for.

It was a long letter and described in detail everything that Ambrose had discovered and experienced in Bingley: how he had managed to make the acquaintance of a family that was directly involved with the baby farming, the father being particularly forthcoming with information when he was in drink and the mother anxious to explain how her niece's baby came to be taken. According to what she said, the woman might be living on a small farmstead out on Ilkley Moor. Ambrose wrote that he was convinced this woman was Fairfax and may have taken the child to Rickard's. At the end of the letter came a surprising *post scriptum* describing his encounter with the mysterious woman in the lane and how she had run off after landing her cart in the ditch. The most important point was that he had a strong feeling he knew her. The comment that Ambrose had met with Rosalie twice and 'was having supper with her' did not escape Edgar, who knowingly smiled to himself.

After he had read and re-read the letter, Edgar shared its contents with his cousin. 'Ambrose seems satisfied that Donald Thwaites's information was accurate and Mrs Fairfax's location was Rickard's which you identified from the man's sketch. This means I can go ahead and keep it under observation from tomorrow. Looking at the map, where do you think might be a suitable place for observation, George?'

The building was off the boundary of George's land, but he was still able to show Edgar its precise location on a large map of the district. Impatient to start, Edgar asked if he could ride out to see it that evening after dinner, but George counselled caution as his guest was unfamiliar with the type of terrain he would be riding into. Looking carefully at the map, he pointed out a small grove of trees about 400 yards from the building and suggested it as a suitable place to tether his horse; from there he could travel the rest of the way carefully on foot. George's knowledge of the ground was that, like all the local moorland, it was steeply elevated with tough tussocks of grass intermingled with stretches of dangerous boggy ground. It would be advisable that he took someone with him, to look after the horses and to provide help if there was any trouble. He thought Peter would be ideal as although he was a very willing worker round the stables, he had not yet become integrated into its daily routines. In any case, he was an extra pair of hands and, however useful, could be spared for the day. Knowing of Ambrose's insistence that Peter should not be involved in this affair, Edgar was hesitant; but, as George observed, this was only to be a reconnaissance, there would be no confrontations with the occupants of Rickard's.

As for Ambrose's encounter with the woman and the cart, George knew of Right's of Halifax who provided carts of all sizes for hire. 'I can tell you, Rodney Right won't be pleased to know that one of his

Chapter 9

vehicles had been driven so carelessly and left with such disregard. I'll make enquiries about the driver; I know RR very well.'

'It's curious that Ambrose should have felt recognition of her so strongly, even from a fleeting glimpse.'

'It will come to him – probably suddenly when he's thinking about something completely different,' said George cheerfully.

'Hmm. It's very frustrating trying to drag something from the depths of your mind!'

Edgar himself was to suffer frustration as the weather on Tuesday was appalling. Visibility was poor and George again advised it would be too dangerous to risk getting lost in unknown terrain. So he spent the day sorting and adjusting provisions and equipment.

By the following morning the fog had completely disappeared, so Edgar and Peter set out together, taking provisions and water for the day. For most of the journey the ground rose steeply, but as they jogged along they noticed the bright acid green of the vegetation on the watersheds which told them there were dangerous springs to avoid, confirming George's warning about keeping to the tracks. Fortunately, these were well-worn, either by sheep or shepherds, and they could travel in safety provided they stayed in single file. Edgar could see that an inadvertent stumble into any of these lush-looking areas with their new growth of cotton grass, which had yet to show its white scut-like fluff, would have serious consequences. He had heard from George how ewes and lambs had been lost in them when an inattentive shepherd had allowed them to stray. There were tales of larger creatures – cattle and horses – coming to the same sticky end.

Edgar wanted to take his time and get the feel of the country and it was not until about an hour later that they reached the copse of ash trees which were coming into leaf and would provide total cover. In front of them facing west was a short sharp hill that obliterated their view. But according to George's map beyond that rise was Rickard's cottage.

Edgar reined in and said, 'We'll tether up here, Peter, and have some food; then I'll go off on foot to spy out the country. I'll take my spyglass and a water bottle and be back within the hour. If anything happens and I've not returned in two hours, you're to ride back to Hoyles and get help.'

'But if there's any danger, sir, should you go? Remember what Mr Ambrose said about not getting involved.'

'I won't take any risks – I can assure you!' Edgar said to the boy, although inwardly he was thinking, 'At least not this time.'

Leaving Peter sitting with his back against a tree and the two horses quietly grazing new spring shoots, Edgar climbed the rise by means of a narrow sheep track and was soon out of sight of the wood. Fifteen minutes later he came to the lip of the hill, fell onto his front and, lying as flat as he could, peered over. He could see the building immediately below him but some way off and taking out his spyglass he surveyed the small walled area around it and then the cottage itself. 'Cottage' was not an accurate description: it was more of a large hut mostly in wood but with a decent turf roof. Neither was it adequately walled around; many of the dry stones were broken down and there were huge gaps leading directly onto the moor between sections that remained standing. Completely isolated on this lonely uninhabited stretch of moorland, the place had been let go.

Edgar could see immediately that there would be a problem getting nearer to it without revealing himself; it was totally exposed from all sides. But as he looked more closely he could see, further to the west beyond the cottage, an outcrop of rock which, if he could access it, would provide closer cover than his present position and a clear but sheltered view of the front of the place. From this current vantage point he could only see the rear and surrounding land of the building, but could ascertain its boundaries. He noticed there was no back garden, only moorland that seemed to stretch away unbroken into the distance. A stream from the north-east passed by the side of the cottage and was obviously its source of water. The whole area had a desolate feel about it and it was clear that the lonely position was why it had been chosen. There would be no reason for anyone to come here.

He asked himself, 'Who's at home?' It was evident that there was someone there, or there had been recently, since streams of thick dark smoke rose from a small chimney. But there were no other signs of life and Edgar waited for a clear 20 minutes before his patience was

Chapter 9

rewarded. A young girl of about 12 or 13 appeared round the side of the building carrying a wooden bucket with a rope handle. Edgar could see she was thin and waif-like even from a distance. She took a shortcut across the garden and passed through one of the large holes in the wall and disappeared down a slope. From his vantage point Edgar surmised she was getting water from the small stream. She reappeared with what was evidently a full and heavy bucket, struggling back through the garden trying not to slop its contents over her feet and clothing. She disappeared again and must have passed through the front door, which Edgar reckoned was the only entrance and exit. Although the place was obviously inhabited, Edgar could see no signs of regular domestic activity; for example, there was no washing hanging outside. He was relieved that there seemed to be no evidence of dogs around the place, at least any that he could hear.

He waited another 10 minutes but there was no further sign of the occupants; indeed, the place remained eerily quiet. By this time, he noticed how damp his clothes had become lying on wet ground and wished he had had the forethought to bring a waterproof. He saw from his watch that his time was up and reluctantly walked back down the hill to the wood and Peter.

'Well, sir, have you found out anything?'

'It's a desolate place, Peter. I would think it's just right for someone to hide away, especially if they didn't want anyone prying into their business. I can't think that anyone would come here. We know the shepherds aren't using it – so the place is completely private. The only person I saw was a small girl who obviously does the menial work. Apart from her I didn't see anyone else.'

'Does that mean you'll be going back, sir?'

'Indeed, and there'll be enough time and daylight for us to return in the early evening and, if that produces nothing, then again very early tomorrow morning when surely things will start to stir.'

The second visit in the evening was more fruitful. This time, having consulted George's estate map again, Edgar took them on a longer, well-defined route that circled round west of the cottage to some trees at the base of the hill with its outcrop of rock that Edgar had earmarked as a safe place for observation. They applied the same routine, Peter managing the horses while Edgar climbed up to the high point, settling himself behind the largest of three boulders where he could keep a better surveillance of the property. This time he had brought a waterproof to lie on. He now had sight of the front of the building where there was a small plot of untended garden. At some point last season it had been cultivated by the shepherd, but was now totally abandoned and overgrown with encroaching reed, nettles and rough grass. A well-trodden path stretched from the front door to a small wooden gate which provided the west boundary, although it was redundant since the walling around the place was almost all broken down. He peered round the side of his hidey-hole, spyglass pressed to his eye, although he hardly needed it. Within minutes he saw the same girl leave the house and walk to the wood chopping-block where she picked up the axe and began to hack away at some kindling.

A middle-aged man followed her out and walked down to the gate, leaned over it and took out a pouch of tobacco. Having filled a pipe, he had some difficulty lighting it, for the breeze was strong and, turning his back to the wind he was directly facing Edgar. While the man's concentration was fixed on lighting his pipe Edgar managed to get a good look at him. He had a swarthy complexion and what looked like grey hair under a small peaked cap. He was not tall but clearly muscular. Edgar found it incongruous that he should be taking his ease while this thin slip of a girl was swinging the axe.

The man had left the door open and suddenly Edgar's blood chilled as he heard the distinctive crying of what he imagined to be a very young child. Even though he had no direct experience of babies he recognised this as the unmistakable sound of one in great distress. It was a piercing, insistent noise designed by nature to produce an immediate response from those around. The man became aware that it could be heard outside the door and immediately told the girl to close it. As she slammed it shut the sounds became much less distinct, although still evident. Edgar wished he could get close enough to peer through the small window at the side of the cottage, but it was too risky. By this time dusk was falling and he waited for the pair to return

Chapter 9

to the cottage. Once inside one of them must have lit a lamp as his last view was of a pale yellow light shining through a small uncurtained window. All went quiet and it was evident there would be no further activity. Disappointed, he crawled out of his hiding place and made his way back to Peter who was anxiously waiting for him.

'Well, did you see anyone else, sir?'

Edgar was less forthcoming this time. He was determined to keep Peter at arm's length; the less he knew the better. He was certainly not going to mention anything about a baby crying.

As they picked their way carefully back along the moorland tracks in the semi-darkness, each wrapped in his own thoughts, Edgar concluded that he needed to find means by which he could keep the place under constant surveillance, rather than wasting time with chance visits that risked producing little of substance. He decided to consult George again.

Back at Hoyles, after some food and wine, Edgar broached the problem with his cousin.

'It seems to me that our original plan to establish a base close enough to keep the place under observation is by far the most practical one, but it must be somewhere remote enough to prevent accidental discovery. As I said, I'm quite prepared to spend days out there – in fact I can see it's the only way to proceed.'

'I agree with you,' said George, 'you need a permanent presence to gather strong enough evidence to convict these scoundrels. I've been thinking about it and come up with a couple of possibilities. Let's get the map out again and study what might suit the purpose.' He went to a shelf and selected a large piece of rolled-up cloth. 'This is the most recent estimation available of the properties and their ownership – it was put together by a group of us landowners about ten years ago; things haven't changed much since then.' George unrolled the map onto the dining table, securing it at all four corners with stone paperweights and as Edgar leaned beside him he saw a detailed painted plan. The owners had gone to a good deal of trouble to delineate all the boundaries and properties of the extant estates and farms. As far as George knew, just about every building in the area was marked –

even the wooden shepherd's huts which, although sparsely built, were refurbished every year as and when they were needed.

'Looking at this I can see a couple of huts that might serve your purpose. Rickard's is here' – he pointed to the cottage which was marked clearly on the map – 'and here's an empty shepherd's hut to the west and still within my boundary line.' The limit of George's estate was not far from the cottage; as the crow flies he estimated the distance of the hut from the cottage as four furlongs. Although it was lambing time his chief shepherd had no use for it as his ewes were mostly grazing on the far side of the estate and the shepherds and their pages were working solely in those areas. It would provide rough, but sheltered conditions and Edgar, once having committed to this enterprise, was not deflected from his goal by the thought of any domestic discomfort.

George peered at the map again. 'Wait a minute! I think this one might be better. It's not far to the outcrop of rock and trees you described due west of Rickard's, but, as you found out, has good cover. Of the two huts I was considering, this one is closer and has the advantage of being in a hollow and therefore difficult to see. Its low-lying position was one of the reasons the shepherd didn't like it – too damp as it's close to the same stream that bypasses Rickard's, but that means there's a ready supply of water. If you look at the contours of the map, you'll see the steep rise you discovered between you and your objective. It has a few bushes on the top, but also large boulders that keep you well hidden. You'd have the place in plain sight from that vantage point. You'll need supplies, of course; there's plenty of water about, but fresh food will have to be brought in. Peter can act as runner for you and bring back any letters you wish to send out – and certainly report to me on your progress, which I can pass on to your friend!'

'This sounds exactly what we need,' and Edgar nodded his head approvingly. Then he asked, 'Do you know anything about these people, George?'

'Local gossip has it that, having been empty quite a while, two months ago the cottage and half an acre of land were taken on by a family – a middle-aged man, his wife and young daughter. It's said they're not too friendly towards us locals. Shortly after they moved in there was trouble with their two dogs which were very aggressive and a potential risk to all the local flocks. I was particularly exercised when one of my ewes was found savaged and sent my bailiff round to challenge the man, although I had no proof it was their dogs that were responsible, but no one else round here keeps such animals. Initially he was as aggressive as his dogs and the confrontation almost ended in blows until his wife intervened and promised the dogs "would be taken care of", although they never actually admitted they were at fault. After that the animals were never seen. From what you've told me about their suspected activities, it would seem the pair don't want any trouble or anything that might attract unwanted visitors.'

'It's not only this family who don't want unwanted visitors! This business of me staying in this remote shepherd's hut is bound to cause comment in this tight-knit community, George. How do we deal with that?'

'Well, we'll stick to the story of you coming here to view sheep farming Yorkshire-style. You've already been out and about with my man and I'll just put it about in the neighbourhood that you're considering major developments to your own sheep flocks and looking at our conditions for grazing. I'll impress on them that you're a forward-thinking man – which you are – and this is the "new way of doing things". They've always thought that you southerners often have strange ideas! I'm recognised in the district as a practical man, a landowner with a keen interest in the running of my estate. I often muck in when it comes to foaling time and regularly visit the far-flung outposts of my land at lambing to see all's well. After the first round of curiosity most of the inhabitants will accept the story, although you may be plagued with questions at times – when they can get at you. We'll have to try to keep you isolated from the curious as best we can!'

Later that evening Edgar wrote to Ambrose to explain the proposals that he had agreed with George; it was essential that they were as informed as possible of what each other was doing. George promised to pass the letter to his delivery man so that Ambrose should receive it the next morning. On that day, with Peter's help, Edgar carted bedding and supplies across to the wooden hut which was a quarter of an hour's walk from his objective. Fortunately, it was a dry though cool April day. He decided that once he had moved in he wouldn't use a horse as there was no facility for stabling and he didn't want the added responsibility of its care.

Arriving at the hut they could see the place was depressingly ramshackle, damp and musty through lack of use. However, overall it was sturdy enough with its newly repaired roof, but it had a dirt floor that would become very damp and probably muddy in wet weather. That would be solved by the application of armfuls of reeds which grew in abundance everywhere. Edgar had supplies of waterproofs, and the truckle bed – which was too short for him by inches – was well off the ground. There was a small plain table, a bench and, hanging on the wall, a manger with the remnants of last year's hay. He imagined the shepherd would bring orphaned lambs here as well as injured sheep. The fustiness was augmented by the distinctly acrid smell of sheep's urine and despite the cold they left the door wide open all day to clear the air. There was a rough fireplace underneath a chimney in the turf roof and the shepherd had left a good supply of kindling and logs for the next occupant – as was the neighbourly custom among them. George had promised to send over a wagon-load of wood should it be needed, but for now Edgar was well set up to maintain a good fire at least.

It had been decided that Edgar only needed Thursday to move in and that he would start his surveillance on Friday morning; he would wait until Peter arrived with fresh supplies, and then set out for the whole day. Now, having seen that Mr Lawes had all he needed, Peter prepared to ride back to Hoyles, taking Edgar's mount with him. With one foot in his stirrups he turned to Edgar and asked, 'Begging your pardon, Mr Lawes, but can you cook? I mean – you can't just exist on cold meat and tea.'

Edgar laughed. 'The answer to your question, Peter, is – what do you mean by "cook"? I can't prepare a meal from scratch but I'm hoping that the kitchens at Hoyles will provide me with soup and stews that I can heat up. You can bring them over in cans and I can make them last. I don't intend to be here longer than five or six days, at the

Chapter 9

most ten. I'm sure I can rub along with what you bring me. Remember, plenty of bread, cold meat and cheese, please! You can be on your way safe in the knowledge that I won't starve. Have a safe ride back. I've a bed to make up!'

Having seen the boy off up the track expertly leading the second horse with one hand and guiding his own with the other, Edgar turned and went back into the hut. He experienced a mixture of feelings: apprehension and excitement, but also at the back of his mind there was fear. He couldn't estimate how ruthless their opponents were. Had they really disposed of the dogs, or were they just keeping them quiet and out of sight?

Dusk was approaching early in this gloomy, low-lying spot and he lit one of his two oil lamps. He would be sparing in their use; he didn't want Peter to be laden down with supplies and he felt sure he could live meagrely for a week. It would be good for him to experience something of how most people lived, many with far less than in this situation. Ambrose had described in graphic detail the filthy slums of Manchester and, looking around the hut at the well-covered bed, the table laden with food, and a generous supply of fuel, he decided it was positively palatial in comparison. He had had a good meal at midday and now he filled his kettle and hooked it over the fire – which Peter had lit for him – and prepared bread and cold beef, washing it down with tea. As the sheep had all moved away across the moor the water was fresh and uncontaminated – at least George had assured him so.

He sat at the table, his hands warming round his mug of tea and anticipated the next few days. For the first time in his life he was alone, reliant only on himself – no Foster to attend to his every whim, no maids to clear up after him. A unique experience and one that he hoped he could come through 'a better and a wiser man'! He stripped off and washed himself down in cold water, standing in the bucket one leg at a time; put on a thick flannel nightshirt borrowed from George; pulled back the blankets and climbed onto the bed, which creaked complainingly at his weight. He soon discovered his feet would stick out, so he put his socks back on and moved the bed closer to the dying embers of the fire. Extinguishing the lamp, he lay in the dark listening for night sounds, but all was silent. There was no breeze, no owl calls, no bleating sheep. As comfortable as he could be in a bed two sizes too small for him, but tired after a day's toing and froing, within 20 minutes he was fast asleep on his back, snoring with his mouth open.

Having been deeply asleep, Edgar stirred and attempted to turn over on his bed. He was immediately awake as the difficulties of such a manoeuvre manifested themselves. The blankets fell off and he all but rolled off after them. Cussing, he swung his legs onto the floor and stood up. Using the light from the embers of the fire, he checked his watch. It was ten past one and everywhere was deathly quiet. To his dismay he realised he needed to relieve himself and there was no chamber pot. There was no alternative other than to go outside, so he put on his boots, breeches and a jacket. Opening the door, he had a job to see; there was no moon and the stars were obscured by cloud. With difficulty in the pitch black he lit a candle and stumbled with it down the track to the bushes. As he walked he became aware of some movement and breaking branches within the trees; something or someone was wandering about. His heart thumping, he walked across in the direction of the noise and almost fell over a ewe which was lying down and in evident distress. He was surprised since George had told him the flocks were far away and not likely to trouble him. Where had this one come from?

He bent over, imagining the animal would take fright and move off, but she stayed where she was and began bleating loudly. Clearly there was something wrong. He put out his hand and there was no resistance from the sheep. Since his source of light was poor he retraced his steps to the hut to fetch the lamp; when he returned the ewe had still not moved. He could see she was panting rapidly and, as he examined her in the light he noticed a wetness coming from her rear end.

'What's the matter, old girl? You're certainly in a bad way.' Setting down the lamp, he attempted to move the animal to make more room, but she was a dead weight. As he looked at her rear, to his horror he saw she was in the process of lambing and was obviously having difficulties. He could just see two small hooves sticking out of her back

Chapter 9

end, but she seemed too exhausted to push the lamb out. There was nothing for it but to give her some help. Although he had occasionally been present at lambing on his own estate he had only once delivered a lamb himself, but he'd helped at the birth of plenty of foals and he thought the process must be similar. Drawing a deep breath, he grasped the two hooves, one in each hand, and as firmly as he dared he pulled on the lamb. To his great relief there was a response and movement; he could see the head which, once out, was rapidly followed by the rest of the body. The little ewe lamb lay on the grass and Edgar pulled aside the birth membrane and wiped her mouth and nostrils clear with his handkerchief. To his great relief she took a shallow breath and then a deeper one. He rubbed her vigorously with his hands to warm her and get her blood circulating before turning his attention to her mother.

By now she was evidently exhausted and bleeding heavily; half dead already, her eyes rolling and head lolling. She could certainly not cope with her newborn. He was in a dilemma; it was not really his place to put her out of her misery, although it would have been the kindest thing to do; besides, he was not anxious to let off a firearm in the middle of the night. There was nothing he could do other than try to make her last minutes as comfortable as possible. Fortunately, her suffering was short and within minutes she breathed her last.

Only then did he take up her lamb, now wrapped in his jacket and, with the lantern in his left hand and the creature on his right arm, 'a biblical image if ever there was one', he walked back to the hut, completely forgetting he had not fulfilled the function he originally came out for.

He made up the fire with fresh kindling until there was a good blaze and placed the lamb in front of the hearth. His next problem was how to feed her; he must get fluid into her somehow. What was required was something approximating a teat and his eyes alighted on a pair of his goodish doeskin gloves. He took a leather water bottle and cutting off the thumb of the right-hand glove he pulled it over the aperture. It was too wide a fit and so he took a piece of twine and wound it round and round to make a tight seal. With his knife, he made a nick in the top of the thumb and holding the whole bizarre apparatus upside down was very relieved to see water oozing through. If he could get the lamb to take the makeshift teat, he could keep her fed until Peter came the next day and took her back to Hoyles. Warming some milk, he poured it into the bottle, reattached the teat and took the lamb on his lap. Holding open her jaws, he inserted the teat; the lamb baulked at first, but, getting a taste of the sweetness of the liquid, started chewing on it and eventually Edgar could see she was gulping down the milk quite successfully. When he could feel her stomach was full he wrapped her in a small blanket and laid her down by the fire.

Sitting back in his chair, he determined he would stay up all night and keep watch; besides, the creature would probably need feeding at least twice before Peter arrived. Reflecting on the night's event he had a sudden feeling of satisfaction. Generally unsentimental about animals, he felt a glow of pride that he had been part of a natural occurrence, something that was happening all over the moor and beyond. He looked across at the lamb and felt possessive of her, almost as if he had given birth to her himself. He conjectured that this was how women must feel afterwards.

He glanced at his watch and was surprised to see it was already three in the morning. Wrapping himself in his blanket, he dozed before the fire until it was time to feed his orphaned responsibility again. He expected Peter to arrive any time after eight and anticipated the thought of human company with pleasure; it had been a long solitary night and there would be many more like it. At seven as it became light he went outside to the stream where he stripped off and washed all over in the icy water. Refreshed, he made himself some porridge, brewed a mug of tea and fed the lamb again. She was now able to stand on her feet and seemed to be gathering strength by the minute; in fact, whenever he came near she bleated hopefully, looking expectantly at him. For the first time in his life he knew what it was to be totally responsible for the life of another creature. It was a new experience – the responsibility to respond immediately to the raw insistence of another that they required feeding and care.

Peter arrived later than expected at nine but with a saddlebag full of supplies and letters from Suffolk.

'Well, sir, this is a surprise!'

Chapter 9

'I'm not sure who was most surprised, Peter, the lamb or me; anyway, she's survived the night and seems to be doing well. I'm afraid the mother wasn't so fortunate.'

'You've done well to keep her going, sir. But I wonder where the sheep came from. Mr Lawes said there were no sheep in the district.' Peter was impressed that Edgar had been willing to literally get his hands dirty and then had improvised so well to keep the little ewe alive. After several feeds and a warm night, the animal was standing up strongly and looking increasingly interested in the world around her. 'She's evidently bonded well with Mr Lawes,' he thought, as she followed the man around the hut bleating loudly. 'Have you given her a name, sir?'

'No, I understand it's not a good idea to make a pet out of them. You'll have to take her back and get one of the shepherds to find a suitable ewe to put her with. I've no idea who the sheep belonged to and I'm undecided what to do with the body. I'm afraid the foxes got at her earlier this morning – they don't waste time – and she's beginning to be mauled. The crows will be down now it's light.'

'Wouldn't it be best to bury her? At least whoever owns her will know where she is and can do what they like with the carcass. There must be a mark of ownership on her. I'll ask Mr Lawes – he's bound to know.'

'Good idea! We'll take some food together first and then dispose of her. There're some tools round the back; we can find a couple of spades and set to work.'

'I'll do it, sir. No need to get your hands dirty again.'

'Peter, while we're on this assignment we're on equal terms and must both pull our weight. We can't stand on ceremony. Besides, I am not paying you for your help in this affair with Ambrose; you're simply an apprentice working for me at Mr Lawes's. On a matter of principle, I wouldn't insist you help me, although I know you do it willingly.'

Half an hour later between them they had dug a large enough hole to take the ewe which was by now beginning to attract flies. Having covered the carcass thoroughly, they felt they had done enough to discourage further scavengers and walked back up the path to the hut.

Edgar scanned through the packages Peter had brought which contained nothing of absolute urgency and he would put off replying for a couple of days.

'Did you have any letters when the post came?' he asked Peter casually.

The boy's face went pink. 'Two, sir: one from William and the other from Miss Alfrey.'

'What did William have to say?'

'Only that he was still enjoying being at his new school and thinks the master is pleased with him. He writes mostly about Rushie Farm and how he has been helping the O'Brien brothers with the lambing at weekends. He's probably as good at delivering lambs as you are, sir!'

'I'm so happy that he's finding his way at last.' Edgar nodded. 'He's going to become a fine young man, I've no doubt. How is Miss Alfrey and what's the news of her mother and Mr and Miss Bradshaw? Is Miss Alfrey still helping Mr Bradshaw with his library?'

'Oh, yes, sir. She writes that he's started her off on cataloguing all his travel books and it's given her the notion that she would like to travel. That's rather worrying, sir; you don't think she'll get the wanderlust and leave Seddon, do you?'

'Not while you're there, I'm certain.'

'Do you think Mrs Alfrey would agree to us getting married, sir?'

'I'm sure she would, when you're both a little older. I believe that all she wants is what will make her daughter happy, and she knows you do that. When we get back I'll talk to her and reassure her that your future is secure and that you'll be able to offer her daughter everything a mother could wish. Now, have you had enough to eat because it's time you went back and took this young orphan with you.'

'What will you be doing today, sir? Are you going up to spy on the cottage again?'

'I certainly am; I intend to be there all day and into dusk if necessary. I aim to find out exactly who's living there. By the time you return tomorrow I hope to have some news for Mr Hudson.'

'You will be careful, sir, won't you? Remember what he said. He thinks these people are really evil and will stop at nothing to hide what they're doing.'

Chapter 9

'I won't take any risks, although I must find out more about their routines, so I imagine it's going to be quite a tedious day. I'm just glad it's not raining!'

Peter put on his jacket and took up the empty saddlebags. Carrying the lamb out to the horse, Edgar waited until he was securely in the saddle and handed the ewe up to him. With one arm round the animal and the other on the reins the lad pressed the horse into action and had soon disappeared around a bend in the track.

The day was becoming brighter and, although the air was chill, there was a faint chance the sun might come out later. Back in the hut Edgar turned his attention to his preparations. He packed some food, water, his notebook and spyglass into a bag that he slung across his shoulders, then he closed the wooden door of the hut and walked out with a determined stride onto the moor, up to the base of the steep slope below the outcrop of rock. Soon, after a stiff climb, he arrived at the small area of bushes and large stones. Taking off his bag and leaving it on a rock, he took out his spyglass and, keeping as low as possible, crawled on his hands and knees to the lip of the hill where he resumed his position of Wednesday evening among the higher boulders. Cautiously he looked eastward across at Rickard's, which was now in clear view, unlike on his previous visit when it had been in the deepening shadow of evening. Without his spyglass, he could see smoke rising from the chimney, washing drying out on the bushes, and the axe and chopping block in the front garden. There was no one outside, but taking up his spyglass he could see directly into the front of the cottage through an uncurtained window where he observed some movement. Satisfied his lookout post would provide more than adequate views, he slithered back to his belongings and, dragging them behind him, moved up again to his chosen spot. He anticipated it might be some time before anything happened and was prepared for a long wait.

But luck was with him as within minutes the young girl came out and filled a basket with wood. She had left the door open and for the first time Edgar could see directly into the room beyond. Although his view was limited, he could just make out a central table and the outline of a man. So, there were still just two of them there. He began to consider how they lived. He could see no means of transport and wondered how they managed to get supplies. Someone obviously brought them in. But if they wanted to keep their dealings completely private, then that person must be part of the activities. George had mentioned 'a wife' and, although there was no evidence of her presence now, it was likely she would turn up later in the day. She must be the Fairfax woman Donald Thwaites had identified and Edgar was very impatient to catch sight of her.

In the meantime, the young girl was certainly kept busy hanging out some bits of washing – a man's shirt and women's linen which she draped over the stone wall. She made several trips to the stream and it was obvious that she was responsible for the heavy work, small as she was. The man seemed content to remain idle, puffing on his pipe and resting at the table. Occasionally Edgar imagined he heard the wail of the child again, but the breeze was up and blowing from the west and he could not be sure what he was really hearing on the wind. At midday he took out some food. He was feeling rather cramped, having been stretched out in one position for an hour and was just about to take a break and stretch his legs, chancing that nothing was going to happen at present, when he heard a call and the rumble of wheels.

Moving back to his observation post, he looked across and immediately in his view was a small horse and cart which pulled up at the front gate. The man and girl hurried down the path and round to the back of the cart where they unloaded several sacks and boxes. The driver gave the reins to the man and climbed down off the seat. Edgar could see it was a woman, rather small and dressed quite tidily in a grey coat and bonnet that hid her face. She walked up to the front door, the young girl staggering behind her under the weight of a heavy sack; they both entered the cottage; the man unharnessed the horse and led it round to the back, presumably to tether it. When he returned he took up the remainder of the bundles and followed the woman and girl into the cottage and shut the door behind him. For the present they were out of sight.

Carts and boxes? Edgar cast his mind back to Ambrose's letter and his encounter with the woman on the road on Sunday evening. From what he had said, that cart had been hired. As far as he knew, Ros-

Chapter 9

alie was arranging for it to be taken back to the owner and would try to ascertain who hired it in the first place. Was there a connection between that event and what he was looking at now? Ambrose said the cart was marked with the owner's name: Right's Carts of Halifax. This cart was unmarked on the side – he had a clear view of it. If this was the same woman, then they had been able to find another cart – either bought or hired – essential for where they had sited themselves. He would be interested to hear what Mr Right of Halifax thought about a customer who abandoned one of his vehicles so casually.

He didn't have the same feeling of recognition as Ambrose when he looked at the woman, but his view had been poor and she was muffled in coat and bonnet. If he was patient she might come out, hatless, and then he would possibly see her face. But it was not to be. No one left the building, other than the girl who came out once to get in the washing as it started to drizzle. His optimism about the weather had been misplaced; the clouds swept in and the moorland took on a gloomy dour aspect which increased Edgar's own feeling of chill. By one in the afternoon visibility was poor and the wind had got up and was blowing in a thick mist. Although sheltered behind large boulders, overall he was in an exposed position, on top of the rise with the wind stiffening from the south-west. Badly needing to boost his circulation, he decided to retreat to his hut and have a warm meal. If this weather persisted it would be unlikely any of them would be moving anywhere until it improved. As soon as there was any sign of change he would go back and resume his surveillance.

A couple of hours later, warmed by the fire and some of Hoyles's cook's excellent stew that Peter had brought across in a small churn, Edgar was relieved to see the weather was lifting. Clouds changed from grey to white, and there was a patch of blue sky among them. He picked up his bag and made his way back to his observation spot. He had brought a waterproof to lie on and, as he stretched himself out and observed the cottage through his spyglass he was relieved to see the cart still there. On a long tether, the idling horse had found its way to the side of the building and was happily munching on the rich grasses. His surveillance grew tedious as nothing happened for a couple of hours, when the man reappeared. He found the horse and re-harnessed it to the cart. Edgar held his breath. Would the woman come out to see him off to wherever he was going? His luck was in. At about half past six out of the door came a small, neat-figured woman dressed in a simple grey cloak and bonnet; as she moved he observed she was wearing a black dress with a white starched collar and pristine cuffs; a cloth bag was slung over her shoulder. She was altogether out of place on this wild expanse of moor; her appearance was more suited to a housekeeper from a country house.

With this thought he had an immediate moment of recall; he drew his breath in sharply. Without hesitation, he brought to mind the woman's small, stiff and upright carriage; he had also seen such well-tended linen before. Even lacking a view of her face, he realised who she was. He knew that, if he was here, Ambrose would too.

Chapter 10

It took Peter only half an hour to ride back to Hoyles. He rode as fast as was possible carrying his small helpless bundle which he slung across the saddle and steadied with one arm. Arriving in the stable yard he found the first farmhand available and handed over the lamb with a brief explanation that fitted as near the truth as he could, but did not include Mr Edgar's part in events. The man disappeared with her into the lambing shed and Peter was satisfied that she now had a decent chance of survival. He tied the horse to a rail, unsaddled her and led her into her stable where, before even considering approaching Mr Lawes, he rubbed her down and made sure she was fed and watered. Harry Valentine had taught him well – the animal always came first.

Fifteen minutes later he knocked on the back door of the farmhouse and enquired of the housekeeper if Mr Lawes would see him. George was in his study and the woman led Peter through the kitchen and into the hall. She tapped on the oak door with its shiny brass handle and informed her master that, 'Young Master Samuels would like a word, sir.'

'Come in, come in, boy!' In his customary bluff manner George ushered Peter through the door and pointed to a chair opposite him at the large mahogany desk.

Peter looked around the room which, although evidently a 'book room' for paperwork, was in complete contrast to that of Mr Edgar Lawes's library back at Seddon Hall. Here were business-connected papers, maps and account books – all scattered across the immense old and well-used desk which was, even in the late morning, illuminated by an oil lamp. A large fire burned in the grate and taking pride of place on an armchair by the side of the fireplace was a small, black and half-grown cat curled up asleep. It occurred to Peter that the animal was out of place in such a masculine room. He might have expected a couple of lurchers or gun dogs at least. But it confirmed to him that Mr George Lawes was a man of many facets – bluff and Yorkshire-influenced if not bred, but also cultured and well-read. Perhaps he felt he had much in common with a cat – self-sufficient and calculating, but also home-loving and fastidious.

'Have you news of Mr Lawes? How are things working out at the cottage? I take it you found him in good health?'

'Most certainly, sir! He's coping well.' Peter went on to describe Edgar's success in delivering the lamb and how he had used much initiative to keep the creature alive.

'I know the brand you describe on the animal. I'll contact the owner and see what he wants doing with the carcass. I'll offer to dispose of it as it's on my land. There's no point encouraging prying eyes around the place at this particular moment.'

'We buried it quite deeply, sir – to keep the foxes away.'

'Good. So, tell me what else has happened? You say you left Mr Lawes to find a good surveillance spot and keep watch today? Let's hope the weather holds, although rain will always be with us this time of year. But there's nothing we can do about that! Now, when you return tomorrow ask him to give you a summary of his journal – I know he's keeping one. I want to feel totally up to date with events. I must say, it's more difficult to keep abreast of Mr Hudson's doings, but I hope he sends another letter via John Walters, my delivery man, on Monday at least. In the meantime – how are you getting on with my horses?'

The trick with George was that he could put anyone at ease within a few minutes. Before he knew what was happening, Peter was having a deep exchange of views on the timing of entering young horses for their first race. By the time he left Mr Lawes's study he had extended his equine knowledge considerably.

Mr Lawes's prediction was accurate; the weather didn't bode well early Saturday morning. Loading up his saddlebags with essential provisions, Peter steered his mount out of the stable yard at seven o'clock and took the same route he had used the day before. He was quite confident that he knew the way and for a mile the horse trotted on quite happily. But twenty minutes into the ride the weather suddenly changed. Before he knew it, he was surrounded by dense wet fog. The cloud seemed to have come out of nowhere and visibility was

Chapter 10

less than a foot all round. Unable to guide his horse, Peter found the beast was inclined to turn and find her way home, but he pressed on in hope rather than certainty. Very soon it was apparent he had left the main track and was well and truly lost. The moor was featureless, relentlessly so in the absence of bold landmarks. He had been warned many times by the inhabitants of Hoyles that getting lost was dangerous in the extreme and could happen in a flash. The advice was to find immediate shelter – a tree or building – and sit it out until conditions improved. The worst thing to do was to wander uncertainly; that way generally led to disaster.

He heard the tinkling of water and realised he was adjacent to a stream. If he followed its course downhill he might eventually come to some habitation close to it. At least he could be steered by it.

Fortunately, a sheep track ran parallel to this small singing brook and he walked the horse along it. The presence of dense fog makes estimations of distance almost impossible, but he thought he had covered about a mile before, to his great relief, he came close to a stone wall. Where there was a wall there must be a cottage or hut. Boundary walls were put up for reasons; out on the moors, as he had already observed, boundaries between farms were generally open to allow sheep to wander freely. Farmers were less territorial up here. This wall must signify the boundary to a garden or smallholding. At least it might be a fixture for the sheep to shelter behind, in which case he would use it for that purpose himself. But he really hoped it signified a building and, sure enough, following the line of the wall, soon looming out of the fog he discerned the rectangular outline of a cottage or hut. There was no door and no window, so he surmised he was at the back of it. He guided his mare down the side track that joined to the front path. He dismounted, and holding the reins in his left hand, walked up to the front door which was split in two like stable doors. He gave the top half a sharp knock; it opened and a man poked his head through. Even in the mist, Peter could see he was old – old at least in the eyes of someone of 15 – and looking suspicious and annoyed.

'What d'you want?' was the unpromising response.

'As you can see, I'm off my track. The weather came down on me and I've followed the stream. I'm completely lost. Could I shelter here for a few minutes until the fog lifts? Perhaps you could give me directions back to—'

The man cut in immediately. 'No, no! We can't help you. Way up yonder on the tops is a grove of trees. Wait there until the weather lifts, then you can see the whole of the moor and work out where you are. We don't take to strangers here.'

Peter was nonplussed by the man's response. Surely Yorkshire hospitality was a byword. Since he had left the workhouse he had never been refused help so brusquely. He bristled. 'Where I come from we take pride in helping strangers when they're in trouble.'

'That's as maybe. We don't. Now clear off!'

Peter stood, uncertain what to do. He desperately needed shelter and a drink. The thought of moving out onto the moor again went against all his instincts of survival. Before the old man shut the swinging door, a young girl, who could be no more than 13 or 14, leaned through and peered at him. She looked scared and apprehensive. He was just about to speak to her when there was the faint muffled sound of a horse and wheels and this made her jump and scurry back into the cottage. Someone had arrived. Perhaps he would have more luck with them. The noises of tethering and items being taken down from the back of the cart were followed by the rustle and flapping of clothes as the driver hurried down the path. The fog was such that he couldn't get sight of whoever it was until they were upon him.

It was a woman, and she started violently as she almost collided with his horse. She cussed, 'What the devil's going on? What's a horse doing here?'

Peter came around into her view. 'I'm lost, ma'am. I wanted shelter until the weather changes, but there seems to be a difficulty. The man inside has refused me.' He couldn't see her face as her head was well covered against the drizzle. In turn, she could not make him out either although, as well as conditions would allow, she regarded him carefully.

She seemed to weigh up the situation quickly and to his relief she said grudgingly, 'Tether up your horse; you'd better come in for a while.' As he led the horse away he heard the man protesting, but he

Chapter 10

was sharply rebuked and went quiet. Peter heard her say, 'I've got it! It's in the cart. We'll bring it in later. They paid the money easily enough.'

Peter relieved the horse of the saddlebags and, returning to the front door, knocked politely and pushed it open.

The woman had her back to him and was taking off the waterproof cape which she shook before putting it in front of the fire. From behind he could see she wore a black woollen dress. As she turned he was first aware of a pair of immaculate white cuffs which, despite the saturating weather, she had managed to keep dry. Raising his eyes from her wrists he took in the face above the brilliant white of a starched collar. He could not believe what he saw. His mind went back to the previous year. The last time he had seen this woman she had been running the gauntlet of the female inmates at Seddon workhouse. She had been woman-handled and thrown out of the place. He had an indelible memory of her sitting in the middle of the lane outside the House with her belongings scattered around her, screaming abuse at Mr Lawes and Mr Lake. She was the only woman he had ever feared in his life and now they were face to face. The question was – would Jennie Calman recognise him?

Once the initial shock had passed, Peter's mind immediately moved to how he could manage the inevitable discovery. He knew that Jennie Calman was very sharp and most likely had a good memory – especially of people who might have crossed her in the past. He had intense recollections of the severe punishments he had received in the workhouse at the hands of her husband, at which she had always been present. He had not been cooperative as a young inmate and would surely not be forgotten, although he considered that he had changed physically. He was at least 3 inches taller and had filled out healthily with the improvement in his diet and the routine exercises of physical work. He might get away with his appearance, but it would not be long before memories would be awakened and realisation would dawn on her.

Her initial reaction was one of raw curiosity. 'What are you doing out on the moor in this weather? What do you want?' There was no hint of recognition.

Peter drew a deep breath and, with a great effort, tried to diminish his accent by slowly mumbling.

At first Mrs Calman took his answers at face value; but as she drew him out further a flicker of recollection passed across her face. She frowned as she searched her memory and then everything fell into place. 'My God, it's the brat Samuels – Peter Samuels! How on earth...' Her voice trailed away.

The man looked puzzled. 'D'you know him, then?'

'I certainly do! He was a workhouse bastard. John and I had many a clash with him. He was an awkward little sod – insolent and devious.' They were speaking as though he was not present.

Peter's stomach went into knots as he wondered what was coming – something unpleasant, that was certain. He was not disappointed.

'Why are you here? Who are you with? That's a fine piece of horse-flesh you're riding. You couldn't afford that yourself. Is it stolen? Don't tell me you've taken to horse-thieving? Who does it belong to?'

The questions kept coming and he barely had time to make up his answers. Remembering Mr Hudson's precept that it always pays to tell as much of the truth as possible when living incognito, he said, 'I've been sent here to stay at some racing stables. I'm 'prentice to a racing man near Ipswich. He wants me to visit Wetherby and see how they do things up here. I do remember you from Seddon; I wasn't sure where you and Mr Calman went after...' He trailed off, not wanting to bring up the undignified ending of the Calmans' last day in the institution.

'None of your business! I'm not sure what you're doing here but it seems too much of a coincidence you turning up like this. I don't believe your story; you always were a little liar. Let's have the truth. Someone sent you, didn't they?'

'Of course not! Why would they? I'm as surprised as you that we've met up again like this. I just want some shelter until the weather lifts.'

Jennie Calman looked troubled and then became angry. 'We can't allow that. We have things to do – we're busy people. I've no idea

Chapter 10

how long this fog's going to last. You'll have to find your own way back – the fog will lift sometime. On your way!'

Unceremoniously she picked up his riding coat and saddlebags and thrusting them at him pushed him towards the door. Peter wasn't sorry. He felt he would rather brave the mist of the moors than spend any more time with the woman, who seemed to have lost none of her old vitriol. He stumbled across to a post in the wall where his horse was tethered and, just as he was arranging the saddlebags across her quarters he heard what he thought was the wailing of a bird. But no bird would be close by in this open ground in such weather. They would be seeking shelter in the occasional bushes and rocks. It came again, a thin screech but with a desperation behind it. That was a human cry and from one very young. Although it was muffled by the dense fog, he turned his head towards the direction it seemed to come from. Walking forward, he came to the front path and followed it to the gate. Looming out of the fog he made out the shape of the cart. He could hear the breathing of the horse which was still between the shafts.

The cry came again, nearer and more penetrating, demanding immediate attention. He clambered up onto the back of the vehicle to find sacks and boxes that had yet to be unloaded. As he waited to pinpoint the exact location of the noise, he saw a pale light coming from the cottage as the front door opened. Within seconds the wailing started up again and he could hear it was coming from a small wooden box at the front of the cart. Moving across the bales and packages he took up the box and with ease took off the lid. Even in the extremely poor visibility he could see what it contained. Lying on some straw, covered in a thin cotton sheet, was a naked baby, newly born. Its limbs were flailing and it opened its mouth to cry. Just as he was about to take it out to cradle in his arms, a voice from behind him hissed, 'What are you doing? Give that to me!'

Everything fell into place and Peter suddenly became fiercely angry. He realised what he had accidentally stumbled on – it was Jennie Calman who was running the baby farming and from this very cottage.

'What are you doing with this baby? Why has it been left out here in a box in this weather without clothing? It can't be yours; you're too old to have a baby.'

Whether it was this slighting reference to her age that incited her, or the fact that Peter now had far too much information, the woman snatched the box from him and shouted to the man for help. 'Take him inside and keep him out of the way. Tie him up and, lock him in the back room. I'll have to think what to do with him when this business is over.'

Although Peter was tall and well-built he had not yet the full musculature that a man acquires with age. Also, despite putting up a stout struggle, his position in the cart was such that he didn't have a firm footing and thus the man was able to drag him out and onto the ground where he was more easily overpowered. Pushing him through the front room, the older man nodded to the young girl to open a small door in the back wall. Looking very scared, she held the wooden door open and Peter found himself propelled into an area no bigger than a very large cupboard. Mrs Calman followed them into the cottage carrying the box, which she deposited on the broad table in the main room. While the man pinioned Peter's arms behind his back, she procured some twine and soon he was trussed up at the wrists and ankles and left on the floor. Although there was no lock, the door was firmly shut as they left him there and he heard something being dragged to block it on the other side.

He was relieved he wasn't to be left in total darkness as there was a small window that let in some daylight. Even though the gloom of the fog eliminated a great deal of the natural light, Peter could just about discern his surroundings. He managed to manoeuvre himself into a sitting position and looked around the room. It was empty apart from some rough wooden shelves, wide enough to hold provisions. It had the dimensions of a large walk-in pantry and was clearly used for storage. There was an unpleasant sweetish smell that he could not identify, but could almost taste as it was so strong. On the shelves were three small boxes, all of wood. He felt a chill of horror as he could see they were the same as the box on the cart that had held the baby.

From the other side of the door came a low murmur of voices, with an occasional angry exchange. Sliding on his backside, he moved

Chapter 10

himself close to the door where he could faintly hear what was being said.

'Well, you say he knows you, so what are we going to do with him?' This was clearly from the man.

'First we'll let his horse loose, but not until dark. It'll find its own way back to wherever it came from.'

'What about the saddle? Should we take it off?'

'No, better leave it on – a pity, we could have got some money for it. But better they find the horse riderless; they'll think he's been thrown somewhere.'

'Then they'll send out a search party!'

'So, what of it? The later the horse gets back the later they'll go looking for the boy. This place is well off the main tracks – that's why we chose it. There's no reason for anyone to come here. Even if they do we can disclaim all knowledge of him. By the time the fog lifts and they've discovered he's missing, he'll be untraceable. We'll use our usual method.'

'I don't like it. He might be with someone important – like Lawes, who's a magistrate; he runs racehorses. If there's any chance he could be connected they'll do all they can to find him.'

'You may have a point,' she said. 'There was a Lawes in Seddon and he kept horses. Perhaps they are related and Peter Samuels has been sent up here by Edgar Lawes. I hope that's not the case because that'll make things even more awkward. In fact, we may have to wind up the whole thing and move on when I've done this next bit of business. It's a pity; I've had enquiries from Leeds. There's a lot of money still to be made in this God-forsaken area. Perhaps you should go in and rough him up; find out what you can about what he's really doing here. In the meanwhile, I must go back to town this evening. I've another bit of goods to pick up.'

Peter heard the girl ask, 'What are we to do with that?' He thought she must be indicating the baby.

'Give it some milk to shut it up. I might be in the way of making more cash from this one. I've been given the name of someone who might take it for a price. If that doesn't work out, I'll have to deal with it.'

The man sounded worried. 'With all this going on and us having to cope with the boy, isn't it too risky to carry on?'

'There's a good sum for us from this deal. The girl's expecting me and she's got the money together. This may be the last time here, but we can't afford to throw up the chance of ten pounds. Anyway, for now get on and see what that little bastard next door knows about our business – and find out how he ended up here.'

'All right, if you say so.' But the man still sounded doubtful.

Peter heard movement and he supposed the girl had gone off to carry out the order. At the same time, whatever was blocking the door was moved away and someone pushed it as Peter was leaning against it. There was no point in resisting, so he shuffled out of the way and let the man in. He was evidently going to frighten or beat the truth out of Peter; the question was how much could he withstand? His breaking point had never been tested, although it had been a source of pride with him that he had taken his numerous punishments at the workhouse with equanimity. He waited for what might come.

Chapter 11

Each day Ambrose rose early and presented himself on time and fit for work at the mill. The labour was mundane and mentally unexacting although he used his muscles more than normal and was glad that he had physically prepared himself beforehand. He continued to keep his eyes and ears open. This morning, Thursday, John Walters had passed him a short but informative letter from Edgar giving details of his brief surveillance of Rickard's the previous day. Although there was yet no indication what the young girl and man were about, at last it was clear there was something afoot at the place. Only careful observation would reveal what it was. It appeared that George and his cousin had moved swiftly. Edgar would be taking up residence in an empty and secluded shepherd's hut on George's land and Peter would provide him with provisions daily. Ambrose smiled wryly to himself. It was likely that Edgar's food supplies would be of a considerably better quality than he was enjoying. It was one of the deprivations he felt most keenly when working incognito. Normally he had a large appetite, especially for good red meat. After all, he was an exceptionally tall man who needed fuelling regularly. Weeks living on poor food did him no good at all and it was one of the reasons he was beginning to consider how much longer he could continue working in this way. Still, he didn't begrudge Edgar his three square meals; he was just glad to have his friend with him. Always used to working alone, he now appreciated the companionship and the thought that others were there to back him up in the event of problems.

He had seen Rosalie briefly, but there had been no opportunity to talk. She had been occupied on the weaving floor and there had been no occasion for him to access that area officially. But today, Thursday, his luck had changed and he found her waiting for him outside the mill gates when their shifts had finished. Standing in the shadows of the surrounding buildings, she was barely noticeable until he felt a tug at his sleeve. She put her finger to her lips and beckoned him to follow her down a narrow entry between a set of terraced houses. The crowd of workers moved as one in the direction of the town, all with the same intent – to get out of the mill as fast as possible to destinations of home or tavern. They paid no heed to Ambrose or Rosalie as the pair walked single file to the end of the entry which joined another in a maze of small muddy alleyways. Leading the way, she walked confidently in the light of dusk to the end of a passage that led out onto a field. Crossing the damp pasture, they came to an old tree where she indicated they should stop.

Ambrose laid down his jacket and they sat side by side in silence for a while. Rosalie turned to face him and Ambrose took in her dark eyes with their finely arched eyebrows. Once again, he noted the tension in her face, but that still could not conceal its fine symmetry. In that regard, she reminded him of Emily Alfrey, the widow of his friend Richard who had hanged himself in Seddon workhouse the previous year. Her beauty had attracted the worst kind of attention from a vicious scoundrel, but one who had eventually met his just deserts.

'Ambrose, I've found out the name of the woman who hired the cart. My neighbour kindly returned it to Right's yard in Halifax on Monday evening after work. I told him it had been left on the lane outside our cottage. As you can imagine the owner was furious but glad to have the vehicle and animal back.'

'Did he give the neighbour any idea who hired it?' asked Ambrose.

'It was our friend Mrs Fairfax who told Rodney Right she was from Bradford.'

Ambrose stiffened. This news bore out his suspicion about the woman he had seen. Mrs Fairfax had taken Meg Foley's baby – Janet Stow had been clear about that.

Rosalie continued. 'It seems she hired the vehicle in early February and there'd been no trouble up to then. She'd paid him three months in advance and he'd heard no more of her since.'

'He must have got an address from her.'

'It was a house in a decent part of Bradford, I understand. She was quite well spoken and neatly dressed and he took her on face value, although the payment in advance probably settled it as far as he was concerned. I've asked around and there's no such number in that street in Bradford.'

'I'm surprised he didn't question why she would hire a cart from

Chapter 11

Halifax. There are plenty of places in Bradford. Also – wasn't he curious as to what she would use it for?'

'I think Mr Right is like any other businessman. When cash is on offer it's unwise to question the customer's business. Anyway, she'd paid him more than he would have to pay to replace either the hack or the cart, which were neither best quality. But he was very grateful to get them both back almost in one piece. The traces had come apart, but otherwise there was no harm done. One of the reasons my neighbour was able to get the information out of him was because he wanted to thank the man for his trouble.'

'Rosalie, this is the evidence we need. It puts the woman in the vicinity of Rickard's cottage as your brother had already discovered. Now we can safely assume there's a direct link between the woman driving the cart – Mrs Fairfax – and the baby farming. You remember I told you on Sunday at the church, when I was visiting the Stows Janet Stow described how they'd contacted a woman by the name of Fairfax who'd offered to take the newly born baby of Meg Foley – that's Janet's niece.'

'Yes, and I wasn't surprised.'

'It seems the woman's been very busy. According to Janet Stow she told them she was running quite a large operation and had several babies to care for. She said she used local girls to help her and had many satisfied mothers who were grateful for the care she gave their infants.'

Rosalie was silent for a moment, then she asked, 'Are you saying that the box that she took up in such haste from the cart might have contained...' Her voice trailed off.

'I'm almost certain of it. She was very anxious to get whatever it was away. If it was an infant, it'll be very hard to find out whose it is. Do you remember in your brother's letter to me he mentioned that he thought the baby farming and the illegal employment of little children were run by an organised gang? Although he didn't have their names, I've been looking out for likely men. Sizewell's definitely implicated and must be linked to Fairfax – Jed Stow identified him as the go-between.'

'He's a nasty piece of work and one of those I think was involved in the cover-up of my brother's death, if not the perpetrator.'

He could hear the anger in her voice, although in the gathering gloom he could not see her expression. 'I've not forgotten your brother's murder. I'll do everything I can to find out more. I must be very discreet at this stage because I can't afford to arouse suspicion, but some of the workers I see regularly are beginning to open up to me, like Jed Stow.'

'So, what's your next move?'

'To try to discover who exactly Mrs Fairfax is. We know where she's operating from. Edgar may have some more information by now from his observations at Rickard's. I feel things are starting to come together, but we must be careful. You mustn't get involved. The fact that these people killed Donald and then ransacked his rooms show how desperate they are. They may try again to find out what you might know.'

'If it'll help, I could ride over to Hoyles and see if there's any news from Edgar. There'll be no more messages via Mr Lawes's delivery man. He's made his scheduled delivery today and won't be back until Monday. We need information before then.'

'Perhaps.' Ambrose was unwilling to put her to any trouble – especially as she had her father to look after as well as her long hours in the mill. 'It's a difficulty not having regular contact, but I'm sure if Edgar had any further news he would use all means possible to get it to me. I'm more interested in what Mrs Fairfax will do next. The fact that she has contacts in the town shows she'll be back again before long. I'll keep my eyes open for her. There's a chance Meg Foley might have heard something from her, although I'm not getting my hopes up. But tomorrow's payday and there'll be plenty of activity at the mill, people moving around to collect their money. Besides, as I said, I've become more trusted and the workers are less suspicious of me when I get them into conversation. I'll seek Janet out and see what she knows. I'll keep Sizewell well in my sights too.' He took her hand. 'As for you, please don't take any risks. You've first-hand experience of the ruthlessness of these people. I couldn't bear to think of you in any danger.'

Chapter 11

She made no attempt to remove her hand; instead she allowed him to hold it even tighter.

He continued, encouraged. 'Rosalie, when this is all over might we – might I – call on you as a...'

'Friend, lover?' She laughed. 'There's no need to sound so awkward. You may have an experienced way with the written word, but you're no use at paying court. I like you very much, Ambrose, and I'll certainly consider what you say, but for the moment I want to concentrate on bringing my brother's murderers to justice. When we have achieved that, well – we'll see! I'll meet you here tomorrow evening; I expect you're running out of provisions.' She fell silent and looked away awkwardly. Then she turned back and gave him such a smile his heart thumped in his chest for a few seconds. A very new experience for him!

As he continued to hold her hand he felt its roughness from persistent heavy work. He said, 'Provisions are the least of my reasons for wanting to see you tomorrow!' Slightly more encouraged than he was a few moments before, he gently squeezed that hand before he let go; he almost kissed it, but something made him hold back. Was it shyness or awkwardness? Whatever it was, the moment was lost – to his immediate regret.

They walked back to the darkening maze of passageways between the mean houses at the back of the town and separated – he to the right, she to the left, both deep in thoughts unconnected with their original reasons for meeting.

Back in his lodgings and after his usual frugal and monotonous meal, Ambrose lay on his narrow bed, hands behind his head, and mulled over the events of the evening. He tried to push the most important development to the back of his mind – the encouragement Rosalie may, or may not, have given him to pursue his intentions more openly – and forced himself to consider the information that was mounting concerning the events of the past few days. He was now certain the Fairfax woman was implicated in the baby farming and that Sizewell was acting as a go-between for her with the local women, but he needed hard evidence.

Thinking about Sizewell, he recollected that the man swaggered around the mill with an irritating insouciance. If he fell short of having the deeds of the mill in his bank, he certainly acted as though he had. His power over the workers was absolute and it was the fault of the owner that this was tolerated. Samuel Richmond inclined to let his manager Sizewell have a free hand as long as production was pushed to the limit and the profits rolled in uninterrupted. The unwritten triangular contract between the owner, the manager and the workers was almost feudal in its operation, but with none of the *noblesse oblige* expected of the few in control of the many. At its base, the workers had no redress of their conditions, could make no complaint without risk of dismissal. The manager and overseers, as intermediaries, held the structure firm and employees in check with threats and physical violence on occasions, but always with the power to end employment and thus condemn to starvation those who were brave enough to complain. Perched comfortably at the top of this arrangement, Mr Richmond sat back, drawing on the profits for a good living for himself and his family. If he was a prudent businessman he would plough some of them back into the business.

Ambrose came to the same conclusion as always: that fundamental to the financial success of the whole industrial process was the overabundance of labour; it was a buyer's market. Individually a man couldn't make a difference because he wouldn't take the risk of losing his job through lone protest. Granted, on rare occasions some had tried. In Dorset five years previously six labourers had been sentenced to seven years' transportation each for the illegal administering of oaths to fellow members of a union set up to seek better wages and conditions.

But during the years immediately following those harsh penalties things were starting to move. Just three years ago in 1836 the newly founded London Working Men's Association began agitating for political and social rights. Two years later saw the launch of the People's Charter, as it had become known, the association's petition to parliament which, among other fundamental points, demanded universal male suffrage and secret ballots. This year, two months before Ambrose had left London for Suffolk, the first Chartist convention had met, and he was in the city as demands for improved political rights increased. Rumour and gossip fuelled agitation and there was always the fear that the more volatile working men, who were in no mood for peaceful protest as a route to reform, would not be contained.

His editor James McNiece erred on the side of caution where revolution was concerned. Like Edgar Lawes, he thought progress should evolve. 'This Charter movement's spreading. I hear it's started up in Manchester and Glasgow, and Birmingham's Political Union has revived and is gearing itself up for a fight. I can only see it all ending in trouble. The government's bound to clamp down and bring in a set of draconian laws to curtail it all.'

Despite his editor's caution, Ambrose's experience told him that this was only the precursor to greater and more universal pressure for reform and he determined in the future to try to record it as it happened. During January, a particularly exciting development for him as a journalist was the launch of the *Charter* newspaper, which was to be the published mouthpiece of the London Working Men's Association; he had a treasured copy of the first edition. The launch of this new political weekly was but one of a series of radical broadsheets that had been appearing and as quickly disappearing over the previous six years. But McNiece's dire warning of punitive action by parliament was confounded when the government made the decision in 1836 to reduce the stamp duty on papers.

Ambrose was cock-a-hoop. 'This'll give a massive boost to our circulation. We must grab the opportunity to get the *Escritoire* out to as wide an audience as possible.'

As his mind continued wandering among the printing presses of London, he wondered whether business at the *Escritoire* would boom, particularly in the light of this increased agitation for reform which was dependent on the press for dissemination of new and progressive ideas. His paper must surely become more deeply involved, but he wondered again if McNiece had the stomach for a change of emphasis. The editor considered himself somewhat of an old Scots radical; he was a great admirer of his compatriot, the enlightened David Hume. But his canny business instincts told him that 'real life' was what sold journals, and that was why he made no dissent, indeed positively encouraged his chief journalist to take weeks away from the office with no contact and no certainty that there would be a story to publish. Ambrose admired McNiece for his faith in him, but knew he had delivered in the past and that his exposure of illegality and inhuman treatment of workers and their families did in its small way contribute to social justice and, from McNiece's practical standpoint, improved the paper's circulation. In fact, sales rose considerably when it was put abroad that Ambrose Hudson had new sets of outrages to reveal. 'McNiece won't be disappointed this time,' he thought to himself, 'baby farming is a barbarous act and particularly rife in the capital.'

However his editor was getting on in years and must soon be thinking of retirement. Although the Scot had always maintained he lived for his work, he couldn't go on indefinitely. There was a tacit understanding between the two men that Ambrose would take the paper over when McNiece had decided he'd had enough and was prepared to re-enter, if somewhat reluctantly, the bosom of his family.

Pondering on family brought him directly to his intentions towards Rosalie. Was he really thinking of asking her to marry him? In the past, women acquaintances had considered him a catch and most certainly wouldn't have turned him down; but none of them seemed to share a passion for his kind of politics. Besides, his way of life was inconsistent with the stability needed for a strong marriage. He was more often away than at home and, up to this point, he doubted any woman he would want to marry would put up with that for long. Now for the first time, despite their brief acquaintance, he felt he had met a woman whose intelligence and integrity shone through and one who would understand and share his political motivation.

'But how could we manage a marriage?' he asked himself. 'Would she be prepared to move to London? What of her father? He's old and frail and it's unlikely she'd suggest he should move with her. Yet she would never leave him behind. Does that mean I must give up the idea of a future with Rosalie? Perhaps if I wait a while, Mr Thwaites, who's old and ill, might not be long for this world and then his daughter would be free.'

Immediately ashamed of this thought, Ambrose wondered if he

Chapter 11

could find work with a newspaper in Leeds or Bradford. But a part of him dismissed this immediately. His roots were in London; that was where the action was and where influence could be applied. Besides, he had painstakingly developed a reputation for writing with integrity and honesty and was now increasingly listened to by those with influence and power. Burying himself for ever in the north would be a mistake.

Despite these obstacles, he nevertheless began to imagine their life together in London. Mrs Bridie – his landlady – had spare rooms available and, combined with his own quarters they would make a substantial enough living space for them both, and possibly a family. The question was, would she accept him if – when – he asked her? 'This won't do!' he thought. 'I'm running before my horse to market,' and with that he came full circle, horses, carts bringing him back to the woman in the lane – Mrs Fairfax. But before he began to go over the same ground again he forced himself to close his eyes, and with a picture of Rosalie in his mind, with her hand in his, he attempted to sleep; but it would not come. After an hour of tossing and turning he came to the conclusion that he must be 'in love'.

'Is this what it feels like? Becoming obsessed with a woman to the point that I can't wait until we next meet? Damnation! I've only known her a few days. How can this possibly happen to me – a dyed-in-the-wool bachelor with no experience of woman, other than the good Mrs Bridie. How can this be resolved?' And his mind wandered for a further hour on the problems such a situation would entail. Finally he drifted off and dreamed he was having an intimate discussion with his Scots landlady, seeking her advice on matters that were making her blush.

Waking at his usual time, just as dawn was breaking, he stretched his long legs as far as possible without falling off the low bed and, hastily putting aside the embarrassment of his imagined conversation with Mrs Bridie, contemplated the day to come. Friday was wages day and he could look forward to collecting a pittance for almost 80 hours' labour this week. He estimated he would receive between six and seven shillings, as the rate for general labourers in this small town was a shilling a day, lower than in London where it could rise to 1s.

6d. Under normal circumstances Ambrose earned many more times as much money as his fellow labourers – and could enjoy it for himself alone.

However, what exercised his mind most this morning was how to approach Janet Stow without causing suspicion, especially from her husband. He knew she was no longer working at the mill, but she had told him how, as well as sometimes collecting her girls, she always attended the wages payout to ensure the children were paid their dues and to collect the meagre sums they had earned. In that way, she could be sure of getting her hands on the money before her husband bullied them into handing it over for drink. Then there was Tom Sizewell. Pieced together, the small pieces of intelligence coming from Edgar and Rosalie, plus the character references given by a few factory hands he had spoken to during the past week, had provided promising evidence that the man was certainly mixed up in excessive gambling, drinking and dog fighting. Ambrose determined he would endeavour to follow up these leads somehow. Perhaps he would find out where Sizewell went after work.

Following a suspect was a skill he had long ago mastered. The crowded streets of a small town provided as many door- and alleyways to dodge into as a large city, and there was less likelihood of getting separated from the quarry. Ambrose had worried at first that his height might be a disadvantage. He was not someone who could easily merge into the crowd, but he had learned to stoop and shuffle along, with his head bent and eyes downcast, never meeting anyone's gaze. Dressed in the uniform grey of the factory labourer he could make himself as invisible as everyone else. With that thought he pulled on his shabby clothes, splashed his face in cold water, took a hunk of bread with a small piece of meat, and set off for Richmond Mill.

There was a change of atmosphere about the place: a degree of expectation and relief was in the air which came straight from the desperation of being short of money for days. He joined in the game of anticipating what would be handed out from the piles of coins on the big table and how it might be spent, if there was any left to spend

Chapter 11

after the necessities; the wise always budgeted for those first, while the feckless had different priorities. There was a shrewd and calculated scrupulousness in getting a whole week's work out of his labourers before the owner parted with a single penny from his profits. Collecting wages was a disruption to production; better it was done in the workers' time at the end of the day.

Ambrose worked steadily through the hours. He didn't catch a glimpse of Rosalie as he had hoped to do, being kept busy in the loading bay with fresh deliveries of fleeces. When the evening whistle blew at the end of the shift there was a surge of eager movement to queue at the steps to the first floor where Sizewell and a clerk would distribute the wages. It seemed to be a human instinct to try to get to the front, almost as though the money might run out and there would be a cry of 'too late' if one was unfortunate enough to be shunted to the end of the queue. But all the wages were minutely docketed in the account ledger. Fines for absence, lateness or careless work were carefully deducted from the final tally. Ambrose was in no hurry since Sizewell wouldn't be leaving the premises until his responsibilities were over and the last man, woman and child were paid.

Instead he watched out for Janet Stow's appearance through the gates against the tide of people returning down the stairs to the loading bay and exiting from the factory. Some hurried with the money clenched in their fists, perhaps to a rendezvous with a creditor, or to the tavern to slake a desperate need for alcohol. Others, women mostly, waited for members of their family and, holding out their hands, took the few hard-earned coins from their children who reacted with emotions ranging from reluctance to resignation – sometimes defiance and refusal which would generate a public argument. Just occasionally a woman would approach her husband and he would sheepishly hand over the contents of his pockets, to his chagrin and the derision of his colleagues. This was generally considered bad form by both sides. Sensible women didn't humiliate their menfolk in this way; rather they should settle their demands privately as they walked out together and before the men reached their tavern of choice.

Then he saw her coming in to wait at the foot of the stairs. He took his chance and stepped up alongside her. 'Good evening, Janet. Best day of the week!'

She looked pale and weak, a face permanently sculpted with worry lines. There was no hint of immediate recognition, let alone a smile.

'It's Frank Barrett. I came to see you the other evening – brought your husband home.'

'Ah, yes, I remember.'

'I thought a lot about your niece and her problems.'

'Why? What's there to interest you?'

'Nothing – except it seemed a sad story, a mother parted from her newborn.'

'It's life round here; happens all the time.'

'Have you heard anything from the woman who's looking after the baby, and about how she is?' He tried to sound casual.

She was defensive. 'We didn't expect to. My niece can always collect her if she raises enough money to pay the woman off. Anyway, I'm sure the child's well looked after. We paid enough, after all.'

'She seems to deliver a good service. I expect she has plenty of mothers on her books who need to have their children looked after,' he commented soothingly.

'Not so many as you'd think; she charges too much. Most can't afford it; it's only those with a real problem – like my niece – who are forced to get the money together. She would've liked to keep the baby, but it was impossible. In fact, there's someone else in the same position in the next street to ours. Someone told me she was in trouble like my niece and had been put on to Mrs Fairfax.'

Ambrose was immediately alert. Had this transaction taken place, or was it in the offing? He asked her casually if she knew when the pick-up was to be.

'I've no idea. I don't really know the family well, just heard the rumour.'

After days trawling for small gobbets of information, here was something he could really work on. If the story was true, it was certain that the safety of this baby could now rest with Edgar and himself. Somehow it had to be rescued, but that might mean that part of the investigation would be exposed, and what would become of their

Chapter 11

enquiries into Donald Thwaites's murder, and the employment of young children, which were all surely connected? Yet he could never contemplate sacrificing a tiny infant even in order to bring all the perpetrators to justice later.

Fortunately for his purposes the queue had been slow, and he had been able to press Janet Stow for as much information as he needed. But their conversation was cut short as she waved her hand at three tiny figures running towards the gates. 'Here are my girls. I must make sure they give me their money before Jed can get to them.' And she called out to three small, underfed and ill-clothed children who ran to her.

Seeing a stranger with their mother, the smallest hid her face in her mother's skirts. The other two, looking sullen and tired, grabbed her hands and placed the few coins they had earned in them. 'Here you are, Ma,' said one. 'Da didn't get it this time.'

'You're a good girl, Annie. Perhaps there'll be a treat for you later. Now let's get home and put supper on. We'll have ours long before your father gets home.'

Bidding them goodnight, Ambrose watched as the little group shuffled off through the archway and then turned towards the stairs. Almost last in the thinning queue, he soon stood before the large deal table where he faced Sizewell and a small bald man, the office clerk. Removing his cap, Ambrose bent his head and tried to look respectful.

The clerk looked up and asked, 'Name?'

'Barrett, Frank , sir.'

The man ran his finger down the ledger and turned the page.

'Last in, so last entry,' Ambrose thought.

'General labourer, Mr Sizewell; has done seven full days and a half. By my reckoning that should be 7s. 11d.'

'Not late then?'

'No. On time every day.'

Sizewell grunted and looked up at Ambrose. His little bloodshot and rat-like eyes scrutinised him from top to toe. 'Oh yes, I took you on last week. You seem to have been satisfactory.'

'Will there be a chance of work next week, sir?' Ambrose asked.

'Probably, but I'm not promising. Come back tomorrow and I'll see. Here's your money.' He pushed across some coins which Ambrose scooped up and put in his pocket. 'Don't spend it all at once. There might not be any next week.'

Ambrose replaced his cap, touched it to the pair and walked back down the stairs. By the time he arrived in the yard the excited stream of humanity had all but dispersed into the town. The last of the queue had been dealt with and Ambrose waited for Sizewell to appear. Hiding himself behind the wall of the factory, Ambrose manoeuvred his position for a good view of the gates. Sizewell would have money in his pockets tonight and like any other man who forgot about or deliberately ignored his responsibilities to his family he would probably be in the mood to spend it. Ambrose wanted to ascertain who he would spend it with.

It was almost half an hour before the man appeared with a couple of others and they swung through the iron gates out onto the road. The streets were busy; shops were open in the expectation of especially good business tonight. Walking purposefully, the three men quickly covered the ground to the centre of town where they entered a large ale-house which was crowded with men, and some women, all with the same idea: to get as much liquor inside them in the shortest time possible. Children ran in and out getting in the way, regularly cussed and boxed round the ears as they invariably tripped up people carrying precious mugs of ale. Sizewell and his party pushed their way into the front parlour which was packed with workers. Ambrose saw immediately that his plan to get close enough to overhear any conversation was impossible, but he had an alternative up his sleeve. He would wait until Sizewell was drunk and incapable, as he surely would be by the end of the night, and then, companionably, he would offer to buy more drinks. That way he might ingratiate himself with the man and strike up an acquaintance that could be carried further during the next week.

But his second plan became redundant too. Squashed into a corner and nursing a single mug of ale, after half an hour Ambrose was beginning to regret the whole venture. But it was not his way to give up and later he was very glad he had not. He had a good view of the door and the comings and goings. The entrance was crowded as peo-

Chapter 11

ple spilled out onto the street, but then, determinedly pushing her way through the crowd, was none other than the woman with the cart. He recognised her neat clothing and distinctive bonnet.

But this time he also had a full view of her face. Fortunately, she was staring directly ahead of her and he caught her profile, but the sharp set of her face was unmistakable. Recognition was followed by a thrill of horror. No wonder he had thought there was something familiar about the silhouette he had seen in the lane. Last time he had seen Mrs Jennifer Calman she was grieving for her reprobate brother, Robert Enderby, who had been gruesomely killed by person or persons unknown and whose body was found in one of the pigsties of the Seddon Union workhouse. Forced to leave, she had been unceremoniously driven out of the establishment by a posse of angry women who perceived that she had been party to his hideous treatment of some of the female inmates there, even encouraging her husband's cruelty to the inmates. What had happened to her afterwards was a mystery, but it appeared that, somehow, she had ended up in Yorkshire and was certainly mixed up in a very grim business. The question was, had she collected her latest victim yet? Mrs Stow had been uncertain when the transaction would take place. He fervently hoped it had not yet occurred.

Then the proof he needed to link Sizewell and Calman became evident. She pushed her way to where the three men were standing and took Sizewell's arm. He seemed unsurprised to see her and Ambrose surmised that they had already arranged to meet here. The place was packed and noisy and he dared not move too close and therefore couldn't overhear what was being said. He did see Sizewell hand money to her which she put in a small cloth bag hanging over her shoulder. She seemed to turn down the offer of a drink and as soon as the cash was safely stored she turned around and made her way back to the door. This time Ambrose had moved to where he could get a full view of her face. Such was her intent to leave the ale-house as quickly as possible that she was unaware of his scrutiny, although they were at one point within touching distance of each other. Ambrose thought the woman looked older, more lined and careworn than the last time he had seen her. Then she had been a woman with status, although not respected so much as feared by the inmates. She always held herself stiff and upright, the thin lips unsmiling and the brown eyes darting hither and yon looking for any mischief or misdemeanour that required correction with the harsh methods common to the workhouse.

It occurred to him that there would be more point in following her than staying to watch Sizewell and his cronies getting steadily more drunk, so he went outside. To his disappointment he saw her retrieving a horse and trap from a small boy who was minding it. She tossed him a coin and clambered up and was off before the boy could pick it up. Even with a fleeting glance, to his great relief he could see the cart was empty. But perhaps she was on her way to pick up the baby. It was clear that she hadn't meant to stay; the meeting was simply to collect money from Sizewell. What their relationship was exactly Ambrose had no way of telling. Where was Mr John Calman? After the affair at Seddon they had both disappeared, some said to America, others to various parts of England. She had always been the driving force in the marriage; he was a weak bully but totally dominated by her. In her turn, she was heavily influenced by her brother and apparently took his loss very badly. How she had arrived in Yorkshire was a puzzle. Perhaps she had relatives here who had taken her in after the Seddon business. They had left the place with nothing but the clothes they stood in. But here she was, operating an iniquitous activity, either with or without her husband. From what he had been told by Mrs Stow, she was very much active in the wider area of West Yorkshire. No wonder she needed an isolated base like Rickard's from which to run her business.

He turned back to the inn and decided not to waste the evening; he would resort to his previous plan and try to strike up an acquaintance with Tom Sizewell. As he predicted, the man was already partly inebriated. His two fellows were matching him pint for pint and the three were in that state of drunkenness where the conventions of normal conversation give way to free-for-all speech, either the boastful or the argumentative. Ambrose noticed that one of Sizewell's companions was examining his pockets as though looking for his money. It was soon obvious to the man that he had run out and he signalled to

Chapter 11

Sizewell that he would be leaving after he had finished his pint. The third man quickly drank up and made a move to the door as though relieved he had been given an excuse to depart. Sizewell remonstrated and seemed to offer to replenish their pots, but both had had enough and, shaking their heads in refusal, pushed their way through the crowd to the exit.

Seizing his chance, Ambrose moved into the space they had left next to his quarry. Seeing Sizewell had almost finished his pint Ambrose said, 'Here! Let me fill you up.'

Looking suspiciously at him through bloodshot squinting eyes, Sizewell slurred grudgingly, 'Thanks, do I know you?'

'You took me on last week; this is just a way of thanking you. I was desperate for the job.'

The man looked Ambrose up and down. 'I remember – tall feller – big hands and feet; caught a bale one-handed. Will you be back next week?'

'Will there be a job next week?'

'Keep buying me pints and there will be!'

'It's a good job you've got,' observed Ambrose casually. 'I'd like to get to that position myself sometime.'

Gratified at the envy, Sizewell became more amicable. 'There are ways and means. You must learn to accommodate the owners, do what they want. It's all about profit, nothing else matters.'

'The mill must give a lot of employment for folks hereabouts; but I guess there's nothing much else. It seems to have brought people in from everywhere. Look at me – I travelled up from Oxford to work here; seems to me there must be a danger of not enough work if there are too many people looking for it.'

'Well, that's what makes the mill a profit. There's always someone looking for work who'll take any wages going. The trouble is most of them have big families, lots of brats to feed. That means we can drive down the wages to the nearest penny we can get away with. They never complain.'

'I hear that in some towns workers are getting together to ask for better pay and conditions. I don't see that here.' Ambrose was aware he was moving into dangerous territory, but felt it was worth it to raise the discussion to the more serious subject of the mill's policy on hiring and firing.

'We're safe from that here. This is a small town and the owners and managers know all the scallywags and troublemakers. We make sure they're never taken on. Any rabble-rousing Chartists and radicals are given short shrift. No – we don't get much trouble, not like they do in Manchester and the big towns. If word gets out they're in our district I've some useful men who'll take care of them. What about another pint? My pot's empty.'

Ambrose obliged and then took a second chance. 'Do you have any trouble with these new inspectors? The bosses down in Oxford weren't happy about letting them in, but there was nothing they could do. The law's the law, I suppose.'

'They turn up here occasionally. We always know when they're coming so we can have the place shipshape. It's the little bastards that cause us the problem. We have to make sure they're all over nine years old now – can't take on anyone younger.' Whether it was the drink, or Ambrose's expression, innocent yet attentive as though he were hanging onto every word Sizewell uttered, the man was becoming more loose-tongued by the minute. 'Sometimes the odd one slips through; there's no way to tell how old they are.'

Ambrose resisted the impulse to remind the man about the possibilities of the new birth certificates and simply nodded encouragingly. 'I suppose you need the really small ones for the scavenging work. We had them down in Oxford and there was really no other way to keep the machines moving; we had to send them in to clean up the jennies.'

'That's it. It's all mutual – we need the little tykes and their parents need the money. Everyone's happy. I can't see what the fuss is about; those Londoners interfering with business. The government's happy enough to take our money in taxes and then goes and passes laws that try to stop us making profits. Still, there're ways round it.' He slurred to a halt as though he realised he might have said too much.

Ambrose stayed silent in hopes of a substantial revelation, but nothing was forthcoming. By now Sizewell was very much the worse for drink and Ambrose was running out of cash. It appeared they would soon part company.

Chapter 11

He tried one more ploy: 'I've got a friend who's got several children, just moved here from outside Harrogate. He's looking to get them employed – would there be any chance at Richmond?'

'Maybe, I can't promise, depends how things are next week. Brats are always needing to be replaced for one reason or another. Mention it on Monday.'

Ambrose had to be satisfied and Sizewell retreated into his pint, supping it in silence. Within 10 minutes they had both decided they'd had enough and pushed their way together through the door. Sizewell tottered slightly as he was confronted with a draught of cool April night air. As though Ambrose had not existed the man didn't attempt to say goodnight, but swung unsteadily down the street and quickly disappeared among the crowds in the thoroughfare. Ambrose thought it was unnecessary to follow him; he had just about squeezed all the information he could hope for from the man; where he lived was immaterial to his immediate purpose, especially as Sizewell was in no condition to do anything other than sleep off the drink.

With his mind in a fervour of activity he made his way back to Mrs Jolly's lodging house and immediately set out paper and pen to write a letter to Edgar. It was important that his friend was informed that their old adversary Jennie Calman was on the scene and deeply involved with one of the mill's overseers. Janet Stow's information had confirmed that Mrs Fairfax, as she styled herself, was active and had negotiated a deal with the mother of another child. If anyone was to prevent the potential tragedy of a child murder it would have to be his friend. With Edgar's status as a magistrate, he could legitimately approach the inhabitants of Rickard's to search the place and rescue the child, if it was not too late. Surely, she would not dispose of the infant immediately she collected it; she must take it to Rickard's as somewhere isolated to do with it whatever she did – he dreaded to think of it. She must have a routine in these matters. Perhaps she'd come back into town to meet Sizewell after she'd left the baby at the cottage with her accomplices.

How to get the letter to Edgar in the shortest possible time was a problem. He couldn't leave the lodging house tonight – the inhabitants were all locked in by ten o'clock and short of risking life and limb climbing two storeys down the rickety pipework he couldn't get out of the building. Instead he decided to rise before dawn and walk to Rosalie's cottage with a letter to Edgar which he'd ask her to deliver. It would mean she'd lose half a day's pay, but he would make it up to her eventually. He couldn't afford any absence since he was on daily rate and could be laid off immediately. It was not the time to be away from Sizewell and the mill.

He spent the next hour writing a covering note to George and a letter to Edgar minutely detailing all he had found out, and the likely movements of Jennie Calman. It occurred to him that his friend might have already recognised the woman as he was observing the cottage where she had her base. Had she seen him? Had his cover been compromised? Rosalie was his only hope; it was important that she agree to ride to Hoyles in the morning. He estimated that she would arrive there before eight o'clock if she left her cottage immediately she received the letters from him. George Lawes would take control and then ride over to Edgar and deliver the news. It would be up to the two magistrates to work out how to proceed. Both men, he reckoned, would be robust in their response.

To settle his racing mind, he stirred himself to take his weekly bath and have a shave. The effort of filling the copper with water from the street pump, heating it and then toiling up and down the stairs with jugs of it was extremely tedious and took him a couple of hours, but it kept him physically occupied and the result was worth it. Feeling a great deal fresher and tidier, he had something to eat before stretching himself out on his bed and trying to force sleep. But he had a sleepless night and was up by four o'clock. He knew the bolts would not be drawn on the front door until then, so he was dressed and in the front hall as Mr Jolly opened up the place.

'Up early, Mr Barrett.'

'I need to be at work as soon as I can – I want to show willing.'

'Well, I dare say they'll be impressed, if that's what you want.' He opened the door and Ambrose walked out into the dark.

It was drizzling and cloudy and looked as though the weather would be foggy when daylight arrived. He walked briskly the 2 miles

Chapter 11

to Rosalie's cottage and, arriving in 30 minutes, knocked urgently on her door.

A dog barked from within and soon her voice called through the door, 'Who is it?'

'It's Ambrose. I need to speak to you urgently. Please let me in, I'm wet and cold.'

She unlocked the door and he wiped his feet as he went into the main room. She took his coat and went to the dead ashes in the hearth and brought the fire to life with some kindling.

'This is an unexpected pleasure.' She smiled. She had a woollen shawl over her nightdress and her dark hair was unbound. You catch me out, Ambrose. I'm not dressed for visitors.'

'I've much to tell you and I need you to do something for me.' He then proceeded to recount all the events of yesterday, and his discoveries. 'Will you ride over to Hoyles this morning and deliver a note to Mr George Lawes and ask him to arrange for this letter to be sent immediately to Mr Edgar Lawes in his refuge? I know it's asking much to lose half a day's pay, but I promise I'll recompense you for any loss.'

'Ambrose, of course I'll do it; you don't have to sound so formal. A half a day's pay's nothing when we're considering matters of life and death. The woman's beyond salvation to be murdering babies. Until my brother had his suspicions I'd never heard of such things, and to contemplate a woman being involved was almost too much to believe. I'll dress and ride over to Hoyles. Edgar will get his letter as soon as possible – I'll take it to him myself if necessary.'

'I don't want you involved in any of this,' said Ambrose sharply. 'Leave it to the magistrates, please.' He handed her the packet of letters and, suddenly feeling tired and dispirited, he sat down on her father's fireside chair and put his head in his hands.

'But, before I set out for Hoyles, I'll get you something to eat. You need warming up with some hot food. A few minutes is neither here nor there,' she said firmly.

He watched her as she moved gracefully round the room preparing eggs and tea. He said, 'It would be pleasant if on just one occasion we could spend time together openly.' He hesitated. 'There are things I'd like to talk to you about – about our future...' And his voice tailed away.

Rosalie was more robust. 'Our future? You've moved along considerably since we last met. Then we were only just deciding whether we were friends or lovers!'

'I didn't want to seem presumptuous. Look, there are many things I want to do in my life, and I've just discovered being with you is one of them. That wasn't very well put – what I mean is, you have become my priority. You must forgive me, it's five in the morning, I've had no sleep, and we're in the middle of a serious business. I've never been able to make pretty speeches no matter what time of day, but you can be sure, however it comes out, my intentions are – are—'

She broke in. 'It's very early – and soon – for a proposal, if that's what this is; and certainly too early and too soon for a response. I promise, by the end of this business I'll give you an answer. I don't want to sound discouraging, but there'll be many questions I'll have to put to you before I make up my mind. In the meantime, you must be making your way to the mill; the six o'clock whistle will have gone before you arrive unless you leave now.' She was right.

'I hope to have found out as much as there is to know about the Fairfax woman and her latest victim. I've decided to watch Sizewell's movements again this evening. Perhaps the woman will return and seek him out once more. I'll come back early Sunday morning to exchange news of progress and perhaps to receive an answer to that most important question.'

Rosalie nodded slowly and then said, 'Please be very careful. I know you're skilled in the art of surveillance, but this woman is, as you have already told me, ruthless in the extreme and she's not remained undiscovered without significant intelligence. She strikes me as the kind of woman who plans and takes in all possibilities. We don't yet know what Edgar has found out, or even what he's been doing.'

Promising her that he would take no unnecessary risks and satisfied that he'd made headway, Ambrose picked up his coat, took her hand and put his lips to it before striding out of the door and up the path to the lane. He felt positively light-headed with optimism, an emotion he had not experienced for some weeks.

Chapter 12

As soon as she had seen Ambrose off Rosalie returned to the cottage to consider what she should do. There was her father to think of and, although he wasn't helpless, he had come to rely on her far more since Donald's death and was now apprehensive that he might lose her also. This anxiety was particularly evident whenever she left the cottage. He constantly questioned her about where she was going, who she would be seeing and when she would be back. He was perfectly able to take care of himself, in fact very self-sufficient when it came to practical aspects such as getting a simple meal and keeping up the fire. Although quite frail, he could still handle a small axe and chop kindling. He continued to tend the chickens and could also manage the pig they kept in the orchard. When Rosalie was at the mill, neighbours often called in with produce, and the more motherly of the women would do a little washing and tidy the place. Rosalie was never affronted by what other women might have seen as interference. She was only too glad of these acts of generosity from those who themselves worked from dawn to dusk.

She hadn't confided in her father how Donald had discovered the murky business of illegal child labour and baby farming. As far as Mr Thwaites was concerned, he believed the coroner's verdict of accidental death. Rosalie did not disabuse him; she would far rather he remained in ignorance, settled in his mind that it had been purely an act of God and therefore unavoidable. Ambrose had been introduced as a new worker at the mill – which was true – who had just moved into the area, which was also correct. She had said nothing about either his investigation or, least of all, his spoken intentions towards her. Marriage had not been on her mind of late – although there had been a few hopeful suitors in the past. The death of her mother six years previously necessitated her assuming all the responsibilities of a wife and, coupled with work at the mill, there was precious little time for 'walking out'.

When her brother had asked her why she never 'took up with anyone' she replied, 'I'm not ready for marriage, Donald, and anyway,

I haven't yet found the man I want to share my life with.' She put it as kindly as she could, but in her head she had never been exactly impressed with the young men who had put themselves in her path – they all seemed rather callow and dull. She was a reader and thinker, as encouraged by her brother, and appreciated a sharp mind and elegant turn of phrase. Neither was there much in the way of stimulating conversation on the power-loom floor. The noise prevented any exchanges between the workers; women had long since learned not to bother to shout, but to use hand signals and gestures by way of communication.

It had only been a short acquaintance, but Rosalie judged Ambrose to own an enquiring mind like her own, which attracted her. Besides, he was a man of the city, specifically London – a place completely unknown to her; she was not even certain exactly where it was down in the south, but she knew it was a wellspring of new ideas and energy. Her mind wandered to thoughts of visiting the capital with Ambrose one day, but she quickly put that idea to one side as premature in the extreme.

'This is all nonsense,' she said to herself. 'We met less than a fortnight ago. I hardly know the man, although I admire his mind – and his looks. He's taller than me, which makes a change, but that's no basis for thinking we have a future together. There are so many obstacles, but there's no doubt I like him and he has all but expressed himself as a serious suitor, even after such a short acquaintance. But I don't really know much about him, certainly nothing of his life in London. He said very little about himself when he visited on Sunday. Perhaps I didn't give him the chance!' For she realised when he left that she had spoken mostly about her own life, at his quiet encouragement. She had read some of his articles and was impressed with his literary powers of persuasion. 'His work's more than a way of earning a living, it's his life. Can I be part of it? Would there be room for me? He travels all round the country following up stories and it's certain I'd be left to my own devices for long periods. What would happen when we had children? Children need a father to be present as much as possible. My father has always been there for me.'

The reminder of her father halted her flow of thought and, tutting

Chapter 12

with impatience at herself, she brought her mind back to the here and now. 'What am I thinking? The man hasn't even asked me formally! I'm racing too far ahead. For the present it's enough that he's interested. But I must set these daydreams aside and concentrate on matters in hand.'

As she had promised, she would ride over to Hoyles and find Mr Lawes. Her father was up and pottering in the garden, despite the mist that had been present since dawn. She went outside and suggested he came in for a meal before she went out. To her dismay it seemed the fog was increasing rapidly and she determined to set out for Hoyles without delay.

'Where are you going? You're already late for the mill!' He was tetchy because he was hungry.

'Come inside and have your breakfast. I'm taking the morning off. I have to ride over to Hoyles to see Mr George Lawes.'

'What have you got to see him about? We hardly even know the man.'

Rosalie tried never to lie to her father, but on this occasion she told him there had been a few outstanding things to be settled after Donald's death; Mr Lawes was a magistrate and she wanted his advice. Mr Thwaites was more concerned with getting his breakfast and enquired no further and so she left him warm and comfortable, with plenty of fuel and a good rabbit stew simmering over the fire. Stowing Ambrose's letters in her bag, she wrapped up warmly and ventured outside to the stable. Saddling the beast of all work they used around the smallholding, she covered herself with an oilskin which she took down from the peg and mounted from the block. Despite the fog that was rolling in like thick bundles of grey woollen cloth, she rode off at a brisk pace up the lane in the direction of Lawes's farmstead.

Even with visibility as poor as it was there was no danger of becoming lost; the track was direct and distinct; within 30 minutes she had reached Hoyles's stable yard. A young stable hand came over and, dismounting, she handed him the reins and asked if Mr Lawes was in the house.

'He's done his inspection of the yard, miss. I think he's in his study,' answered the boy.

Having taken off the oilskin, which the boy put over the back of the mare, Rosalie walked over to the front porch and rang the bell hanging over the large oak door. The housekeeper showed her in and soon Rosalie was standing in front of George Lawes's large mahogany desk, piled as always with papers, prints, stud books and, incongruously in such a masculine room, a small silver rose bowl that contained some spring flowers – the housekeeper's touch, she thought. The cat commanded its usual place.

'Good morning, Miss Thwaites. This is an unexpected pleasure; we last met at your brother's funeral. I hope all's well with you – your father's well?'

'All's as well as possible, sir. Mr Thwaites does quite well, although he's a little frail and was considerably knocked up by my brother's death. Friends and neighbours have been kind and we are coping as best we can. It's not about myself or Father that I've come. I understand your cousin Mr Edgar Lawes is staying with you. We met some days ago, with Mr Frank Barrett. I'm sure you're aware of all the circumstances, sir.'

'Indeed I am. Tell me your news. Young Peter Samuels has just ridden off to Edgar's station – a well-hidden shepherd's hut – to take provisions. I'm worried about this weather which came down more thickly after he left. I hope he reaches Edgar while he can still see clearly. It's not an easy journey, especially for someone who doesn't know the ground. Still, he's a resourceful lad and won't take risks. I expect him back later this morning.'

'That's a pity, sir. I've a note for you and a letter for Mr Lawes from Mr Barrett. Peter could have taken it. When the weather clears I'll take it myself; can you give me directions?'

'In that case I'll come over with you. I'd like to see how my cousin's doing living rough! In the meantime, let's move to the sitting room and you can show me the letters. Mr Lawes, Mr Barrett and I are all completely in each other's confidence in the matter. It would help me to know what Frank has discovered.'

'He's taken me into his confidence, sir – I think we might call him Ambrose. It'll save confusion.'

Sitting in one of George's comfortable easy chairs in front of the

Chapter 12

warmth of the fire, Rosalie took out the package and handed it over. Having read the covering note, George broke the seal of the letter to Edgar and scanned its contents.

After a minute or two he let the letter fall into his lap and said, 'Well, here's a fine thing. Ambrose has evidence that the Fairfax woman is an old adversary from his days in Suffolk. Her real name's Jennie Calman. My cousin related the whole sorry tale of events in the union workhouse last year. I heard about the Calmans, especially how they were driven out neck and crop by the women inmates. So, she's turned up here, has she! If she's involved in this business of baby farming she'll get short shrift from the women round here if they discover she's done anything more than look after a few unwanted babies. But I'm afraid, from what I have been told, she's ruthless enough to do anything for money.'

'I had no idea of this woman or her past; Ambrose didn't tell me anything about it. I think he's anxious that I don't become mixed up in it because, as you say, he knows how ruthless these people are. But I know it too because my brother lost his life because of what he found out about both Sizewell and Fairfax. I'm glad you've shared the letter with me. At least I know what and who he was dealing with.'

'Your friend is very wise to keep you away from this filthy business. I'm sure both Ambrose and Edgar will do all they can to bring these villains to justice. What is most important now is to get this letter to Edgar as soon as the fog lifts.'

Rosalie spent the next hours fretting as the weather showed no sign of change. George offered to take her round the stable yard, hoping it would provide a distraction, but although she was very polite, admiring the horseflesh and the immaculate state of the yard, her mind was clearly elsewhere. The time ticked by; midday dinner was served and then it was teatime. By four o'clock George also had begun to worry, but about Peter.

'I hope he's been sensible and stayed with Edgar until the weather cleared. Even so, the lad should've been back by now. At least the fog has begun to lift and there are signs of the sun coming through at last. But it shouldn't take him more than an hour from the hut to Hoyles and it's four o'clock now.'

'Perhaps Edgar persuaded Peter to stay the night in view of the weather and his lack of knowledge of the moors.'

'That's a possibility I suppose,' agreed George, but reluctantly. The boy had promised to return and, even on short acquaintance, George felt the lad would always try to keep his word.

But by six o'clock the fog had returned. Rosalie was anxious to get back to her father before dark and while she could still make out the track. 'I've stayed longer than I intended, Mr Lawes; I must get back before my father really starts to worry. As it's Sunday tomorrow, I'll arrange with Ambrose for us to return to Hoyles early in the morning.'

'Yes, I'm sorry you've been delayed. I think we can assume that Peter has spent the night at the hut – poor weather and lack of local knowledge would have persuaded both him and Edgar that it was the right course.'

Her horse was saddled and brought round to the front. George gave her a leg up and waved her off as she turned down the drive to the track and home, but he was seething with frustration that Ambrose's letter would have to wait until the morning before it could be safely delivered.

Chapter 13

At about the same time on Saturday morning as Ambrose was making his way back from Parsloes to Richmond Mill, Edgar Lawes was rising early because the stiffness in his back and the coldness of his feet drove him to it – despite two layers of socks. He would never get used to the bed which was far too small for anybody other than a midget. He lit the fire with kindling chopped the day before and went outside for a wash in the stream. The spartan life was all very well, but there were times when he wished he could simply call his housekeeper and order jugs of hot water to be brought to the hip bath in his dressing room. He was eagerly awaiting Peter's visit as the lad should be bringing some decent food to eat. But the weather was turning foul with heavy watery fog that began to surround the hut, reducing visibility to inches. It occurred to him that Peter might not come; George would not encourage the lad out onto the moors in such conditions. Meanwhile he made do with his usual porridge, the consistency of which was improving as he became more practised at gauging proportions of oats to water and milk.

Warming his hands around his second mug of strong hot tea he thought over yesterday's events. He still remembered the shock of recognition when he saw the woman at the cottage; it was certainly Jennie Calman. What on earth had brought her to Yorkshire? There had been so many rumours about her subsequent to her violently forced exit from Seddon Union last year and no one seemed to have an accurate account of what had happened to either her or her husband John. There had been no sign of him at the cottage. Perhaps he was staying in the town, or not even here at all. She may have cast him off after their experience in the House; she was, after all, the stronger partner in the marriage. But now it appeared she was heavily involved in this abysmal enterprise, perhaps even running it. He had considered her an exceptionally hard woman when he had come across her in the workhouse. She had been highly valued by the chairman of the board of guardians, Jack Shepherd, precisely because of her propensity for strictness and unstinting observance of the disciplinary code; this she followed through with severe application of the punishments as ordered in the regulations. Ambrose's account of how she dealt with the young children had sickened him, so perhaps it was not so strange that she would involve herself in the disposal of tiny babies, although it was an egregious escalation of inhumanity and went much further than marking young backs with a rod or locking girls in cupboards for hours on end.

Edgar cursed the weather. What he really should do was to continue his surveillance of Rickard's; perhaps even find a way to get inside if the occupants ever left together, but his observations so far made that seem unlikely. It was the woman who took the cart for provisions; the man and young girl were left to look after the place. So – how to gain entrance? He considered he might simply ride up, knock on the door and ask for directions as though lost. He was not known in the district, although it would have to be done when Mrs Calman – or should he call her Fairfax? – was not at home. She would recognise him immediately. He decided that when Peter arrived he would take the boy's horse and ride up to the spying place. If the cart had gone and he could be sure she was not there he would ride down to the cottage and see if he could get himself invited inside – risky but it might prove fruitful.

He waited for the boy for two hours but there was still no sign of him and the dense fog had not lifted. While he was waiting he wrote a letter to Ambrose describing all he had discovered and alerting him to the involvement of their old acquaintance, Jennie Calman. He also dealt with the estate business his manager had sent via Hoyles which Peter had delivered to him yesterday. The lad could take all the correspondence back to Hoyles and George would see that the letter to Ambrose was passed to John Walters for delivery on Monday morning. By midday the fog showed no signs of clearing and Edgar, having tidied up the hut, chopped wood and drawn a supply of water, settled down to read. He always carried a selection of books and was grateful to his friend Hugh Bradshaw for introducing him to the novels of Charles Dickens. Until last year he had been dismissive of what he considered to be 'romances', having always veered towards philosophical works, under the influence of his father and his classi-

Chapter 13

cal education. Dickens, however, had a philosophy of his own that concerned the workings and interaction of people from all strata of society. He had the rare gift of telling a story and painting pictures for the mind at the same time. His evocation of life in the workhouse had particularly resonated with Edgar at a time when he was closely involved with the Poor Law process himself. Now he settled down to read his new purchase of *The Pickwick Papers* in book form that had cost him twenty-one shillings plus carriage. The text and illustrations were very amusing and for a few hours Edgar immersed himself in the world of the eponymous hero and his miscellany of acquaintances.

However, by about three o'clock he noticed the light was changing in the hut and opening the door a pale shaft of sunlight came through; the fog had almost completely lifted on this part of the moor. He went outside to stretch his legs, walking half a mile up the path in the hope that he might see Peter coming down it, but the track was clear of anything or anybody for as far as he could see. He went back into the hut and an hour passed and there was still no sign of the lad.

Tied up and in a most uncomfortable position, Peter had waited what seemed like hours for whatever punishment was likely to come. Would they kill him? There was a possibility they would. They were all implicated in murder and had nothing to lose by silencing someone who was a serious threat. He was not at all sanguine about the thought of dying. He was too young and had too much to live for. Besides, providence would surely not want to take away all he had been given in the last year – this new life after the dismal start he had been handed. As usual, his thoughts flew to Caroline. The thought of having come so far, almost to the point of marriage, and have it torn away from them by this evil woman increased his anger and frustration. It was fear of that loss that scared him; he had been used to severe beatings – indeed had often received them from the hands of Jennie Calman's husband John when Peter had committed some petty misdemeanour or had been judged to be insolent and disrespectful to the House authorities. Jennie Calman always watched these proceedings with relish. Enderby had been the worst – Mrs Calman's brother – who took a perverse delight in tormenting the smaller children, clouting the boys and assaulting the girls. No, anything the man in the next room could throw at him he had experienced before and would be ready.

Not that he had been sitting idly waiting for the visit; he had done his best to loosen his bonds, but twine was almost unbreakable and the more he twisted and pulled at it the tighter the knots became; there was no give in it as there was in good hemp rope. His wrists had become sore and his shoulders ached from the unnatural positioning of his arms behind his back. He had looked around the room for sharp objects with which he might cut his bonds, but there was nothing suitable. Besides, in that gloomy room it was hard to discern any features, except he could make out the eerie rectangular shapes of the wooden boxes on a shelf above him.

Now, as Peter moved out of the way to let the man in he was momentarily dazzled by the light that came through the door. It seemed the weather had changed and there was sunlight shining into the main room. He looked up and was relieved to see that the man had no weapon in his hand. Perhaps he was just going to shake him up a little.

The man got straight to the point, 'What are you doing up here? You're a long way from Suffolk.' He took hold of Peter's arm and with a vicious twist hauled the boy onto a chair. Peter looked him full in the eye. In Peter's mind the man was old, possibly in his fifties – he looked about the same age as Mr George Lawes, and Mr Edgar had told him that his cousin was 20 years older than himself. He was short, stocky and probably strong with muscles that had been worked hard, like Harry Valentine's.

Peter gulped and said, 'I'm here staying at Mr George Lawes's farm, learning about racehorses. Mr Lawes's cousin in Suffolk had taken me on as an apprentice and sent me here for a few months.'

'So, what were you doing out on the moor in this weather?'

This was a tricky one and Peter thought for a second. 'I went out early this morning to one of the far pastures – the fog was not so bad then; I was sent to look for a mare that was about to foal, but the weather got worse and I was lost. I must have wandered for some miles before I found this place.'

Chapter 13

'Don't know that I believe you. This place is hard to find – well off the track.'

'That's the point; my horse took me off the track. I was stupid because I thought if I was slack on the reins she'd find the way back to Hoyles on her own.'

At that point Jennie Calman pushed her way in and said impatiently, 'What are you doing? Have you found out what he's about? I know this bastard – he's sly and a liar. There's more to this than he's telling.'

'He says he's staying at Hoyles – been sent from Suffolk to learn about racehorses with George Lawes.'

'I knew it! There must be a connection.' She approached Peter and hit him twice with an open hand hard round his face. 'Now, tell me why you're really here!'

Peter felt the stings and tears of pain came into his eyes. 'I can't tell you any more, that's the truth. I'm staying at Hoyles and will be for three months. I've done you no harm, and there's no need to treat me like this. You can't keep me a prisoner for ever. My people will get suspicious and come looking for me.'

'Your people, indeed! My, we have gone up in the world. Whether that's true or not, it's obvious to me they can have no idea where you are and it could take days of searching before they get here. In the meantime, you must stay here until I've decided what to do with you.' With that she took a small cosh from a pocket in the folds of her skirt and, as it came down on the side of his head, he heard her say, 'This'll save us trouble for at least the next few hours.'

As the weapon found its mark Peter was knocked sideways off the chair and fell to the floor out cold.

'What shall we do with him now?' The man was concerned.

'Leave him where he is. But I don't like this at all. The place might not be as safe as we thought. I know he says he came here by chance, but they're going to be searching for him, especially when the horse arrives back without him. Let the animal loose after I've left – wait till dark. I'm not taking any risks. We'll probably have to pack up here and move on somewhere else.' She looked down at Peter's body, trussed up like a Christmas goose. She shrugged. 'Anyway, it was his own fault.'

Equipping himself with food, water and warm clothing, late in the afternoon Edgar climbed from his hut up to his spying place and settled down to observe the cottage for the rest of the day. The weather had become murky again, but he hoped to stay out until full darkness, which wouldn't be for another few hours. He had left a note for Peter as he was certain the boy would try to keep his promise to visit every day. By now he assumed the lad had stayed at Hoyles until the weather cleared. The moor was no place to be out in the fog without knowledge of the ground.

Settling himself in his usual place, his eyes swept across the land in front of him. The mist was damp on his face and the ground shone bright green after its soaking. There were still pockets of heavy fog above hollows and dips in the ground where the breeze couldn't reach. But the cottage was illuminated with its yellow light and Edgar could just see peaty smoke rising from the chimney. Everything was quiet; there was no movement, except for the horse which had been tethered to a fence. The cart was there, so Calman was in residence and Edgar's plan to visit would have to wait. At one point the young girl came out with a wooden bucket, went down to the stream and came back with water. Nothing else happened until nearly dusk, when the man came out carrying a lantern in one hand and a bucket of food for the horse in the other. Edgar was gratified that at least the animal was being cared for adequately, whatever was going on in the cottage. As the man returned to the house he shut the door and Edgar imagined the bolts being set and the trio settling down for the night.

But, just as he was considering giving up – it was now fully dusk – the door opened and the woman and the man came out. She was heavily dressed for the weather. He disappeared and then returned with the horse and soon had it in the traces of the cart. The woman climbed up, lit a small lamp and drove out onto the track in the gloom. The man went back into the house, shutting the doors behind him.

There was no point in remaining out any longer. Wherever the woman was going he could not follow her. By now he needed his

Chapter 13

own lamp to light his way home, but he made sure he didn't use it until he was well under the breast of the hill. As he approached his hut he hoped there might be a light on to signal Peter's arrival, but he was disappointed. The building loomed up in the darkness and he stumbled through the door. Setting the lantern down, he looked around for signs that the boy had been and gone – new provisions perhaps, or letters – but clearly he had not arrived and would not do so now. His own letter was unopened and propped up against a mug where he had left it. Perhaps George had insisted he stay at the farm rather than risking the weather.

But he began to worry. Peter was reliable and had never let him or Harry Valentine down; if he had ventured out from Hoyles anything could have happened to him. He may have taken a fall, or the horse might have cast a shoe and he was stuck out on the moor somewhere. Would the boy be resourceful enough to see the night through in such exposed conditions? He comforted himself with the thought that Peter had been through very tough times from early childhood onwards and lived in extreme privation, particularly permanent hunger; it was likely that he could survive a night on the moor. If the boy was lost the hunt would be on for him by early morning. George would spare no one in the search. He would walk to Hoyles himself tomorrow and see what had happened. The surveillance would have to be postponed; the boy's safety was his prime concern. He stirred up the embers of the fire, made himself a bowl of porridge and tried to settle on the uncomfortable wooden chair to eat it before he condemned himself to the narrow confines of the truckle bed.

When Peter had set out from Hoyles the weather had been dull but clear; the fog came down suddenly, as was often the case out here. George had hoped that Peter would have reached Edgar before then and waited it out until visibility made it safe to cross the moor. By eight in the evening, as darkness came, there was still no sign of the boy and George surmised he was staying the night at the hut, even though there had been a short respite from the fog in the late afternoon. But it had come down more severely during the evening and

Edgar would never have allowed the boy to venture out in it. All the same, George went to bed uneasy in his mind. He was even more troubled when he was woken by his steward some hours before dawn on Sunday morning.

'Sir, sorry to wake you so early.'

'Has Peter returned?'

'No, sir. But his horse has returned saddled and in a lather. She's unharmed.'

'Now I'm really worried. We never specified what time the lad should return, but he's normally straight back by dinner-time. I thought when he didn't turn up yesterday that he'd stayed with Mr Lawes until the fog lifted. But his horse returning without him just adds to my concern. I suppose there's just a chance the horse broke loose from her tether and instinct made her return to her stable. We can't do anything while it's still dark. But as soon as there's enough light, if he hasn't returned, we'll start a search.'

As dawn broke there was still no sign of Peter and, as soon as the light was sufficient to see clearly, George made up his mind to wait no longer. He hoped that Ambrose and Rosalie would arrive before the search party moved off. The weather this morning was cold and damp with permanent drizzle in the air. There was always a chance that the fog would return; George didn't relish being stuck out with his men on moorland terrain. However, he called them all together in the yard. 'Young Peter Samuels has gone missing. We were expecting him back yesterday midday from his errand, but he's not yet appeared, although his horse has returned fully saddled. I fear the boy's wandering about out there somewhere. He's no experience of the ground, nor knowledge of the district. He was heading south-west of here, so we'll fan out in that direction as best we can and see if we can pick up a trail.'

As the men were preparing to leave a shout was heard and, looking up, they saw a horse with two on its back trotting into the yard. At first George thought one of them might be Peter, but as fast as the wishful thought came into his head it disappeared. As promised, Rosalie and Ambrose had arrived.

Quickly George explained what had happened. 'Can't think where

Chapter 13

the lad has gone. He was obviously lost in the fog. Let's hope he found shelter last night and is waiting it out. The horse has come back of her own accord and is unharmed, which may mean the boy has been thrown and that will be serious. If he's been lying injured out there through the night I don't honestly give much for his chances. We're just ready to go so will you join us? We'll give you five minutes for Charlie Anderson to saddle a horse for Ambrose and we can be off. I suggest you both ride to Edgar's in advance of my main group of men who'll sweep the ground slowly. I'll put Jem with you, one of my hands. He knows the way to the hut and will keep you safe. I hope you've had breakfast. I've arranged for provisions for us as I expect to be out for some hours.'

Shocked at George's news and very concerned about his young protégé, Ambrose walked over to the stables with Anderson who provided him with a large but gentle mount.

'You should be all right on Bonny, sir. She's very quiet as long as you don't pull on her mouth.'

Ambrose looked the horse squarely in the eye and she, unblinking, looked back at him down her long nose; he swore later that as he had taken the reins he had seen her wink her left eye. He walked her out to join the rest who had gathered round George for instructions.

'We'll head off on the route he would normally take to the shepherd's place; I take it neither you nor Miss Thwaites saw any sign on your way here?'

'None,' said Rosalie. 'I wonder if he even got halfway. We saw how fast the fog came down yesterday morning. He was probably completely disoriented by it and could have veered off the track anywhere. Let's hope the weather brightens up today. The clouds are still low.'

George nodded and seeing Ambrose's evident distress said gruffly, 'Don't worry, I'm sure the boy has enough common sense to get into some shelter. Even if he was knocked out he must come round and will realise we'll be looking for him and put himself on a track where he could be found. He strikes me as a resourceful young man and, from what you tell me of his beginnings, able to withstand tough conditions. We'll find him!'

Ambrose remembered George Lawes's alarmist opinion of a few

minutes ago and fervently hoped this newly found optimism was not simply intended to comfort him.

The party moved off down the drive. Rosalie, Ambrose and Jem trotted to the front and as soon as they reached the track they parted from the main body of men who began to fan out, picking their way carefully through the tufts of moor grass and avoiding any vivid green vegetation which always heralded treacherous boggy ground. Although it was brighter there was no sun today, and a stiff chilly wind had blown up in the last hour. Ambrose thought how wet, cold and hungry Peter must be in this miserable weather; but he knew the boy would expect a search party and that must give him hope. Besides, the lad had something to cling on to: the possibility of a future with Caroline Alfrey was now his main preoccupation and that, if nothing else, would keep him focused on staying alive. If they found the boy and he was safe Ambrose promised himself that he would take steps to enable the pair of young lovers to tie the knot sooner than had been anticipated. Life was too short for them to wait interminably. If they needed money to make an earlier start he would provide it. Perhaps he was simply trying to salve his conscience at having been persuaded to bring Peter here in the first place. But he needed to think of a practical way of making amends; and securing what would make Peter most happy didn't seem like a bad idea.

Soon the three riders were out of sight of the rest with Jem leading the way and keeping up a brisk pace. By eight o'clock, having taken less than an hour, they saw the smoke of Edgar's fire and soon the hut came into view. Ambrose was relieved to see Edgar outside, clearly ready to be off somewhere, with a pack on his back and well protected against the weather with oilskins.

'I'm so glad to see you – and Rosalie too. Peter didn't arrive yesterday. I assume that he was persuaded to stay back until the weather improved. There was a short break in the weather in the afternoon and I went out to survey the cottage, leaving him a note, but he never arrived. I'd just decided to walk back to Hoyles to find out what has happened to him.'

Ambrose dismounted and, as he was tethering the horse explained, 'We fear he was lost in the fog after he set out to you early yesterday

Chapter 13

morning. He hasn't returned to Hoyles, but his horse came back on her own in the night and we fear the lad might be out here somewhere and possibly injured. George has organised a search party to cover the route from Hoyles to here. We've come on in advance to see what news you may have.'

Edgar frowned, looking anxious. 'From what you say about his horse returning, like you I fear he may have taken a tumble and could be lying anywhere. We'd better go inside and plan what to do. Jem, it might be best if you join the others and tell them Peter never arrived. They can concentrate the search more accurately. Tell Mr Lawes we're heading over towards Rickard's and he should follow us there when he can.'

Jem touched his cap, turned his horse round and cantered off. Edgar, Ambrose and Rosalie went into the hut.

'Why Rickard's?' asked Ambrose.

'I've written you a letter which I was going to give to Peter. I've important news for you, but it seems less so as I think about the boy and what may have happened to him. But I think the place holds the key to all this, and besides that Peter may have stumbled on it in the fog by accident and sought shelter for the night. It's the only habitation in the area and the chances are he could have found a track leading to it; in some ways I hope that's not the case, but I think we should seek out the occupants and ask them if they know anything. First I've much to tell you about them; I've discovered who the woman is!'

Ambrose interrupted him. 'Likewise. I've a letter for you that Rosalie would have given to Peter yesterday – but she missed him by half an hour. What I wanted to tell you was that the woman who turned the cart over is none other than Mrs Jennie Calman, the disgraced matron of Seddon workhouse. She—'

Ambrose was interrupted himself by an exclamation from Edgar: 'I know, I know! I spotted her at Rickard's and managed to get a full view of her. She's operating from there with an older man and a young girl. She arrived on Friday afternoon. I couldn't believe my eyes! What's she doing here?'

'I've confirmation that she's the woman behind the baby farming and she's also connected to Tom Sizewell. I saw them meet in an ale-house and he passed money over to her. I'm certain he's her contact in the mill; that meeting and what one of the women who's involved in giving up a baby said, made that plain. He obviously has access to all the local tittle-tattle and gossip and can pass her useful information. How she's found her way to Yorkshire I don't know; perhaps she has family connections. Anyway, there's no sign of John Calman in Bingley. He's not here, is he? At Rickard's, I mean?'

'I've seen no sign of him, just this old man and the girl. They seem to be living in a very isolated way – neither of them leaves the place. But as I said, I saw the Calman woman arrive midday on Friday with provisions; she left in the evening – that's when I recognised her – smartly dressed, with her trademark collar and cuffs. On Saturday, after the fog lifted I returned to the place and saw her drive off in the late afternoon when the mist was less thick. She seems to know her way round the tracks even in bad weather. I always knew she was resourceful, as well as being cruelly calculating.'

'My source told me she collected another baby, possibly on Friday. Those "provisions" you saw could have included the child – dreadful thought!'

'I don't know what I'd have done if I'd known that! I would have had to try a rescue. But there's no telling whether the child is in the house now. At first I saw no signs of movement from the cottage when I viewed it yesterday. The cart was outside and the horse untethered. Then about half past four she came out and went off in the cart. I wouldn't have wanted to drive a vehicle in those conditions.'

'Was she carrying anything?'

'No, she had nothing with her.'

'That's interesting and ties in with what I saw. Last night immediately after work I was determined to follow Tom Sizewell again. I thought there was a chance Jennie Calman would return to town and seek him out and I was right. Seeing them together in the tavern on Friday evening proved they have a connection, particularly as money was exchanged. Anyway, last night, after a couple of drinks in the ale-house he walked out into the town and I followed him through the better streets until he stopped at a house in the middle

Chapter 13

of a small terrace and went inside. I presume that's where he lives. I stood observing the place, and my luck was in. Within an hour the woman turned up on foot, knocked on the door and Tom Sizewell answered; I could see him framed in the light from the hallway. She went in and, although I waited as long as I could – I must be back at the lodgings by ten o'clock – she didn't show herself again. It appears she would spend the night with him in town. What their exact connection is I still don't know, but the link is clear. I decided I'd resume my surveillance early this morning, before coming across to Hoyles with Rosalie. At five Calman appeared out of the front door and I followed her to the back of the houses where she retrieved her transport. I saw her driving the cart on the road in the direction of Bradford and the moors.'

'Undoubtedly she'll have arrived at Rickard's by now. Who knows what mischief she's up to? But I'm most concerned about Peter. There's been no sighting of him since he left Hoyles yesterday morning. I can't think where he might be. As I said, the nearest occupied place to here is Rickard's. That's why I think we should chance going over and see whether he went there for help.'

'As you say, Jennie Calman has probably arrived there by now and I'm not anxious that you and I should show ourselves at present. We really need to catch her in the act. There's no doubt she'll cover her tracks once she recognises us.'

'But I could go,' suggested Rosalie. 'She's no knowledge of me; we've never seen each other.'

Ambrose was immediately anxious. 'This woman's completely ruthless; we all know what we think she's capable of, even though we haven't exactly spelled it out. I'm not happy about you walking in there alone.'

'I'll simply be making enquiries as to whether they've seen or taken in a stranger in trouble on the moor. If I think there's more going on than they're telling me, I'll make an excuse and come away at once.'

'I'm still not happy. These are dangerous, nasty people.'

'What danger is there in knocking on the door, making an enquiry and then leaving? I won't set foot over the threshold. But I may discover something just by seeing inside. I won't give my name; Calman probably knows it already from Sizewell. She may be mixed up in my brother's death for all I know.'

'I still say it's too dangerous. Better to wait for George – he's a magistrate and can insist on an official entry.'

Edgar shook his head. 'I don't think we have time for official action. Peter may be in there – already dead for all we know! Rosalie's right – the Calman woman doesn't know her from Adam and we'll be close by.'

Finally, Ambrose reluctantly agreed that she should make the attempt: 'As long as you make no move to enter the cottage. But let's hope George arrives soon with adequate reinforcements if there's trouble.'

The three made their way on foot up the steep hill to Edgar's spying place and looked down on the isolated cottage. Smoke rose from the chimney and, sure enough, as Ambrose had guessed, Jennie Calman's vehicle was tied up at the dilapidated gate; the horse, still harnessed, was browsing on the rough moorland grasses but there was no sign of the occupants. The weather was dull, chill and damp, but visibility was reasonable and, using his spyglass to look through the small window at the side of the door, Edgar could make out some movements inside. The two men pondered on how they could get nearer to the place without being seen. The cottage was very exposed with no tree or bush cover. The only chance was to skirt round the property very stealthily and site themselves at the back of the building where there were no windows and they would be out of sight from those at the front and side. From this position, they should be able to hear what was being said and immediately provide help to Rosalie if necessary. It still seemed very risky to Ambrose, but Edgar continued to assure him that between them they could easily protect her from an old man, a young girl and a small woman – however vicious she was.

'Anyway,' said Edgar, 'I'm sure it won't come to that. Rosalie has too much common sense.'

Having agreed on this course of action it was now time to see it through. The two men plotted the route they would take down the hillside and, keeping as low as possible, sometimes on all fours, at others on their stomachs, they crept and slithered inch by inch towards the cottage. Rosalie went off openly in the opposite direction, boldly swinging down the hill and round to the track that led to the front of the building.

It was profoundly dark. He could just make out the shape of the small chair, and objects that must be shelves hanging from the walls. Having managed to open his eyes and move his head, Peter was immediately aware of a sharp pain that stretched from the side of his head, spread round the back of his skull and found its way to his forehead. He was also suffering badly from pins and needles that had numbed his hands, his wrists being so tightly bound. Lying curled up on the stone floor, cold and in pain, he tried to recollect where he was and why he was in such a strange position. As his brain cleared he began to remember how he had been caught out by Mrs Calman and shut in the back room of Rickard's.

'How long have I been here? What time is it? Is it day or night?' These questions came into his aching head as his eyes adjusted to the dim light of the room with its one small window obscured by a dirty rag of a curtain. He was extremely thirsty and his mouth had dried out completely; he found it difficult to move his tongue when he tried to moisten his lips with what saliva he had left. His parched mouth made it impossible for him to make a sound other than from the back of his throat. Desperate for a drink, he wriggled himself into a sitting position and shuffled across in the direction of what he could see was the outline of the door. Facing it, he braced his knees together, raised them and struck the door hard with both feet several times.

There were muffled voices that stopped momentarily and then the door opened, catching him a glancing blow as it swung into his shoulder. A stream of daylight shone into the room and he squinted in its unaccustomed glare. In the doorway was haloed the outline of the man, who entered and swore at Peter, who managed somehow through his gasps to indicate that he needed water. His jailer disappeared for an instant and returned with a tin mug and proceeded to pour the precious liquid down Peter's throat.

Now able to speak, and emboldened by pain, thirst and hunger, Peter said angrily, 'What gives you the right to treat me like this?

Who's responsible for keeping me a prisoner? I have friends who'll be searching for me. When they find me, you'll be for it. Mr George Lawes is a magistrate.'

The man refused to engage in any dialogue but he untied Peter's wrists, brought the boy's arms to his front and retied them so that he could at least access the mug of water himself. The door was firmly shut again, but Peter brought his ear to it and found he could make out some faint conversation taking place in the next room. He remembered seeing a young girl when he had arrived, and it seemed she was expressing concern about their captive.

'What are we to do with him?'

'We'll wait till the woman comes.'

'We can't get rid of him like the others. People will be missing him soon. He must have family or friends who'll be looking for him.'

'He'll be long gone before they arrive here. She chose this place because no one comes. It'll be days before they come out here and we'll have left by then. She says it's all up with the business in Bingley and we should be moving to Leeds where there're still good chances – more people for a start, and a bigger place which means we can merge in better.'

'I don't want anything to do with getting rid of him!'

'You'll do what you're told, you little whore! Otherwise you'll go the same way. You've been willing to take the money and food on offer which has kept you off the streets. You must pay us back for that by helping. Now, go and get some water and wood. Fairfax will be back soon and we'll need food before we start packing up.'

Peter heard the front door open and the girl evidently left the place to carry out her chores. By now he was very scared. He was aware he had fallen into the hands of some exceptionally ruthless people. Mrs Calman he already knew was capable of great cruelty, especially to the young. She had, it appeared, moved on to child murder. What chance would he have with the erstwhile matron of Seddon Union? He had never been a favourite of hers. There had been a mutual loathing between himself and this virago and one of the most satisfying aspects of being plucked out of the workhouse by Mr Edgar Lawes was never

Chapter 13

to clap eyes on her again. Now he was at her mercy, and he knew she had none.

He tried to focus his mind on more practical thoughts, like how to escape. Now that his hands were in front of his body he tried to work the knots in the twine, although it was very painful as the thin plaited strands cut into his wrists and showed little sign of loosening because, as he had already discovered, they had no give in them. Even biting at them was useless. The man had known what he was doing when he first tied him up. The water he had been drinking, although the most welcome draught of liquid he had ever tasted, was now beginning to work on his bladder and he became desperate for the privy. Despairing, he banged on the door again with his feet and called out for someone to come.

He heard the front door open and the sound of the woman's voice. She asked the man what the noise was about, and how long it had been since Peter had come round. He told her it was a matter of minutes and then Peter's blood chilled when he heard her say, 'Let's do it now. No point in waiting. Go and get him and we'll deal with him and the other at the same time. I can't afford to risk a search party coming here to look for him.'

The man muttered something that Peter could not catch, but he braced himself as he heard footsteps approaching the door. As it opened he decided he must put up a fight; he couldn't lie there supine and allow them to simply dispose of him. He prepared to kick out at her in the hopes of causing her at least some injury and pain if he could manage nothing fatal. He knew in his heart there was no hope – it was two determined and ruthless adults against one bound young man. But he would go down fighting. He only hoped he wouldn't wet himself in the process. As she pushed the door open he swung his legs up and out and kicked her full in the stomach.

Caught completely unawares, she momentarily lost her balance and went flying backwards through the door again. She struggled to her feet and advanced with a look of fury on her face. 'Fucking bastard!' she shouted and went for him with hands and nails.

While warding off her attack as best he could with his arms tied together, he continued to thrash his legs around. The man came to her assistance and between them they began pulling the boy through the doorway, dragging him by his arms and legs.

Just as they had pulled him into the main room the young girl came in through the front door followed by a tall woman, a stranger. The girl opened her mouth to explain that she had found the woman in the garden and she was asking about a lost young man; she wanted to know if anyone here had seen him. But her words faded as the sight of Peter shocked her into silence; he was lying trussed and bound on the ground, towered over by the man and woman.

The stranger was also clearly surprised at the sight and looked suspiciously at the pair, asking sharply, 'What's happening here? What are you doing to this boy?' At first Rosalie had no idea she was looking at Peter, never having met him, but instantly she put two and two together and realised it must be the young man; clearly, he was being kept a prisoner here.

Jennie Calman, flushed and dishevelled from the struggle, also knew that she couldn't provide a satisfactory explanation and didn't stay to try. With a stream of invective aimed at no one in particular she picked up a small cloth bundle from a wooden box on the table and bolted for the open front door as though making for the cart. To her dismay she found a tall man standing close to the door and almost blocking her way; another was approaching down the path. Swiftly she swerved away under the first man's arm and at lightning speed avoided the second's outstretched hand. For a moment, she looked from one to the other and, realising she was possibly trapped, took her advantage of surprise, hitched up her skirts and with the bundle tucked under her arm, raced across the ground and through a gaping hole in the wall out onto the moor.

Rosalie had followed her out, brushing past Ambrose at the door. Realising that the woman was attempting to escape and guessing what she had under her arm, she called to Ambrose and Edgar that Peter was inside and followed the woman out through the same gap in the wall, gathering speed away across the moor.

The two men responded instantly and went into the house where they found Peter on the floor and the man and young girl standing

Chapter 13

by helplessly. Aware that Rosalie was after the main quarry and must need help, Edgar turned and ran out of the building while shouting to Ambrose that he should get word to the search party; they would surely need it to hunt down this woman. As he ran out to the edge of the property he could see two figures not far off, one behind the other, racing up a steep slope of moorland. By his estimation, Rosalie appeared to be gaining on the Calman woman but soon both were out of sight as they breasted the hill and disappeared over the top. Edgar followed their undeviating route and, panting hard, came over the hill and saw them running down to a brilliantly green patch of ground. On first sight, it was uniformly iridescent and beautiful, but as he drew nearer he recognised the fatally deceptive appearance of a dangerous piece of bog.

As Edgar approached the mire he saw Jennie Calman standing on its fringes. She raised her arm and threw a small bundle into the swamp where it lay for some seconds on the surface, its covering of rags holding it up momentarily as they spread out across the filthy water. Instantly Rosalie rushed forward from behind the woman and into the mire where she stretched out her arms and pulled up the bundle, cradling it just before it started to sink. But in her haste to rescue the child she had stepped into deadly danger; her feet and lower legs were already sinking into the ooze. Aware of her plight she tried desperately to extricate herself, but the force of the black mud was too strong and she found herself slowly sinking into its gurgling mass.

Meanwhile, turning around, Jennie Calman saw Edgar running towards her. Wildly she rushed past him and headed off across the moor and out of sight. Edgar ignored her, knowing she wouldn't get far on foot and the search party would soon surround the area and pick her up. Instead he concentrated on getting Rosalie and the baby out of the mire. He searched around desperately for something to throw them, but there was nothing; the area was devoid of any loose branch or bush that he could get to her for support. Besides, her arms were taken up with carrying the child. He shouted to her to throw the baby to him so that they would be freed to grab whatever he could find to help her pull herself out. She offered up the baby laid across her two hands in a fruitless sacrificial gesture, as though pleading with him to take the child, but then realised that the only course was to throw the bundle to Edgar for him to catch. She brought both hands towards her breasts and then, raising her arms and with a great effort, gathered enough power to ensure a trajectory that would bring the baby safely beyond the edge of the marsh and into Edgar's outstretched arms.

He watched as the baby seemed to float across the marshy ground, then almost as if in slow motion, he moved forward to catch it, his eyes focused exclusively on the object, as though a fielder after the long curve of a well-slogged cricket ball to the boundary. The baby fell firmly into his arms but bundled as it was in layers of muddy wet rags its arrival was well-cushioned. He found a dry tussock and gently laid it down as he turned his full attention to trying to save Rosalie.

In the brief instant of her throwing and him catching the tiny infant she had sunk further and was now almost waist deep. To his horror he realised he still had nothing to assist her – no branch or fence post by which, combining both their strengths, he could pull her out. In desperation, he took off his coat and laid it across the mire as close as he could and lay down on it, attempting to grab her hand. To his intense frustration and dismay he was still well out of reach. But he was close enough to see the look of horror on her face as she began to accept the inevitable. At that instant they both realised she was beyond his help.

Then, as her shoulders began to submerge, her courage and intelligence came through and she called across to Edgar. 'Tell Ambrose the answer would have been "yes". I wish I'd been able to tell him myself.'

He looked back into her eyes, helplessly but no words came from him, although he nodded his head slowly.

Edgar stumbled to his feet and stood looking at her face as it slowly disappeared. He turned away with tears in his eyes as her mouth and nose vanished beneath the mud, not bearing to look into her eyes as they must close in acceptance of her inescapable fate . When he turned his head to look again there was nothing to see – not even bubbles. But he heard a sucking sound, and he thought the marsh was licking its lips. The tears in his eyes began to spill over until they were running down his face. He had never in his life felt so futile and he

Chapter 13

stood numb for a moment, until a brief whimper from close to his feet reminded him that he had another to take care of, a small life that could be saved.

Tenderly he picked up the child and pushed the filthy rags from its face. Looking down he saw the brown eyes of the baby, which he estimated could not be more than a week old, looking back at him. He was instantly reminded of the eyes he had just seen before they were swamped by black slime. The baby's small mouth puckered and frown lines appeared on the tiny brow as it prepared to wail its protest at being so manhandled. The grubby little face became redder as it let out cries that became increasingly demanding. Fighting loose of its wrapping, its clenched fists began to flail in anger and Edgar noted it was a little girl. He knew she must be hungry and this imperative exerted him to action. He must get help for her, but he was loath to leave Rosalie alone in that desolate place, although he knew she was gone for ever. He had nothing with which he could make a marker of where she had met her end. He tried to keep a mental image of the exact spot where she had gone down, but the landscape was so uniform in its structure that within seconds he could no longer identify the place.

Reluctantly he turned his back on the sickly green swamp and made his way slowly up the hill and down the other side back to the cottage. Undoubtedly Rosalie Thwaites had been the bravest of women, giving up her own life for the poor scrap of existence he carried in his arms. As he walked he repeated her words aloud '... the answer would have been "yes". I wish I'd been able to tell him myself.' On no account must he forget the message, although it remained a mystery to him as to its meaning; whatever its significance Ambrose was going to be appalled and devastated. He wondered how he was going to describe to him the manner of her death and his own impotence to save her. He was relieved that it was he who had witnessed the tragedy and not Ambrose, although the sight would remain in his mind's eye for ever. Edgar had realised some time ago that there was more to his friend's feelings for the woman than mere admiration of her integrity and courage; that would compound the horror he would have felt if he had witnessed the last desperate gasps of the woman he loved and whom he hoped loved him in return. More than likely Ambrose would blame himself as much as anyone, but Rosalie had been involved in these desperate matters long before they had met. If there was guilt to be endured then surely Edgar must take his share.

But rationally the blame lay squarely with Jennie Calman who had instigated this dismal business. She was directly responsible for Rosalie's death, as she had been for the murder of at least three children that were known of; there were probably more. When she was caught she would surely hang for all the misery she had caused.

By now in sight of the cottage he slowed down as he began to formulate what he would do next. The priority was to find someone capable of taking care of this infant which had become ever more fractious as they made their way back. Indeed, such was the power of her cries that Ambrose, who had been at the rickety gate looking out for them, came out onto the moor to meet him. Taking a deep breath, Edgar approached him, slowing down as though reluctant to meet his friend. When they came face to face he said simply, 'Ambrose, a most dreadful thing has happened…'

Chapter 14

Hoyles,
Bingley,
Yorkshire

6am, Monday, 29 April 1839
   Dear Mr McNiece,
   Although we have never met I feel I am acquainted with you through the warm regard our mutual friend, Mr Ambrose Hudson, expresses for you. He has talked of you often, and I feel I have come to know you as an 'absent friend'. Knowing you are well acquainted with the reasons for Ambrose's journey here and understanding that he has, as far as possible, kept you abreast with events, it now falls upon me to enlighten you further with the most recent sad developments. I have set down the appalling events as I remember them. I do not have the skill of a journalist, but have written them as succinctly as I can and enclose them separately as they are as faithful a record of all the events here as I can muster.
   The horror of it will live with me for the rest of my days and telling Ambrose was the most distressing thing I have ever had to do. He is, understandably, completely broken now. I was unaware that he had made overtures of marriage to Miss Thwaites, something that she referred to in her final words; it seems she reciprocated his feelings and now she is lost. You know him well and I must assume that sometime in the future he will come to himself again. I am doing my best to rouse him to normality by reminding him that he has done some excellent work here, which is yet unfinished as Mrs Calman has not been caught. We assume her contact in the mill, the manager Tom Sizewell, may be aware of what has happened.
   As things stand at this moment the search is still on for this

evil woman. Her accomplices, the man and young girl, are currently temporarily held in the town lock-up awaiting removal to Wakefield Jail and have been only too anxious to lay all the blame on their mistress for the crimes, both denying they had any involvement in disposing of any babies. We will probably never know the truth of that, but undoubtedly they are complicit in murder and will possibly be hanged alongside the main culprit who, I am certain, will be apprehended shortly. The word is not yet out generally as to what she has done as we are anxious that there should not be a witch hunt. Mrs Calman's actions will strike horror and revulsion in all women and especially the mothers of young children. My experience of the vengeful women at Seddon Union workhouse last year tells me that many of those in this neighbourhood would take it upon themselves to avenge such awful crimes and possibly in the most ghoulish ways. It is our aim to see her safely in the dock to answer for her crimes, and then to be publicly hanged so that all can see justice has been done.

After the day's grim occurrences Ambrose insisted that we immediately visit Miss Thwaites's father to break the news to him. The man has now lost both his children in the space of a month because of this woman and the villainy of her gang; he also is completely broken down. The neighbours have rallied round and a kindly woman is now living in at his farmstead and taking care of him until permanent arrangements for his future have been made. However, since he is already a frail old man I feel that it will not be long before there is yet another casualty of this affair.

Last night I tentatively broached the idea that Ambrose remains in Yorkshire for a few weeks to recover, while under no illusion that he would agree, preferring no doubt to return to London where there are no reminders of what might have been. To my surprise he agreed without resistance and when I asked him what would retain him, apart from recuperation in the good

Chapter 14

Yorkshire air, he said he 'still wanted to get to the bottom of the business'. He is minded to interrogate Jennie Calman when she is caught to try to uncover what could possibly motivate a woman to take up the practice of 'commercial' infanticide. His journalistic spirit of enquiry is so strong that it overrides any consideration of his own feelings. He has said little about Miss Thwaites, but I hope one day he may bring himself to talk about her to us both. He is also concerned to stay with young Peter Samuels who remains seriously ill after his treatment by Calman. The boy is being well looked after by my cousin's housekeeper and the surgeon who says, 'he will soon be on the mend'.

I cannot tell when we will be returning. My estimation is that it may be within the month; certainly, our stay will encompass the trial. In the meantime, the hunt for Calman goes on and when there is news of her inevitable capture and incarceration I will write directly.

Yours respectfully,
Edgar Lawes

Edgar laid down his pen and sighed. He still retained the image in his head of Ambrose's face as he relayed the details of Rosalie's last few minutes. When he had repeated her words to his friend, the man's face became frozen as he absorbed them. Then he gave such a cry of pain it touched Edgar's heart; with tears in his eyes, his friend's shoulders sagged and his knees buckled. Edgar had reached for a chair and pushed him down into it. There were no words to be said that would not sound crassly inadequate. Instead he turned his attention to Peter who was lying unconscious on the floor covered by Ambrose's coat. Ambrose had cut the twine and Edgar winced to see the cruel red and black bruises across the boy's wrists. Taking some water from one of the buckets, he placed some in a bowl and ordered the young girl, who was standing helplessly by, to bathe them with a cotton rag. The man whom Ambrose had wrestled to the floor had sustained a bang on the head and was half-sitting in a dazed state.

Peter lay totally still and looked very pale; Edgar saw the violent bruise on the side of his face where the woman had struck the blow that had laid him out cold for many hours. The boy was clearly in a bad way and needed urgent attention. He hoped George would soon appear with his party and that he and Ambrose could escort Peter back to Hoyles, a warm bed and treatment for his various injuries. He estimated that the lad had been held with force for over twenty-four hours.

Edgar was anxious to interrogate Calman's accomplices thoroughly before they were taken away by George Lawes since he was the local magistrate. The pair were both in states of shock and fear, and he felt he could get answers out of them in that condition, which might not be so easy when they had time to calm down and consider how best to save themselves. He turned to the young girl cowering in the corner for more precise details as to what had happened to Peter while he had been kept against his will.

'How long has this boy been here? Why is he in such a state? Who's done this to him?'

'It was Mrs Fairfax. She walloped him with her cosh and then he was left in the room tied up. We wasn't allowed to go near him while she was away.'

'You mean you left him unattended when he might have died? I call that "attempted murder" and you can hang for that. Now, tell me. What's been going on here? How do you know Mrs Fairfax?'

'She says she's some kind of auntie of mine,' she said sulkily. 'I don't know nothing about her. She turned up one day and asked me to help look after some babies she was fostering. I just fetch the water and do some work around the place.'

'What do you know about the infants she brings here? Where are they? The mothers pay her to look after them – so, where are they?'

She looked really frightened now and began to cry. 'I didn't want any part of it; she said we had to do it because we couldn't look after them ourselves and besides, they weren't wanted and would have miserable lives if we left them where they were. It was better to put them out of their misery.'

'Are telling us that you stood by and let her murder small babies and never said a word to anyone? I can't believe even a young, stupid girl would allow that to happen without reporting it.'

Chapter 14

'I was never allowed to leave. I've been here weeks and she wouldn't let me into town. I had to work to earn my keep, like the old man.'

'What about your parents? Where are they?'

'I don't have none. She brought me out of the workhouse; told them she needed a servant.'

Edgar turned to the man, who by this time was much more alert and clearly now very scared. It seemed he was a genuine relative of Jennie Calman's, an in-law of sorts. At first, he professed ignorance of all her affairs, but after some physically menacing threats from Edgar he admitted he knew what her business was, although he denied he had any involvement in the disposing of the infants.

'You're both guilty of at least conspiring to commit murder and will hang for it,' said Edgar. 'If there are any other details you've missed, then it might help you if you tell me now. For instance, you must know where the Calman – Fairfax – woman would go? She's on the run and needs friends to hide her.'

The man spat derisively. 'Friends! She has none. She isn't the type to make them or need them. As far as I know she works alone.'

'Have you heard of a man called Tom Sizewell?'

The man gave a start at the mention of the name. 'May've done,' he muttered evasively. 'She went to see a man in town some nights. I think she might have said she was going to Tom's.' It was clear he was beginning to see the sense in cooperation. 'I don't know where he lives though, and he never came here.'

'Are you the only people she knows in the district, besides Sizewell? Where is she likely to hide? For instance, does she know other ways to get off the moor to escape?'

The man was sullen and shrugged his shoulders. Edgar felt like hitting him, but restrained his anger and repeated the last question. It had sunk into the man's consciousness that he had no way to escape a trial and conviction and decided it might eventually be to his advantage to be helpful; he laid a proposition out to Edgar.

'If I give you places she might go, would it go easier for me later? I'd rather be transported than hanged.'

'I can't promise anything,' said Edgar with truth, 'I can only say I'll do my best to let the judge know you cooperated.'

'Jennie and I have some mutual relatives, a mill-working family living in the shacks down by the canal. I've never been there, so I don't know exactly where it is. You'll find it difficult to track her there; it's like a rabbit warren – everyone living on top of everyone else. A good place to hide, I'd have thought. As Bingley's probably sealed off it's her last chance. She wouldn't go out on the moor – she hated it and always used the same tracks to and from the town. She said she didn't want to end up under the mud.'

Edgar shook his head at the irony of the statement and then moved on to question the man about the other crime connected to both Sizewell and Calman. 'What do you know about the death of Donald Thwaites?'

The man and girl both looked mystified and he thought genuinely so. Ambrose had by this time roused himself slightly, especially when Edgar referred to Rosalie's brother and listened intently as Edgar continued his interrogation. The pair both flatly denied any knowledge of or connection with his death and Edgar felt it would be fruitless to pursue it. Instead he turned back to the matter of the baby farming.

'I'll ask you both a straight question, and I need a correspondingly straight answer. How you answer might help you when you come to trial; it may mean the difference between hanging and transportation. If, as you say, you weren't practically involved in disposing of the children, tell us how Mrs Fairfax went about it. The more honest you are the better it'll be for you.'

They looked one to the other and fell silent as though weighing their options.

After a few seconds the girl burst out, 'She threw them in the mire! I know because she took me there one day and I saw her do it. She told me I'd have to do it sometime so I might as well know how. I'm really scared of her. If she could do that to babies, what would she do to me if I crossed her? But I swear I've never done it. The last one she took was a couple of days ago.'

Edgar was silent for a while as he digested this grisly information. Then he asked, 'How many are we talking about?'

Chapter 14

The man replied, 'I know of about six or maybe seven since she came here – that's about eight if you count the one you brought back.'

Ambrose and Edgar looked at one another. That many! The latter felt sick and looked at the tiny bundle of humanity wrapped in rags and lying on the table. The baby had given up on her demand for food and gone to sleep with the obliviousness of the newborn to its surroundings. Edgar tried to keep the picture of the mire from his mind, for not only did he see the last pleading look on Rosalie's face, he could also imagine this infant slowing sinking into the filthy mud to be covered, smothered and lost completely.

Edgar looked at Ambrose. 'How could a woman do this in cold blood? I've come across some very hard cases in my work as magistrate, and I expect you've met a few in your work too. But I can't think of anyone to match the callousness of Jennie Calman. She seems to have a remarkable facility for escape and I can't bear the thought of her getting away and setting up somewhere else. I know you're full of grief, but we need to think clearly about the man's suggestion as to where she might have gone. We must do everything we can to apprehend her. Can you bring yourself to help me form a plan?'

Ambrose certainly was 'full of grief', a pain he had not felt as intensively even when his parents died. To know that, in such a short space of time he had experienced pure joy at the anticipation of a future with a loving partner, one whom he could love and respect in return, only to have it snatched away and by such appalling means. He had at first instinctively refused to believe Edgar as he described the events out on the moor, hoping it had been a dreadful mistake and that Rosalie had somehow managed to extricate herself from the foul mud and slime, and would swing through the door to relay her adventure. But as his friend fell silent his reason returned and he knew it was the truth and she was lost to him in the most appalling way. The painful recollection of their last meeting and Edgar's reiteration of her final words for him choked him into tears and, unashamedly, he broke down despite the presence of two strangers who looked on in silent embarrassment to see a grown man cry.

He was at first oblivious to Edgar's questioning of the young girl and Calman's accomplice until he heard the name Thwaites which roused him from his abstractedness. The whole business of Donald Thwaites's murder, the baby farming and the evilness of the Calman woman rushed into his head and temporarily subsumed his grief. Now vengeance overcame sorrow and his first desire was to apprehend the woman and see her brought to justice. Edgar's plea for help roused him and as he realised the extent of the crimes committed and who was responsible a sharp pang of pure rage almost shook his body, and his mind wrenched itself from misery on to revenge.

Ambrose frowned. 'If the woman's able to obtain some form of transport, she could quickly disappear into the environs of the town, assuming it is right that she has relatives who might hide her. The only solid information we can follow up is her link to Sizewell and I think it's most likely she'll go to him for help. We must arrange for a watch to be put on his place. Whether he'll be prepared to hide her, especially now their business has been exposed for what it is, is another matter. As this man has told us already, she came to this part of Yorkshire because she has relations living here, somewhere down by the canal, which is another useful lead.' But it occurred to him there was a significant problem: neither he nor Edgar were aware of the extent of her acquaintances in the wider district of Bradford and Leeds should she escape the town. Perhaps she had family there too. The words 'needles and haystacks' came into his head.

As he was expounding his thoughts to Edgar they were both relieved to hear thudding hoofbeats on the turf outside and the calling of voices. Presently George entered the cottage, and in his bluff, uncompromising way demanded news. As Edgar unfolded the catalogue of events, his cousin was horrified at the news of Rosalie's death; became very concerned for Peter and Ambrose, and then extremely angry that the woman had made good her escape.

'Curse the woman; if I'd caught her I'd have horsewhipped her before handing her over to the constable! So, what's to be done now? What about these two?' And he pointed at Calman's accomplices with his whip.

Edgar suggested that two riders took both away to Bingley lockup where there would be no opportunity for them to have contact

Chapter 14

with their mistress. George ordered the men to take up an immediate watch close to Sizewell's house after they had delivered the two prisoners; they were to report any sightings of the woman. He arranged for the bridges and other exits in the town to be covered so that she couldn't escape into a wider area.

Edgar was concerned that Peter should be taken back to Hoyles immediately so that his wounds could be treated and he could be fed and rested. The boy was now in a state of unconsciousness and neither Ambrose nor Edgar could tell how badly he had been concussed. They commandeered the cart which was made as comfortable as possible before they laid the boy in it and George arranged for two others of the search party to accompany him back. Hoping for the best, the three men watched as the vehicle was driven out of the gate and across the turf to the nearest track.

Returning to the cottage, George wondered if the pair shouldn't return to Hoyles themselves for some food; but Ambrose, now stimulated into action, was anxious to see the matter through.

'I won't rest until that woman's safely locked up in Wakefield Jail,' he said through gritted teeth.

'Well, you're going to need some transport. Take the horses from my men; they can remain here in the unlikely event she returns. What'll we do with the baby by the way?'

'Take her with us and reunite her with her mother as soon as possible.'

George looked down at the whey-faced infant who was quietly sucking her thumb in lieu of anything more sustaining. 'Looks a poor little thing – are you sure she will last?'

'We'll wrap her up well and hope for the best. I'm sure if I can get a lamb to survive I can do the same for this little one,' said Edgar, taking charge of the bundle and cradling her between his arms. 'This will be the only decent thing we'll see in all this – the smile on the mother's face!'

The three men mounted up and set out for Bingley. Ambrose was determined that Rosalie's father should be told of her death immediately. As they rode, George, worried about both Ambrose's physical state as well as the burden of his grief, did his best to persuade him get a night's sleep.

'Two of my men have been sent to watch Sizewell's place and report back if there's a sighting of the woman. I think it's unlikely she would move out of the house if she'd gained entry; she'll know it's too risky for her to be seen in the town once word gets around as to the crimes she's committed. Look – I still think you should come back to Hoyles and rest up. You'll feel more refreshed and better able to cope with things.'

By the time they reached Mr Thwaites's smallholding the pressure from George, with Edgar's support, was very great and Ambrose was on the verge of submitting to their suggestion that he return to Hoyles and sleep on a plan he was evolving, which he could appraise in the morning with a refreshed sense of purpose. The interview with Mr Thwaites clinched it, as Ambrose felt physically drained when he came out of the place. Seeing the sense in his friends' argument, he capitulated to their pressure and turned his horse towards Hoyles.

It was a sad, damp and bedraggled group who dismounted in the stable yard at around four o'clock and entered the house. All three had been up very early and out in dull, wet and clinging mist; their mood matched their appearance. Edgar immediately passed over the infant to George's housekeeper who clucked over her and whisked her away, shaking her head. The three men's priority was to send for a surgeon to examine Peter's head wound. The lad was by now unconscious again and lapsed into delirium from time to time. He had been put straight to bed in Edgar's room which was the largest guest room in the house while they waited for professional help. Edgar and Ambrose stayed by Peter's bedside, while George ordered hot water and food. Ambrose, already undergoing severe shock himself, was now weighted down with the idea that Peter might die because of his investigation. If he had not suggested this adventure in the first place, Rosalie would not have died and Peter would have been spared his injuries. When he suggested this to his friend, Edgar attempted to rouse him by pointing out that none of this was anyone's fault except the Calman woman and her accomplices. Peter was a strong young

Chapter 14

man who had survived the Seddon Union with no signs of any physical effect. He was certain he would pull through this crisis, especially with expert care. Two hours later the surgeon had examined Peter and declared he had a severe case of concussion, but which was not fatal and would surely respond to bed rest for several days.

After a meal, which Ambrose hardly touched, the three men withdrew to George's study to discuss what to do next. Two men had been posted to keep watch all night on Sizewell's house and report back if any sightings were made of Jennie Calman. If she was seen entering they were to make no move to follow her into the property. The exits of the town had been covered so that should she try to slip out she would be immediately apprehended. Nothing was heard from any of those on lookout until about nine o'clock, when one who had been watching the house sent a rider to say they had seen a woman slipping through the front door which had been opened by Sizewell. She had been on foot and there was no sign of a vehicle. The man was sent back to resume the watch; George, Edgar and Ambrose agreed that it was unlikely Calman would move that night; she had nowhere to go and no transport. Perhaps she was going to put up at the house for a few days until she thought things had calmed down, although she might have known there would be a full hue and cry at some time as the news of what she had done filtered out through parish-pump gossip. To that end the men from the search party had all been sworn to secrecy. It was imperative that the woman was left uncertain what the response would be from the authorities. Satisfied that nothing would happen until the morrow, the three men turned in for a few hours' sleep.

Over breakfast they discussed how to bring about the arrest of Jennie Calman. George was all for taking a few of the local militia and making a full-scale raid on the house. Ambrose thought this would be counter-productive; such a hullabaloo would alert her before they could get inside. She would probably be clever enough to bolt into the interminable back alleys of the tenement quarter of the town and make her way to the relatives whom her accomplice had mentioned.

'I've been working on an idea that could enable us to get at her. The more I think it through, the more I think it'll work; it's devious and matches cunning with cunning. The victims of these crimes are obviously the infants, but also their mothers and I believe they should have a share in bringing this woman to justice. We can use them to flush her out. There are possibly seven mothers in Bingley and beyond whose offspring have been brutally murdered by someone offering to care for them. There's also one whose baby has fortunately been saved. Besides the grief and anger they'll feel when we tell them what's happened, they're also going to feel guilty they were complicit in giving away their babies to a stranger in the first place, however much they had been cornered into it. The combination of grief, sorrow and rage will be a powerful incentive for them to seek this creature out and bring her to justice. They know the town, its back alleys, cellars and shacks and I'm sure they'll spare nothing to find her. The only risk would be if they got to her unaccompanied by anyone in authority; it's likely they'd tear her limb from limb. But if we plan it well we can minimise the risk. Besides, from my point of view it's worth taking. The woman's crimes were such that no decent female would tolerate her presence. Look, I think I can persuade Janet Stow to help us. I believe she has good standing among the tenement occupants and they'll listen to her. She was, after all, the great-aunt of one of the victims and she knows the mother of the one we saved – by the way, we must return the child to her as soon as we can.'

But Edgar was very dubious. 'That sounds much too risky to me. As you say, if they got hold of her before us they'd probably kill her. No one would take absolute responsibility; it would be a collective act and defeat the object of bringing her to a public trial where all her crimes could be exposed. By bringing this plan to fruition we could be accused of condoning riot and murder.'

'There speaks the lawyer,' muttered Ambrose. 'I'm convinced we can control events and use the women, not as a bloodthirsty mob, but by co-opting them to make a citizen's arrest, all perfectly legal as you will know. As I understand it an Englishman has been entitled since medieval times to apprehend a wanted felon at the behest of the sheriff without being sworn in as a law officer. I presume it applies to females as well?'

'Just because it's legal if it's been sanctioned by a magistrate or sher-

Chapter 14

iff, I'm still not sure it's the right thing to do; we may be unleashing all kinds of mischief. Remember what happened to the Calman woman at Seddon when they drove her out. It was the females who instigated that, and the power of their anger was such that they alarmed me. The crimes she's committed this time are way beyond cruel treatment, they strike at the very core of a woman's maternal instincts – infanticide is beyond reason. I think they'd mete out reciprocal punishment.'

George interrupted: 'I've some sympathy with your view, Edgar. As a local magistrate, I'm not keen to see disorder in my neighbourhood, neither would I condone murder, however justified. But in this instance, I know my men and I can assure you we'll intervene at the slightest hint of trouble. They'll be armed, but no muskets will be fired unless necessary. There are more effective ways of controlling a would-be mob; since Peterloo my men are well-versed in them. We train in the event of trouble in the factories.'

Ambrose sighed. 'You wouldn't need to be prepared for trouble if conditions were improved.'

'Now I know you are coming around to your rational self' – Edgar smiled – 'but this is no time for radical debate. Between you both I'm reluctantly persuaded. Now, how are we to achieve this miracle of control?'

'Speed is essential if we're to catch her before she can make a permanent escape. It was well thought out by George to cover the exits from Bingley; now obviously we must return to the town and question Sizewell as to Calman's whereabouts. As a magistrate, George, you'll have a right to enter the place and make a search. If she's there well and good, but I can't help thinking she'll somehow give us the slip. That's when the women will come into play. I'll arrange things with Mrs Stow.'

Edgar enquired, 'Where is the child, by the way? She seemed to disappear when we arrived yesterday evening.'

'A stable hand's wife has taken her in for the time being, until she can be reunited with her mother. But we must inform whoever she is that the child is safe,' said George.

'More reason for us to move quickly and get into town,' suggested Ambrose, who was now in full readiness for action. He had tucked his grief away for a while; his prime motivation was now revenge and his anger was white-hot. Never mind what the women might do to Jennie Calman, it was what Ambrose might do that worried Edgar; it was not difficult to read his friend's thoughts.

The two men made their way to Peter's room and were relieved to see him propped up on the pillows and being fed from a spoon by the housekeeper. He managed a faint smile and, although pale and bearing a black eye and a livid bruise down the side of his face, he could converse a little, obviously pleased to see them. Edgar was aware that Peter was likely to remain out of action for some weeks and it struck him that he might benefit from some special company. He promised himself he would write a couple of letters immediately he returned to Hoyles after their business in the town was completed. He hoped there would be better news by then.

Horses were saddled ready in the stable yard and the three men were soon on their way to the town. Coincidentally they met one of the men posted to watch the Sizewell house. He reported that the manager had left the premises and had been followed to the factory.

Ambrose thought for a minute then observed, 'So, he's going to work as though nothing has happened. Either she's not told him of yesterday's events, or he knows and is covering them both by behaving normally. The question is – is she still there? If there was only one man watching while the other followed Sizewell, and if she suspected the house was being watched, could the woman have escaped out of the back? She's so devious I wouldn't be at all surprised if she isn't at large somewhere. She may have even got out in the middle of the night – through a window or something.'

'My men are very reliable,' said George robustly. 'If she did manage to escape, she must be near invisible.'

'Dressed entirely in black and at night – there was no moon last night – even the sharpest-eyed lookout might miss her,' replied Ambrose.

'Then I suggest we break in and search the place,' said George. 'At least we'll know one way or another!'

'I'd rather we did nothing so dramatic. I still say we shouldn't stir up the town; breaking down doors and effecting searches will only make

CHAPTER 14

tongues wag and rumours fly. Instead I propose we go to the factory and take Sizewell to one side and tell him we know all. I understand, George, that you're acquainted with the owner, Mr Richmond. Can you rouse him now and ask him to come to the mill on a matter of urgent business? You could brief him on the way so he knows what he'll be involved in. I want Sizewell to recognise the game's up and put pressure on him to tell us where the woman is. The presence of two magistrates and his master should be enough to make him come clean. My impression of the man is that he has the looks and qualities of a rat – he'll soon want to gnaw his way out of this sinking ship.'

George and Edgar glanced at each other. Edgar said, 'Yes, I think this would be useful as it could possibly deliver three outcomes all at once.'

'And they are?' asked George.

'Uncovering the whereabouts of Jennie Calman; second, exposing the baby farming issue to those in positions of power in the town. Third, revealing other breaches of the regulations like the employment of under-aged children. Including the mill owner in this is an excellent idea.'

'There's no doubt Richmond will be shocked when we let him know,' said George.

'I'll relish the expression on his face when we tell him of the egregious crimes being committed by his manager.' And Edgar looked almost triumphant.

George was, as usual, pragmatic. 'What happens when we go piling into Richmond's office? Surely people will begin to talk. As we've agreed, it's imperative we keep the news of Calman's business quiet until we have her cornered. If word gets out where she is then I don't give anything for our chances of getting to her while she is alive, let alone seeing her in court.'

'I can't see why two gentlemen such as you and I shouldn't visit Mr Richmond at his place of work without causing gossip,' responded Edgar. 'In the meantime, Ambrose can visit Janet Stow to explain what's happened; break the news about her niece's baby and reassure her that her neighbour's child is well and in good hands. What will you say to Mrs Stow, Ambrose?'

'I'll tell her the truth. I can be frank with her – her husband will be at work and I'll be able to see her alone. I gauged her as a sensible woman and I think she'll be able to galvanise other women in a search, while holding them back from any desperate action against the Calman woman.'

There was general agreement that this was a useful plan and as they approached the outskirts of Bingley, George deviated off to the high area of the town, where the professional men had built their large villas, to seek out Samuel Richmond; Edgar and Ambrose set off in the direction of the low town. Having arranged to return to the mill as soon as he had finished arranging things with Janet Stow, Ambrose parted company from his friend. Realising he needed to stable his horse as he would go on foot to visit her, he found an inn where a small boy took his mount and, for a sixpence, agreed to feed and water the beast. Ambrose then walked with long determined strides towards the Stow family lodgings.

In the meantime, Edgar rode up to the mill; as he approached the gates to the yard he saw that work was continuing in a normal fashion and called a labourer over to enquire the whereabouts of the main office as he wished to see the owner. Dismounting, he left his horse tied to a post and was led across the yard where he saw John Walters, George's delivery man, standing with a labourer checking the bales as they were hoisted into the mill. Edgar was taken up the steps to the first floor and shown the door to the office. Hearing the noise of movement in the room, but knowing that his cousin George and Samuel Richmond could not have yet arrived, he was uncertain whether to knock and enter. Most likely it was Tom Sizewell inside as, according to Ambrose, the manager regularly used the office; the fact that he was there was a relief since he would not have to be sent for, which might have roused his suspicions; Samuel Richmond had designated days when he might have visited the office and Monday was not one of them.

Edgar was looking with curiosity round the lobby in which he was standing. He could hear the persistent reverberation of clatter and banging from the machines in the spinning shop beyond doors to his right. They were slightly open and he could make out vague move-

Chapter 14

ments from people and machines. What most struck him was the pale grey dust that had escaped from the shop to the waiting area and permeated the air with its grease. Within minutes he felt his hands and face were sticky with this residue. He wondered what its long-term effects were on the lungs of the workers permanently exposed to the contaminated air and it reminded him of the miasma left by the residue from the oakum, the hemp rope unravelled by the workhouse inmates in Seddon Union and how he had seen it drifting through the sunbeams in their workroom. There were no hints of sunbeams in this place; the dim light that came through the tiny barred windows was diffused by this grey mist.

Wondering how long it would take George to rouse Samuel Richmond, Edgar estimated that Sizewell would soon become aware of someone outside his office. Anxious to meet this man, having heard something about him from Ambrose and feeling he had nothing to lose as they had never set eyes on each other, Edgar tapped briskly on the door and, responding to the order to enter, he stepped into the room. It was a place of business with a large desk covered in ledgers and loose papers; lining the walls were record books; in the corner stood a mighty iron safe with a large wheel at its front.

Sizewell looked up from his accounts. 'Yes? Who are you?'

Edgar did not remove his hat and responded truthfully, 'My name is Edgar Lawes, I've come to see Mr Samuel Richmond on a matter of business.'

Looking Edgar up and down, Sizewell could see he was a gentleman and therefore deserving of due deference. 'Mr Richmond does not attend the mill on Mondays I'm afraid, Mr Lawes.'

'Well, today I think you'll find he'll be joining us,' responded Edgar obliquely. 'May I sit down?'

'Please do.' Sizewell mustered as much politeness as he felt was necessary. If the owner was to make an unexpected visit he did not want to be reported for rudeness. That would be yet another problem to solve. All the morning he had been preoccupied with the business of Jennie Calman and how they were to get her out of the town; now, just as he was preparing to leave to try to organise her escape, his boss was making an unannounced visit.

Edgar sat bolt upright on his chair. He made no attempt to engage the man in conversation, and Sizewell, lacking those skills of politeness that mark out a gentleman, was at a loss to know how to fill the silence. He looked uneasy and began to shuffle papers from one side of the desk to the other. As the man fidgeted with files and dockets, Edgar noted his rat-like features and how the man did his utmost to avoid visual contact. He was, as Ambrose had described him, shifty.

At least five minutes passed until they heard voices and footfall on the stairs and then the door opened. A thin man of average height stepped through followed by George Lawes. On first viewing Samuel Richmond had a dour demeanour; a slightly over-large, hooked nose gave him a hawkish look which was augmented by piercing grey eyes.

'Edgar, let me introduce you.' George tried to undertake the social niceties as Tom Sizewell started to his feet when he saw his employer.

But ignoring Edgar's outstretched hand, Richmond, in a white-hot fury, advanced towards the desk. 'Yes, get up, Sizewell. The story I've just heard leads me to believe you no longer deserve to sit in my chair.'

The man went pale. His eyes darted between the three men; his tongue flickered over his top lip.

Richmond continued: 'I know everything you've been involved in: the woman Fairfax or Calman – whatever her name is – and her connection to you. You're a liar and a murderer as far as I can tell, and I'll see you on the gallows. Now, tell us where the woman is. Is she still in your house or has she moved elsewhere? Lying won't help, neither will playing for time. There are men watching at all the exits to the town and she can't escape. It may be better for you at your trial if you can deliver her to us. It'll certainly be best for her because if the women of Bingley get hold of her before the law does we can't guarantee her safety. If you have any sense you'll tell us everything you know.'

Sizewell fell back into the chair; his eyes continued to dart from one face to another. He was clearly trying to think his way out of this predicament. It flashed across his mind that there was a chance he might escape the rope if he gave evidence against his erstwhile accomplice. After all he had not been directly concerned in the dis-

Chapter 14

posal of the children, only providing cash investment in the enterprise in the early days, collecting the fees for the transaction and passing them over to Calman – less his commission. If they had become over-friendly as a result, that didn't make him a murderer. Within seconds he decided to cooperate and try to extricate a promise that his collaboration would be considered at his trial. His tongue continued to flick out to moisten his lips which had dried up with fear.

'She spent the night at my place. I told her to stay there while I found a way to get her out. As far as I know she's still there.'

'What about these distant relatives of hers who live down by the canal?' asked Edgar. 'What are their names and where exactly are they?'

'Don't know anything about them. She didn't mention anything to me.'

'Is there anyone else in the house besides her?' asked Edgar.

'Only a lad, my nephew, who's lodging with me.'

'My men didn't report any sighting of a boy,' said George.

'He hasn't left the place; he's only been there two days.'

Samuel Richmond was anxious to be rid of his manager as soon as possible. He asked George what he intended to do with him. 'You're a magistrate, won't you arrest him?'

'We'll call the constable to place him in the lock-up while arrangements are made for him to be taken to Wakefield. I can't see any point now in interrogating him further about this business. We'll have to speak with him later about other matters, but for now he's given us what we need – the whereabouts of the chief culprit. I suggest we get over to the house immediately and fetch her out. May I use your desk for a moment, Samuel?' He reached for pen and paper and scribbled a note for the constable which he sealed. A worker was sent for and told to deliver it with all haste. Despite their best efforts to keep matters discreet, the rumour mill was soon grinding fast with the news that Mr Sizewell was under restraint in the office with Mr Richmond and two gentlemen standing guard over him. The place was rife with extravagant speculation.

Hurrying through the cobbled streets down the hill to the tenement buildings, Ambrose rehearsed the conversation he was about to have with Janet Stow. He was gambling somewhat on her common sense; that she would not immediately think of a terrible retribution, but rather understand his logic that justice would be best served through a public trial and a public hanging. Tearing the Calman woman limb from limb would make all involved as tainted as her.

It was fortunate that, because of her injury, Janet Stow was still working from home. As he approached her lodgings, he heard small children quarrelling, and the exasperated shouting of their mother. They were all confined to one room and Mrs Stow was expected to complete a daily quota of work. Just as he had raised his fist to knock on the dilapidated door, it flew open and out tumbled three raggedly dressed infants, followed by a scrawny and dishevelled young girl who looked about 12. Janet Stow was screaming at their retreating backs, 'Get out, and stay out! Don't come back till I call you.'

The small unwanted scraps of humanity rushed against Ambrose's legs, almost toppling him over. The young girl following looked surprised to see a stranger, but, mindful of her charges and the clout she would get if she didn't pursue them, rushed off in full flight calling to them to come back to her. He watched as they disappeared to the end of the lane to a large communal midden heap where, he supposed, they would spend the next few hours in 'play'. The door now standing wide open on loose hinges, he stepped into the room unimpeded. Mrs Stow, bent to her work on the table, didn't see him at first, but becoming aware of someone in the room thought it was her niece returning and stood up to remonstrate. Startled when she saw Ambrose, she put down the scissors and mechanically rubbed her greasy hands down her filthy dress.

Her visitor immediately tried to put her at her ease. 'Good day, Mrs Stow. I hope you're keeping well, and your leg is improving. I'm glad to see you're at home. I've some things I need to talk to you about, and it's best you're alone.'

She was immediately suspicious. Only men with devious intentions visited other men's wives when they were at home alone. 'My husband's at the factory, where I suppose you should be. He wouldn't like it if he found you here when he was away. You may drink together,

Chapter 14

but he told me he thought there was something not right about you, and he's not sure whether to trust you. You don't talk like a mill-hand. What do you want?'

'He's quite right, Mrs Stow. I'm not what I appear to be. I suggest you sit down and let me tell you why I'm here.'

She looked even more doubtful and suspicious, but curiosity overcame her and she motioned him to one of the only two chairs in the room.

He continued: 'There are two reasons I want to talk to you: first, I've some tragic news to tell you that concerns your family and second, I need your help to obtain justice for your niece, and other young women of your acquaintance.' Now he had her full attention and she took her place in the other of the two rickety chairs at the table. Ambrose wasted no time and started by outlining Jennie Calman's crimes, although he gave no details of the way in which she had disposed of the babies. Before he could, she interrupted him.

'You say she's not looked after the babies she was given, but got rid of them in some way? Tell me, what's she done with them? What's she done with Margaret?'

Ambrose hesitated. How could he tell her she had probably been literally thrown away, and sunk without trace in the mud of a mire? Yet it was pointless to lie; everything Calman had done would be exposed in open court, however graphic the evidence. He drew a deep breath. 'She put her in a bog out on the moor and watched her sink.'

Mrs Stow gazed at him, blinked hard and shook her head. 'No! I don't believe you – no woman could do that. I know of women who've got rid of stillborns, trying to hide them, but never in all my life have I heard of one throwing a live baby away and into such a place. Our family scraped together money we couldn't afford and gave Mrs Fairfax – Calman – our little Margaret on the understanding the child would be cared for. Now you're saying the woman has pocketed the money and killed the baby, and not only my niece's child, but seven others. That is wicked – wicked indeed!'

'There were seven babies killed that we know of, but possibly more. One piece of good news is that the child of the woman you told me of who gave up her baby last week has been saved. I need your help to reunite that little girl with her mother.'

'Where is she?'

'She's being well looked after over at Hoyles farm, and is no worse for the experience of being in the clutches of one of the evillest of women I've ever come across. Besides bringing the baby back to her rightful place, there's another task that has brought me here. I want you to help us catch Jennie Calman. So far she's been very clever and quick in giving us the slip, although I'm assured she can't leave the town. Watchers are posted on all the exits. She may be hiding in the house of the mill manager, Tom Sizewell—'

'That bastard!' Janet Stow spat on the earth floor. 'How's he involved?'

'The Calman woman knows him and he's been sheltering her. We've been luckier with him – now my friends who are both magistrates are questioning him about her whereabouts.'

Janet Stow was silent for a moment as she took in the information. Then she looked Ambrose squarely in the eye and asked, 'Tell me, who and what are you? It seems Jed was right when he said there was more to you than he first thought.'

Ambrose did not want to go into a full explanation of what he had been doing in Bingley, but felt she deserved to know something, so he told her what he was; that he had come to the town to investigate the suspicion that baby farming was going on in the district.

He was not altogether surprised when she responded indignantly, 'You mean you've been spying on us? Coming here, pretending to be neighbourly when all the time you were trying to get information out of us. I don't think that's a right thing to do, it's underhand and it's not the behaviour of honest folk.'

'You're partly right and I don't take any pleasure from it, although I've been using those methods for some time now – because they work. But whatever you think of them, my intentions are always to try to make things right and get justice for those who might not be able to do it for themselves. Now, I want that justice for these dead children and their mothers – and all the others there may be! That's all

Chapter 14

I can say and I hope you believe me. I can't defend myself any other way.'

There was a long silence while the woman pondered on what he had said. Finally, looking directly into his face, her small button-sized brown eyes searching for answers, she asked, 'And what do you want of me?'

He gave an inward sigh of relief that she seemed to be accepting his explanation. 'You know this area well; if Sizewell has been hiding her and she's slipped out of his house, she'll surely have gone to ground in this end of the town. There are so many alleyways and derelict buildings here for her to hide in. We've been told that she has relatives living down by the canal, although we don't know where or who they are. She may be thinking, once the hue and cry's died down, she'll be able to make an escape – even if that takes a few days. She's certainly one of the most cunning people I've come across, and no doubt she'll have planned it out and have food enough to last while she lies low. I want you, with a small group of women you can trust, to work with me to search the area and find likely hiding places.'

'Why the women – why not involve the men? Anyway – how would you keep them out? They'll want to show her a thing or two when they get hold of her! That's not to say the women won't!'

'That's why I've come to you particularly. I rate you as being level-headed and sensible.' He didn't add that he was impressed with the way she put up with a drunken lazy husband while keeping her family from starvation. 'Also you're someone with authority in this neighbourhood. Your reputation among the women is well known. I've heard them talking in the mill about how you try to help families out with food and advice, even though you struggle with a large family yourself. The fact that you've taken your niece in when she was in trouble, and scraped together the money you could ill afford, tells me a lot about you and I can understand why your neighbours look up to you.'

Mrs Stow looked momentarily taken aback. Praise from one's neighbours – and a stranger – was a new experience, and her normally grey face flushed dog-rose pink with pleasure. But, lacking the skill to accept a compliment graciously, she quickly brushed his words aside.

'That's as maybe, but what are you going to do? What do you want me to do?'

'As I see it, the most important thing besides catching her is to keep her safe for the hangman. When she's up on the scaffold you'll all have your revenge as you watch her swing. But it must be done officially. If she's torn to pieces by a mob, then the law will be after all of you and the moral and legal victory will be lost.' He held his breath while she absorbed this truth. Would she see the sense of it, or would her thirst for revenge overcome the desire for official and public justice?

'I still find it hard to know how you'll keep the men out of it. As soon as it gets out, there'll be a riot in the town until she's found. How do you think the men will take the idea of a group of women leading the search, finding her and handing her over in one piece?'

'Fortunately, at the moment very few people know about this. All those involved have been sworn to secrecy by the magistrates. We'll arrange things so the search will go on when the men are otherwise occupied – that is in the taverns after work. If you don't mind me observing, Mrs Stow, your husband spends most of his evenings in the ale-house and when he returns is not in any state to organise a search party. The same goes for many others. My estimation is that the women of this town, as in most others in the country, are the true organisers who keep the family and community together.'

'You're saying my husband's a drunkard?'

'To be honest, I've spent several evenings with him, and he has a certain capacity for ale!'

'I can't argue with you. He's no good either as a husband or a father, but he's all we have. You're quite right, it's us women who keep things going. While you've been talking I've thought of several good wives who will be reliable and discreet. We wouldn't need many to search these rat holes. Whether we should include the mothers of the babies who are already dead I'm not sure. I think it would be best if we keep them out of it for as long as we can; in fact, we shouldn't tell them anything until she's under lock and key. Besides, the two I know of – my niece and the other one – are both very young and would be of little help. We need some of the older women who have good sensible heads on their shoulders. I would think eight at the most. We

Chapter 14

can split up into pairs to search if we must. Two of us will be able to restrain the woman when we catch her.'

Ambrose was gratified that Janet Stow had fallen in with his plan so effectively and was already mentally organising things using her refined local knowledge. He hastened to tell her that he would be coming with them, along with a JP who could authorise an arrest, but that should anyone come across Calman first, they would be entitled to make a citizen's arrest. He also pointed out that members of the militia would be on hand, discreetly, but available should things go wrong and there was likelihood of a riot.

'Hmm! Where would we be without the militia?' she asked sardonically.

Within half an hour the plan had been finalised. Mrs Stow had the names of possibly seven or eight women whom she trusted would carry the search through to its desired conclusion. Ambrose now needed to return to the mill to see if there was any news of where the Calman woman might be and told Janet he would return within the hour. If Jennie Calman was still at Sizewell's then their strategy would be redundant, she would be detained by the militia and sent off immediately to Wakefield Jail. If she had managed to escape then it would be up to Ambrose, Edgar and Janet Stow to put their own plan into action. Once that was decided, Mrs Stow said she would need half an hour or so to gather her women together, to inform them of their strategy and to set up an organised sweep of the district. Ambrose offered to come along with her to explain things, but Mrs Stow felt he would be a distraction. He was impressed with the way she had questioned him closely and then immediately put a plan together, and so was satisfied that he could safely leave her to gather her group together as necessary. What he was really hoping was that Jennie Calman was still hiding in Sizewell's house and it would be a simple matter of extricating her from there.

As Ambrose walked briskly back to the mill he heard the church clock chiming midday and realised that he hadn't eaten anything since a scant meal early that morning. It also crossed his mind that the factory workers would be stopping for their dinner in half an hour. It was important that he and his friends had left the place before the workers began milling about in the yard; it wouldn't do for Sizewell to be led out in full view of the whole factory, as though he was under some sort of detention. He increased his pace and in five minutes had arrived in the office, ignoring the starts of recognition he received from fellow labourers in the yard and the questioning looks they gave him as he ran up the steps three at a time. Arriving in the office, he found Edgar, George and Mr Richmond standing over a cowering and deflated Sizewell who was slumped in the chair. After a brief introduction to the mill owner, Ambrose asked, 'Has he said anything as to her whereabouts?'

Edgar told him that as far as Tom Sizewell knew she had been in his house when he left for work four hours previously. There had been no word from the men watching the house, so it could be presumed she was still there. Edgar and George had already planned how to bring Sizewell out discreetly so his appearance would engender no gossip. They were all aware that it was approaching the dinner break and it was decided they must leave immediately and deliver their suspect to the constable. Richmond would stay behind as he had no direct involvement in the current matter, although Ambrose told him he would be back to talk to him about 'some dubious aspects' of the running of the mill. The owner raised a questioning eyebrow, but as he opened his mouth to enquire what those aspects might be, Ambrose had disappeared through the door and caught up with Edgar and George, with Sizewell, head bowed, walking between them.

There were some curious stares from workers in the yard, but the group managed to make their exit through the factory gates casual, as though they were on their way to some business or other. Once out of sight of the mill George delivered their prisoner to two of his men waiting in the street, with instructions that they should take him to the constable who would put him in the town's lock-up until George gave him further orders. The rest of George's party of farmhands were waiting outside Sizewell's house, which was a few minutes' walk from the factory.

George approached them and asked immediately, 'Has the woman left?'

'No woman has left, but a young man did – we heard he was

Chapter 14

Sizewell's nephew. He headed off into the town about a quarter of an hour ago. She must still be in there.'

'There's no question then, we must break in and root her out,' declared Edgar.

Quickly the men formed themselves into a file and George knocked firmly on the front door several times, shouting for admittance 'in the name of the law!'. There was a resounding silence and so he gave the nod to one of his men who shoulder-barged the door which, being cheaply made, easily gave way. The men piled in behind George and Edgar and the party went through the house from top to bottom. In the cellar they found a young, slim and tallish youth cowering semi-naked who, when he was asked who he was and what he was doing there, whimpered that he was Mr Sizewell's nephew.

'Who else has been living here?' asked Edgar. 'Has a woman called Fairfax been staying here?'

'Yes, but she's gone.'

Light dawned on Ambrose; as someone who adopted disguises himself he knew when he had been hoodwinked. 'She's taken his clothes and is masquerading as a boy!' He turned to one of the men who had been watching the house. 'When did you say you saw the boy leaving?'

The man looked defensive, as though he felt he was to blame that she had given them the slip. 'Quarter of an hour ago, like I said, he – she – walked out cool as you like and headed off towards the town. She was carrying a large pack.'

'Well, she'll be well and truly hidden in the rat holes of the low town.' Ambrose was fuming, not at the men who had been charged with guarding the place, but at himself for underestimating Jennie Calman's cunning and coolness under pressure. 'I'll go straight back to Janet Stow and tell her the hunt is on. Most of the women she needs will still be working and not available until after six o'clock but if all the exits to the town are tightly sealed – and I'm sure they are, George – we can afford to wait until dark to find her. There are no escape routes for her beyond the town's boundaries. The one thing that must be done immediately is to alert all the watchers that they're looking for a woman who is now in disguise as a young man. It's my guess

Calman won't plan to move from wherever she is for several days. You may be sure the pack she's carrying will contain enough provisions for her to sit it out until she thinks it's safe to move. Talking about provisions, I think we should all get some food, it's been hours since we ate.'

His friend's comments heartened Edgar. He had noticed a change in Ambrose since early this morning. The need for action had galvanised him, and underlying it all, he knew, was Ambrose's thirst for revenge. He couldn't blame the man, he would have felt the same in those circumstances, but he wondered how far Ambrose would go to satisfy his urge for vengeance. Although he had been insistent that the women should not lay a finger on Calman but leave her to official justice, he wondered if his friend could resist a physical attack on her when she was caught. There had been no chance for them to talk in depth about Rosalie, his intentions towards her and certainly not the manner of her death; the man had been too deeply shocked and withdrawn and Edgar, in respect of those emotions, had been unwilling to broach the subject. Now, it seemed, the man was on fire for action, doing what he did best – planning and directing strategy. It's the best medicine, he thought, and just as well his appetite's returned.

They turned into the town and found a quiet, clean tavern where they ordered ale and food. Keeping themselves to themselves in a corner hidden from the bar, they talked over the events of the morning. Edgar and George reported that Sizewell had denied all knowledge of the baby farming and any involvement in the murdering of infants. They would have to wait until Calman could be interrogated to confirm his version, but there was general agreement among the three men that he was deeply implicated in the business by accepting money from the mothers, even if he hadn't committed any murder. But there was the question of the death of Donald Thwaites which Edgar had raised in Richmond's office. At the mention of his name Sizewell's demeanour changed, from indignation that anyone would think he could be involved in such things as the murder of babies, to a more furtive and defensive guise. He persisted in the notion that Thwaites's death was accidental – after all, the coroner had said so – but Edgar pushed him hard, hinting that there was evidence of foul play. At that Sizewell really looked worried: a magistrate with evidence was not to be argued with but, nonetheless, he doggedly stuck to his story that there had been witnesses to show that the man had leaned too far over the barrier and that he himself had been in the office when the incident had taken place. Again, Edgar realised how necessary it was to get hold of Jennie Calman. She probably knew the truth – the question was would she cooperate? Knowing the woman as he did he was doubtful.

Well-refreshed and in a fever for action, Ambrose was anxious to return to Janet Stow and tell her she and her cohort of women would be needed after all. There had been a discussion between the three men as to what role they should each play in the search. George, with his local magistrate's hat on, was anxious to 'protect public order' as he put it. He was still not altogether reconciled to the idea of a band of factory women roaming the back streets of Bingley looking for a murderess. He had only Ambrose's assurances that the Stow woman could be trusted to command her small company and he was all for joining the group as a means of keeping overall control. Ambrose was confident that he and Edgar could exert sufficient influence over the women, and Edgar supported him by suggesting that, although the back streets of Bingley were honeycombed with courts and alleys, it was not an extensive area – nothing like searching the moors – and it would probably not take too long to locate their target. George proposed that he and the few men remaining who were not helping the militia guard key exits from the town would station themselves by half past six at the entrance to the low town, so they would be ready to assist in the woman's capture if necessary. In any case, he must be present to formalise the arrest and see her safely delivered to Wakefield Jail; a demand that Ambrose could hardly deny given the man's position. For the moment, George decided he would remain with his men while they patrolled the exits to the town and the canal bridges. In that way, he could be sure to be on hand should there be any signs of disorder. Having come to this arrangement, the three men set off in their various directions: Edgar and Ambrose to Jed Stow's lodgings and George back to collect the horses from the factory yard and arrange for the two mounts to be properly stabled for the night at the nearest inn.

Janet Stow was standing outside her door remonstrating with two of her children who had been fighting and presented a sorry sight of mud and bruises. 'The little buggers are always scrapping. My niece can hardly manage them, small as they are. She's inside and I've told her the news. I'm not sure that it's sunk in properly but you can go in and have a word with her. Perhaps you'll be able to get through what's happened. Have you caught the bitch yet?'

'Unfortunately not – she's given us the slip. I suggest we step inside.'

Mrs Stow, having given both the children a box round the ears, which almost lifted them off their respective feet, ordered them to 'behave – or else!' and they went whimpering away into the gloom of the alley. Ambrose and Edgar followed Janet Stow through the rickety door into the dim interior of her lodgings. As they had walked through the myriad passageways of the low town Edgar had taken in the scene with increasing horror. In Suffolk, as landlord to many tenants on his estate, he had at times visited their cottages on business and, although they were in some cases squalid, they did not compare in filth and degradation to the courts and tenements he observed here. All round him was derelict: broken windows, damaged structures and, underfoot, a mass of polluted earth; an accretion of detritus thrown willy-nilly from the houses into the passageways and pounded down underfoot year by year. His farm workers, poor as they were, had the benefit of being surrounded by fresh air; here there was a miasma of dust and a stench that was sickening. He thought about reaching for his pocket handkerchief to cover his mouth and nose, but, sensitive to the fact that he was a visitor, and taking his cue from Ambrose, who seemed oblivious to the malodour, he gritted his teeth and bore it as best he could.

Entering the main room, he noticed no improvement. There was no distinction and no respite from the foetid air outside; it was as though the external and the internal were at one in their squalor. A young girl was sitting at a stained and shabby table with her head in

Chapter 14

her hands. She looked up as the two men entered and her eyes showed her fear. Edgar supposed they were intimidating and tried to smile encouragingly at her to put her at her ease.

Janet Stow introduced them. 'Mr Lawes and Mr Hudson know about your trouble, Meg, and are going to do something about it.'

'I'm so sorry about your little girl, Meg,' said Ambrose. 'Your aunt, this gentleman here and I are going to try to bring the Fairfax woman to proper justice.'

'Is it true she killed my Margaret?'

'I'm very sorry to say it is. There are no words to describe how wicked she's been. You're not the only one to have suffered; there are other mothers here who have lost their babies the same way.'

'Why did she have to kill her? We gave her money to look after her. I was going to get her back when I was a bit older and I've already started to save up some money. Here, I've got coin – look!' She took a grubby piece of rolled-up rag from a pocket beneath her apron and opened it up. Inside were a few coppers.

Edgar was very affected by this and turned away so as not to show his distress; it was all so pathetic. The girl was too young to have a baby and most certainly shouldn't be going through the agony of losing it in this way.

Ambrose took her hand gently. 'I don't know how one woman can do this to a baby or cause such distress to its mother. Perhaps at the end of this I'll find out and tell you. In the meantime, we have to catch Mrs Fairfax so that she can be brought before a judge and tried for her crimes.' He turned to Janet Stow: 'Mrs Stow, we'll need the help of both you and your women. We've been to Sizewell's house where she was being sheltered and it seems she slipped out sometime this morning disguised as a young man. I've no doubt she's still in the neighbourhood because all the exits to the town are well sealed. Sizewell thinks she doesn't know anyone else in Bingley apart from him, but as I mentioned to you, we've been told she might know people living down by the canal. That's where she could be hiding out until she thinks the hunt's been called off. If you and your women, with our help, can carry out a sweep of this area of Bingley, Mr George Lawes, the magistrate, will be using his men and some of the local militia to search for her elsewhere in the town. I think it's his intention to bring in dogs if we're unsuccessful this evening. Let's hope for her sake that won't be necessary.'

'Seems like a good idea to me; being hanged for what she's done is a light sentence; torn to pieces by dogs or women would be a fairer one.'

Ambrose frowned. 'Remember, I told you this isn't an opportunity for raw vengeance. The whole town needs to see her in the dock and then officially punished publicly. Are you absolutely sure you'll be able to control your women?'

'Don't worry, I agree what you're saying is the best result for us all and if you can get an explanation out of her as to why she could do this, poor Meg might find it easier to understand. As for the women, I've already got the ones I need in mind. When they come back from the factory I'll call them together and you can explain what they must and mustn't do.'

Ambrose was relieved at this suggestion. Mrs Stow had evidently reconsidered and now saw the advantage of his presence. He felt easier that he would be there to gauge the mood of the women before they set off. Edgar's mind flew to the events he had witnessed at Seddon workhouse, when Jennie Calman and her corpulent husband had been evicted by the female inmates. He had not witnessed it, but was told later by one of the male inmates that Mrs Calman had been subjected to a physical attack that involved her having her undergarments stripped off. He did remember seeing her drawers hanging from the spike on the pediment over the front door of the building. It seemed, when fully roused, women's anger could be extreme and he thought of what the Bingley women would be capable of if they became truly hostile when they found their quarry. He hoped that between himself, Ambrose and Mrs Stow the situation could be controlled, otherwise George's misgivings would be well founded.

Chapter 15

Ambrose and Edgar arranged to return to Janet Stow's lodgings when they heard the factory whistle blow at the end of the shift at six o'clock. Meanwhile they determined to explore the canal area for themselves. It would be as well to know the ground before a search was made. Neither man had ventured into that quarter of the town, although they remembered passing sections of the waterway when they had first arrived. It was a straight walk down a newly made track from the courts and alleys of the low town and they carefully picked their way through the rubbish thrown out by its careless inhabitants until they were in sight of the water, which stood unmoving, dark and somehow haunting. As they came down to the edge of the canal they joined the towpath that ran alongside and which Ambrose informed Edgar was the means by which horses or men tied to the barges would drag them through the waterway. Edgar's knowledge of canals was limited, although there were some in his native county that had been built in the previous century.

In his professional enquiring way, Ambrose had researched Bingley and its area long before he arrived there; consequently, he was able to give his friend a conducted tour and an explanation of how the Leeds and Liverpool Canal system worked.

'From my research, I found the whole thing has been a masterpiece of ingenuity. If we move along the towpath I'll show you what I mean.'

A couple of hundred yards on Edgar was confronted with the sight of what looked like a giant staircase rising above him.

'This is known as the Five Lock Rise because the boats and barges are lifted and lowered in five stages. We're lucky – look, the locks are working.'

They stood fascinated as the boats moved into each chamber, the enormously strong wooden gates swinging shut on one side and opening on the other as the water poured in to raise the boat to the next level. It was a long and elaborate ritual, guided entirely by several lock-keepers. Impressed by the intricacy of the operation and in wonderment at the mind that designed it all, Edgar could have stayed longer, but Ambrose reminded him why they were there and reluctantly he turned away as the lock-keeper explained it would be at least another 30 minutes before the whole process was completed.

Moving down the towpath to explore the area further, Edgar was surprised at the amount of wildlife that had taken up residence on this newly available habitat. Mallard ducks in particular seemed to appreciate what was in and on the water, plunging their heads into the turbid stream. Already Edgar could see the canal was becoming a repository for the rubbish of the town, most notably a dead dog, already bloated and floating downstream on its side, slowly and gracefully. To his relief, quite soon they came to a tavern – the Locks Inn – but to his disappointment Ambrose, who was intently conscious of the work in hand, insisted they resist the temptation to step inside.

'Much as I would like to stop for some ale and warmth, we have a job to do. Although I know that many people from far and wide visit this engineering wonder, we're still strangers and would probably have to parry all kinds of unwanted questions.'

Heading north for about a quarter of a mile they came to a group of cottages, some wooden and decrepit, a few more substantially built of stone. This quarter seemed familiarly run-down, in keeping with all the area of the town leading down to the River Aire and the canal. The late April afternoon was cool and damp and the men were glad of their heavy coats. There were few people about; one old man in working clothes and sturdy boots was sitting on a home-made wooden bench outside a dwelling smoking a briar pipe.

He looked at them without curiosity and, taking his pipe from his mouth, asked, 'Come to see the locks, have you?'

'We certainly found them interesting,' replied Edgar. 'The whole canal's very impressive. Are you connected to it at all?'

The man shook his head and, pulling on his pipe, said, 'No, but my father and grandfather were – they helped to build it – came over from Kerry in old King George's time and stayed after it was finished.'

'So, what do you do?' asked Ambrose.

'I help with a bit of loading and unloading, do a bit of this and that. I've got a garden and we live all right.'

Chapter 15

It seemed he had plenty of time to sit and reflect and Edgar wondered how much work he managed. Ambrose was more interested in what the man might know about his neighbours and began to gently probe in his clever subtle way – starting with the general and moving on to the particular.

'You must have seen a few changes here since the mills have opened; I expect there are many more strangers coming into the district for the work.'

'Hundreds! They come in from the land because they think they can make a living in the factories, but as far as I can see, all they get is misery. See these wooden houses behind me – well, they were built by the navvies, temporary like, but people are still living in them. My place isn't a palace, but at least it's got a stone floor and a good stout door. I wouldn't give you tuppence to live in any of those huts, but people do.'

'They can't stay for very long, surely.' Ambrose pursued his course. 'Who'd want to stay any longer than necessary?'

'You'd be surprised,' said the old man. 'Some of them have been here for years – raised families and have grandchildren. Little brats some of them are – running about and getting into trouble; they often end up in the canal and have to be fished out.' He was warming to his audience. He clearly enjoyed himself when visitors stopped and canvassed him for information and was in the mood to expand to anyone who seemed genuinely interested in what he had to say. Besides, if he played his cards right there might be a pint in it.

'You must know them well, then,' commented Edgar.

'We pass the time of day and I see one or two of them in the Locks Inn. I don't know where they get their money from, most of them don't work regular, but they seem to be able to afford a drink. They've all got children – lots of them; my wife and I don't have any.'

'Perhaps they work in the mills?' suggested Ambrose. 'The children must work too. I know the mill owners aren't fussy about taking on small children.'

'I suppose they do. I know the Taylors next door have four and they seem to disappear during the day so they must be working. They certainly don't go to school. Likewise, the O'Clearys – I see their two boys go off at five in the morning. I'm not sure about the Enderbys – never see much of them; they keep themselves to themselves.'

Edgar and Ambrose simultaneously jerked their heads up and then looked at one another in disbelief. The name Enderby was well known to them both. Robert Enderby was Jennie Calman's brother and the prime cause of the trouble at Seddon. He had been murdered there in the most graphic way and his killer had still not been brought to justice. Before Edgar could wade in and start questioning the man hard, while not wishing to alert him to the fact that they were extremely interested in that family, Ambrose said quickly, 'The O'Clearys are obviously Irish – I'm not so sure about the name Enderby. I think it originates in Lincolnshire; I did know of a branch of a family with the name that lived in that county.'

'You may be right. It's not a common name round here,' replied the man. 'I've no idea where they came from, but they've been here about six years now – husband and wife and several young infants.' He puffed away at his pipe for a few seconds as though he was now happy to bring the conversation to an end, but Ambrose and Edgar had only just started.

Following Ambrose's seemingly random style of questioning, Edgar said, as casually as he could, 'It must be difficult living in such conditions with a large family. Better that they live in a decent place like yours if they have young children, but perhaps they couldn't afford the rent?'

The man looked almost smug and said, 'No, we worked hard to pay for this place. People like the Enderbys can only afford one of the shacks.'

Ambrose drew a deep breath and took Edgar's cue, 'I can't imagine anyone wanting to live in any of them; which one is it?'

The man took the pipe out of his mouth and waved it vaguely in the direction of the end of the row, towards a wooden house that had a small garden to the side; from their vantage point it seemed larger than the rest. This might be the end of their hunt and now they couldn't wait to get away from the man and follow up his information. But to avoid suspicion they lingered for a few minutes while he expatiated on the virtues of hard work and thrift, disparaging his

Chapter 15

neighbours who were, as far as he was concerned, nothing but shiftless idlers with too many children. His invitation for them to step inside his cottage to meet his wife was politely but swiftly refused with the excuse that they were intent on reaching East Morton before nightfall and must therefore be on their way. Wishing him 'Good evening!' they sauntered away as casually as they could until they rounded a curve in the towpath out of his sight.

They came to a halt. 'Well, here's a bit of luck at last! It can't be a coincidence,' Ambrose exclaimed. 'Enderby – Calman – there must be a connection. This is obviously the family that her accomplice mentioned. What relationship they are to her we don't know; whether they'll be prepared to hide her is also another question, especially when they discover what she's done.'

'What do you suggest we do for the time being?' asked Edgar. 'Should we wait here and see who comes and goes? We must be getting back to Janet Stow.' He took out his pocket watch. 'It's getting on for six. Perhaps one of us should stay here and keep the place under observation.'

'I think it's imperative we do that. Now we might have narrowed the search considerably we need to keep a close eye on this place. I'll go back to Mrs Stow to talk to her women as I arranged. I'll also explain this new development. You stay here.'

'On what pretext? Might our man here not be suspicious if I changed my mind and decided to accept his offer of some tea?'

Ambrose thought quickly. 'We passed an inn – the Locks – you could call in there and buy a couple of pints in a jar and take it to him. Think up a story as to why we've parted company and you've had to come back. Perhaps you've decided it's too far to walk to East Morton after all and you need to rest up for a while. I'm sure you can be creative!'

Subterfuge was new to Edgar and he'd never considered himself as someone with much imagination, let alone an ability to dissemble. Ambrose seemed to have the knack and could get out of tight corners. Edgar supposed it came from the type of work he undertook and his long experience of assuming the guise of impostor. Despite his misgivings he would try his best and began to rehearse a short explanation along the lines his friend suggested. Having agreed to meet back where they were as soon as possible, Ambrose headed off the towpath back into town, taking one of the many short alleyways that wound between the shanties.

Edgar made his way back to the inn where he fortified himself with a quick brandy before ordering a jug of ale to take out. Within minutes he was knocking on the workman's door which was opened by a plump woman with a pleasant face.

'Good evening. My friend and I have just been talking to your husband and he was kind enough to invite us in for some refreshment. We had both planned to continue to East Morton, but I'm suffering slightly from an indisposition and wanted to rest. I've brought some sustenance for us in the way of ale and hope I could prevail on your kindness for a while until I am ready to follow him.'

There! It had not been as difficult as he had imagined. Perhaps it was the brandy, but it sounded plausible to Edgar and by the time he had got it all out the man was peering over his wife's shoulder.

With a grunt of recognition, he ushered Edgar inside; as his eyes alighted on the jug he became even more welcoming. 'There was no need for that, but you're very welcome. Missus, get us both some bread and cheese.'

She hurried away and Edgar, keen to be able to observe the Enderbys' shack, despite the dampness in the air, suggested they went outside with their pots and platters – on the pretext that he was interested in watching the barges and boats pass by. As they sat together on the bench, the man rattled on about life on the canal while Edgar kept one eye always on the row of wooden shanties to his right. Smoke was coming from a stove pipe, which stuck through the wooden roof of the Enderby place; there was obviously someone at home although there was no movement in or out. Now more people were passing by on the towpath in front of them as their shift in the factory finished and they returned home.

Having cleared their plates the man suggested that, as the weather was closing in and as his new companion had said he was suffering from 'an indisposition', perhaps they should go back inside to the warmth of his fire. There seemed no point in arguing and Edgar

Chapter 15

reluctantly entered the cottage. He quickly observed that, if he took a place next to one of its small front windows he could observe the towpath and anyone passing by. But he had no view of any of the wooden houses. He had to trust to luck that nothing would occur between now and when Ambrose returned.

If his view was restricted, his hearing was not. Fortunately, the man was garrulous and enjoying his audience; Edgar could sit back and let him rattle on with small grunts and facial signals of encouragement. He absorbed very little of what was said and afterwards he could never recall any of the information the man had been at pains to relay. At one point, surreptitiously glancing at his watch, he saw that there was at least 30 minutes to wait before Ambrose might arrive. Raising an eyebrow at a particularly hair-raising account of the sinking of a barge full of wooden poles, he sighed inwardly and hoped he could keep up the pretence of interest. Hurry up, Ambrose! he thought as he sipped his dregs of ale and prepared to be entertained by yet more tales of the canal bank.

Ambrose was hurrying – but not in Edgar's direction. He heard the six o'clock whistle as he reached the main area of the workers' tenements. He found his way to Jed Stow's lodgings, but the niece was the only one at home. She told Ambrose that her aunt had gone to meet some of the women at the factory and was bringing them back with her. She would be here soon and had said that Mr Hudson should wait. Hoping that Janet Stow could restrain the women's curiosity until she arrived back and he could take some control over what was said, he sat himself at the shaky table and waited. The room was silent; Meg Foley was still in shock and had no words for this strange, exceptionally tall gentleman who had brought her the horrific news about the death of her small daughter. She couldn't fathom how a woman could be so wicked as to destroy something as perfect as a newly born baby. It gnawed away at her, but she didn't have the language to describe her feelings, particularly to a stranger, so she remained mute. Ambrose respected her silence and made no attempt to intrude on it.

Soon he heard voices and the clatter of pattens on the cobbles. The door opened and in crowded a group of seven or eight working women. On first viewing they all looked the same: pallid faces from years of a poor-quality diet; facial expressions almost petrified by hardship; harsh grating voices tuned to overcoming the constant noise of machinery; and all clad in a uniform thin-quality grey clothing. Even as they jostled for space in the small room, crowded together, they terrified Ambrose and he thought of the French *tricoteuses* with their interminable knitting as they sat under the guillotine waiting for heads to fall into the basket; if it came to a fight the women here would surely give a good account of themselves. Janet Stow endeavoured to induce some order and brought the women's attention to Ambrose.

'Some of you will know this man who works as a labourer at Richmond's.' Ambrose nodded and she went on, 'His name is Frank Barrett and he's had me bring you here for a purpose – but I'll let him explain it himself.'

Some of the women made murmurs of recognition and, anxious to dispel any confusion, he decided to be completely honest with the group from the outset. After all, the subterfuge was no longer needed and he had to instil some credibility. As he stood up the women became silent and he cleared his throat.

'Some of you recognise me from the factory and know I've been working there for the last week as a labourer. But I must confess to you that I'm not what I seem. My name is not Frank Barrett, it's Ambrose Hudson and I'm a journalist and writer from London. I'm especially interested in investigating conditions of work in factories and mills, and most particularly how your children are treated.'

A murmur went around the room and several women opened their mouths to speak, but Ambrose raised his hand. 'Please, let me explain first and then you can question me afterwards.' He went on as briefly as he could to outline why he had first come to Bingley and what he was investigating. He found it very difficult to put into words an explanation of what Jennie Calman had been doing, but there were no fine descriptions to couch it in and he had to be graphic. The result was an initial stunned silence, then uproar. When the women heard how she had disposed of the infants she had been paid to care for, in one voice they began to scream for retribution. Ambrose could see

Chapter 15

which way things might go; at any moment, they could stream out of the room onto the streets as an anarchic mob and ransack every building they came across until they got hold of the woman. At all costs, he had to prevent a riot. Interposing himself between the women and the door, not for the first time he was glad of his height. He was at least 3 inches taller than the tallest woman in the room and, holding up his arm, he shouted above the din, 'Listen to me – all of you! We can and will get justice!' His compelling presence caused a momentary lull in the turmoil and recognising he now had their attention he asked them to hear his tactics for retribution. To his intense relief Janet Stow also raised her voice in support of him. Slowly their indignant chatter was reduced to muttering and then silence.

Throwing her weight behind Ambrose, Janet Stow exhorted the women to listen to him as he 'talked a lot of sense'. Between them they managed to calm the group before proceeding to lay out their plan for catching the woman. Ambrose described how she could be somewhere down by the canal and that he had a companion, a magistrate, who was watching the area. He suggested they took lanterns and went together to search. He assured them all that the law was on their side and any of them could make a citizen's arrest. He noticed an energy in the room that was fuelled by a mixture of rage, determination and anticipation. Finally, he asked every woman present not to take any physical revenge. If they came across Calman they would make sure she was unharmed by the time the constable came to take her away. Short of making everyone swear on the Bible, he had to accept their verbal promises. In return, he said he would ensure they would all be in the front row at her public hanging. 'So, you see, we all want the same thing – the end of Mrs Jennifer Calman as she dangles from a rope in full view of the world; but we can only do that if we keep within the law.' One of the largest of the women, assuming some leadership, reassured Ambrose that they all understood what he had said and would restrain themselves and each other as the best way of getting justice. He could only hope they would keep their word.

Some women went off to their homes to fetch lanterns and very soon returned; now it was time to move off. The group, nine in all, proceeded as one with Janet Stow and Ambrose at its head. As silently as their pattens on the cobbles would allow, they passed with the ease of familiarity through the dense areas of the courts and alleys, finding their way as effectively as cats at night in the darkness. As he walked beside them Ambrose considered that everyone worked on the principle of territory; they knew their ways round here as well as he knew the streets of London. Within 15 minutes they had arrived within sight of the Five Lock Rise and the towpath. There were a few people about, most still making their way home from their places of work. Some looked curiously at the raggle-taggle group of women and the tall rangy man who stood with them; others, with heads bent and eyes on the ground, were intent on getting back to their homes, or the warmth of the Locks Inn.

Once the group was out on the towpath it strung into a double file, like a crowd of charity school girls out on a walk with their school mistress. The grimness of their mission had reduced them to silence; there was no idle chatter, each woman set her face in hard determination, lips drawn together and frowns of concentration between the eyes.

They reached the cottage where Edgar was waiting for them and he came out of the door, careful to close it firmly behind him, shutting in its occupants whose curiosity had been aroused by the crowd of females. As Ambrose stopped, Edgar saw the women move out of their file formation and stand as a group behind him.

'Edgar, here's Mrs Stow and her friends. Ladies, this is Mr Edgar Lawes, a magistrate from Suffolk.'

The women looked one to another and shook their heads, having no idea where or what Suffolk was.

Edgar stepped forward and tipped his hat to them all. Turning to Ambrose he said, 'There's nothing to report here. As far as I could see no one's entered or left the shack, although I must admit my view of it wasn't perfect. What's your plan now? We can't approach the place as a mob, can we? If the people inside have nothing to do with Jennie Calman, and it's always a possibility, they won't be happy confronted by an angry crowd at their door.'

'There are just too many coincidences for it not to be the place. Calman's accomplice in the cottage was certain she had relatives living

Chapter 15

down by the canal. The name Enderby's not common round here – and we know that was her maiden name. I think we can be sure these are the people. The point is, is she here or not, and if not, do they know where she is? I suggest I approach the place, knock on the door and enquire whether they know her. If it becomes obvious that they do and that she's in the house, I'll explain that we've come to arrest her. If there's the slightest hesitation on their part, that's when we can bring up the women. A little of their menace should do the trick.' He turned to Mrs Stow. 'Go with Mr Lawes and take a couple of women and hide round the back in case she makes a run for it that way. I'll approach from the front. The rest of you ladies keep yourselves in the shadows of the bushes as much as you can. If I raise my arm like this' – and he held his long arm up above his head where everyone could see it – 'it means she's inside the house. Move forward towards me, but slowly and as a group. Remember, no one is to do anything rash.'

Excitement and nervousness assailed Edgar as he moved through the wilderness of the garden round to the back of the property. Ambrose, having assumed leadership of the enterprise, wished to delegate to Edgar the pleasure of some action and he was fully confident of his friend's ability physically to manhandle Jennie Calman if necessary, particularly with the help of three angry women. As his group disappeared into the shadows behind him he stepped forward and gave the thin wooden door three sharp knocks. For some seconds, there was no response and then he heard a muttering of voices and at last someone shuffled to the door. In just enough light to see without a lantern, Ambrose made out a young boy at the door as it opened; he couldn't be more than 10 years old. The child stood stock still and said not a word.

'Is anyone at home here? I'm looking for Mrs Jennie Calman, or a Mrs Fairfax. I've reason to think she's been staying here,' explained Ambrose.

The boy hesitated and then looked behind his shoulder. There was the sound of scurrying – like rats in the attic – and then a chair or table was knocked over and a stream of expletives was heard.

Wasting no time, Ambrose lifted his arm and the women moved out of the shadows; following him they pushed their way into the shanty, careless of the child who fell back into the room and was in imminent danger of being crushed. One of the women stopped and pulled him clear, pushing him into a chair in the corner out of the way, where he sat unmoving and terrified. Now the whole group was in the room, just in time to see the skirted rear end of a woman escaping through a window in the back wall of the house.

Ambrose shouted to Edgar, 'She's coming through!' Then he heard a scuffle and a woman shouting, 'Got you – you bitch!'

Rushing back through the front door, Ambrose was relieved to see Edgar coming around to the front of the building with the captive. It was as easy as that. Unprepared for such an assault, Jennie Calman had been taken completely off guard and she now stood between Edgar and Janet Stow with her arms held behind her by two burly women. Although no weapons had been used, she had not escaped unscathed: there was a deep bruise beginning to spread under her eye where she had been punched and her clothes had been torn in the scuffle. As she stood flanked by the women and the two men, she was face to face with the rest of the group who projected so much menace it was almost tangible. But Janet Stow was watchful and checking for any signs of attack. The women responded to her call for calm, but suddenly, out of the shadows, a young woman rushed forward, hands and nails ready to claw. She flew straight for Jennie Calman's face; defenceless with her hands restrained, her cheeks were like a blank canvas. Taken totally by surprise, her captors were unable to prevent the nails doing their work.

Meg Foley screamed, 'That's for my Margaret, you witch!' Janet's niece, overcome with anger and a need for vengeance, had broken ranks. Calman's face, already bearing the cut and bruise from the blow to the eye, was now scraped and bleeding from the action of grimy fingernails. Blood from three deep incisions poured down her cheeks and pink rivulets found their way into the corner of her thin mouth.

Mrs Stow stepped forward and caught her niece's arm. 'What are you doing here, Meg? I told you to stay behind.'

'I wasn't going to let this hag go anywhere unless I had a go at her first. She shan't go in the lock-up! Let's stone her now – baby-killer!' And she looked round at the women: 'She killed my little girl, my

Margaret!' And she put her hands over her face and howled with raw grief.

With real affection Janet took the girl in her arms and whispered, 'No more, Meg. Let's have proper justice from the judge. We'll see her hang together.' She led the girl back to the rest of the women who had been standing in silence; Ambrose noted that they all gave a little cheer of approval as she returned to them and he felt it was time to leave before there were any further individual attempts at revenge. He would hardly blame the women if they did take it into their heads to imitate Meg.

Standing in front of Jennie Calman, and with all the authority he could muster, perched as he was on the edge of a canal, in the dark and surrounded by a group determined that he would keep his word and deliver bona fide justice, Edgar explained that she was now under arrest on suspicion of the murder of seven infants, possibly more. She showed none of her usual haughty arrogance, but instead was dazed and uncomprehending; the blows she had received had clearly shaken her. With her arms still held, the women marched her away up through the alleys of the low town with the two men in the rear.

Their procession was soon joined by neighbours and casual passers-by, who, having heard there was some excitement going on, fell in behind and quizzed anyone they thought might know what was going on. The press of bodies in the narrow alleyways restricted easy movement and the trail came to a halt, particularly at bottlenecks where paths crossed or turned sharply angled corners. Edgar and Ambrose became concerned for the safety of them all as the crowd behind them began to swell; they were also aware that there could easily be a serious reaction by the townsfolk once the facts of the case spread among them. For the first time that evening they felt things could go badly wrong. They became conscious of low murmurs of indignant conversations and gasps of astonishment and disgust as the news spread. Their only hope was that George was not far off and they could deliver the woman safely into his hands. To that end they tried to speed up the pace, pushing the group in front of them on at a faster rate until they came out of the last alley into the broader street of the main town.

To their great relief George and his men were waiting. 'I see you've been successful,' he said, 'but you seem to have collected a rabble behind you.'

'Not at all, George,' replied Edgar smoothly. 'I told you it would work. These women have been instrumental in helping us. Not only that, they've behaved with great dignity and common sense.'

George walked over and examined Jennie Calman's face. 'I see she didn't come off lightly.' Then he stiffened himself into a formal pose and announced, 'Mrs Calman or Fairfax, I am placing you in the custody of the constable who will accompany you to Wakefield Jail tonight, along with your accomplice, Tom Sizewell, and two others connected with your crimes.'

Jennie Calman licked her dry lips with her reptilian tongue but made no reply, to the disappointment of her escort who, Ambrose felt, would have liked an expression of sorrow or an explanation. Two of George's men stepped forward and the women who still clung on tightly to her arms let her go, wiping their hands on their grimy dresses as though to rid themselves of some awful contamination. The crowd, taking its cue from those in the front, became perfectly quiet as she was taken away, her arms now tied behind her back. The hatred in the silence spoke more than any jeers, whistles or catcalls.

Ambrose and Edgar shook Mrs Stow's hand, thanked her and her neighbours for their help and wished the group goodnight, Ambrose confirming his promise that they should have ringside seats at the hanging. The women melted back into the darkness of their courts and alleys, now able at last to express their feelings about one of their sex who had gone against the female grain so horribly; it was really beyond belief. For some minutes, even as they were walking away towards the inn, the two men heard the hum of voices which eventually pierced the air as they rose in indignation.

Chapter 16

A week later, Peter's convalescence had greatly advanced and he was in the very best of spirits. The severe blow to his head had caused a concussion which took some time to improve; for several days he had remained very drowsy and incapable of conversation. He was aware of the presence of the housekeeper who hovered watchfully by his bed and tended to his every need. Slowly he began to experience longer periods of lucidity when he could exchange a few words with Mr Lawes and Mr Hudson who took it in turns to sit with him.

On 7 May, a Wednesday, as he lay awake looking at the cherry tree now in full leaf immediately outside his window, there was a gentle tap on his bedroom door. Puzzled as to who it could be – the housekeeper did not bother to knock, and neither could it be either of his other regular visitors who, he knew, were all elsewhere – he invited them in.

To his intense joy, disbelief and confusion, who should walk into the room but Caroline Alfrey, followed by her mother Emily. True to the promise he had made himself, on the day after Jennie Calman's arrest and when they were all settled back at Hoyles, Edgar had written to Hugh Bradshaw, Emily's employer, informing his old friend that Peter had been in a bad way and it would be very good for him to see his best-loved friend. He suggested that Hugh send Caroline with her mother in Edgar's coach and let Fred Lodge, his estate manager, chaperone them on the journey. He could then send Fred back on the mail and later, after the trial and sentencing of Jennie Calman, use his coach to transport the whole party back to Suffolk. Hugh wasted no time; within a couple of days the two ladies and an excited Mr Lodge were on their way to Grantham.

Waving away any idea of food or rest, Caroline asked to be taken to Peter immediately and was relieved to see him sitting up in bed and looking cheerful. She had spent the four days of the journey anxious as to what she might find. She didn't know the full story, only that Peter had fallen foul of some madwoman and been severely knocked about. Shyly she sat in the visitor's chair next to his bed and took his hand.

Her mother placed herself discreetly in a corner of the room, trying to give them as much privacy as protocol allowed. Not wishing Peter to be tired by all the excitement, she suggested they stay only for a few minutes, but that they would return later in the evening and perhaps Caroline could read to him before he went to sleep.

Happier than he had been since he arrived in Yorkshire, when they had gone Peter lay awake in a state of complete euphoria. The housekeeper was glad to report this change in condition to her employer and his friends. Edgar was congratulated on his initiative and all were very relieved that it seemed clear the boy was on the mend.

The ladies joined them for dinner. Edgar was glad to have report of his friends Hugh and Deborah Bradshaw, but particularly anxious to have news of his own estate. Before dinner he had spent an hour with Fred who assured him everything was running well, the crops were advanced because there had been sufficient rain, as well as some warm spring days and little frost. Lambing had been uneventful and Fred was very interested to hear about Edgar's management of the orphan lamb. He was particularly taken with the idea of Edgar's fine doeskin gloves being used as a feeder. Fred was to stay for a couple of days before making his way back to the estate, giving Edgar time to catch up with other aspects of estate business and correspondence which his manager could take with him.

During dinner and post-dining conversation with the ladies, they tried to avoid the subject of Jennie Calman, but the two women were insistent on hearing the whole story, gruesome though it was. Ambrose and Edgar felt they had a right to know, since Calman had gone out of her way to make their lives a misery in the workhouse, as she had done for all the inmates; she was particularly implicated in the suicide of Emily's husband Richard.

While horrified at the nature of Jennie Calman's crimes, Emily expressed no surprise at the woman's hard-faced attitude towards what she had done.

'I always knew she was a woman without a heart. It was evident from the way she treated the children in Seddon workhouse that she had no feelings at all for anyone – apart from her brother. I wonder how she'll conduct herself at her trial.'

Chapter 16

'Do you wish to attend it, Mrs Alfrey?' Edgar asked her.

'No, neither Caroline nor I wish to be reminded of her since she made our lives so miserable. We just hope justice will be served and she'll be suitably punished.'

In the week before the trials, which would take place in Wakefield, Ambrose took time to confront Samuel Richmond, the owner of the mill whose indifference to its management had, he reasoned, contributed to the sorry events of the previous months. Richmond's lack of oversight of what was afoot on his own property was a scandal and Ambrose sought him out to tell him so. George Lawes, in the uncomfortable position as friend to the mill owner, but now fully aware of the man's shortcomings in terms of protecting his workers, supported Ambrose and arranged the meeting himself in the mill office. He suggested to Richmond that he had no choice but to hear some unpleasant truths about how the factory was run, the illegal practices that he, because of his lack of supervision, had allowed to take place, and the possibility that Donald Thwaites's death was no accident, but a murder that had gone unpunished because it lacked rigorous investigation either by himself or his overseers.

Ambrose approached the interview clear as to his intent – which was to acquaint the man with his evidence little by little, giving him time to rebut or defend himself. He was not seeking an aggressive verbal confrontation which would surely result in Richmond becoming defensive and obstinate when faced with inevitable demands for change, which was Ambrose's objective. His approach would be to suggest that improvements were in the best interests of not only the workers, but of production and consequently profit.

Samuel Richmond must be alerted to the fact that under-aged children were being employed; that certain workers were feeding on the desperation of parents and taking money from them, and that his manager, Sizewell, had been allowed to intimidate ruthlessly anyone who stood in his way. Sitting in the office, the two men faced each other, Richmond looking increasingly uncomfortable as Ambrose quietly revealed the extent of the malpractice.

'I can't be blamed for the death of Donald Thwaites,' he protested, 'it's been judged an accident by the coroner. There's no evidence the man was pushed.'

'That may be the official view. However, there is and always will be an element of uncertainty about the death. But as Sizewell's crimes and motives are exposed it seems very likely to me that he arranged to have the man pushed over the balcony. If it was not investigated fully because these "accidents" happen regularly and are accepted as an occupational hazard, then you as owner are condemned for lax protection of your workers. If it was an extraordinary occurrence, then it deserved a much more rigorous investigation than it was afforded and that can also be laid directly at your door.'

'First-class sophistry!' Richmond was becoming defensive, clearly resenting the intrusion of this man sitting in his office, so ready to criticise. He went on the attack. 'I know of your underhand methods, Hudson. Why not investigate openly and tell us what you intend? I'm sure my colleagues here and in Lancashire would open their doors to you rather than you take on these foolish disguises while trying to infiltrate us.'

'Then I'd put myself in the same position as the factory inspectors who not only post notice of their intended visits, but are guided round the places and shown exactly what the owners want them to see. My method – and I agree it's underhand – gets me closer to the truth. I can take you onto the three floors of this mill and identify children as young as four, scavenging at the bases of heavy machinery at great risk to their limbs and sometimes their lives. I know that when the inspectors come the children are sent home for the day – without pay as well. The law's clear: no child under the age of nine can work in factory, mill or mine. Neither do you follow the regulations that demand owners provide education for children working legally. I think it's also likely that youngsters in your mill between the ages of nine and thirteen are working more than the eight hours a day laid down in the 1833 statute. I can quote it to you if you wish.'

'That's not necessary, I'm fully aware of what the law says. Look, we're a small concern here and the parents of these children have no truck with education. They wouldn't thank me if I hauled their offspring out to teach them their letters. They're only interested in the

Chapter 16

money they can earn for their families. These reforms are directly in opposition to what the families want. No one has complained to me because I've not set up a school.'

'That's most likely because most of them are ignorant of the law. You've no excuses because you can read it for yourself. Like others of your "brethren" you're effectively condemning a whole swathe of humanity to illiterate ignorance. Somewhere and at sometime soon this pattern must be broken.'

'I see you're a zealot for reform, Mr Hudson,' Richmond sneered.

Ambrose felt he wasn't making the progress he had hoped and changed tactics. The discourse was moving from the particular to the general and he was keen to steer it back to Richmond Mill and the plight of its workers.

'Mr Richmond, I'd hoped I could persuade you through logic that your interests are best served by, first, applying the law as it stands, and, second, considering how you treat your workers. I've evidence to show that improvement in working conditions has a direct impact on profits. If you don't take my word for it I can direct you to others in your position who've had cause to change their approach and have reaped the benefits. For my part, I'll go away now and write up my experiences, sparing no one. I'll also be reporting my findings to the Factory Inspectorate in London as well as my contacts in parliament. Whatever deals you may have with the local inspectors, I'll ensure that men from outside the area will be sent in immediately – and for several days – to go over the place minutely. You can be sure they'll give an objective report. Who knows – it may close you down.'

Richmond bristled and for the first time looked alarmed. 'That's a grievous slur, Hudson! I refute the suggestion that I manipulate the inspections. George Lawes knows me well and will confirm my integrity.'

Ambrose curled his lip. 'As a friend of Mr George Lawes myself, I'd like to think he's right and that it's simply a matter of dereliction of duty on your part. It seems to me you've been too content to allow Sizewell free rein. It's more a question of laziness and neglect on your part than viciousness; am I right?'

Richmond squirmed. If he disagreed he was condemned as

unscrupulous out of his own mouth. If he agreed he looked negligent because of lack of interest as to what was occurring on his own property. Clearly weighing it up, he was now keen to see this man off his premises. Anxious not to be shamed in any newspaper report and certainly not to be discussed in the Houses of Parliament, he suddenly capitulated.

He sighed wearily. 'What is it you want me to do, Mr Hudson?'

Ambrose wasted no time in giving him a short list of priorities and in return promised that the mill, although fully described in his piece, would remain anonymous – at least if the reforms were put in place immediately. These included a full and thorough investigation of the ages of all the children and the hours they were working; provision of a school for all those between the ages of nine and thirteen; an insistence that parents bringing children to the mill for employment had official papers to prove how old their offspring were. As a parting shot, Ambrose informed Samuel Richmond that he would be returning to Yorkshire in a couple of months to make sure the reforms were up and running. The two men shook hands, if a little stiffly, and went their separate ways.

Chapter 17

The newly built courtroom in Wakefield was packed on the day Jennie Calman was led out to face her accusers. The militia were in evidence to forestall any attempt at rough justice and they found themselves in action when there were unseemly scuffles as people tried to get into the courthouse, which was bulging at the seams. Enterprising voyeurs took ladders to the courtroom windows; the pedlars and traders did a roaring trade in the streets and alleys around the courthouse. All was set for an 'occasion' and Bingley folk were in the majority. The women most concerned had been allocated prime seats in the room, looking appropriately serious and dignified, but unable to resist waving familiarly to Ambrose and Edgar across the court. Edgar remarked to Ambrose that the women must have come on foot or hitched wagon-rides and he wondered where they would stay the night. Ambrose thought the local people might be willing to put them up in return for all the details of the case. Peter had not been called as a witness since the defendant was pleading guilty to all charges, including grievous bodily harm.

From the outset of her trial Jennie Calman insisted she needed no one to speak for her. She would conduct her own defence, although she was directed by the judge that she had no alternative other than to plead guilty because her two accomplices had testified against her to clear themselves from charges of murder. At the end of their trials, some 10 days since, they had persuaded the judge and jury they had been intimidated into helping Calman and feared her extreme temper. Both strongly asserted that they had never disposed of any babies; Calman had seen to it herself. The jury found them guilty of assisting, but, acknowledging it had been under extreme duress, they both avoided the rope and the judge condemned them to transportation for life.

At his trial held at the same time, although Sizewell denied any involvement in the baby farming, witnesses from the mill came forward to confirm that he had passed on details of the 'service' to several young women whose babies had subsequently disappeared. There was also Ambrose's evidence that he had seen money pass between the two. In the dock Sizewell rejected the accusation that he knew Mrs Calman had disposed of the children in such an appalling way; but given the fact that the pair had a physical liaison the judge ordered the jury to consider there would be no secrets between them under those circumstances; there was also no doubt that the accused had aided and abetted his accomplice with money and protection. The jury consequently found him guilty of conspiracy to murder. As far as the death of Donald Thwaites was concerned, Sizewell maintained that he had nothing to do with it; it had been an accident confirmed by the coroner and at the time it took place he had secure witnesses to prove he had been in his office. To Ambrose's acute frustration, the jury found Sizewell not guilty of the murder of Donald Thwaites, despite Jennie Calman's testimony that he had told her he arranged it because the man was getting too close to the truth about their activities. But this verdict was ameliorated in Ambrose's eyes by the guilty verdict for his part in the conspiracy to murder babies for monetary gain. He was condemned to be hanged within the same week.

At no time during her trial did Jennie Calman express any remorse for what she had done to the helpless infants or pity for their mothers. As the acutely vicious nature of her crimes was revealed, she offered no defence for her actions or any explanation and when the judge came to deliver the sentence she remained perfectly still and composed. Her face remained expressionless while she stared directly at the Bench as the judge put on the black cap and condemned her to death by public hanging at '10 of the clock' on Friday next at Wakefield Jail. Never did she reveal the exact numbers of infants condemned to the boggy mire at Rickard's and the nature of the terrain meant they could not be recovered and given Christian burials; a fact that compounded the misery of their mothers.

Ambrose felt a powerful need to speak to the woman. While he found her repellent in all ways, nonetheless his curiosity was piqued as to how she could have done such things. To that end he wrote a letter to the prison authorities requesting an interview with her. To his disappointment he received an immediate reply that she would see no one. It would have given an extra insight to the story he would write

Chapter 17

in the *Escritoire*; but now he could only rely on the spectacle of her on the scaffold.

Two days before the execution, the three men sat in George's study after dinner, a bottle of brandy close by. The ladies had gone up to bed and the housekeeper, who had become very fond of Peter, insisted her charge also had an early night. It had been their final day at Hoyles and he had been up and about round the stables. Fitter by the day, although not yet ready to risk himself to ride, he was able to undertake a few light chores in the stable yard and glad to be back with the horses. Fred Lodge had brought news from Seddon Hall of the mare that was due to foal in July; she was well and all was expected to come to a happy conclusion. Of course, he would be back home by the time of the birth and, when he was not thinking of Caroline, he anticipated the event, wondering in the manner of an anxious father whether it would be a filly or a colt.

Peter had enjoyed these last weeks at Hoyles, particularly since Caroline had appeared, but now he was ready to return to Suffolk and the familiarity of Seddon Hall. He had no wish to see Jennie Calman hanged, even though she had brought him perilously close to death. There had been so much misery caused by the woman he was just glad that she would be no more trouble to anyone. He hoped she made a swift end. He was ambivalent about the death penalty, but he regarded it as a punishment that did not fit any crime other than murder; it was too extreme for anything else. Some people, like Mrs Calman, evidently deserved it; but he wondered how many innocent people had been wrongly convicted and hanged. Perhaps it was better not to hang anyone at all, just take away their freedom for ever or send them permanently to the wilderness that was New South Wales.

He had heard Mr Edgar Lawes and Mr Hudson discussing the rights and wrongs of it and knew that they disagreed. Most of the time as Peter listened he couldn't follow their arguments. He understood he was badly educated and had a limited understanding of the world in general, whereas they had both been well taught and were widely read. But there was no desire on his part to improve his knowledge on that score. His life was horses and he would spend all his time learning everything he could about their welfare and all the possibilities connected with them. Politics and philosophy were not for him and knowing the topics would arise and continue late into the night, he was glad to retire to bed early as suggested by his nurse. Immediately after dinner he said goodnight and left them to it.

Settling themselves in front of a good fire – although it was now the middle of May, the evenings were still cool in Yorkshire – the three men began to discuss arrangements for the morrow. Edgar proposed that they wait until after midday to travel to Wakefield, which would still give them plenty of time to arrange rooms and have a good supper.

'I'm not coming with you,' announced George. 'I've seen enough public hangings and I'm not needed. The Wakefield militia will be there and I've no official function to perform. Besides, I'd have to ride with you separately since you're not returning to Hoyles. I think I've enough to catch up with here, so here I'll stay.'

'So, this is our last night together,' observed Ambrose. 'It's a pity, but I suppose it was inevitable that we all return to our own daily lives. George, I hope I'll see you again soon. Perhaps we could meet when I return in a couple of months to see what improvements Samuel Richmond has introduced. I know he's your friend and neighbour, but I'm sure you understand why I'm insisting he carries out these reforms. After all, it's in his best interests, as I explained to him.'

'I do understand and I'm part way to agreeing with you. But, like my cousin, I'm not so sure about the kind of rapid changes you radicals are urging. I like things to be done at a gentler pace – let people get used to ideas before rushing them into practice. Still, I was as horrified as anyone to hear of the outrages perpetrated at Richmond Mill and grateful that you've exposed them and justice is being done. I also think it's gentlemanly of you not to publish names, which would result in national humiliation; I'm sure Richmond understands what's at stake here and will keep his word. It's been a pleasure and privilege to have you as a guest and I've particularly enjoyed our debates after dinner. You give Edgar a run for his money on that score!'

Ambrose nodded in acceptance of the compliment. 'I've also enjoyed them, although I know we continue to agree to differ on

Chapter 17

many issues, not least the type of spectacle Edgar and I will observe on Friday. I still say that a public show of punishment leaves everyone with no doubt as to the seriousness decent people feel about one person taking the life of another. I suppose this goes against the grain of my radical views, but I feel this most deeply.'

'Public hangings are reducing in numbers as many crimes once considered capital have been ameliorated to transportation or long imprisonment,' said Edgar. 'I think our attitude towards this form of punishment is changing, even if slowly. Although I believe there's an atavistic drive in us all for retribution, I'm just not sure that a public execution is apposite in our civilised society. In many ways we've progressed beyond that in our humanity.'

'And those ways are?' asked George.

'Well, for a start, there's a change in some quarters as to how we treat animals. Parliament's now decided that bear- and bull-baiting are inhumane.'

George shook his head. 'That was only five years ago – it's taken us centuries to realise it. I believe the last bull-baiting around here took place on the day the law was passed – a bowman's gesture of disapproval if ever there was one. These old country sports are still in the blood. You'll be telling me next that parliament will outlaw hunting foxes sometime!'

'I'm sure it won't be in our lifetime, George, especially while there are still old buffers like Colonel Shepherd back in Suffolk. But can't you see there's a progression in the way we think and deal with what is cruel and unacceptable. Look how we used to treat inmates in lunatic asylums. I read somewhere that earlier this century people were still going to look at "freak shows"; for a penny, they could take a stick and poke the poor devils incarcerated in the Bethlem mad house, for example. But I know attitudes are changing and enlightened men are demanding better treatment for these unfortunates. It seems to me there is an inevitability in this benevolent push to inform social progress and which eventually will not be denied.'

'People still like to see their villains hanged,' protested Ambrose.

Edgar had been nonplussed when his friend had first expanded on his view of capital punishment. He thought a man of letters, living in London close to modern thoughts and attitudes would have been more enlightened. As Ambrose admitted, his views 'ran against the grain'.

'Why do you feel so strongly that it's right and proper for a man or woman to be publicly killed by the state? Someone who has such liberal principles on other issues. As I see it official executions are carried out purely for revenge and "*pour décourager les autres*". I think it's time to dispense with them altogether. It's clear the tactic's not altogether successful; the murder rate hasn't diminished as far as anyone can tell; history's littered with capital crimes carried out for all kinds of reasons.'

'But surely it's a matter of justice?' objected Ambrose, shaking his head.

'Justice – yes, there's always the matter of those who are innocent and hanged because of miscarriages of justice; there's no redress for them.'

Ambrose fell silent and Edgar wished he hadn't spoken out so vehemently. He knew Ambrose thirsted for revenge and his misery at losing Rosalie and the horrific manner of her death would be tempered somewhat when he saw Jennie Calman swinging from a noose. Neither was it the time to point out that the woman had not actually murdered her; Calman's crime lay in her actions which had indirectly led to the accident. In the same regard, Sizewell was surely guilty of involvement in the murder of Donald Thwaites, yet ironically it could not be proved. But there was no question the Calman woman had, with her own hands, murdered a significant number of infants and her motives were clearly mercenary. Sizewell, although tainted by his association with her, may or may not have been aware of her actions and Edgar thought, as there was an element of doubt, his sentence might have been reduced to transportation.

He sighed to himself. There would be very few people turning out to watch Calman hang at Wakefield Jail who would have any sympathy with his arguments; they would all be at one with Ambrose. For the moment Edgar remained silent and avoided engaging in any censure of what he considered barbaric views; consequently, he left the subject for another time when his friend might be more amenable to

Chapter 17

listen to reasoned argument. However, he conceded to himself that the description 'thirsting for vengeance', as it applied to Ambrose and those others who had been cruelly robbed of those they loved, was an accurate one. The desire for retribution must be like the all-consuming need for water after too long without. When it came at last it satisfied and was relished like nothing else.

George was more interested in protecting the countryman's right to kill anything that moved. Born and raised in an area where hunting was meat and drink to all landowners and those who followed them, he had a hard-nosed view of anyone who sought to disrupt the old habits and customs. He was as unyielding in his attitude to the traditions of country pursuits as Ambrose was for upholding the utility of public executions. By the end of the night Edgar felt out-talked and out-gunned.

As he lay in bed he wondered how best he might pursue some of the ideas that he felt he had articulated well, but to an unyielding audience. It had done him good to come up against firm opposition and although he had not been successful in persuasion, he was satisfied on his own account that he had expressed himself clearly and satisfactorily. Full of ideas, sleep would not come; but after an hour, with the beginnings of a challenging plan in his head, he finally succumbed and, stretched out on his back with his mouth open, was soon snoring heavily.

Chapter 18

Edgar, Ambrose, Peter, Caroline and Emily rode out from Hoyles to Wakefield for a second time, on this occasion in Edgar's equipage; although a capacious carriage, they were still somewhat squashed. The journey took a few hours and they expected to reach the city later in the evening; their intention was to stay again at the main coaching inn, the Strafford Arms, which George had previously recommended as having a reputation for clean rooms and bedding. The next morning Edgar and Ambrose would view the execution of Jennie Calman; Peter and the two ladies would wait at the inn and afterwards the group would begin the long journey back to Suffolk. Although curious, as he had never seen a hanging, Peter finally decided he didn't want to join the crowd after agreeing with Ambrose that although it was considered a public spectacle it was not intended for the purposes of entertainment. Besides, Peter had already experienced a scene of violent death which, as Ambrose pointed out, was probably enough for his lifetime.

Wakefield was crowded and busy. They had heard a little of the city's history from George.

'We had a major battle here in the 1400s. The Duke of York and King Henry VII's wife, Margaret of Anjou, fought on fields just outside the town. The duke lost that particularly bloody encounter, along with his head which was later stuck on a pike above the gates of York by the very vengeful queen.'

'Real public humiliation, George!' Ambrose laughed.

'Certainly, but it was common practice in those days. At least the Calman woman will have a quiet burial in the prison grounds.'

'I imagine many of the Bingley women would pay money to see her head stuck on a pike,' said Edgar. 'But you were telling us about Wakefield. What else has happened there?'

'That wasn't the only battle. Two centuries later the city was fought over by the Roundheads and Cavaliers, being a royalist stronghold, but eventually captured by the Parliamentarians. Wakefield Jail, where Calman will be hanged, was originally a Tudor house of correction. Although new additions have been planned for the building, you'll see it still retains its overall air of ancient gloom and despondency.'

'Much like Seddon workhouse,' thought Ambrose.

Arriving at the coaching inn they found accommodation was difficult to come by, but the landlord recognised them and Edgar's practical addition of a sovereign into the man's hand saw the two men and Peter welcomed into the largest room upstairs in the front. The host had seen fit to move a couple of merchants already settled there to a smaller room, placating them with the promise of a free dinner. The sovereign minus the cost of the dinner still left him with a handsome profit on the deal. Emily and her daughter were shown to a small, clean and comfortable room with a good-sized bed and brightly burning fire. Soon, well fed and becoming drowsy as the fire in the dining room threw out its unwavering heat, they decided to retire to bed; by half past ten they were all asleep, except Ambrose who lay awake wondering what Jennie Calman was thinking as she prepared for her last night.

They were all wakened early by the general bustle outside their respective windows as people flocked into the inn for breakfast. The landlord and servants were kept on their feet by the increase in trade that the hangings had brought to the city.

'None for a couple of years, then two within a week of each other! It's all good for business,' he told them cheerfully.

Having broken their fast and packed their small valises from the overnight stay, Edgar and Ambrose made their way with the throng in the general direction of the jail. As they approached the building the two friends looked out for the women who had been instrumental in bringing Mrs Calman to justice, but it was impossible to pick them out in such a horde. The crowd in front of them came to a halt but with deft use of their height and evident status the two men managed to push their way to the front. It was soon clear that the barrier preventing the crowd from moving forward was a tight line of militiamen with their rifles shouldered. The captain stood close at hand and both Ambrose and Edgar recognised him as the official whom George

Chapter 18

had ordered to take Mrs Calman and her accomplices to Wakefield. They nodded to each other and to the surprise of the two men the soldier made his way across to them.

Taking off his helmet he held out his hand. 'Mr Lawes and Mr Hudson. Mr George Lawes has asked me to provide you both with a seat seeing as how you've played a major part in this affair.' He took them beyond the barrier into a large space in front of the prison doors in the centre of which was the scaffold. To their great pleasure Ambrose had kept his promise and a double row of 10 small wooden chairs had been set up in front of the walls and in full sight of the grisly device, the plain wooden platform with its hanging rope. The seats were occupied by the very women they had been searching for. It seemed that George – who had influence in many quarters in the West Riding – had suggested to the prison constable that everyone who had participated in the prisoner's capture should have a view concomitant with their involvement in the affair. Seven of them had lost babies by Calman's murdering hands and an eighth baby had only been saved by the ultimate heroism of a woman who would never see justice done. The rest of the women had been instrumental in bringing the Calman woman to public retribution. Janet Stow had taken her place at the end of the front row and by her side was her niece, looking scared and tearful. The rest sat in silence, oblivious of the stares of curiosity from the crowd who could see them. As Edgar and Ambrose took their places at the end of the back row the captain handed Ambrose a thick package.

'The woman asked me to give you this, Mr Hudson. The jailer said she's been writing something for days.' He looked curious and they could see he was willing Ambrose to open it there and then, but the journalist disappointed him by slipping the envelope inside his coat pocket.

The large wooden doors to the jail were pushed open by two sturdy soldiers as the minute hand of the prison clock high up on the front wall moved to five minutes to ten. Through the doors came first two more soldiers, then the turnkey together with the chaplain, followed by Jennie Calman. Behind her were two more soldiers and three more officials.

Neither Edgar nor Ambrose had any idea what to expect from the crowd. They had experienced noise, shouting, catcalling, whistles when previously witnessing public hangings. But to their intense surprise the crowd fell completely silent as the small procession came into view. The only sound that the two men could hear was the chaplain intoning parts of the burial service as the party made its way towards the scaffold, where the six soldiers took up positions around its base. Mrs Calman was a short woman and, at ground level, had been dwarfed and hidden by them. It was only when she had climbed the steps to the platform and was in full sight that those at the front of the throng had a close view of the 'termagant', as the papers had called her. It was she they had come from far and wide to see – a woman who was guilty of the worst crime one of her sex could commit. Some were disappointed at her smallness of stature, as though they thought the size of her physique should match those of the dimensions of her crimes. As she mounted the steps of the scaffold and appeared into the view of all, a woman shouted, 'Bitch! Getting what you deserve. Why didn't they just throw you in the mire instead of wasting money on a hanging?' But surprisingly her shout raised no response from either the prisoner or the rest of the crowd as militia-men, drafted in to keep the peace, moved forward, hands on their rifles.

The woman's arms were pinned to her sides with a leather belt. They learned later that, pristine in her habits to the end, Jennie Calman had asked as her last request to have her linen laundered and starched. But prison regulations denied her; instead she made an unimpressive sight in a plain black dress. Her customary gleaming white cuffs and collar were absent; the neck was bare in order more easily to accommodate the noose. She stood silent and expressionless, neck and head erect, staring into the crowd. For the first time Ambrose and Edgar saw that her hair was quite grey; previously it had always been hidden by a full cap. Whether the stress of the trial and finality of the verdict had turned it from another shade they could never know. Today she had scraped it back severely and tied it in a knot on the back of her head. Her pale face was fully exposed to the gaze of the crowd. It was expressionless, the narrow lips drawn together in a thin line, the nose pinched and the cheeks hollow. The

Chapter 18

silence continued as the crowd appraised her. Disappointingly, they found she looked ordinary, a woman who wouldn't attract any specific notice in the street. There was nothing of the monster about her, but Edgar still shivered as he looked at her. It was that very commonplace appearance that made her crimes the more shocking. How could such an unremarkable-looking woman commit such unspeakable acts?

The hands of the clock had moved three minutes and the hangman stepped forward. He took the noose and placed it around her neck where it loosely rested. As she stood staring directly in front of her he offered a cloth covering for her head. Jennie Calman shook her head vehemently and murmured, 'I won't have it!'; a final dismissive gesture of defiance. As the chaplain stepped forward to say some last words to her she was clearly heard to snarl, 'There'll be no cant here! I'll take my chances. Take your God to the devil and go with him!' Startled by this unexpected and aberrant curse, the poor man stepped back perilously close to the edge of the platform. As the hands of the clock moved towards the hour the hangman tightened the rope, adjusting the knot until it rested on the back of the woman's neck; he moved over to the wooden lever. Nothing was left to perform other than a signal to the executioner from the constable of the jail. As the clock struck 10 the man stepped forward, released the lever and the trapdoor opened.

The body fell through the space a short distance until the pre-calculated length of rope was played out and the feet dangled a few inches from the ground. The legs and feet twitched for what seemed minutes, but which was in fact 10 or 15 seconds at most until the body became still. This was no more than strangulation and Ambrose was immediately taken back to the sight of Richard Alfrey's body as it hung from the beam in the yard of Seddon workhouse; although a suicide, that had also been a slow asphyxiation. A prison official listened for heartbeats and then pronounced her dead and the party on the platform moved off back inside the prison. The body would remain for some hours to ensure complete absence of life, and as an unsubtle warning to others, before being cut down and buried without ceremony in the prison graveyard. Four militia-men were posted at each corner of the scaffold to deter anyone from attacking the corpse.

The crowd lingered; when those in the front had had their fill, they melted away leaving space for those behind. Edgar and Ambrose had taken note of the reactions of the seated women. There had been no show of malevolence, nothing to compare with the women sitting at the foot of the guillotine, for example. The whole group had behaved in an exemplary and dignified manner. At the precise moment of Jennie Calman's death there had been a collective sigh, as though a chapter had been closed. There was no outward show of jubilation as they rose as one and filed out of the place, melting anonymously into the crowd.

Edgar did manage to catch up with Janet Stow, however, and persuaded her to stay for a while so that they could talk. They moved away from the jail and found a bench beneath a tree where they sat together. The men had already decided they would like to reward her in some way for her cooperation; they had been impressed with the cool way she had managed the group of women. It was entirely through her efforts that there hadn't been a serious riot on the evening that Jennie Calman had been detained. Edgar had put ten sovereigns in a small leather purse and placed it in her hands. She was at first confused by this gesture and unsure whether to take it. Persuading her that she had earned it and exhorting her to put it to good use, the two men each shook her hand and they parted as friends.

'I only hope she manages to hide it from the drunken husband!' said Ambrose.

'We have to hope for the best on that score. But she has a good deal of common sense and I rather think she'll know exactly what to do with it. I wouldn't be surprised if it's not shared out with the rest of them. Still – it wasn't our place to tell her how to spend it.'

The crowd was beginning to thin, although there was a large group clustered around the front window of the nearest inn. Curious as to what they were looking at, the two men peered over heads and saw the front page of a broadsheet in the window. The headline was 'The Last Words of the Child Murderess as she Spoke them on the Scaffold'.

Chapter 18

'Damn it!' said Edgar. 'Someone's been quick off the mark.' Reading on, they saw in black and white the imprecation made to the chaplain. Jennie Calman had her epitaph straight from her own lips.

'How did they get this out so quickly?' asked Edgar.

'I suspect one of the soldiers standing by the scaffold was paid to report to the printer all her final words; he would have the full story already from the court proceedings. To add these words would have only taken a few minutes and then it would be complete. The broadsheet could be run off the press immediately and circulated.'

Having read all they wanted, they pushed their way out of the crowd and began to make their way back to the inn.

'Has today's spectacle changed your mind about any aspects of public executions?' asked Edgar.

'No. I'm relieved the woman's dead and that she was despatched in full view of us all after an open trial. I'm particularly glad for the victims who can now be certain she'll never kill any more infants. I'm also glad for Emily that the second of the main culprits concerned in the death of her husband has been punished. Calman may not have killed Richard Alfrey, but by colluding with her brother she certainly contributed to his suicide. For myself, I'm also grateful that Rosalie's death has been publicly avenged, even if there never was a guilty verdict.'

'So, you cling on to the precept of "an eye for an eye"?'

'I do.'

Back at the inn their friends were waiting eagerly for news, but the two men were disappointingly unforthcoming with details. They were particularly aware that full descriptions of a public hanging would resonate unfavourably with Mrs Alfrey, no doubt bringing back images she had done her best to forget during the previous year. Instead they diverted their companions by concentrating on the journey to come, insisting they check that all the luggage had been packed and nothing left behind. By eleven o'clock they were ready and took their places inside the coach to make the first stage of their journey to Doncaster and the Great North Road.

They had been on the road for an hour when Peter requested that he be allowed aloft with the driver. On their journey to Yorkshire he had been exhilarated by the stories the coachmen had told him of life on the road and hoped for more. His exit to the top of the vehicle freed up some space which everyone took advantage of and it was not long before the two women were fast asleep; directly opposite Ambrose, Edgar was close to nodding off himself.

As Ambrose shifted position, he heard the rustle of paper coming from his inside pocket. Putting in his hand he withdrew the package he had received from the captain of the militia. He turned it over; it was unsealed; the paper of poor quality. Clearly several sheets were included as the package was of some substance, the loose sheets held together with grubby twine. He slipped off the string and straightened out the six pages. At first glance, the writing was almost illegible, large, thin and spidery, but as his eyes adjusted to it he could begin reading quite rapidly. The letter opened with no epistolary niceties:

Wakefield
May 1839
To Ambrose Hudson,

I was told you asked to see me. What reason you could have had I cannot think, but I have no desire to see you. I imagine you are anxious to obtain some kind of explanation from me; something that will help you come to terms with your loss. I have no desire to comfort you in any way. I remember you as connected to the rabble that drove me out of steady and well-paid employment at a time when I had just lost my brother. If you expect an apology you will be disappointed. What I will do, through you and your newspaper, is give the world my side of the story. I know I will go down in history as the bitch who murdered babies – so be it – but I want my version to be made public.

I hate men, but I hate women more. I'm sure it was women who killed my brother. My motivation has always been revenge. They robbed me of the only human being I ever loved and I resolved, by whatever means, to avenge him. I discovered baby farming practices when I was living in London, immediately

Chapter 18

after Calman and I had been driven out of Seddon by those hags. I could see immediately this would be a way of making money, but above all, I would be taking away something precious from those slatterns and trollops, the likes of whom took away my brother. My chance came after John died. He fell down the stairs, drunk as usual, broke his neck and never recovered. 'Good riddance!' said I. He was a millstone round my neck. Once he was gone I was free to go my own way. The coroner questioned me as to whether it had been a fall or did I push him? Someone had heard us arguing but the police did not pursue it as his reputation as a drunk was well known in the district. In the end, the verdict was accidental death.

It was a bad time. I had no money. Calman had drunk away most of what we had and there were no savings, but I took up the idea of fostering young babies and put advertisements in the papers. There was no shortage of work. I was surprised at the numbers of young women who ended on the streets out of desperation. I offered a service that they needed. Soon I had too many babies to look after on my own and I did not want to share the profits. So, I began to dispose of them, making out they had 'unfortunately passed away'. It was too easy. The mothers either did not care, or were too upset to enquire too deeply, so I was making a pretty penny for some months, until one of them got too curious and started asking questions about how it was that so many babies had died in my care. I could see the officials would soon be snooping round and I knew it was time to move, but where to?

I remembered my brother and I had distant relatives in Yorkshire and I scraped the fare together and travelled up north with the intention of setting up a similar business in a place I was unknown. I found out about northern factories and mills and how people were moving off the land to work in them and that they took young children and women to mind the machines. This seemed an ideal place to start again. Surely the women would need help minding their innumerable brats? I was right! I linked up with Tom Sizewell and, having sounded him out, he confirmed what I thought – there was no shortage of babies to farm; those mill-hands were as often or not in trouble and I looked upon it as a service. Those babies were mostly unwanted bastards; if they had lived they would have led miserable lives. Better they were put out of their misery sooner rather than later. You can be sure that even when I'm gone there will be someone else setting up to take my place. I was asked how many brats I had disposed of. To tell the truth I cannot remember; I did not keep account of that side of the business – only how much I was making. The money, by the way, has mostly all gone. Sizewell, well named, took a sizeable amount. Anything that was left has been spent on food and laundry in here.

If you were here to question me you might ask, 'Would you have done the same thing if you'd had children of your own?' And 'Did you ever think they had a right to life – however miserable? They might either by luck or hard work have made something of their lives later.' The chaplain said this to me when, in vain, he came to absolve my mortal soul.

You must think of Tuttle and Daniels in that regard. Oh, yes! I heard all about your 'kindnesses' to masters William and Peter. I always thought there was something funny going on when you were in the dormitory teaching Tuttle not to piss the bed. 'Now,' I thought, 'why would a man be interested in a young boy who was no relation?' It could only mean one thing. Calman and I used to joke about it.

I never wanted children; screaming brats about the place is not my idea of living. They make a mess and are good for nothing until they're old enough to work. The government's idea about raising the age when a child can work is stupid. Once a child can get up on its feet it should be found something useful to do. Those children in the workhouse were always kept busy. I hear they're all being taught to read and write now – that will bring

Chapter 18

nothing but trouble. Children getting grand ideas – that is a bad idea!

I am writing to you to make sure you realise I do not give a tuppenny damn about what has happened to the children – or Rosalie Thwaites, or her brother. They should never have poked their noses in and she should not have tried to save the bastard. Believe me, I take no responsibility for her death. It was entirely her fault. Well – she got what she wanted, a heroine's death and a sticky one. I'm not sorry she's gone in the mire with the brats. Is that what you want to hear?

As for my death, it can't come too soon for me. I've had enough of this stinking world. Once my brother had gone, there was nothing else in my life that gave me any pleasure – apart from making money. My one regret is that I won't live to see my brother's murderer or murderers found. I am certain it was carried out by women from the House. You might ask, 'How can that be? He was horrendously mutilated, why would a woman do that?'

My advice to you is: never underestimate us, Mr Hudson; women can be just as merciless as men. We can feel the same surges of anger and hatred as you and – as I have shown – are quite capable of carrying them out in extreme ways.

I will end this letter now as I wish to prepare myself for tomorrow. I am determined to look my best – or as far as I can under the circumstances. They have taken away most of my clothes and the laundry here is dreadful. No doubt you will see me on the scaffold. I hope I can look everyone in the eye and say, 'All of you – go to hell!' I sign myself in the form I wish to be remembered.

Jennifer Enderby

The vitriolic tone of the letter with its bald statements of defiance and hatred shocked even a hardened journalist like Ambrose. It was made more disturbing by the fact that she was a woman with such a low opinion of her own sex. He wondered how she had spent her last days. It was obvious she had abjured all approaches from the chaplain. 'Poor chap! A thankless task,' thought Ambrose. Presumably she had accepted that these were to be the last days of her life. No appeal for pardon had been made to the authorities and the sounds of hammering as the scaffold was erected under her window would have been a reinforcement that her hours were numbered. He considered she was such a hard case that she would show no fear. But was she so obdurate that she had no feelings at all? He doubted it. Her deep feelings for her brother showed she was capable of empathy at some level, but at heart she was an unrepentant misanthrope, completely lacking in any womanly tenderness. Her comments about Rosalie hurt him deeply and, as usual, as soon as he started to think of her he had a vision in his mind of her beautiful head just above the bright green mire calling out her message of love for Edgar to deliver to him.

The question was, what to do with this letter? The journalist in him recognised it as an essential part of the story, partway to explaining 'why'. It would be sensational. 'Somehow I have to translate this piece of vitriol into a report that readers will accept,' he thought. 'They'll all be thirsting for explanations, but there's no way I would have this published as it stands. It's a troubled woman's final desperate testimony and should remain private between us. I'm not sure I'll even show it to McNiece. The only other person who should read it is Edgar since he's been as deeply involved in these matters as myself. I can't hide it from him. But I'll pick my moment to show him.' Having made that decision, he lay back in his seat, closed his eyes and attempted sleep himself.

Swaying, rumbling and bouncing along, the coach headed southward and home.

Acknowledgements

Thanks go to Lesley Taylor and Carolyn Box for their constant encouragement and good advice.